a METAL & LACE NOVEL

CAMELOT BURNING

KATHRYN ROSE

Woodbury, Minnesota

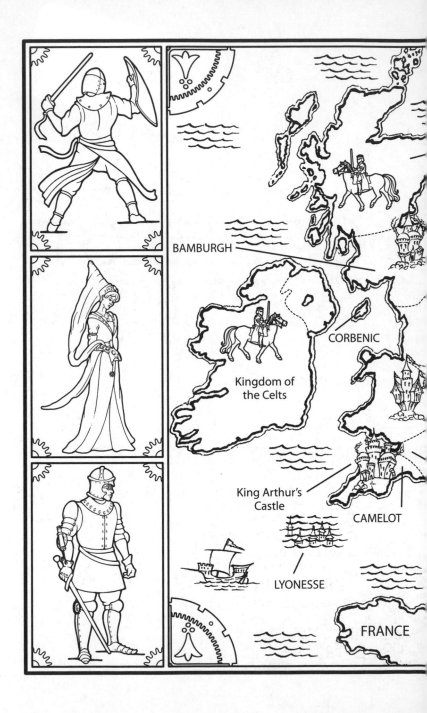

BAMBURGH

CORBENIC

Kingdom of
the Celts

King Arthur's
Castle

CAMELOT

LYONESSE

FRANCE

CALEDONIA

N
W   E
S

Castle Blanc

BEAUREPAIRE

BEDEGRAINE

SARPENIC

Morgan le Fay's
Fortress

GLASTONBURY

BRITANNIA

For my mother.

An epic tale of magic versus machines

Seventeen-year-old Vivienne lives in a world of knights and ladies, corsets and absinthe, outlawed magic and alchemic machines. By day, she is lady-in-waiting to Guinevere, the future queen of Camelot. By night, she secretly toils away building steam-powered gadgets as apprentice to Merlin, the recovering magic addict.

When Morgan le Fay, King Arthur's sorceress sister, comes to seize Camelot, Merlin enlists Vivienne's help in building the perfect weapon to defeat her: a mechanical beast powered by steam and alchemy. To activate it, they need Sir Lancelot's squire, Marcus, who Vivienne starts to fall in love with, despite his forthcoming vow of chastity. In order to save Camelot, Vivienne will have to risk everything she holds dear—her apprenticeship and her love for Marcus.

First Edition
First Printing, 2014

Book design by Bob Gaul
Cover design by Kevin R. Brown
Cover illustration by John Blumen
Interior map illustration by Chris Down

Flux, an imprint of Llewellyn Worldwide Ltd.

This is a work of fiction. Names, characters, places, and incidents are either the product of the author's imagination or are used fictitiously, and any resemblance to actual persons, living or dead, business establishments, events, or locales is entirely coincidental. Cover models used for illustrative purposes only and may not endorse or represent the book's subject.

Library of Congress Cataloging-in-Publication Data
Rose, Kathryn.
  Camelot burning/Kathryn Rose.—First edition.
    pages cm.—(A metal & lace novel; #1)
  Summary: Seventeen-year-old Vivienne, lady-in-waiting to the future queen Guinevere, is secretly apprenticed to Merlin, the magician, and helps him try to create a steam-powered metal beast to defeat Morgan le Fey, King Arthur's sorceress sister, when she declares war on Camelot.
  ISBN 978-0-7387-3967-0
[1. Courts and courtiers—Fiction. 2. Apprentices—Fiction. 3. Automata—Fiction. 4. Merlin (Legendary character)—Fiction. 5. Wizards—Fiction. 6. Magic—Fiction. 7. Camelot (Legendary place)—Fiction. 8. Kings, queens, rulers, etc.—Fiction. 9. Knights and knighthood—Fiction.] I. Title.
  PZ7.R71715Cam 2014
  [Fic]—dc23

                                        2013041681

Flux
Llewellyn Worldwide Ltd.
2143 Wooddale Drive
Woodbury, MN 55125-2989
www.fluxnow.com

Printed in the United States of America

ONE

When a mechanical falcon takes flight from Merlin's tower, it means the sorcerer is bored or drunk on absinthe.

I wonder if anyone else in Camelot stargazes enough to know this.

The scarlet curtains of Merlin's window catch on the bird's "feathers" when the absinthe is especially potent, and today is no different. An arm stretches the falcon out the window. From the height of Lady Guinevere's bedchambers, the tattooed words of magic on Merlin's forearm aren't visible. But I know such words are there: faded and old from his travels to the Holy Land before sorcery was purged in favor of the mechanical arts and, with it, his addiction.

The back of his hand flicks the machine into the air. I wait for the sorcerer to reveal himself, a wind-up controller in hand with copper wires attached to the falcon's artificial brain.

Instead, a wire-free bird plummets toward the ground, and my heart stops. "No . . . " I breathe, careful not to speak too loudly in case my lady would hear. The mechanical falcon will be smashed to bits. Weeks of construction for nothing! My eyes squeeze shut, and I wait for the explosion of cogs, copper, and brass on cobblestone.

But then, "Extend!" Merlin calls, his voice demanding obedience.

The shining wings crack, one plate at a time, to a span of nearly three feet. They catch the breeze and spread across the sky, steering upward without any wires.

My eyebrows lift; my lips part. This is new. Even more: Merlin demanding a mechanical falcon obey him and fly freely is nothing short of alarming. Knowledge of his former vice alone might make people wonder if he's turned back to magic.

I glance at the dressing table in my lady's chambers, making sure I can steal a few more seconds of sky watching. Guinevere tugs at the golden skirt of her gown—another brilliant low-cut style from Lyonesse that initially shocked Camelot's prudish subjects—and resettles herself in front of her mirror, whispering in a high-pitched voice to the birdcage beside her. A canary whistles back. She's occupied. Perfect.

Outside, the falcon eclipses the setting sun.

"Return!"

From the valve on its head, steam whistles, identical to a real falcon's telltale caw. It swoops over the gardens' violets and returns to the highest window in the castle, where Merlin waits wearing a leather glove. For tradition, of course, never mind the sharp brass talons.

The curtain draws across his window, so I lower my viewer, my incredulous smile no longer subtle.

The falcon flies, but its miniature boiler isn't sophisticated like an aeroship's and cannot rely on steam power to soar through the clouds. It's simply for show. For applause. For Merlin's own amusement. Tonight, Caldor doesn't fly because of the mechanical arts. Caldor flies because of Merlin's words.

That's *remarkable*.

"Vivienne?" Guinevere calls.

I've got my hair caught around my fingers, twisting the tail of my blonde braid into a knot. After three months of being Guinevere's lady-in-waiting, I know how she hates it when I play with my hair. Clearing my face of any excitement, I pry my fingers loose. My other hand collapses my viewer into a metal disc—barely indistinguishable now from a coin—and then into my pocket it goes, safe from the eyes of those who might ask how a handmaid came across an inventor's toy. I drag myself from the window, smoothing out my long sleeves that are tied up with soft, pliable copper and embellished with pearls.

My back straightens as Guinevere approaches. *Greeting royalty,* my governess taught me, *requires poise.* "Yes, my lady?"

She sets her thick chestnut hair over one shoulder. Usually I use the coiled brass comb to steam and straighten her locks into a more fashionable style. Today, she didn't want to bother.

"Are the alterations ready?" she says, her voice devoid of emotion, though sometimes it's simply the way she says certain words. "Almost French-sounding, even if Lyonesse was technically part of Britannia," Merlin once declared at court after several pints of ale. "And I don't trust the French other than to make a fine absinthe."

I nod. "My mother's finishing them up as we speak."

Wondering how to remove so much fabric, more likely. The task of creating a wedding gown a lady of Lyonesse would approve has kept Lady Carolyn working later than Merlin himself. It took her weeks to gather the courage to allow her seamstresses to alter the gown's satin front to Guinevere's liking, low enough for a liberal amount of feminine curves.

Bawdy laughter from the knights' quarters flows through the window with the breeze. Quite possibly Arthur is there on his last night of bachelorhood, knights serenading him with vulgar sonnets or creative ways to show a wench the Round Table. I breathe a sigh.

"Ale turns them into rascals," Guinevere says, too ladylike to comment any further on what else they might be up to.

She's looking for a way to distract herself from tomorrow's events, and I don't blame her. "I think 'rascals' is putting it lightly," I say.

She smiles. Despite her cold disposition toward others, to me she's never been anything but warm. "If Arthur and I had married in Lyonesse, my friends and I might have acted the same." Her eyes well, and she must look away before it's obvious I've noticed.

My heart falls, as I know what it's like to mourn being here. I search for any possibility of happiness within these stone walls; I squeeze my eyes shut and think of what it'd be like to be away from Camelot, in a warmer land where my future wouldn't consist of tending to the queen, but something greater. Something I've wanted since I was ten years old.

I disregard fantasy. For now. "Was today a good day, my lady?" Seven words I've asked every night since the start of our companionship three months past.

She lifts her chin. "Yes. Much more than yesterday." Five words she's memorized as a response. "I love Arthur, Vivienne."

"He loves you, too."

Truthfully, the king has never been happier, and all of court has noticed. It's just a matter of time before Arthur and Guinevere are blessed with an heir. I hope, by some miracle, I'll be relieved of my handmaid duties by then, but really the only way out is through marriage. I cringe at the thought.

Guinevere peers through the window at the descending night. "I just never thought my wedding day would be in a strange land. Or that none from my kingdom would witness it."

I'm certain she never imagined being an entire kingdom's lone survivor either. Lyonesse was the last castle in the civilized world to expel magic and accept the mechanical arts. Being the only person left alive raised suspicions about Guinevere. Her trial was supposed to end in execution, but miraculously didn't when an anonymous witness testified on her behalf.

That wasn't the only talk of death associated with Lyonesse. When I was a girl, my brother Owen told me how the kingdom was slowly descending into the waters between Britannia and France. To frighten me, surely, but it captivated me more. Lanterns in our bedroom would let him bounce shadows off walls. Owen would speak of men who went insane by stealing magic, of men handing their souls to the devil if it meant feeding their euphoric addictions. Of men like Merlin. My brother would go on and on until our father stormed into our chambers to silence us and whip the boy for telling me such dark tales. The strokes across Owen's back would fade. The exhilaration over what world lay beyond Camelot would not.

Guinevere waves a light hand at the memory of her former home. "Silly to think of what could have been." She kisses my cheek and makes her way to the parlor.

I know this land doesn't bring her peace or joy. Her smile is solely for appearances with the hope its melancholy goes unnoticed. And now, I hear nothing but the clock tower tick and feel ashamed that I mourn each minute lost.

But Guinevere said today was a good day, and tomorrow will be better. Soon she'll go to sleep. Early, considering she'll need to be up at dawn. While all of Camelot retires for the night, I'll be free. Free to escape this life for a secret one of my choosing. Free to discover more about the incredible revelation in machinery I just saw.

A wire-free falcon.

Caldor.

Just several weeks ago, Caldor was but a pile of sprockets, but now the sorcerer has sent the mechanical bird into the sky, only controlling it with his voice. Morning is ages away. Plenty of time before I'll have to return to the conventions of Camelot.

"I'll draw the curtains now," I call to Guinevere, sweeping

thick, rich fabrics across the window to hide the clock tower from view. All evidence of Merlin's enthralling endeavor has now vanished.

Cannot be magic. Merlin wouldn't return to a life of immense danger. I'm nearly certain.

Nearly.

TWO

I'm careful as my boots hurry over some of the softer stones in the hall, worn down over the years by the king's former lovers. At this time of night, the lanterns' glow casts shadows upon the curvature of the corridor, making me think someone's there even though, other than the knights, everyone is asleep.

No, not everyone.

Rough, urgent voices from the castle's northern gates stop me at a window, reminding me that guards stand alert day and night in Camelot. Curious, I lift to my toes and look down. A dozen guards by the extendable steel drawbridge point across the way to someone riding from the castle.

I continue to the rigid stairs, pulling the cream-colored veil from my shoulders and resting the hem on my head so the edges float down my back.

" ... word le Fay's breached the English shore," a guard from the city walls whispers to two at the door. "Heard him plain as day shout it up to the blokes on the wall this morning. Let him in, they did."

Before they see me, I press against the doorframe and peek around the corner, at upright weapons and blades pricking at the stone floor. Chain-mail gloves grasp the curved hilts of those blades where iron firelances were fused, allowing them easy access to more than one deadly form of weaponry.

Le Fay. The name of the king's sorceress sister is one I know well: a monster's name whispered into the nightmares of children. The details of her exile have been exaggerated to the point of legend. I myself admit to the occasional sleepless night because of what Owen's told me of her.

"That's preposterous. With the mark on her head after they outlawed magic?" the second replies. "Wasn't just a drunken bard looking for a pretty penny?"

The third looks unconvinced. He's much younger, and perhaps this is the first time unsettling news has arrived while on duty. His fingers fumble with his weapon. I wonder if he's forgotten the small trigger by his thumb, which would extend the firelance's barrel and set it off. He might lose a foot.

At the gates, the commotion grows stronger. There are calls to reinforce the perimeter. But the sun's already set, the clock is ticking, and my mentor awaits. I have little time.

A soldier with a crossbow strapped to his back beckons the three. "Word from Corbenic!"

The skeptical guard is first to move. "Cannot be." They leave. More exhilarated than is necessary considering King Pelles of Corbenic is Arthur's ally. According to Owen,

Lancelot sometimes frequents Corbenic on his way beyond the English shores.

But now's my chance. I run from Guinevere's tower, watching every corner in case someone would spot me running this way, when our family's quarters are in the exact opposite direction. I lift my dress's hem past my boots, moving faster. Smoke races for the sky from the clock tower's chimney as I bolt through jasmine-scented gardens. So quickly, it's only after I've landed atop the cobblestone in the village that I realize the dreadful *thump* was, in fact, my viewer tumbling out of my pocket and onto the street.

"Blast!" I turn and gather my dress in my fists to duck and retrieve my viewer, but another hand is quicker.

"What do we have here?"

I'd recognize Stephen's thick voice anywhere, but if not that, I'd recognize the appalling condition he's kept his leather boots in. "Give it here, Stephen."

He's Owen's friend and a fellow squire, and there are two more behind him, but neither is my brother. This lot of three prefers to mimic the ridiculous dandies of Camelot by acting foolishly around ladies and looking for trouble. If their respective knights were worthy of Arthur's praise, perhaps these squires would follow suit.

Stephen's long face widens into a mischievous smile. "Oh, hello, Viv. Fancy meeting a fine noblewoman such as yourself out here."

I reach for my viewer, hoping Stephen's reactions are as slow as his wit, but no such luck. He tosses it to Ector, who dashes around me to catch it.

"Shouldn't you be prettying yourself up for the wedding tomorrow?" Ector adds. He's much taller than me, so there's no use in jumping. "Or have all of Camelot's lords and dandies passed on star-gazing, quiet-as-a-mouse Lady Vivienne? What will your father do now?"

I set my hands on my hips and wait for them to lose interest, my long, overdrawn sigh of exasperation somehow too subtle for them to notice. I'd offer a smart remark in return, but they're tragically too oafish to ever feel the sting.

"How does this—" Ector mumbles, fiddling with the viewer's edging until he's found the switch to lengthen it. "Oh, there we go."

I cringe. "Blast it all, Ector. You'll break it, you buffoon!"

My fingers dart for my viewer, but Ector jerks it high above his head, narrows his eyes to the right, and throws it at Bors, who nearly drops it.

"Should be inside at an hour like this, Viv," Bors tells me. "Especially tonight." He's the slowest or perhaps the nicest of the three, and lets me take back my inventor's tool. I hold up the lens to the gaslight. God help them if I find any scratches on the glass.

"Why is that?" I mutter. I use the soft wool of my pearl-studded gloves to wipe away some pebbles and dirt.

"Hold on," Stephen says. "Don't tell me rumors of Morgan's return didn't reach the nobility this afternoon! Hasn't your brother told you anything?"

They speak of Morgan, just as the guards did. Though the idea of crashing gray waves and a haunting fugitive of magic breaching them is an exhilarating fantasy, surely aero-ships would never be permitted to bring le Fay here.

I must look surprised, because even Stephen's disposition softens, likely misinterpreting my expression for fear. "But I'm sure it's only a rumor. Don't worry." Stephen gestures the other two to go with him into the village. "G'night, Viv."

I follow them down the shadowy streets. "Wait. What rumors? My lady will want to know of this."

Stephen looks sideways at me. But I have a valid reason for demanding more, considering Morgan's connection to Lyonesse. He shrugs, like he's realized the same. "Bards wandered the countryside declaring it for weeks, but it was only this morning that Arthur's sister was allegedly spotted on the English shores. Pelles told Arthur to kill her on sight if she returned to Camelot. His messenger just left."

It sounds like a proclamation of superiority over King Arthur, who Pelles knows did not come about his reign by normal—or even desired—means. But this cannot be right. "How could Morgan still be *alive*, let alone back in Britannia, unless the whole world has forgotten her face?"

Bors is quick with a response. "Rogues, of course. Every man has his price. Theirs is much more competitive."

Ector scoffs. "Air pirates everywhere are occupied enough these days, not just the ones who took control of the Spanish kingdoms. Lancelot will attest to that once he returns. Empty-handed, granted. Again."

They walk too quickly, as though trying to lose me. I must pick up the pace. "What do you mean? Empty-handed? What aren't you telling me?"

Stephen halts in the middle of the silent streets. "Viv, we told you all we know. Word is Morgan might return to Camelot. If that happens, Camelot must kill her or face the wrath of Pelles and the other kingdoms of Britannia. End of story." He pauses. "Why are you out here, again?"

I'm out here because of a standing appointment with Merlin. But I cannot tell them that. Instead, I lift my chin through the utter discomfort of three pairs of eyes on me and stare the squires down. "I might ask you the same. Shouldn't you be preparing your knights' vestments for tomorrow?"

They know I've caught them. Stephen cocks an eyebrow. "We won't tell if you won't." He taps Ector and Bors each on the shoulder, and the three dash down the streets.

I return my viewer to my pocket for the second time tonight, then I turn on my heel and run the other way. My veil tumbles from my head, catching on my copper hairpin, but I straighten it, ensuring my blonde locks don't give me away.

I hurry through the town square, black leather boots clambering over the wooden stage of the gallows. More of a decorative landmark in a kingdom where there are no executions, it's mainly used by dandies who smoke *hashish* and hope nobility will notice their hawked hair. A patrolling guard gives me a curious stare, but I hold a finger to my lips for silence. He looks the other way, but not before gifting me with an obnoxious wink I choose to ignore.

———

I race through a blur of empty tanner shops boasting specialty leather corsets; I pass deserted optic boutiques, whose monocles are worshipped by perfectly-sighted dandies. Twisted iron lanterns illuminate bare cobblestone streets. Even the crimson flags with gold dragons, sharp black studs as eyes, are free of birds atop their poles.

I reach the painted sign of the blacksmith's shop in front of the sorcerer's tower: tall, thin, unstable-looking as though a slight wind would send the rickety structure crashing to the ground. From the streets below, the clock is monstrously large: black and white with decorative iron numbers and curled hands that wrap around an enormous golden cog.

I dash behind the workspace, and freeze.

An iron mask on a giant's face turns my way. The blacksmith. Bashing smoldering metals against his anvil or not, he hides his eyes from the kingdom. Now he stands by a bucket of water, soaking callused hands. I pause, unsure of whether I'll be able to continue to the cellar door by his feet. After a moment of shared silence, he steps to the side and pulls the heavy iron ring himself, gesturing for me to descend.

I'm hesitant. This is the first time we've come face to face as I usually sneak by late at night, but he doesn't say a word, and intuition assures me he'll keep my secret. As illogical as that may be, I step down, letting him draw the cellar door over my head, stealing my light.

My hands grip the ladder, rotting from age but reinforced with steel handprints and leather-covered steps to maintain grip. I climb down to the earthy cellar and feel my way toward a wooden wheel that lets a fake wall fall into paneled plates, mimicking the fold of an Oriental fan. Behind the secret compartment is a wooden door leading to the steps of Merlin's tower—the only entrance, at his request. My heart pounds in anticipation of hearing how the sorcerer got the mechanical falcon to fly.

I twist the iron knob, throw open the door to the stairs, and jump.

Because Merlin is already here.

Couldn't wait either, not after what happened with Caldor at dusk. The lantern's light in his tattooed hand reflects in the steel piercings in his ears, eyebrows, and nose. Unwilling to follow tradition, Merlin's head is completely shorn, his facial hair a small goatee woven with a phoenix feather and glass beads from a lover he took in Africa. He's never looked older than fifty, but must be as old as the world itself. His entire body is a journal of his life: dates inked on his knuckles, limp requiring a cane.

A wave of excitement rushes through his amazed blue eyes, lined with gold.

"You won't believe what's waiting upstairs."

THREE

"Come quickly. You have a busy day tomorrow tending to Arthur's pagan woman, and we need every minute until then," Merlin shouts as we climb the spiraling stone steps.

One day I counted: three hundred, but it feels like a thousand. The sorcerer's legs must be as strong as a mule's; despite his limp, he can still scamper up two at a time even as the fashionable restraints of black trousers and a crimson cloak bind him. His antique blade, the craftsmanship of which he likes to show off at court amongst Arthur's advisors, clacks against each step, creating a song with the rustle of his cloak. The pristine firelance he calls a *pistolník,* he holds steady at his waist. A gale-force wind passes through the windows as we venture above Camelot.

"How did you—" I gasp as the bone lining of my corset digs most dreadfully into my waist.

"There'll be plenty of time for questions soon enough!"

We arrive at a red door with an iron ring in the center.

Merlin throws all his weight into the pull, and it creaks open, giving way to a circular floor that might fit several of Guinevere's elaborate chambers. Some of his gas lanterns are already lit, Merlin's first invention after establishing the mechanical arts in Camelot. A way to be forever rid of candlesticks that would ruin his journals when knocked over.

He adjusts the gauge of the lantern by the door and draws a dark velvet drape across his bedposts. A quirk of his, uncomfortable with others seeing where he sleeps unless his visitors are Arabian dancers with time and erotic energy to spare.

I search about for Caldor. "Where—"

A flash of copper blinds me. Caldor flits around in midair, forcing me to step back into shelves of scrolls and globes. I catch balance on a map of India and gasp in delighted surprise.

"Return!" Merlin calls before snatching the falconry glove from his work desk. The falcon twitches, clicks and whistles its only voice. Merlin trades the lantern for the glove, pulling it onto his left hand and extending his arm. Black glass eyes study Merlin before the bird scurries over to its master. As Caldor becomes more mechanical by the second, Merlin pulls up the plate from its back so the residual steam can escape. The falcon eventually goes still, head resting on its breastplate.

"Yes, very good," Merlin mutters. He gives the bird an affectionate touch of its chest where real feathers would otherwise be. A lazy hand sweeps the desk of its half-completed copper inventions, goggles, and old-fashioned weapons to create an open space. "Magnificent, isn't he?" Merlin says. When a sharp whistle splits the air, he faces the fireplace and watches his new pulley system click over the piping-hot kettle. "Although, you saw him earlier, didn't you?"

Nothing gets past him, even from afar. My answer is a smile, and though I'm dying to know more, preparing a proper cup of tea comes first. Not the novelty from the far east, but the good raw stuff from a tribe of Druids that Merlin met during the period of unrest between Camelot and the Celts. How a gentleman appreciates tea is sometimes a better indicator of character than political loyalties, and Merlin keeps the Celts' company to this day.

"I saw Caldor lifelike, without wires."

Merlin beams. "Yes."

After pouring hot water into a waiting teapot, he hobbles over to his desk where there's an iron safe and a padlock the size of my outstretched hand. He reaches for a ring of skeleton keys and selects the mightiest to unlock the safe. I try to peek inside, but Merlin senses it and steps in front of me as though his shorn skull tattooed with tribal symbols would ward off my curiosity. He glares over his shoulder, a twinkle in his eye telling me he's not entirely angry.

"You could be more discreet, Vivienne. I would have thought seven years of apprenticeship would have taught you that." He pulls a stone mortar and pestle from the safe. When he sets it on his desk, sparkling smoke bursts from the impact. I reach to touch it, but he smacks my hand away with the handle of his cane.

"Do not touch what you don't yet understand," he scolds as he gauges the mortar. "At midnight, Azur brought me payment for the aerohawk."

I imagine the excitement in Azur's bright eyes when he saw Merlin's newest invention: a steam-run hawk. A flying vessel large enough to carry one passenger, styled like a miniature aeroship with brown and gold wings. Now Azur can fly across the ocean, the moors, as far as he wishes— as long as there is sufficient water and fire to power the craft. To depend on private aeroships instead might send the traveling alchemist from Jerusalem straight into poverty. Much more convenient for Azur Barad, who taught Merlin the mechanical arts years ago in order to free him from the old pagan ways.

Merlin has yet to share how he and Azur stay in touch so easily, but that's merely one secret of many the sorcerer has hidden in Camelot.

"Vivienne, I present to you the next advancement in eastern alchemy," Merlin says, lifting the pestle. The powder is gold, as I expected, but it shimmers with a barely audible sound: a woman's whispering voice. I lean forward. It's almost fluid.

"Azur called it *jaseemat*. No longer does an alchemist simply change rocks into precious stones or metals. Now, we can drench moveable objects in *jaseemat*, made out of gold derived from common charcoal, and have whatever it touches respond as though it's living."

My eyes widen at the insinuation. "Only magic could do that, Merlin."

He shakes his head. "This is not magic. This is an instruction to the elements. A conversation, if you will. The words I say are nothing more than a gentle prodding, but the elements obey, Vivienne. Thankfully in English as well as Azur's native tongue, for practicality's sake." He points at my hair. "Your pin."

I release my mother's copper hairpin, forged in the shape of a dragonfly atop a violet, and hand it to him as my bangs fall across my eyes.

He sets it on the table and shakes atop some *jaseemat*. It glows as it falls.

Merlin's voice goes low. "*Yaty ala alhyah.*"

We watch. The shimmer fades. I frown, but Merlin grunts at me, bringing back my attention. Then, the hairpin twitches. I hold my breath, my eyes fixed open though they desperately want to blink. The pin turns, as though on an axis. Slowly at first, and then the whirring of metal against wood speeds up, rendering it a spinning top. It lifts from the table into the air, only inches from our faces, turning and turning, the residual dust falling, giving the illusion of a grand, golden skirt.

"Merlin," I gasp.

His eyes are enchanted like he wants to burst with happiness. He licks his lips and speaks. "Now fly."

One at a time, the wings of the dragonfly break free of the copper entrapment. They're translucent and shimmery, batting against the air. The dragonfly weaves through long tapestries hanging from the rickety ceiling and nearly flies out the window.

"Return!"

It stops in midair and jets backward to the waiting hand of the sorcerer. He lets it rest on his finger, wings still beating, and hands it to me.

"He won't hurt you. Hasn't pulled out your hair yet, has

he?" The bug jumps to my waiting finger. Its tiny feet tickle my skin. I breathe a smile of amazement. "Look," Merlin adds.

The bug's arms move back and forth over the flower, which I now realize is also twitching.

"What in—" I whisper.

A dark-green bud presses through the bronze, twisting skyward, covered in cracked metal and alchemic dust. The lifeless violet turns scores of exquisite shades of purple; the dragonfly settles itself onto the stamens of the flower and lowers its wings.

Speechless, I gawk at Merlin, who does nothing but regard his mortar with the most delicious amount of praise.

"How can this be?" I say. "How long will it last? What is to become of my hair, old man? Is this life?"

He holds up his hand to slow me down. "For centuries, we've limited life to what we can create organically. We've never looked at its basic elements and compiled them differently. Alchemy has finally given us other options. Unlike its war with magic, the copper in your pin shares a blissful marriage with alchemy. But is this life as you and I live? Alas, no. The amount I dusted onto your jewelry will last for but several minutes. This is my own version I concocted using Azur's as a guide, while his remains safely locked away. It'll take me years to develop my skills to match my old friend's."

As he speaks, the coppery shade grows bolder, the dragonfly's wings less luminescent, the flower less purple. Seconds pass, and it's nothing but a hairpin again.

I frown, a spark of strange despair coming over me as the pin goes cold.

"Don't be saddened by it, my dear. Nothing is permanent, and everything in life is merely waiting to become dust." Merlin's cane helps him to his window. He pulls back the curtains to get a wider view of the stars.

I pocket my mother's hairpin and join him at the window. In strong winds, the top of this tower feels as rickety as it looks, though Merlin has assured me many times there's nothing to fear.

My eyes strain beyond Camelot to a world I've never known other than from the sorcerer's journals and letters. If I listen carefully, I can hear waves crashing into the high cliffs to the south. For seven years, Merlin has entertained me with stories of his journeys to the icy northern lands, of seas and airs patrolled by Vikings and Spanish rogues, and of the infinity of hourglass sands in the Holy Land.

So much I'll never see if I stay in Camelot.

But staying here is not the plan. I steal a glance at the sorcerer who's been a dear friend and mentor for years. And yet, a future in Camelot has only one ending for me and wouldn't involve continuing with the mechanical arts, but would rather consist of cross-stitching in my bedchambers, and a husband who'll likely have the personality of a prickly winter pine.

A future in Jerusalem, working alongside Azur, however . . .

Merlin hands me a cracked cup of tea. Black, as it should be, and cool enough now to swallow in one gulp.

"Seventeen years of castle life and you still have bad manners at tea time." Merlin clicks his tongue as I set down an empty cup. "I suppose I can't blame you. The rubbish they serve in the castle is no match for O'Ciaragain's." He finishes his own cup and sets it down with a satisfied gasp. "Now, to work! Your lazy compilation of pulleys and sprockets is inexcusable. If you don't strengthen Terra's wings, she'll live up to her namesake and crash to the earth the second you send her into the sky. Fix her so Caldor can have an *aerial* friend."

Terra hangs like a marionette above a small table I've claimed as my own. She's made of hammered-out copper I soldered together myself. More of a nightmarish skeleton than Caldor's meticulously-constructed body.

Merlin shakes his head at Terra's sharp metal appearance, her face like a barn owl's instead of a falcon's. "Painful, but your next one will be more ... accomplished. Surely."

I return his scowl with a wicked smile. "Another remark like that, old man, and I'll make sure she attacks you in your sleep."

"Ha!"

Then he's at his work desk, welding mask pulled over his eyes, setting a soldering torch to the frame of a looking glass. One of his many side projects in a clock tower rich with copper for inventions and mechanical falcons alike. A way to make a fortune off the nobility who might believe in the serfs' myths that sheets of reflective glass act as windows to the soul.

I pull a set of goggles over my eyes, blinking as I adjust to the oversized, cloudy lenses. Terra looks back at me, lifeless. What sort of life could she ever live? What more could she be capable of herself?

"Merlin, why not use Azur's blend on Caldor? If his powder is more powerful, why not spare a bit for your pet?"

"The same reason Azur and I choose not to share the

secrets of how to derive gold from the elements. We must not play as gods of the world. Azur's alchemy is priceless, Vivienne. I'd wager even more than Arthur's damned sword." He snorts at the allusion to Excalibur, but when he lifts his mask there's a touch of envy on his face. "For now, until the rest of the Round Table idiots return, Azur's *jaseemat* shall remain untouched. God forbid, if we ever urgently need it, the castle will already be in grave turmoil, something my old incantation could not protect against. We cannot waste what is precious."

He gives me a cautious look, and as he does so, he resembles my father, Lord William, who has yet to discover my seven-year lie of omission. Each day is one day closer to *someone* finding out about my apprenticeship with Merlin. The daughter of one of the king's advisors, the sister of Owen, Galahad's squire, learning about the mechanical arts and alchemy...

Even if only to satisfy my curiosity about something as legendary as Excalibur, which Merlin himself is too proud to speak of, it would be the talk of the court for a handmaid to appear so interested. It'd be nothing less than scandalous for that same handmaid to be discovered as Merlin's apprentice.

I hate that I worry about that. I can only hope the next time Azur arrives, he's considered my request and agreed to it, foregoing his aerohawk for a vessel big enough to bring back a second person to Jerusalem. Perhaps he'll surprise Merlin and arrive tomorrow to offer congratulations to Arthur and his new queen. I could be away from Camelot in mere *hours*.

Azur understands there's no life for me here—he must. And while Merlin might understand, too, there's nothing he could do to change my destiny in Camelot. I don't know how I'll finally break it to him that I simply must leave.

The old sorcerer says nothing else, but regards the clouds gathering above all that is Camelot—city, castle, countryside beyond.

Simply a change of weather over the farmlands, surely.

FOUR

Court-appointed jugglers toss flame-throwing firelances—
eight at a time—into orbit in Camelot's June gardens.
Children reach into one juggler's braiding arsenal, knowing the clown-faced entertainer with spinning wheels on
his stout hat is also an accomplished mechanic. The entertainer does not disappoint and flicks the hammer of each
firelance when it returns to his hand. Instantly, the jug-
gling instruments click inward, transforming into spinning
copper figurines meant to be exaggerated representations
of the knights seeking the legendary Holy Grail, much to
the children's innocent delight.

It's all so dramatic seen through a veil of textured black
fabric over my eyes. Two nights past, Guinevere suggested
I wear something daring to her wedding, something never
seen before in Camelot. She'd kissed my cheek and set *lace*,
of all things, to the black brim of a rounded ladies' hat, letting the veil eclipse my face. Perhaps the poignancy came

from knowing such a rare decoration was from Lyonesse mere months after the alleged twenty-year-old curse of Morgan le Fay finally passed, sending the kingdom to join Atlantis at the bottom of the sea.

"Girls in Lyonesse didn't wear trinkets in their hair," Guinevere had said. "Lace was the fabric of lovers. The keepsake a lady's champion would give her. We used to say, 'Wear black at night, wear lace in the day. Wear both one night, and you will find your way.'"

It's grand enough to surpass my usual desire not to stand out in a crowd. With that lace covering my eyes, I weave through jugglers, entertainers, and gemstone-peddlers in the gardens toward the grand hall. I'm antsy leaving Guinevere's chambers ahead of her, even if she did ask for a moment alone for prayer, but the gardens are calming.

I know every path that tours them blindfolded. Every tree, favoring the elm planted before I was born that now stands a masterpiece. One day, as a girl, I hid in its branches while my father searched the entire castle for me, thinking I'd finally run away from my declared *prison of Camelot*. Now, as I slip between lady-in-waiting and apprentice to a snuff-addicted former sorcerer, I come here, where I've hidden tools and scraps Merlin wouldn't miss for a side-project of my own: a one-handed crossbow attached to the wrist with a leather cuff.

From years of watching Owen master archery, I've seen the drawbacks of Camelot's clunky crossbows. A miniature-sized one would be of better use in hand-to-hand combat. I've buried it and some arrows under the elm's heavy root, where it lifts and the occasional mouse makes its home. I've kept

Merlin in the dark about this because I want to make something that is truly mine. Besides, the old fool would likely tinker with it whenever I wasn't there.

A minstrel with a wind-up harp has gathered the attention of those by the grand hall, strumming the same Celtic ballad I recognize from my mother's music box. But a tipsy knight gesturing the gates with his pint glass is louder than the minstrel's song.

"The prodigal son returns! It's Lancelot!"

I reach the edge of the gardens and look across the courtyard at heavy doors rumbling open and steel gears spinning. Chains draw each port inside and back. As the doors slam open, a handful of knights by the grand hall raise copper pints and cheer. Their eyes are blood-red, their lids smudged in kohl.

A stallion trots inside draped in red and gold and carrying a man I recognize: his dark, curly hair longer now, his skin bronzed. A twisted dragon tattoo climbs Sir Lancelot's neck, and a long metal piercing goes clear through two spots on the upper cartilage of one ear, required branding of all Knights of the Round Table. Sir Lancelot's brows cock arrogantly above kohl-lined eyes, but the pompous look quickly fades to a smile.

"We rode through the night to arrive in time!" he calls, flashing white teeth and leaping from his horse for his brothers-in-arms.

"We expected you months ago," his former squire Sir Galahad says. "God, in three years, you might have made time for a bath." Galahad shoves Lancelot back a few steps.

"I had to see which refined lady Arthur tricked into marrying him." Lancelot swings a friendly arm around Galahad's neck.

And show off the squire to fill Galahad's shoes, I think, shielding my eyes as the boy in question rides in after Lancelot, stopping a good distance away. His shoulders are slouched, disguising what would be a tall frame. A gloved hand rakes messy, dark hair flat as he takes in Camelot and its extravagant celebrations. A smile I admit I find dazzling crosses his face at the wealth of colors and mechanical trinkets soaring through the air. I feel my feet inch closer to get a better look, but peddlers and nobility crowd in front of until I can no longer see him.

"Out of the way, please, my lady!"

I must duck quickly to avoid the juggler's fiery arsenal of transforming firelances as he and his audience of children stroll past.

I leave the gardens, crossing the courtyard for the grand hall's entrance, where inside, the ceremony will take place. Now there's no sign of the boy who arrived with Lancelot, and I'm forced to pass through Camelot's finest, who hastily ensure Arthur's champion kisses a pint glass or three in the meantime. I should hope their new blended sword-firelances they call *fusionahs* are empty of silver bearings. Lancelot shows off one he claimed while away—it boasts an iron hilt whose grip is black leather with a long metal barrel twisting against a shining blade. The novelty of the mechanical arts hasn't worn off yet, it seems. Galahad seizes the fusionah in good fun, mocking the delicate engravings on the barrel too demure for a roguish knight, but Lancelot is quick to return it to his holster.

The stink of them hits me before I reach the doors. They watch me pass and whistle as I keep my head down. Lancelot among them is the loudest instigator with eyes already red from ale.

"I've missed the fair ladies of the kingdom. Your greeting flatters me, love, but alas, my loyalty is to Arthur."

The lot of them laugh, and those who've been on the quest with Lancelot tell tales about him that would set a blush to the most daring harlot's cheek.

I shoot him a nasty look. Up close, he's nothing more than an obnoxious drunk with messy facial hair.

———

The grand hall is composed of lords and ladies greeting each other with air kisses and compliments just as sincere, all too boisterous for my liking. I weave through them, noting how Guinevere's Lyonesse style has caught on: ladies wear bold colors, copper and brass ornaments, low-cut gowns, luxurious nighttime corsets. Glittery jeweled brooches shine in polished hair. Men adjust their rounded black hats and twitch their waxed moustaches.

Trumpets sound, and Guinevere is first to make her way to the altar. The queen-to-be has magnificently covered her prized curves with an angelic veil under which violets and doves' feathers lie attached to her hair. A Lyonesse tradition. For luck.

I search for my mother in the crowd of nobility. With her lovely blonde hair and Owen's intense brown eyes, Lady Carolyn cannot help but stand out in Camelot. She's near the front, and I slip past a handful of dandies to her side, hoping my arrival goes unnoticed.

No such luck. My mother does a double-take when she spots the never-before-seen lavender gown Guinevere loaned me, corseted with thin white mesh and asymmetrical in how it falls. Too strange to be from Camelot; too low-cut to have been made by one of her seamstresses. Her fingers note the black hat and daring lace. I wait to see if the pagan costume I'm wearing warrants a scolding from Camelot's master seamstress.

"Guinevere asked me to—"

"You look lovely. The hat's a bit much." She flicks a fingernail against the brim, and the veil pops up. "Suitors might try to distract you from the toast in that." One hand reaches for mine, lacing our fingers together. "You have my hands, Vivienne. Right down to the fingertips."

I breathe in sharply as we both stare at the forgotten soot under my nails. Her eyes rise to mine, giving me a look.

"And perhaps next time you could make a stronger effort to return from Guinevere's chambers *before* midnight."

I nod, scrubbing my fingers on the underside of my dress. The garment's skirt is terribly loud—

"Ahem!"

The forced cough draws my attention to the squires across the hall, where my brother Owen rudely seeks my attention. He waits for the king's bride to pass before glaring for my loud shuffling. I promptly return the glare, and

Owen shakes his head, showing a flash of silver in the upper rim of his ear, mostly hidden by his curly blond hair. A little early for such a decoration, but Owen is ambitious, and it's only a matter of time before he'll have the ink to match.

When the trumpets sound, we stand straighter for King Arthur. At the hall's entrance, the king glances about at nobility with green eyes younger than his thirty-five years, as though still the boy who took rule of the kingdom twenty years past. He sets his gaze upon Guinevere, his walk indicative of his confidence but lacking the authority a castle-bred king might have boasted.

Like the gentleman I've always known him to be, he nods politely at those who meet his eyes, even as the hammered gold of his crown and his morning jacket lined in red silk must surely weigh him down. A boyish smile crosses his face at the sight of Lancelot, and if Arthur's curmudgeonly advisors at the front weren't so concerned with propriety, the king might have dashed into the crowd to embrace his champion. He settles for a salute to his knights, who lift their arms in return. Lancelot, now with a rather melancholic disposition, is the last to do so. The scoundrel surprises me. I would have imagined he'd be elated to see Arthur so happy.

Lancelot lowers his arm as Arthur passes, and the knight is inebriated enough for his elbow to clumsily hit a flagpole. It nearly topples over, only caught at the last second from smashing into a stained-glass window by the boy standing there.

It's his squire, whom I can see much closer now. A boy not quite twenty, rather tall indeed with a lean build that rivals the knight he serves. His hair is much darker than I thought:

nearly black and would probably hit his chin if it weren't so wild, scattered about his forehead. Some of it falls over his big eyes, and he pushes it back, but it refuses to stay put.

He looks at me and when he does, it's not by accident. I look closer. Violet eyes, like the flowers in my lady's hair. Unnatural, unusual, heavy in a fashion that must always look like he's just awoken. And looking right at me.

When I realize how long I've been staring, I snap back to the Latin ceremony and the droning priest whose monocle tumbles onto his Bible.

From the corner of my eye, I watch the squire shuffling in place as though the prospect of standing still for this long is impossible. With as much casual nature as I can muster, I glance back. His eyes pierce mine, and one corner of his mouth lifts in a smile. My cheeks go warm, and I dart my gaze to the stage.

Arthur and Guinevere hold hands, and the bishop wraps their wrists together with a ribbon to signify the union. Though the mechanical arts are new to Camelot—and with it, the embrace of science in addition to Christianity—some traditions must be kept. The usual chatter of nobility goes silent. The significance of this moment doesn't escape me either.

A knight slips through a side door—Owen's childhood friend, Percy. His beeline for Lancelot is quick, and he whispers in the knight's ear as Arthur repeats the bishop's words to his bride. A look of worry comes over Lancelot's face. Signaling to those around him and tapping his squire on the shoulder, Lancelot follows Percy out the door, a bevy of urgent whispers accompanying them. As much as I block out the bishop's empty declarations of faith, I can't make out a word they're saying aside from several mentions of the Round Table.

The violet-eyed boy is last to leave. He doesn't look at me again as he disappears outside. And while I'm curious about why they're leaving, I also find myself wondering why that'd disappoint me.

━━━━

After the ceremony, the new queen must return to her chambers to change into a proper Lyonesse gown now that the Christian ceremony is complete. But I know it's partly because the ridiculous veil atop her head is cooking her in the hot June sun.

I'm supposed to accompany her, but she smiles and tells me not to worry, that I'd be of no use to her with the many hooks and buttons so different from the gowns of Camelot. Her orderlies can handle it without me, and so I wander the courtyard with my eyes on the sky, hoping by some miracle Merlin is wrong, and Azur has decided to visit for Arthur's wedding. But maybe the old fool was right.

"Knights to the northern gates!"

The sudden shout startles me. Knights rush past me for the drawbridge. Urgency sobers up a man quickly, and their wits have returned. I wonder what's happening.

Two squires jog past me from the walls. When I recognize my brother, I grab his arm. "What's going on?"

Owen stops, but instead of answering, he flicks my hat. His eyes are smudged from sweat and likely his fingertips' unsuccessful attempts at relieving the kohl's itchiness. "Where'd you get this? Embracing Lady Guinevere's exotic roots?"

The other squire stops as well. It's the boy, the one with violet eyes, still kohl-lined and just as messy as my brother's, with dark hair tangling in his lashes. He blinks and cocks a smile to the side.

Owen glances at him. "Marcus, this is my sister, Vivienne, the queen's lady-in-waiting." His voice is cloaked with newly drunk ale.

Marcus inclines his head to me. I mock a curtsy and turn back to my brother. "What's happening? All the commotion—"

"Someone's drunk the last of the green fairy, Viv," Owen jokes. He knows how much I love the licoricey spirit. "Nothing for you to worry your little head about, I'm sure. *We* don't even know. Back to the other children with you."

I frown. I hate it when he does this.

"Maybe Galahad thought it unwise to tell you because you handle serious news about as well as you handle your ale." I cross my arms. "One pint before you're calling for our mother."

Marcus coughs into his fist to hide his laughter. He runs his fingers through his knotted hair at the back. It makes him look even wilder. "Are you always this brash, my lady?" His posture is poised.

Owen's loud scoff saves me. "On the contrary. Only when she's bored." This time, his narrow-eyed look comes from the embarrassing truth I revealed, but usually, he makes his envy of my newly acquired social status no secret. His archery skills had to be the epitome of perfection to become Galahad's squire, and it's still not an easy road to knighthood. Owen wouldn't find the requisite decorum exhausting, being constantly bowed or curtsied to, but I'd much rather be sent to the gallows than deal with the many strangers at court.

Owen slaps Marcus on the back and jogs toward the hall. Marcus lingers behind.

"I like brash," he whispers. Then he leaves, too.

I glance around to see if anyone's overheard, but I'm alone, thank God. And as immobile as Caldor without a taste of *jaseemat*.

My eyes fall upon a familiar scarlet-cloaked figure in the shadows: Merlin, ignored by proud and sheeplike nobility as always. He limps awkwardly in stiff trousers for the other side of the grand hall, pointed black shoes giving away his tendency for scuffing his feet. Covering his inked skull is an exquisite silk hat I've never seen him wear, tall and black.

Pausing at the corner before a field of untended greenery, he beckons me with a jerk of his head. I'm discreet as I follow.

Merlin leans against the side where there is no one to bother him. An exhale of green smoke snakes into the air, and his eyes close with pleasure. He drops the rolled *hashish* and steps on it. "What are those fools doing over there?"

I don't want to tell Merlin about rumors of le Fay in the land. It'd only distract him from what the knights can certainly handle on their own, without depriving me of several days of learning about the mechanical arts.

Besides, it might be dangerous to remind Merlin of magic.

"I don't know." God forgive my selfishness. "Neither does Owen."

Merlin stares at the guards keeping lookout on the wall. The sorcerer's fingers layer one by one over the green stone embedded in the smooth round handle of his walnut cane. He shuts his eyes, like he can somehow hear the heated conversation from where we stand. Magic might let him know, but he wouldn't give in to that temptation.

Finally, the commotion calms, and it seems everything has been settled. Laughter is meek, but the knights return to the celebrations.

"Owen," Merlin says. "A lot of sleeping demons in that boy."

More like a lifetime of seeking control over the stupidest things.

Guards sound their trumpets. The daylong feasting and dancing is set to begin. I'll be needed once Guinevere returns.

Merlin waves at me to go on without him. "I forgot my hookah in my tower. Caldor needs a bit of wind anyway. I'll be down at nightfall."

It has nothing to do with his forgotten pipe and everything to do with watching Caldor soar through the night sky. "See you at the feast, Merlin."

"Aye, but don't stay out too late. On Camelot's day off, we'll meet in the clock tower at eight sharp."

"Of course," I reply with a smile, letting myself feel the cool anticipation of an entire day where no one will seek me for errands or tea.

"Oh, and Vivienne? Squires become knights. And knights take vows of celibacy."

Surely, he can't be that naïve to think none of the knights visit the harlots in the countryside when the rest of Camelot sleeps. Even the king himself can't believe otherwise. Besides, what does that have to do with—

"And some will actually need to take it seriously, dear girl."

Owen bursts from the grand hall with flasks spilling ale onto his hands. Marcus strolls out, too, shaking his head at my brother's antics. Owen's laughter is infectious, intoxicating enough that Marcus doesn't need as much as a sip to succumb to the same ecstatic level. Our eyes meet, and he smiles with sincerity I've never seen before in the kingdom.

"Marcus!" Owen calls. He's halfway to the knights' quarters already.

Marcus runs off, spinning backward at one point to make sure I'm still watching.

"For some," Merlin mumbles, snorting a pinch of snuff and wiping his nose clean, "life depends on the knights."

It twists my stomach, my awareness of him possibly witnessing the brief interaction I had with Lancelot's squire. But the implication is preposterous and the least of my concerns right now.

I leave the sorcerer sitting in the field and take to the courtyard where servants have set up tents and tables, gas-burning torches and banners, and steam-run carts flying over us on iron pathways in the sky.

FIVE

By nightfall, that sky is speckled with stars and a crescent moon. Just as intoxicating as this past harvest's ale, reserved for tonight and kept safe from the knights' thirsty lips.

At tables in the tents, servants struggle to keep goblets full. Furs cover chairs; platters of apricots and figs and cheeses are never-ending. Maids drop their sleeves from their shoulders at only a glance from Lancelot, leader of the knights. He stands red-faced and drunk, looking too often at Arthur and Guinevere's private table on the stage. The glowing happiness she and Arthur boast is indeed enviable.

Squires ask Lancelot how the commotion at the gates finally resolved, to which he bemoans, "Oh, spare me! Send the children to hide because Morgan is surely on her wicked way!"

Even the most proper of guests ignore the roasted hogs, beef stew, and freshly baked breads. They drink spirits and live in their own inebriated worlds where the fantasy of Camelot overrules the reality of tomorrow morning's blasted headache.

Merlin sits in the corner, in the same spot he found me as a girl of ten: bored at a feast, disassembling his hookah to build a toy aeroship for some crying children. When I was caught, he was too drunk to be mad. He was delighted. Tonight, he puffs away on the reassembled hookah's mouthpiece. The smoke is lovely and willowy, winding through the braid in his beard. Scantily-clad dancers flock to him, but he pulls the brim of his hat over his eyes, not to be disturbed.

I sip my lukewarm ale as seldom as possible. Even but a few drops are horribly vile.

"Perhaps Owen can hold his drink after all, my lady."

I turn toward the voice. Marcus, goblet in hand, gestures toward my brother sitting with the knights. Empty pint glasses sit in front of Owen, whose laughter is so strong, tears have seized his eyes.

I flick an eyebrow. "So far. Being Galahad's squire might increase your tolerance." Though it's still uncharacteristic of Owen. Rather refreshing now, actually. "As you get to know my brother, you'll realize these moments are quite rare."

A few knights lean over Owen, laughing at him. They take pity and call over a servant with a tray of sweetmeats, anything of sustenance my brother could use to soak up the poison.

"I'll remember that." Marcus lifts his goblet to mine and shrugs. "To Camelot," he says. We clink them, but neither of us drinks; instead we regard the warm brew with our own version of disdain.

I look at him. "You don't care for it either?"

He lifts a shoulder. "My parents don't drink much ale in the farmlands. I don't quite get the appeal, I'm afraid."

I smile. "They'll toast with green fairy before the night's end."

Another shrug. "Never had absinthe before either." In the dim light, his irises have a bit of gold. My cheeks feel warm, but maybe it's the few sips of ale on an empty stomach.

"It's the perfect night to try it. Quite possibly the most exciting part of a celebration being in Camelot."

"Really?" He looks around. Knights woo the harlots they brought inside, women more than willing to lift their skirts to their thighs, or trace a gentleman's chest to his belt buckle. "Maybe these folks have already had their green fairy." Marcus's eyes return to mine. "And I thought seeing Excalibur tonight would be excitement enough."

He has my attention and with one look, he knows it. But what he's saying is impossible. "You've seen Excalibur?" I ask.

"You haven't?" He lifts a teasing eyebrow.

"You've just arrived!"

"The Round Table met after the ceremony. I saw it then." But he doesn't say why and shuts his mouth as though biting back a secret, scrutinizing his pint as though it might be at fault for his traitorous words.

I playfully narrow my eyes. "Liar."

He shrugs with a mischievous smile and pretends to entertain himself with the lanterns swooping over grounds. Dancers arch their stomachs toward the sky, and their legs kicks the stars. Hawk-haired dandies whistle as they take in the show.

I should admire the skies, too, in case Azur might arrive, but…

No. What Marcus said is *impossible!*

I want him to tell me so. No one's watching us, and so I set my pint on a nearby table and step closer, touching his blazer's sleeve to get his attention just as he seized mine. The daring lace I wear must be what has granted me such courage. Normally I'm not this bold.

"Really?" My voice is quieter than I expected. "You've seen Excalibur?"

His lips part as though he's going to confess something wonderful, but he forgets to answer when his eyes get lost in mine. This close, the dim light turns them a bit gray, fading from violet. I should drop his sleeve, move away, keep to propriety, but I can't break free of this moment, and I'm not certain I want to.

Clearly, I'm being absurd, but then blessed bursts of bright lights—red and blue and green—slam against the sky, as though fired by cannons, saving me from my own foolish thoughts. We both jump, awkwardly stepping apart. An array of exploding colors cascades over the entire kingdom. Dancers toss their veils high enough to flutter down like flower petals escaping a storm.

Out of the corner of my eye, I see Marcus turn back to me. "I'll show you one day. If you like."

I smile. It's an impossible offer, and we both know it. "Will you, now?"

He smiles back, and enough confidence has returned

for him to lean closer. "Of course. But it'll put us in grave danger, and we'll have to run away. It'll be scandalous."

I laugh as purple and yellow explode in the sky and trickle down, my solemn nod a promise one can only make under such dazzling colors. Colors that let one indulge in a small bit of fantasy, even if only temporarily.

At the beckoning of Lancelot, the whole court raises their goblets to Arthur and Guinevere.

"To the king and queen!" Arthur's champion bellows, his voice rowdy, his face hot. He goes still when his eyes rest on Guinevere. It's understandable to be caught off-guard by the queen's exotic beauty, especially in her full white corset and flowing skirt puckered into a sensual shape. A small circular hat releases a cascade of white lace across her cheeks. Her smile is genuine as she awaits his toast.

"To prosperity!" Lancelot calls, resettling himself. He forces his eyes back to the crowd. "To Camelot!"

"To Camelot!" we cry, clinking our pints. Even Arthur's stuffy councilmen cheer, and Marcus and I join in. Somehow, the ale isn't that horrible now.

As the celebrations threaten to deafen us, Stephen throws his sloppy arm around Marcus's shoulders. "Oi! Did I hear Lancelot's squire say he's never kissed the green fairy?" A handful of squires surround us—Ector and Bors, too—and their eager eyes dart between Marcus and me.

Ector's eyes are wide and bloodshot. "Hold on. It was *Viv* you meant?" He smacks Marcus's chest with the back of his hand.

Marcus's cheeks flush red. "Blast it, Ector, shut up," he whispers, avoiding my eyes most obviously.

People notice—inebriated lords from Arthur's council, flirty noblewomen who keep company with my mother. I feel their gazes fall upon us, and I step further away from the very unavailable squire. What does Ector mean?

The music becomes louder, faster, more festive. The smoke from the sorcerer's long pipe and bowl creates a fog, the illusion of rainless clouds. Knights crowd the king, pulling him from the stage. Their chants are contagious. *Music! Green fairy! Dancing!*

"Yes, it must have been Viv!" Stephen says. "Come on, Marcus. To hell with Owen. There's nothing immoral about talking with a beautiful girl—you said so yourself. I'm sure Viv would love to dance, wouldn't you, Viv?" Stephen shoves Marcus straight into me.

I look up into Marcus's eyes, just as surprised as mine. His fingers linger on my waist a few seconds too long before he yanks them away. "Apologies."

I back away and force a proper smile of forgiveness. "I shouldn't," I say. "The queen might need me."

I'll have those squires' necks, if it's the last thing I do. Guinevere doesn't need me, but Marcus is not available for my amusement. He should know it as well, even if all of this is in good fun. One foot takes another step backward, but Ector and Bors are standing behind me, blocking what should be an easy escape. Knights spot us and don't seem to care, but these days, I simply cannot afford to be seen flirting with a squire.

Stephen and Ector aren't finished yet. "Oh, come on, Viv.

Not even a full day in Camelot, and this one's already got his eye on you," Stephen slurs, arm slung over Marcus's shoulder. "At least give him one dance before he signs his life away to the Round Table. Poor bastard's been dying to ask you—"

"Oh God—" Marcus's eyes fall shut fast.

"Yes, and he had to hear Owen's spitfire declarations about you being off-limits to *everyone*, not just squires, obviously. What, with you about to be married off, and all!" Ector adds, ale on his breath. Stephen and Bors laugh.

I touch my own face, and then my hat and veil to make sure I'm still covered, hoping my reddening cheeks from these silly words aren't noticeable. Marcus was talking about me? To my brother?

What will Owen tell our mother?

It should be easy for a handmaid to slip away from horrid crowds unnoticed, but suddenly, the guests tonight have forgotten about the servants carrying trays of absinthe. All because of a trio of outspoken squires and a fourth who should know his place. I'm mortified. I cannot stay here any longer.

If I'm to run, I should go to my family's quarters. "I'm not … off-limits." I don't understand why Ector's words even crossed my lips.

Marcus looks humiliated, but he should be. So many watch the squire of Arthur's champion and Guinevere's lady-in-waiting with curiosity. But I won't lose my freedom to escape to Merlin's tower because of him.

Marcus steps forward as though to explain. "I'm sorry. I wasn't—"

But I'm already running to the gardens.

SIX

The music is still ringing in my ears by the time I realize what my traitorous feet did: flee an embarrassing moment the rest of Camelot just so happened to witness. I don't look back, but it's out of sheer humiliation that I can't bear to see if Marcus and the others are watching. Instead I push on, passing the trees lining the gardens. Finally, out of sight, I stop and keel over, thankful for the silence.

Silence interrupted all too soon.

By something less celebratory.

At the city gates up ahead, no more than twenty meters from where I stand amid the trees, guards hiss at one another. And then I read a single phrase on one's lips: *she's here*.

I hide under an evergreen's low branches, in view of both the tense gates and enraptured celebrations. In the tents, drunken nobility are in a happy state of ignorance. No one looks past the courtyard or everlasting feast. Marcus stands in shock, squires punching his arm in a teasing manner as flirtatious dancers surround them. He's without a smile, and that tugs at my heart.

"What is it?" the smooth and confident voice of Galahad calls. Heavy footsteps follow.

I press against the tree to hide myself as the knight storms past, fusionah unsheathed.

It's because of the guards' whispered words that Galahad's usual stoic disposition unravels. He paces, hair ruffled and face blurred. It's unlike him.

When a disheveled Owen arrives, Galahad wastes no time. "Arthur said not to shoot until he's seen her for himself." Galahad nods once. "Get the king."

Owen sprints for the courtyard, leaving Galahad lost in troubled thought. The minstrels' instruments go abruptly quiet as my brother reaches the tent. The eerie silence following is so much louder.

And then, a woman's voice, wobbling between panic and distress, reverberates from behind the gates.

"Camelot is in the business of keeping those in danger waiting this long?"

She's afraid or in pain, and her voice is colder than ice, and I know who she is. Archers on the wall are quick to aim; they declare they were ordered to shoot her on sight. They wait for Galahad's command. But he hesitates. His balance is unstable from a day's worth of self-poisoning.

"Only those who've been exiled," his voice cracks, striving for ferocity. The echo is unnerving.

Silence is her response, but in it lingers the quietest rumble of footsteps. Many footsteps.

Through the low branches, I watch Arthur follow Owen to the gates. Several knights have joined, though Lancelot is strangely absent. They're close enough that I can hear their voices.

"Be calm," Arthur says, bringing whatever discussion he was having with Owen to an end. "If Galahad is certain, no one else can know. Tell the minstrels to continue."

Owen doesn't blink. "Yes, your majesty." He runs at full speed back to the tent. The music returns.

Arthur acknowledges the guards. "Open the gates."

They relay his command, and five engage the mechanism at the door, cracking back solid wood to reveal a white horse carrying a tall, frightfully thin woman in an old-fashioned cloak and hood.

The anxious steed forces its way inside; the woman glances around too often to be sure of her own safety. Guards click back the hammers of their fusionahs. Archers raise their bows. A row of men circle the entrance, goggles pulled down from helmets in case their weaponry would recoil in its emission of fire powder.

They shout and shout and shout, "Stay where you are!"

But the king won't order fire, and the woman ignores the threats. "Let her pass," Arthur declares in a voice barely confident.

Her blinking silvery eyes search each corner of Camelot. They fall upon the king. "Arthur!"

She drops from her saddle and rushes to him, letting her hood fall, revealing long white hair coiling down her back. Arthur freezes as her skeletal arms go around his waist, apple-red nails resting at his hips. My eyebrows rise at that.

"You're here," he says. "They said you'd come, but I didn't believe you'd be this foolish."

She steps back. Her heavy eyes go wider than the kohl extending their corners. "Foolish? The African kingdoms were going to kill me!"

The kingdoms she speaks of are allied with Camelot, just as Corbenic is. Masters of architecture and science, they'd be the last in the world to carry out an execution without the most irrefutable evidence. This truth does not bode well for the woman in Arthur's arms.

But she is relentless. "They believed a lie, doubted my own word, even when the past twenty years proved otherwise! Even when I had proof!" There's a purse at her waist, and she pulls out folded letters. Her lip quivers. "I had no choice. You have to help me. You have to clear my name!"

I frown as the footsteps grow louder, and I strain my vision in the darkness for those who must be behind her.

Then I gasp.

A shine of moonlight piercing through the clouds reveals a black-armored legion carrying torches and gas lanterns. They're in the hills, on the other side of the wall blocking Arthur and his knights from seeing them. But anyone standing where I hide wouldn't miss a sight such as this: scores of soldiers too tall to be men wear black helmets, undignified and savage. Their eyes glow like the fiery tip of an iron that's been blasted in a furnace. Steeds the color of midnight have the same vile, demonic features. Flags blow wildly, black and red, nothing like the elegant crimson of the Pendragon flag.

As quickly as the moonlight reveals them, they disappear. Now, only vast farmlands. I blink quickly, searching. I'm tempted to fetch my crossbow, even if it wouldn't do a blasted thing. But I cannot risk being seen.

Arthur is shocked by the woman's presence. "No more than a day ago, Pelles ordered us to kill you. My God, what he says you did all those years ... " He glances at the watchful eyes of Galahad and the guards. "Merlin would be furious to know I've let you inside."

The woman presses Arthur's hand to her face. "Then don't tell him. You cannot believe those accusations, Arthur. I'm your family!"

Arthur looks toward the celebrations. There's no sign of the hookah-smoking Merlin. "Family."

She nods, and her eyes shine with cold hope like she knows Arthur's greatest wish.

Arthur hesitates. "They mentioned Lyonesse."

The icy disposition in her face shatters. "Cruel lies. Your bride. Her home, her family. Arthur, I loved Lyonesse."

He cannot be fooled by this woman's words. When Guinevere first arrived, her despair from losing her home, from her trial, from nearly being executed because of charges of sorcery—these were enough to keep anyone bedridden with grief for weeks. The stories she told about those unable to leave the damned kingdom ...

Arthur wouldn't believe this woman, would he?

"You *know* me." Slow and purposeful, her voice warbles

like a chant. "You fought for me because you knew to execute me would mean the true perpetrator of Lyonesse's demise would stay free. Remember, Arthur?"

And he must. Arthur's eyes look elsewhere as though reliving the moment all those years ago. Harps and fiddles and horns from the celebrations mix with the tension here. Knights hold back stumbling drunks boasting empty goblets. Arthur and the woman are quiet, but the guards won't rest just yet; their weapons are just as steadily aimed on her.

If this is really Morgan le Fay, then King Pelles might lead a battalion of soldiers against the disobedient King Arthur of Camelot.

What insanity has come over our king?

Arthur pulls her shoulders to his chest. "And that perpetrator was never found." He takes a long breath. "I haven't seen Merlin tonight. Let's keep it that way. We'll put you in the main castle for now." Arthur signals to the guards to raise the bridge. "No one here is to speak a word about this under penalty of death." Each syllable expresses the utmost seriousness of Arthur's order.

"Thank you," the woman breathes into his chest. "Brother."

The guards blink in disbelief as Arthur's command forces their weapons low. They pull on the levers that activate the gates' closing mechanism, and the sanctuary of Camelot accepts the woman. And still, not far off, there are footsteps. So quiet, I'm fighting with myself as to whether I've imagined them. I inch forward to hear better, fingers digging into the soft earth—

A hand grasps my shoulder, pulling me from the tree's greenery. As a scream leaves my lips—all secrecy of my whereabouts be damned!—a hand clamps over my mouth.

"Quiet, you foolish girl," Merlin rasps. I face him as he drops me, his hookah against his shoulder, warm and full of smoke, and a fierce challenge in his eye as he watches Arthur lead his guest into the main castle. A stark difference from how Merlin regards the uninteresting nobility of the court. He looks at the woman like she's his equal.

"Morgan's returned!" I hiss with more fright than I knew was in me. "Why would the king allow this? She was exiled! Corbenic said there'd be war!"

Merlin doesn't look the faintest bit surprised by the woman's arrival. He sets his mouth in a firm line and lifts into a crouch, resting on the stone of his cane. "Yes, that's her. Morgan le Fay, the king's older sister."

With that, Merlin turns for his clock tower. I try to catch up with him, but his feet are surprisingly quick. "She's become much more advanced in her thievery of magic," he calls over his shoulder. "Azur must know before I confront Arthur on his blatant disobedience."

Shadows chill my skin, and I lock from my mind the ghostly images I saw. Magic could certainly render black-armored soldiers able to disappear and reappear at will.

We pass through the blacksmith's workspace for the cellar. Merlin lifts the heavy door and climbs down. I follow. "She said she was innocent—"

"Ha! She's a damn good sorceress now, I'd wager, from the looks of her. Even an accomplished healer like le Fay couldn't resist the taste of magic for that long."

The memory of the woman's strange, silver eyes sends a haunting through me. I won't sleep well tonight. "Why would she return?"

The door to Merlin's tower opens. He carries himself up, two steps at a time.

"Oh, a multitude of reasons. Perhaps she's telling the truth, and there are other kingdoms more dangerous for her than ours. Maybe she's changed—stranger things have certainly happened. More likely, she wants control of Camelot." I'm panting as we round the spiraled steps, but Merlin's breath is steady. "She's wanted it ever since her falling out with Arthur, twenty years past. Excalibur chose him to be the rightful king based on lineage. But Morgan—"

"Morgan's older," I finish, recalling the sorcerer's initial description of her. "Morgan didn't agree with the declaration that Arthur was the rightful ruler."

"Aye," Merlin says with a nod as the last door cracks open. "She thought if she'd had the opportunity to extract Excalibur, it would have chosen her instead, leaving her Camelot's resources, including the Round Table and, well, me." He watches the celebrations from his window, the blasts of color in the sky. His hand finds his pocket, and fingers lift a pinch of snuff to his nose. He draws in deeply.

"Was she right?"

Merlin hesitates as he considers my question. "No," he decides. "I was there when Arthur extracted Excalibur. I was there when he was crowned."

"Why wait twenty years for Camelot, then?"

"So she could master magic."

"Arthur believes she's here in good faith."

"Ha! I wouldn't trust Morgan to know the concept of *good faith* any more than I'd trust Caldor to have blood in his veins. When she left all those years ago, she vowed Camelot would be hers. Arthur would be foolish not to sleep with both eyes open."

"And still he let her inside? Why?"

Merlin leans back in his chair. "Because he didn't believe she was at fault for Lyonesse's demise. There was no proof, after all, and she was his sister, his only family. For years, he had no one other than a step-brother, Kay, and me. And I only met him when he was fifteen, already a man and about to lead an entire kingdom. Losing his sister over a crown he didn't exactly want broke his heart." His eyes dart about like they do whenever he's thinking, and for a brief second, the light hits him the wrong way, and a glint of white fire flits about in his pupils. When I look again, it's gone. Skewed moonlight and eventful evenings are no match for overactive imaginations.

"I hope to God I'm wrong about Morgan. I wish, I wish I'd never spoken with her that final day." His fingers trace the handle of his teacup.

"Why? What happened?"

He regards me, the mixture of moonlight and colorful bursts in the sky combating the patterns tattooed on his temples.

"On that last day, I told her about alchemy."

SEVEN

Blinding sunlight pours through the tall windows of the main castle as guards escort my father and me to the assembly room. I wring my wrists to forget nightmares of militia ghosts advancing through a fog. Of digging my fingers into dirt, contemplating seizing my crossbow to fire at a rail-thin woman who Merlin would later tell me does not come in peace. But it was a trick of the imagination. Certainly we're here for something else.

The clock tower strikes eight. I was supposed to have reported to Merlin, but Arthur summoned his council not two hours ago. Glancing out a window, I can see the top of Merlin's tower peeking over the gardens, acres away and might as well be so much further.

The guards open two wooden doors at the hallway's end, revealing a band of disgruntled knights and advisors surrounding Arthur.

The king leans on a long wooden table decorated with a

crimson runner, only straightening sporadically to speak up against an outspoken advisor. Lanterns form to imitate candelabras, glowing an unnatural orange to match the fiery tension of Arthur's most trusted knights and holding their shape instead of dancing as real fire would. Silver trays offering tea and biscuits are ignored entirely, even by the ever-still Guinevere, sitting calmly in a wrought-iron chair off to the side.

The queen is lost in thought, far away until I've touched her shoulder. "My lady?"

She forces a smile. There are dark circles under her distraught eyes.

"Letters of correspondence should not matter!" an advisor named Lord Henry says in a vicious tone. Behind him, the eleven other lords in Arthur's council, of which my father is a member, nod in agreement. They might look to resolve this quickly, before Merlin would hear of this—none of them likes how the tattooed former sorcerer is the closest advisor to Arthur, and the unofficial head. "Every day, Spanish rogues grow closer to finding that which we seek, and you, Arthur, want to abandon the quest to reopen discussion about Lyonesse?"

I miss Arthur's curt explanation for why his council was called. Looking around, I note the state of the knights after a day's worth of celebration, their respective squires in tow. Smudged eyes are heavy. Hair is disheveled from uneasy sleep or graceful feminine fingers.

Owen is frightfully pale-faced with a frown he's destined to wear until at least the afternoon. He barely registers my presence.

A twitch rolls around in my stomach as I realize if Galahad's squire is here, then perhaps Lancelot's would be, too, even if the roguish devil himself isn't. Over my shoulder and by the window I recognize Marcus's lean frame, but cannot risk a direct look. *Why would a squire inquire so much about a handmaid?*

"Did Pelles's warning mean nothing?" my father questions the king.

In Arthur's hand are letters. "These were verified," he says.

"By whom?" Lord Henry retorts.

"By your king," Arthur responds, eyebrows drawn as he asserts his status. "Morgan was wrongfully accused of sorcery. Framed for Lyonesse's demise—"

The lethargy of the morning finally breaks for clarity. A gasp escapes my lips, loud enough to warrant attention from Guinevere.

But then the door bursts open and in storms Lancelot, clear-headed, able to manage his steady gaze upon Arthur and then the woman he drags in by the hair. Her cries are stricken with pain. The wrinkled clothes beneath Lancelot's gentleman's jacket are no indication of his mental state. His eyes are sharp; his sense of vengeance, strong.

"Release me!" the woman screams through her pain.

"Knights on guard!" Lancelot shouts. His grip around her hair loosens, and he tosses the woman to her knees in the middle of the room.

Guinevere is to her feet instantly, and my hand squeezes

hers tightly. Morgan le Fay, the legendary monster of my childhood dreams, only feet away from me.

"Oh God," I hear myself whisper.

Knights seize the fusionahs at their waists, Lancelot's the first to steady on Morgan. Hammers click back, and barrels aim at the mark. By the window, Marcus is slack-jawed and takes the longest to register Morgan's presence, staring like his worst nightmare has come to life.

Morgan cowers by Lancelot's feet, her eyes on the audience of hungry barrels and merciless faces, her upraised arms only rendering her more vulnerable.

"To your feet, witch, so we can send you to hell," Lancelot growls. "She was in the main castle, Arthur." The king's champion glowers without the appropriate respect for a king. "Either your guards got into more ale than the rest of us, or you've been easily swayed by a sorceress, and please tell me it's the former, Arthur. Please."

Guinevere is eerily silent. Her chest rises and falls with fast, angry breaths. She was likely taught never to show emotional distress, lest she should be seen as hysterical. Perhaps this is why she stays quiet when the contrary would be more rational.

Arthur steps toward his champion. "Lower your weapons."

The silence resonates with the men. Morgan's cheeks are wet with tears I didn't think a rumored witch could shed.

Lancelot's wide eyes show no indifference toward Arthur's guest. "Arthur, you cannot be serious!"

"Believe me, I am."

Lancelot obeys as the rest do.

"She *is* here, then," Guinevere whispers, shaking with anger. "Why is she here?"

I squeeze her hand. "Your highness—"

Her eyes flash at mine. To hell with accusations of hysteria. "No, Vivienne." With a voice close to a shuddering sob, she regards her husband. "Arthur, how could you?"

Arthur doesn't answer in the quiet that follows. Under Lancelot's steady glare, Morgan crawls toward her brother, her lip quivering.

But those who have seen the curse of Lyonesse are surely not ones to toy with. Guinevere storms toward the unwanted guest, seizing her husband's fusionah and aiming it at Morgan. Her thumb is quick to force back the hammer, but Arthur halts the queen before her claws can come out.

"She is not welcome here!" she screams as Arthur reclaims his firelance.

Morgan doesn't dare meet Guinevere's eyes; the alleged witch grovels with a servant's humility. Her voice is shaken, but still elegantly melodic. "I am innocent, your majesty! I was framed—"

"No! Twenty years overdue the justice you never got!"

Lord William seizes the violent queen from Arthur's arms. Guinevere swallows gulps of air. I'm at her side in an instant. Morgan is submissive now, but I'd feel better with my crossbow in hand and hope my narrowed eyes reveal as much.

"Arthur," my father says without as much as a glance at Morgan. "There will be war. And Camelot's subjects … this could cost you your crown."

Arthur sits his sister at the table. "You're weak. Eat. Drink."

It's unnerving how Morgan resembles Arthur in shape of angular face, in purposeful speech. When her brother pushes a cup of tea in front of her, thirsty lips inhale it. She reaches for a red apple amongst a plate of fruit and pricks it with the point of a silver knife, slicing through its core. Dark-circled eyes catch a glimpse of those who would be by the window, where only Marcus stands. With darkened lips and ears full of jewels, from the lobes all the way up the cartilage, Morgan might as well be the female ghost of a Camelot knight.

"Before we return to the quest," Arthur says, "we will clear Morgan's name. I will not have it on my hands that innocent blood—blood Morgan and I share—was spilled when we had the power to change that. We will meet with neighboring kingdoms to remove the tarnish. Her connection to the Pendragon name, and therefore Camelot, depends on it."

The demonic eyes of black-armored men flash in front of me. I see the jumbled images whenever I blink. Was I their only witness? I press my fingers against my temples.

Even if Arthur is desperate for family, even if it is Morgan, deep down he must know how wrong this all is.

Is there nothing I could possibly say?

"I faced charges of magic, Arthur," Guinevere says. "I faced hell and noose, and perhaps they were the same. Someone of mercy would have let me die."

"No—" Morgan reaches for Guinevere's hand. "Your father, all of Lyonesse, you were mistaken. Claims I was responsible followed me wherever I went. I was cast from kingdoms, tortured in dungeons equipped with the mechanical arts until I craved death. Those lies—"

"They weren't lies!" Guinevere screams. She wrenches her fingers free. Her words bounce off the colorless bricks and gas lanterns of tapestry-dressed walls.

A slam of hard wood breaks the tension. My eyes dart to the door. Through it storms Merlin, cane in hand, cape trailing behind him. He regards Morgan.

"Merlin, you were not summoned," Lord Henry says with impatience. "This does not concern you."

Merlin strides past Arthur's advisor without acknowledgement.

"Morgan le Fay, back in Camelot," he says as Morgan gets to her feet and clambers around the table. Merlin follows, forcing her to Arthur's side as the rest of the assembly steps back.

I sigh in relief. Certainly Merlin will set things straight.

"You clearly forgot nothing goes unnoticed here. Especially an enemy trying to sneak in under an old wizard's nose."

Arthur narrows his eyes. "Stop this, Merlin—"

But Merlin ignores the king. "How did you do it? What ports did you land at? What aeroships did you bribe? What magic did you steal to get yourself here? Was it all for Camelot? Excalibur? To observe the knights' quest or claim coordinates to a place you have no right to find?" His cane advances his walk toward her, but she keeps the long table between them.

"Or perhaps you're here for me, Morgan?" The sorcerer pauses to let Morgan state her intentions.

And she's quick to do so. "I needed the sanctuary of Camelot!"

The sorcerer is unaffected. "Word has passed through

the Holy Land about you. Horrific tales of the sorcery you've mastered, torture you've inflicted. Tales that would have made the most powerful witches of Lyonesse tremble with fear."

Morgan's eyes flash. "It isn't true."

"Don't lie, Morgan," Merlin whispers as though scolding a child. "With how advanced you must be after twenty years of thievery, you can certainly show a former sorcerer the respect he deserves."

Arthur takes a step. "No, Merlin. You didn't see her arrive, alone and—"

"No. There were others." My hand flies to cover my mouth.

The room goes silent. My heart falls still, like I'm Caldor and my *jaseemat* has run out. I look at the faces that have all turned to me, Morgan's the first. Silvery eyes blink, brows knit, lips frown. Then those lips curl into a quiet snarl, and the rest of the room disappears, rendering her ghostlike frame the only thing I see. Letting her know and study and memorize my face.

Memorize me.

EIGHT

My father is the first to speak. "Your majesty," he says, "Vivienne is but an imaginative—"

Arthur holds up a hand. "What did you say, girl?" It isn't out of anger, but curiosity.

I look around. At Merlin's face of warning. At Guinevere's empty eyes. At Marcus standing by the window. At his posture tensing, and his eyes falling shut with a strange sadness.

My hands shake. "I mean—"

"Don't be afraid. Speak, if what you have to say is the truth."

Morgan's eyes narrow as though to caution me. It sends a chill over my skin. I rub my arms, pulling my sleeves tightly over my wrists. "I saw men outside the city walls. They wore black armor, and they…were not human."

Merlin hesitates at my revelation, and his eyes search mine as though wondering, *What is it you might know?* I don't miss Morgan catching how Merlin's temper has now softened.

The sorcerer clears his throat. "Arthur, you cannot ignore this, boy."

Arthur shakes his head. "I saw no one beyond the draw-bridge—"

Morgan laughs. "Because there *was* no one. Arthur, the girl is lying. For attention, for a reward—for God knows what!"

I can't help but steal a glance at Marcus by the window. His shoulders slump over from fatigue; his eyelids are just as smudged as the rest. But unlike his companions, Marcus stands unthreatened by Morgan. He stares at me, full of melancholic questions, as though an alleged witch is not mere feet away. Out of embarrassment we should both look away, but don't.

"It's the truth," I whisper, despite how Morgan's glare could shatter crystal.

"Morgan, your lies blacken your soul." Merlin steps in front, holding out a subtle arm between the witch and me. "Blood is not thicker than the poison in your heart."

Morgan clenches her fists until that blood drips to the floor from long, pointed nails. There's no sense of pain on her face, and I'm wondering if she is human. "I came in peace, Merlin."

Lancelot's hand rests on the belt underneath his jacket, where his weapon lies. Fingers drum against his fusionah. He exchanges a peculiar glance of understanding with Guinevere. He might disobey the king, if needed.

And then what?

"Peace," Merlin mutters, circling Morgan like a cat gauging a wounded mouse. "The witch is more likely to become with child again than issue a true statement of peace."

Morgan's eyes snap up. Her hands are quick. Blood-stained fingers find the knife atop her plate, and soon the blade is piercing through the air for the sorcerer.

I scream, "Merlin!"

Merlin catches the knife before it can gouge out his left eye. He lowers the blade with the smallest smile. "It seems I've hit a nerve."

Morgan's skin turns to a shade of harsh sunlight. Her eyes drop to the floor.

"You haven't lost your touch, Merlin," she says in a cool voice. "I can't hear you inside my head chanting *Sensu Ahchla* so I know you haven't stolen that spell to read my mind and learn its contents. Knowledge of our kind alone has entrapped me." She sighs. "I suppose I've waited long enough, now that you're here."

Merlin frowns.

Morgan casts outstretched fingers toward him. Eyes lift, stark-white. Dark lips pull back over teeth.

"Laohchandrith!"

A ripple of blinding light twists in her hand.

Then vanishes.

Morgan's eyes flash with confusion. Her body recoils.

Lancelot's fusionah flies from its holster into his hand. The tarnished steel glints, every dent in the barrel, every twisted design, shining. He clicks back the hammer. The other knights follow suit and draw their weapons, as Percy loops Morgan's arms with his, binding her still.

Merlin is unfazed.

The whiteness in Morgan's eyes fades as she struggles against Percy. "Magic protects the kingdom. Merlin, you hypocrite—"

Merlin doesn't move. "You didn't know I'd stolen an incantation to protect Camelot? It was before the mechanical arts took rank over magic. Before I'd freed myself of my thievery of it. Seems my memory is going, or you'd already left to curse Lyonesse for being the last kingdom to abandon the pagan ways. You hoped to use a particular spell once you got here, didn't you, Morgan? One that needed to be done from inside the city walls, right in front of your targets, lest you would fail from afar. A quick, disarming spell I dare not repeat to weaken me first? Tsk, tsk. Has my own life taught you nothing?"

He approaches her. "What was that spell in question, though? Oh, blast. It's one of the inscriptions on my lower back. Wait—*Telum Paret,* yes? 'The Obeying Weapon'? Very dangerous. Takes years to perfect. A terrible thievery of magic indeed. It would entrap us to your will, to anything you desired. You could have taken Camelot easily, and my own mind would have been nothing more than the empty teacup left here at your spot. Perhaps you would have entertained legend and sought impossible, lost coordinates. And I would have become the slave to help you."

He leans in close to study her. Gold-rimmed eyes shine against her agonized gray ones. "Yes, it would have been quite the accomplishment, twenty years in the making."

Morgan struggles against Percy. The knight glances up at Arthur. "Your majesty?"

The king is broken. "Unhand her."

"Not so fast!" Merlin barks as he turns quickly to face the king. "You're out of your mind, Arthur. War will be on its way if Corbenic discovers this. And they'd be justified, boy."

Guinevere glances up from my arms, her face incredulous. The entire court regards the king, all with identical faces reading *Arthur, you fool.* I shake my head. I don't understand. Surely his tie to Morgan cannot be as strong as this.

The king walks to his trapped sister. "We share blood, Morgan."

She bares her teeth. "Unwanted blood," she growls as she struggles against Percy. "Uther Pendragon's legitimate heir should be the one to rule Camelot, not the garbage born to the whore our father never should have lain with! You speak of blood but disregard it! To hell with your tyranny!" She spits in his face.

The king's eyes shut. He wipes away the spit. "Let her go, Percival." Then, to Morgan, his voice shrouded in devastation, "Leave Camelot. Don't go back to your kingdom in Glastonbury, and don't dismiss my mercy. Keep your word, and you'll escape without any trouble. We could have had an allegiance if . . . " But Arthur is unable to finish that thought.

"You're mad, Arthur," Lancelot growls. "Listen to your advisors. To your *wife*." He bites the word, like to speak of this might tread upon personal insult, and darts his eyes to the queen.

Guinevere shakes with anger. "I will not live in a place where the murderer of my kingdom's people escaped without justice. She's a liar, Arthur."

Morgan cocks her head toward the queen, and while she admits to no evil, the tiniest smile blossoms, and I'm certain Guinevere sees it, too.

"All of Lyonesse would tell you if the dead could speak. You deserve any war to come," the queen declares in a voice that rattles porcelain. She tears her arm from my grasp and storms out.

With haste, I follow. But when I reach the door, Arthur calls me. "Leave her, girl. The woman I know will mourn only in solitude."

I let the iron ring in my hand fall against the wood but cannot find the courage to turn. I pray for Arthur's dismissal as Morgan's eyes surely cast knives into my back. *What was I thinking, speaking up like that?*

But then a flash of movement forces me to turn around. The knights shout in warning. But Morgan's strides are too quick to be human, and suddenly, her arm is around my neck, her skin like ice or metal. I scream, but her bony hand silences me.

Clicks of firelances. More cries.

My fingers dig into her arm. I feel my heart choke my lungs and throat, suffocating me into a terrifying high.

We face the court. Shouts are not as loud as the blood pounding against my eardrums. Morgan lifts me until I must pedal backward to stay upright. Another bone-slicing click sounds by my temple. She's kept a golden miniature firelance holstered to her thigh. Now it threatens to end my life with one wrong move.

I'm her captive.

My father storms forward, armed with his personal fusionah. "Unhand her! She has nothing to do with this!"

Owen is the first squire to unsheathe his firelance. "Your majesty, give the order!"

Morgan hisses with disapproval.

Knights and squires follow Owen's lead. All but Marcus. Marcus, whose breathing is forced and uncertain. But then he locks eyes with me and boldly follows, clicking the hammer of his fusionah back with purpose. I see the reflection of Morgan's icy eyes in his, how they stare at one another like they're long-acquainted adversaries. Though calmer than my brother, the squire steps closer like his presence would be enough to free me from the witch's grasp.

It's Merlin who has to hold Marcus back, a cautious glance at Morgan whose clothes are breaths of dried herbs and days of stark sunshine. He gives a quick look to the squire, one that reads he'll consider his thoughts later.

The sorcerer looks out from under drawn eyebrows. "Release the handmaid, Morgan."

"Ahhh. She's important, Merlin? Not just insurance I'll leave without an army following?" Her hand falls from my mouth. "What does this one know?"

I shake my head, my eyes steady on the firelance's shine. "I'm no one," I whisper in a haggard breath. "I'm the queen's attendant—"

"If that were true," she whispers against my cheek, "the fool Merlin would have slapped your face the moment you spoke up. You might know more than you realize, girl. Or is it that you work alongside the sorcerer while the rest of Camelot sleeps?"

Firelances are pointed and ready, but it's only one girl's life, I realize, and perhaps they'll give up. Or maybe further negotiation is King Arthur Pendragon's plan. Maybe he doesn't order fire because I'm the last hope for the family he wants.

But there's no hope on Arthur's face. "The girl stays here. Release her."

Morgan's arm digs into my neck as she drags me toward the door. "Not likely." She's called her brother's bluff. And Arthur knows it.

I glance at Marcus. He won't look at Morgan anymore. He watches me, his firelance aimed at the witch. The vengeance in his face disappears, and what replaces it is a look of certainty. *It's all right.*

It's enough to calm me.

But my wide-eyed response to Morgan's whispered comment has certainly given me away. "You're not just an attendant or a minion of Merlin's. You're the one I need, aren't you?"

"I don't know what you mean."

"Lies."

We're out the door; we've left the hall, but not the danger. She marches us down the front steps as guards scream, "Unhand her or have your blood replaced with lead!" But that only forces the rounded mouth of her firelance deeper into my temple. I breathe in sharply and bite my lip to keep from crying. I hate how Morgan knows I'm afraid.

"Soon, I'll know for myself," she says. "Once we reach a place where my magic holds power. *Vivienne*, was it?"

She speaks with her lips against my face, eyelashes batting against mine. Her pupils swirl whiter as she leads us away until I think there's no way I'll ever get out of this alive.

We pass over the platform as guards bellow, scores in formation with raised fusionahs. My nails lock deeper into Morgan's skin as I search for anything that might save me.

But then, on the other side of the drawbridge, Morgan halts. Struck by something. Blessed with an epiphany. Her skin warms as she turns back to the kingdom. I'm outside, outside of Camelot, but I can't gather the courage to regard the world I'm seeing for the first time. All I see is how they've lowered steel platforms to cover the moat in case they'd have to charge.

"But wait," Morgan whispers, not to me. "What is this I feel?" Her grip around me loosens. A ringing sound invades my ears, like an aura has penetrated the space with me in it. A cunning smile broadens her face, and I watch her eyes swirl with that same whiteness as her sharp nails grip my temples. A heavy whisper slices my mind in half, and I wince. "Much sooner than I thought. Let's see what you know."

Sensu ahchla tetay meo loqui havahchi …

Words tasting like metal, pricking at my skull. I have to shut my eyes, but it does nothing to temper the explosion in my mind, colored like blasts in the sky. I see a castle build itself, brick by brick, but I cast away the image when something inside tells me it's not for the witch to see. I open my eyes to hers rolling into the back of her head and yank away, but she holds tight.

I hear the thunderous gallops of guards storming toward the gates. I hear Arthur's shouts beneath the strength of those gallops, Lancelot calling, "On guard!" Merlin screaming at Morgan to drop me.

Sensu ahchla tetay meo loqui havahchi...

Flashes of a chalice that rings of a fairy tale. I banish them from my mind.

I realize Morgan has forgotten the barrel warm against my skin. Now, there are only seconds. Seconds before she'll seize this image. Seconds before the opportunity to escape will pass. She's called her brother's bluff, so now I must take care of this myself.

I glance at the castle. At Marcus, who's amongst the knights. At him realizing what I'm about to do.

"Wait! My lady!" he shouts, dropping his fusionah and breaking into a run.

Merlin catches the plan forming in my eyes. "Vivienne, don't!"

But it's too late.

I release Morgan's arm from around my neck. She growls, but I've already thrown my elbow into her shoulder. When she tears away her hand, one of her red nails swipes across my cheek with a sharp sting. The miniature firelance flies from her grasp, but there's no time to watch it fall. I have to get back inside, where magic will not kill me.

"Run, you foolish girl!" Merlin yells.

I run across the drawbridge, my boots miraculously able to keep me upright. Somehow my father pulls me into his safe embrace, and Owen's hand falls on my shoulder.

"Are you all right?" Owen breathes. I nod. "What were you *thinking*? Don't you realize you could have been killed?"

I look at Marcus, not far off. He's watching me, relieved, and reclaims his dropped fusionah.

I watch the witch straighten, miniature firelance back in hand. She doesn't run after me. On the contrary, as Arthur continues across the drawbridge, likely expecting surrender, she glares at her brother with nothing to lose and nowhere to go.

"With one word, I could have you killed, Morgan. Give up your magic—"

"You don't know what you ask," she snaps and just as quickly, that smile of victory disappears. "This life saved Mordred. It kept him alive when nothing else could. Not prayer, not the mechanical arts, not the goodness of others. It can eat at my soul all it wants, Arthur, but our son has been spared, and I'll be damned if I lose him when Camelot's resources could make him strong!"

Arthur freezes at the words. "Our son."

Their son? I back away in disgust. The king glances sideways at all who have heard such a shameful secret, and I have to wonder if this is why he won't order his knights to fire. Morgan steps off the drawbridge.

The king has not yet crossed the threshold. "How will your life affect our son?" His voice lowers, and he takes another step. Morgan flicks a victorious eyebrow. Once Arthur has stopped beyond the city walls, she smiles.

"No!" Merlin bellows, pushing his damaged legs toward the gates.

"Get her to the towers," Lancelot tells my father in a tone that will not concede to disobedience, before running after Merlin. I back away, but only a few steps until I'm forgotten.

My hand reaches for my cheek, and when I pull it away, the faint line of blood on my fingertips is enough to make me shake. Waves of horror come over me. I was so close to death.

Morgan's voice wavers. "He needs but a drink from the chalice you seek. Is it evil, Arthur, for my magic to save another?"

She grasps Arthur's face with her pointed nails and pulls him close. She kisses her brother. Bites his lip. Arthur wrenches away in shock, hand at his mouth. With a sharp inhale, his eyes go blank. White.

"I'm sorry, darling," Morgan says with dark eyes. "It could have been quick and painless. I wouldn't have made you suffer like those traitors in Lyonesse. But know the wizard's a fool to think his ancient incantation would suffice." She backs away, thumb to her mouth as her tongue darts out to taste it. "You're as I remember, Arthur. Haven't aged a day." A girlish chuckle escapes her lips.

"Arthur!" Merlin rushes through the gates, seizing the king to pull him back inside the city walls. Lancelot is close behind. He turns to call forth knights while squires fall back to retrieve armor or steed in case, God willing, Arthur orders his sister dead.

But there was something different outside the city walls. Morgan's epiphany made her forget me as her shield. Something urged her to invade my mind with skull-crushing force. What did she think she could take from me? What did I see in my mind's eye?

The sorcerer has the king by the shoulder, but that only amuses the witch.

"Too late, Merlin," she chimes. "I cannot use *Telum Paret* anywhere near Camelot, but I'm nothing if not resourceful with my magic. I'll come back for what is rightfully mine. I have creative ways of getting what I want." She rolls her eyes until they're sheathed in white once again.

"Essah tah Merlin evanescehah oblivnohamehcha! Essah voucha Arthur yeit Camelot sanalah ladieriah!"

Her arms spread wide, and a translucent orb appears, surrounding her, encasing her. It hums with power. She releases the sphere with bared teeth, letting it shatter into waves blasting against Merlin and Lancelot. The sorcerer grunts with pain as they pull Arthur inside. The waves hit the advancing knights; their armor is ill-suited to repel such ruthless magic. It strikes them down, temporarily blinding them.

Ignoring the blood on my cheek, I run to Percy's side to help him up. "All right?"

He nods, his brow furrowed.

Lancelot calls up, "Fire!"

The guards are quick, but an invisible wall shields Morgan from their bullets' ear-shattering blasts. She fires back, wearing a grin wide with confidence. Several guards fall from the wall dead.

I jump in shock. I've never seen someone die.

"My lady," Marcus says, suddenly beside me, his hand on my elbow. "Go back inside." His eyes plead for this like it's the only thing to soothe the horror surrounding us. I back away for the castle steps as he, Owen, and more squires run forth, equipped with fusionahs and crossbows.

Morgan mounts a horse too demonic to be one of God's

creatures as Lancelot seizes Arthur's arm, pulling him from danger. She gallops away, and only her laughter remains. I steady myself against the main castle's stone wall.

Lancelot growls, "To hell with firelances! Crossbows!"

Flocks of square-headed arrows whistle through the air to no avail. Guards grunt as they pull crossbows taut, reload, aim, fire. But Morgan rides on.

Arthur's trance breaks. He sees the attack on his sister and yanks himself free from Lancelot's hold. "Stop! Cease fire!"

"No, Arthur..." I whisper through clenched teeth.

Arthur watches Morgan flee, demonic hooves digging into rocky ground as her monstrous horse soars across the land.

"Arthur!" Lancelot growls. "She'll return to destroy you!"

Merlin nods. "He's right, boy. She won't rest until she's taken Camelot for herself. Kill her before whatever spell she's cast takes effect."

Morgan's white hair whips around her, mingling with black shadows.

"You said Camelot was protected, old man," Arthur says.

"The city walls divide the kingdom into that which my incantation protects and that which is...less important. It was never adjusted when the kingdom expanded." Merlin looks on in regret.

Morgan is getting away. Lancelot seizes the king's arm. "Arthur, send your knights after her!"

Arthur opens his mouth to speak. But before he can say a word, Morgan le Fay vanishes.

NINE

But Morgan would not leave.

In the middle of the night, a violent blast shakes me from a nightmare and bolts me upright in my pitch-black bedroom. I leap from my bed for the window to see smoke crowding the sky. Flickers of red and orange silhouette the city walls.

"My God," I gasp. My long, corseted jacket lies on a chair by the window, and I throw it on for warmth, fastening the copper clasps and letting the hood hang loosely around my neck.

The western farmlands are immersed in an ugly fire fighting to surpass the mountains. At least twenty fields go up in smoke. One by one, they fall victim to loud blasts, like the flames are alive, able to think and seek prey. I hear terrible screams. "Oh God, the people."

I avoided death's call no more than a day ago, but it's returned for others. I squint through the thick smoke, making out scores of figures scampering from the hills. Some have survived. But those who won't make it follow in desperate attempts to change that, their hair and clothes just as luminescent as the fields they've left. Their screams are the loudest.

In the courtyard, Arthur and a handful of knights are already rushing for the gates as guards stand shocked and helpless subjects watch. Knights call for their steeds. In his eveningwear of a thick woolen robe and dark trousers, Arthur shouts loudly enough that even I can hear from my chamber's height, "Open the gates! *Now!*"

As the heavy doors peel open, I see the disaster is so much worse.

Trees have been devastated: black and lifeless, mere skeletons of the full, lush branches Camelot knew. Serfs lucky enough to have lived close to the city walls take to the sanctuary inside, faces black, limbs burned.

The door to my bedroom bursts open. I jump. My mother has a thick woolen robe tied around her shoulders with the hood covering her hair. "They need help," she says. I nod and move to join her, but she shakes her head. "No. You stay here. Your father doesn't want you leaving these chambers." She sifts through my boudoir, finding several blankets to take with her.

I feel my eyes widen. "What?" This is the last thing I want. "That's absurd! I can help!"

"Not now, Vivienne. There are some things in this world even you cannot fix."

I'm trying to figure out what she means, but before I can object again, the door shuts behind her.

I listen to the chaos spilling through our perfect kingdom.

With only distant shouts as company, I'm alone with thoughts of Morgan's icy eyes threatening mine. Of the melodic way her voice called my name. Of her invading a section of my mind I'd never explored before. The scratch on my cheek is raw under my fingers. I could have died at her hand. But I cannot think like this. I have to be rational.

A heavy sound brings me back to the present. Slow, like heavy blocks of steel churning against each other. Like the drawbridge when they let it fall across the moat...

"The lock."

No, I won't be confined here.

I rush to the door and burst through it in time to just miss a long, iron bar falling across the hallway in these quarters. A preemptive locking system that would confine nobility to their chambers, in case the castle fell under attack. No doubt my father was behind these orders to keep me out of danger.

I back up against the parapet. The air is cool, and I close out the chill from my draping sleeves. The bar thuds across the doors; I jump as it slams. A long, iron hook snaps out of a compartment and threads itself into a carved-out loop I never noticed on the frame, and then back into the heavy iron ring in the middle, creating an unbreakable circuit that won't let up until the wheel at the bottom of these quarters is engaged and rotated.

There's silence in these parapets. No one else has left their quarters, but commotion sounds from inside as they hear the contraption lock. I've managed to slip out in time, the only one to do so.

And now I'm going to the courtyard.

Squires run horses toward the gates as knights and guards call for supplies. Woolen blankets, buckets of water, newly-developed iron wheels that build up leather lungs with pressure and expel their contents across a field. As much dried grain as they can muster to temper the fire. Knights' saddles are already equipped with iron canisters that blast flaming fuel by way of a trigger, used in the fiercest battles. As I pull the hood of my jacket over my hair, I watch Galahad test one. An inferno streams from the barrel.

"Fill these with water," he tells a squire.

My heart pounds as I search for ways to help, but I'm useless with a weapon. I can tend to the wounded, though, and they're using the courtyard as a makeshift hospice for serfs and peasants unlikely to see it through the night. The infirmary must be full.

"Put me to work," I tell a young nun who eyes me up and down with a scoff, noting the linens about me too expensive to belong to an orderly. I reach for her shoulder. "Don't refuse good help." She nods and leads me through rows of injured people the knights have just brought in. All have someone caring for them but one.

I nearly pass out from the devastating sight of a girl no older than me with skin red and bloody. She bites down on her screams. The air reeks of smoke, and as often as I can manage, I use my sleeves as a woolen filter. The nun sets a bloodied bowl of moon-reflecting water next to me and hands me a cloth. My head spins as she explains how to care for burns. The girl lying on burlap falls in and out of sleep, the skin on her face bubbling. I'm not to touch that skin; I'm only to set the cooling cloth to patches that are already burnt. Her skin flakes like charred wood, and she clutches my hand tightly.

The gates spill open next to me. Percy and his squire drag inside a large barrel they drop at the king's feet. There's an iron ring for its circumference. A lever pulls forward, and then back, and the barrel's face falls to the ground.

"Fire powder," Percy says, soot and horror on his cheeks. "And fuel to spread the flames."

Just one barrel of either wouldn't do that to nearly half of the farmlands. But two more squires lead in wooden carts packed with more, all marked with the seal of Glastonbury. Bags of fire powder land in front of Arthur. It bursts into the air, just like Azur's *jaseemat* did when Merlin first showed it to me.

The girl in front of me coughs roughly.

"It's all right." We both know it's a stupid thing for me to say, but her eyes thank me for trying nevertheless. I press the wet cloth to her temple, and her eyes fall shut with relief.

Percy watches the kneeling king stare in awe at the unassuming weapon spilling through his fingers. "Morgan, your majesty."

Arthur's stunned, and I can't imagine the bonds of siblinghood tearing like that. I can't imagine how someone as evil as Morgan could be human. The sense of overwhelming loss paralyzes Arthur. Numbly, he steps forward, an emotionless machine regarding his land.

"How could this still have existed in Glastonbury?" Percy asks. "It's been abandoned."

"She couldn't have done this," Arthur says in amazement.

"You should have slain her when you had the chance, Arthur," Merlin's voice echoes throughout the courtyard.

Tumultuous with anger, the sorcerer storms for the king, his long scarlet robe tight around his shoulders. I draw my hood across my face as my mentor strides past. "Now you have no choice but to kill her before she returns." He seizes the king's vestments with the semblance of a father disciplining his wayward boy. "You might not have chosen this destiny for yourself, boy, but I taught you better that this. The decisions you make do not dictate your life alone. You have to consider the lives of those here!"

Arthur grits his teeth and looks over his shoulder. He tears Merlin's hand from his robe. "My horse! We ride out tonight!"

The king's order is relayed until it reaches the royal stables. Merlin grasps Arthur's robe again. "No, Arthur. Send your knights to kill Morgan. For you to leave Camelot now is exactly what she expects. If you leave its protection, I can do nothing."

Arthur faces Merlin, enraged. "I'm not going to kill her. I'm going to find her before anyone else. Have her tried and humiliated more than Uther stripping her of the Pendragon name ever could."

Merlin's mouth parts in surprise. "Are you mad?" He gestures toward the burning land. "See what she's done! See the devastation! With one order to Lancelot or Galahad, you could have Morgan dead before dawn!"

Arthur leans in close. "You ask for my sister's blood twenty years after you dreamt of a just paradise such as Camelot. I am not in the practice of carrying out an execution before a trial. Besides, there is much in this life she'd find worse than death."

A squire brings a saddled horse to the king, complete with firelances and strapped with sheeted armor. The king trades his robe for proper riding gear and mounts the horse, much to Merlin's dismay.

"At least bring Excalibur."

"I don't need it."

"Arthur, don't be a fool—"

"Old man, your point is made." He spots Galahad. "Gather five. Leave the squires. We're going after Morgan."

Galahad nods without question. He throws a whistle at five more knights who gallop toward the gates and leads them out of Camelot as Arthur holds back a little longer. "She's not just blood, old man. She gave me an heir. I cannot ignore that."

Merlin is silent. It could be too early in Arthur's marriage for a legitimate heir to Camelot. To have Morgan alive might mean finding the illegitimate one. What would he do to that boy?

Arthur exhales, speaking louder. "Make sure the perimeter is surrounded. Guinevere must be well-guarded in case Morgan would try to use this diversion to enter Camelot quietly."

Merlin doesn't believe that. "Her magic is useless inside. She'll wait until that's remedied."

"After what happened to Guinevere's handmaid, both will need guards—"

"I don't think so," Merlin says. My heart stops at the idea of being confined to Guinevere's tower or mine because of what I said. It makes me want to storm through the flames myself, if only to escape, shake the insanity from Arthur Pendragon's head while I'm at it. "Even if the handmaid was a witness of magic, Morgan knows the girl was just that: a handmaid. As long as she and your queen stay within the city walls, there's no reason to send for extra guards. It's control of the castle Morgan's after."

The king considers it and nods at the sorcerer's logic. I offer a silent prayer of thanks to whoever would listen and set the wet cloth to the girl's reddening neck. God, the pain she's in.

"Camelot is in Lancelot's charge." Arthur extends his right arm for Merlin's to pass on his power. "The knights will defend it. Godspeed, old friend." Arthur yanks his steed's reins, and the horse gallops through the gates, leaving a bewildered sorcerer behind.

"Merlin!"

I peek at the royal stables. Lancelot rides into the courtyard in time to see Arthur lead six knights into the burning farmlands.

"You just missed him," Merlin says. "He went after Morgan."

Lancelot nods. "Here's hoping he kills the witch before the next moon."

Merlin fumes. "Arthur, always the diplomat. He won't kill Morgan. He wants his sister to be tried for this and for Lyonesse."

Lancelot freezes. "What?" Angry, as he should be.

Merlin presses toward Lancelot, his eyes steady. "He leaves you in charge until he returns. You, with access to his Norwegian steel. Let me have it. Arthur's quest for justice will do nothing but bring more danger. Camelot must be ready, and I must build a weapon."

"A weapon?" I hear myself whisper.

I speak too loudly. Merlin's eyes follow the echo of those words to find me behind them. I'm quick to glance down at the girl holding tightly to my hand and whisper words of comfort. Just as quickly, Merlin turns back to Arthur's champion.

Lancelot is silent as the enormity of Merlin's request registers. He runs a hand over his tired face and pulls uncomfortably at the gentleman's jacket he's not gentleman enough to wear. "Wizard, have you lost all sense of time and memory? Don't you realize what it could do to you?"

"You don't know how much worse it could be. You don't know what Morgan is capable of."

"I can't. You'll need Arthur's consent."

Merlin says nothing but eyes the knight in subtle judgment and suspicion.

He told me about the king's supply of Norwegian steel when Caldor was but a skeleton and I was a year younger, tasked with tightening the bolts in Merlin's construction of woven copper feathers. With relish, he spoke of an alloy of translucent gold from the north, forged and enchanted by the ancient demigods centuries ago with a rare incantation that made it impenetrable. When stolen by men, they realized it boasted a different kind of magic: a loophole the demigods did not consider. Just possessing it wasn't enough to count as thievery of magic. But to touch it, the euphoria would send a man straight into madness.

I cannot deny how fascinated I was to have heard this. I imagined how the steel would shine on Caldor as the falcon flew against the sun like Icarus, despite how immensely dangerous it'd be for Merlin's old vice.

Lancelot continues: "The girl at court, who was she?"

"Vivienne, daughter of Lord William. Guinevere's lady-in-waiting." Merlin's eyes are wide and unblinking. He's ignoring me purposefully now.

"As she was the only one to see those... demons, she'll be brought in. If Arthur fails, I want to know what I'll have to fight."

"Very well."

Lancelot rides into the farmlands to help save those still alive. He leaves behind a sorcerer deep in thought. Merlin's eyes flicker toward mine, and then away.

Surely, he would realize I'm not the kind to let this sort of thing go.

Horses arrive from the knights' quarters, their hollow footsteps barely heard in a panicked kingdom. Squires, including Marcus.

Marcus, who sees what lies beyond the city walls. I press the cloth to the girl's forehead and watch the upside-down scene of squires lining up in the rippling bowl. As ribbons of blood float around them, the squires still their horses, waiting for further instruction.

Marcus doesn't.

He rides to the gates. Dark-circled eyes look to the eastern farmlands just barely spared. People pass, but he's distracted, and his mouth parts in dread as the truth of what happened catches up. I watch him grip his horse's reins as though tied by them. Squires cannot leave the castle without permission, especially in an emergency such as this.

"Marcus!" Lancelot calls from the farmlands, throwing his fingers between his teeth and whistling when the boy doesn't turn. I look up as Lancelot rides for his squire.

"I need to make sure they're safe," Marcus says, unable to look his knight in the eye.

Lancelot contemplates it, glancing back at the courtyard in case someone were watching. "Tell no one, and be discreet."

Marcus takes a deep breath and glances across the range of people. He finds me amongst the dying, eyes so expressive but possibly not even registering mine. He kicks his steed, galloping past those returning with more wounded.

The burnt girl lying before me emits a pained cry. Her eyes roll into their backs as she shudders for breath. "My lady," she rasps. "Tell me a story. A song. Anything. Please."

Ladies of the court take up the dreaded practice of song, though I've never been very good. But I understand the request. Whenever ill as a child, I'd ask the same of my mother. I choose the one I know best:

> *"By the trees in Avalon,*
> *Machines guard that which Camelot's son*
> *Will one day find should all go well.*
> *Rogues of España will come to dwell*
> *In clouds above three kingdoms past*
> *Following enlightened thinkers vast*
> *Where sea and sky meet with a kiss,*
> *The Grail, our hope, cannot be missed."*

My voice breaks with the last line. The girl's eyes are strange. "We didn't know it that way. Surely, the legend of Avalon was different in your world." Her lip quivers, and her eyes lose focus, as though gazing into a childhood of farmland clouds and fields of grain. "No mentioning of the kingdom being in the sky."

Calls from the burning land draw my attention back to the gates. I glance up as Marcus disappears through the smoke.

Arthur's advisors have found Merlin. As they fume about the absent king, the sorcerer catches my eye. He holds up a hand so naturally that the rest wouldn't notice, but his palm facing me is a message, one he's given me scores of times. When frustration at my inability to fix Terra builds so much, I'm near tears. When worries of my future, and who would decide it, make my stomach turn so horribly, I can't drink his tea.

When a witch assumed something about me, something I don't understand myself.

Fear not.

But Merlin makes no further acknowledgment. He never would with so many people watching. He disappears as the clock tower strikes four.

The sleeping girl clutching my hand stops breathing. Her fingers go limp. Death has chosen her, not me, and what a strange thing to see.

I stand in a crowd of many who are close to their own escapes from Camelot. The queen is amongst us, serfs unaware of who she is despite tanned skin peeking out from under her cloak's sleeves. She kneels before a man twice her age with blackened feet, teeth grinding in torment, and mutters quiet words. A prayer, likely one Camelot wouldn't condone.

I stay with the nuns even though Merlin has left. All concern for my safety has waned: my mother doesn't bat an eye at my disobedience when she finds me helping. The knights come and go as the hours pass.

Guinevere clutches a scarf wrapped around her wrist. From time to time, she holds it to her lips. It must be a memento from the king, her champion.

I look closer. It's lace.

Lace that must have been from someone in Lyonesse, because Arthur never would have heard of it here in Camelot.

TEN

"What makes you sure you saw them to begin with?"

Even though it's only Lancelot, I feel like the entire world must be waiting for my answer. Behind him, Guinevere sits on her wrought-iron throne, slouched and annoyed at how he practically harasses me as members of Arthur's council whisper beside her, glancing frequently at their timepieces.

They stopped the fire from spreading east, and the days that followed were bleak. A cloud of gray ash hangs over Camelot even still to remind us of what Morgan can do. When it disappears, the stark quiet might be interrupted all too soon by King Pelles's army for the retribution promised. If that isn't enough, word passes through the court that Arthur fled Camelot despite the wizard's protests. Reasons as to why run rampant. Days have passed without even a minute to escape to the clock tower.

And right now, while everyone else in Camelot either remains oblivious to what I blurted out in front of Arthur or couldn't possibly care less about the imaginative concoctions of Morgan's temporary captive, Lancelot is the only one who demands to know more.

"I'm not sure," I whisper as my fingers touch the faint red line on my cheek, unable to recall any additional details about the black-armored soldiers. It's not the answer he wants.

But I'm too tired to think straight. Too exhausted to believe half of the farmlands are gone. I carry guilt on my shoulders at the thought of my bedroom untouched by Morgan's flames; I carry fear in my heart for what more she could have done. It could have been me in their place. To dream of demonic soldiers in what little sleep I've gotten is nowhere near penance enough compared to what the serfs have gone through.

Each one I pass in the courtyard is a reminder I haven't seen Marcus with the knights tending to what's left of the farmlands.

I find myself worrying about him more than a lady should of a squire.

"Then why speak up at court when it's not your place?" Lancelot growls. Once again, his gentleman's jacket appears too restraining for the fire inside.

"I don't know," I whisper.

Guinevere keeps a steady eye on him. "Stop this, Sir Lancelot."

From what my father has told me about the wild knight, I shouldn't be surprised by his short temper. If he were a squire, I'd lose my patience. But he wants to believe me.

His eyes shut. "If there was something at the gates, I need to know all I can." They open to mine. "Think, girl."

"I said already: there were hundreds. They wore black armor, their eyes glowed red. They were ghosts if I didn't imagine it." My fingers clutch my temples. My head pounds from sleepless nights. One of Arthur's waxed-moustached advisors rolls his eyes at the waste of time he must think this is.

But maybe that's enough for Lancelot. "Then we'll have to be ghosts ourselves as we hunt." He makes his way for the door without a dismissal or goodbye.

The same advisor perks up as the rest of the old men awaken. "Sir Lancelot?"

Guinevere stands, her gaze never leaving the knight. "Where do you think you're going?" Her champagne dress with a magnificent bone corset is dramatic for the early audience. Unkohled, natural eyes watch Lancelot make a point to ignore her and storm off, his walk like a devil's.

She marches after him, grabbing his arm. "Orders were to stay here!"

"There's no time for orders as such. Arthur will one day see my intentions were to save his kingdom. In a day, I could have the witch dead. Your handmaid's account is proof of the evils Morgan'll bring."

"Do not think you know more than me about Morgan's evils," the queen declares. Her eyes are unafraid to challenge his in the way one argues passionately with a companion, not a member of court she has just met. "Your duty is here."

But Lancelot is not ashamed by her scolding words. "I've never known you to defend irrationality."

I try to internalize Lancelot's strange words, but I must

ask, "How would you kill Morgan if her legion is real? They were not normal men."

Lancelot stops at the door. "I have to try." His voice lowers to an angry hush. "Arthur should have stayed in Camelot. I've never been so angry about his judgment."

"*You're* angry?" Guinevere's voice rises. "I awoke to an empty bed, the last to know my husband left to seek the sister he barely knew while the farmlands burned!"

"I know Morgan's guilt as much as you," Lancelot says. "We both saw what kind of darkness there is in the world." A foreign lightness appears in his eyes, one that reminds me of Morgan's translucent skin. It soon vanishes. But he steps even closer, able to touch the queen if he so wished.

That lightness appears in Guinevere's eyes, too. "Stop it." Her voice lingers on a cliff of tears.

Lancelot glances sideways at her. "I don't mean to belittle your feelings." The angry edge in his voice strives for a softer tone.

"Of course not! Like always, your eyes are on the prize—"

"I admit it's true! Had Arthur sent a handful of knights instead, the problem of Morgan would be long forgotten now, freeing up our time for more important matters. We cannot grieve forever."

I hate that I agree with the scoundrel. "My lady, there's merit in what—"

"That'll be all, girl!" Lancelot growls impatiently.

My eyes narrow, but it's no longer my place to speak. Guinevere waves me off with a silent apology. I curtsy and leave behind the muttering advisors who will seek a pint after this.

I look back only once at the queen and champion regarding each other with zealous, vehement anger. Guinevere's eyes dart to mine. A cold-white glow turns them into two full moons laced with dishonorable intentions.

I pull the door shut behind me. She's never looked at me that way before.

There's a strangeness spilling into Camelot.

———

The court will dine in the grand hall tonight. To keep the faith while Camelot mourns her dead. To live our lives in the midst of tragedy and danger. To indulge in the curried beef they'd already made anyway.

Guinevere makes no attempt to recover her lavender gown. "As many as you wish, Vivienne. Take them all."

She searches her boudoir, tearing out gown after gown. When she offers a smile, I can't tell if she's putting on airs, ignoring how she threw cool eyes at me earlier. "Keep the veil, too." She shrugs. "Lace was so *common* in Lyonesse. Millennia could pass without me needing to see that wretched thing again." She speaks too much about trinkets and costumes after such anger overcame her earlier.

Tonight, I am a doll for her to dress up. A way to distract, I suppose. She chooses for me a scarlet gown whose sleeves drop to the floor with grace and copper ties. There's a bronze corset atop, and she loans me a wire necklace that barely fits the circumference of my neck, letting a bronze pendant fall onto my décolletage the dress so liberally exposes.

As she braids the corset's back, I wonder about Merlin. He hasn't appeared at court. "It's like Morgan cursed him to disappear," my irritated father complained to my mother.

"Ready?" Guinevere asks, eyes unblinking once she's tied the corset's final knot.

I nod and quickly set my hair into two long tails, pinning them up. There's a knock at the door, and I move to answer it. But first, she gives me a pair of silver-hued boots with clacking heels to wear, instead of my black lace-ups that simply do not match, and shall be left behind.

———

My mind is clouded during the feast.

Scores of tables are lined up in the grand hall, but the mood is different from the wedding. Ale isn't even offered, especially after the hangovers most recently faced. We sip water as servants lay out spreads of sweetmeats, pastries, and the sumptuous curried beef.

My plate is bare and will likely stay that way. I'm more curious about the sealed letter delivered to Guinevere, not to mention her sudden decision to forego the feast, than the caliber of the kingdom's cuisine. There's an odd silence in the grand hall as no bronze-lined china passes to and from hungry hands. Wooden bowls and plates haven't had any role in Camelot since Merlin brought the mechanical arts from Jerusalem, and with it, a mishmash of European styles and conventions of the Holy Land. I've grown used to the tinkering at supper.

Knights and squires lean their elbows on their table, sipping tea and nothing else. Decorative silver breastplates weigh on them from under red-lined gentlemen's jackets. Their heads are low. Lancelot is not there.

Owen is, but next to him, an empty seat.

A squire leaves home when he becomes a knight, but some bonds cannot be completely severed. It was unlike Lancelot to give Marcus permission to leave in such an emergency. I wonder who's in the east. I wonder if they're all right.

There's movement in the far corner, and my eyes flicker toward it.

Merlin.

Merlin, who sneaked inside unnoticed. Smoking his hookah, as though he must always have it to avoid conversations with those uncouth enough to scold him for rings of smoke in their faces. Like the rest of us, he's distracted, entranced by a spot in the room as he mindlessly puffs away.

Build a weapon.

Not even the slightest hint as to what that might have been, but the wheels are spinning behind his eyes until they find mine. He rises to leave.

If Morgan were to return, as she promised, the sorcerer would want to be ready. I heard him ask Lancelot about the king's steel, and I want to know more.

And so, I stand to follow him.

"Viv," says Owen as he and a few other knights step in my way. I glance over Owen's shoulder at Merlin pulling his hood atop his head, slipping out the door and into the night. Damn it all.

Owen ducks to put himself back in my line of vision. "Hello?"

"What?" I ask with impatience.

My brother's eyes widen. "What are you doing?" Behind him, a handful of knights watch me with worry, and their squires stare with interest.

My fingers clasp my temples to soothe a budding headache. "Leaving. Returning to the queen." My lie comes off my tongue with ease. "Why?"

Owen steps closer. "You're appearing at court? After what nearly happened?"

Though my disposition is anything but patient, I do what's expected and smile politely. "Well, no one pressed a miniature firelance into my temple tonight." I push past him with my eye on the door. "Excuse me."

But Owen grabs my arm. "Hold on. We need to have a word."

ELEVEN

My brother refuses to look at me now.

I put forth a frown as though I couldn't possibly understand what the lot of them would want, but it's clear Lancelot wasn't the only one curious.

"Come along," Owen says, dragging me to their table. I sigh inwardly at the dreadful inconvenience of it all, craning my neck toward the swinging door behind two dandies who've finally succumbed to the ale's tempting call. Outside, the hooded figure of Merlin reaches the gates and disappears beyond them, as does the only chance tonight to ask him about the weapon.

I sit as the knights surround me. No sense in joining me at the table, it seems, when it's not a friendly invite to break bread or share the sugar-dusted figs, but an interrogation. I glare at each of them. "Well, then?"

I'm half-expecting a knight of status to be the interrogator, but they push my brother to sit before me.

Owen's eyes rise to mine. "You spoke with Lancelot at the assembly today."

"I told Sir Lancelot nothing different from what I said in front of the king."

"And Morgan," Owen reminds me. "Arthur wanted as few people as possible to know about that. But do you know how dangerous the castle is now, considering Morgan evidently thought you were someone of importance?"

My throat is suddenly dry. "Dangerous?"

"Only if she were to leave Camelot, Owen," a knight named Darcy says. "And for a handmaid, that's impossible. No need to worry the girl."

But Percy holds up a finger to silence Darcy. "There's a reason Pelles ordered Arthur to shoot Morgan on sight, Vivienne. There's a reason Arthur had to strengthen the perimeter. We've been wondering if perhaps the queen mentioned something, or if you overheard information that was not yours to know. What would make you an attractive hostage? This is serious, you know."

I eye Percy with anger. "Serious? You don't say, Percy." I tremble from the memory of a firelance's barrel against my temple. It takes all of my strength to keep myself from collapsing in a fit of tears or rage. "She threatened my *life*—"

"Yes," Owen says. "And to get away, you were stupid enough to risk your neck. Now we're all wondering why Morgan chose a handmaid to take captive before abandoning her plan to overtake the castle."

They think I know something. Something important. I feel my cheeks redden. Perhaps there are only minutes until everyone in Camelot will discover my apprenticeship with Merlin. Only minutes before Morgan will hear as well and know her suspicions were correct. But it couldn't have been that she suspected my apprenticeship—that's not enough. There was something else.

"Because I revealed the magic she brought with her! Is my life not worth taking?" It's but a way to distract. The end of my time in Merlin's tower cannot be *this* soon.

"This is why you should be guarded around the clock," Owen replies curtly. He fumbles with the teacup in his hands. "Instead, you're strolling around the kingdom like nothing happened," he adds under his breath.

"That was the sorcerer's decision." Percy says, crossing his arms.

My brother scoffs. "Shouldn't the very name of what Merlin once was be illegal?"

Percy looks at me and ignores my brother's commentary. "With a shortage of knights, extra protection for a handmaid isn't of the utmost urgency, Owen. Forgive me, Viv, but it's true."

It won't cancel out nightmares of Morgan, but it lifts a weight from my shoulders nonetheless. This is good. This gives me more time to find out about the weapon Merlin wants to build.

Percy leans on the table. "Be cautious. Stay out of sight and keep to the towers at all times."

A squire laughs quietly behind me. "Stay away from squires, while you're at it. Poor Marcus." It's Ector, the buffoon. There are a few laughs, but more harsh words to stay serious. Owen says nothing to defend the friend who isn't here or the sister he won't acknowledge.

My eyes go chilly. "Noteworthy advice from boys who have years before they'll be men." I face Ector. Stephen and Bors are laughing with him. They hush up, their hands raised as they back off. I glare at Owen. "Any other words of wisdom you wish to bestow upon a lowly maid?"

Owen's silent, but Percy's patient, shooting angry glances at the idiots behind me. "Vivienne, Morgan said she'd return for a kingdom ill-equipped to fight her magic. If anything else comes to mind, please let us know." Percy beckons the others. "You'll excuse us." They exit the front door as the eyes of the court watch.

It leaves Owen and me alone with too many thoughts drifting between us. One being how the entire castle clearly think I'm as dense as the pastries they've served tonight.

"I didn't realize the knights had so much leisure time to spend on a humble lady-in-waiting," I say. "Granted it's been days since you were all granted your rations of ale, so perhaps you're bored."

"Vivienne—" Owen says, exhaustion woven in his voice. "Please. You only got angry once Ector mentioned Marcus."

Dauntless stares from the nobility make me fidget. My hands clutch the folds of my dress, crinkling its silk. I wish I'd worn my hair down so that my reddening face would at least be covered. Even a simple veil would have been better. "That's absurd."

Owen rubs the stubble on his cheek. I sometimes forget

my brother is a man; at twenty, I suppose he is. "I need to tell you something you may not like to hear."

"Oh, good. More advice from Camelot's finest. The stars were certainly aligned in my favor."

My brother takes my hand. "Be careful, Viv. Marcus isn't like the others. Word is he only agreed to be Lancelot's squire because his mother grows ill and needs the castle's infirmary. There are no healers in the farmlands anymore."

Lives depend on Marcus. I knew this already.

"But when Arthur knights him, he'll take a vow of celibacy like the rest of us. It won't do any good to your reputation."

"What are you saying?" I feel my eyebrows furrow, my cheeks go hot. My hand pulls free. "I'm not looking to ruin his honor or mine, if that's what you're implying."

"I'm not implying anything." He sips tea, cringing at the sharp taste. "But Camelot is not blind. People saw him look at you, and they saw you look back. It's just a bit of boyish fawning, certainly, and should pass, but…" He shakes his head, and something strange inside ignites my temper at his flippant assumption. "Perhaps knights can get away with those types of shenanigans, but you're the queen's lady-in-waiting, and he's a serf. I won't have scandal tied to our family."

Too still I sit in disbelief. His lecture is certainly not meant for me, especially at a time like this. But he isn't smiling. He isn't joking.

I have fire in my eyes and humility on my cheeks. "Of course not, Owen. Not when you're so close to knighthood yourself."

I grab the folds of my dress and storm out.

The dimmed gas lanterns in Guinevere's tower tell me she's retired without dinner. I'm relieved of duty early tonight. I try to feel excited about that, but I want to drink proper tea with Merlin, perhaps tinker a bit with Terra. The *jaseemat*—how wonderful it'd be to create life with it. How I long to set some upon my own mechanical falcon just to see what would happen. For now, though, I should go to the gardens to test my crossbow—anything to extinguish my anger toward Owen.

What did the sorcerer want to build? My imagination explores the layout of the clock tower for clues in an attempt to eliminate any twitches of my heart regarding a certain squire.

Just as I've reached the courtyard, the clock tower chimes eleven. The front gates creak open. A familiar face appears.

Merlin's returned.

He dashes inside, missing me as I duck into the gardens. I watch him shove a small purse clanking with coins into a guard's waiting hand. Merlin gives him a reassuring slap on the shoulder and walks in the direction of his tower, his distinctive limp faster than normal.

The gas lanterns are too dim to see another person properly, so long as the individual in question is well-camouflaged. Thank God for beds of bright-red poppies hiding the hem of my skirt.

When Merlin's crossed the courtyard, I decide to forego my crossbow and follow him instead. I must know more about the weapon.

But as he turns the corner, I stop. It must have been a trick of the mind, something the dimness is to blame for.

Because for a split second, it looked as though Merlin's feet had disappeared.

TWELVE

Perhaps it was the gas lanterns.

A logical conclusion, but one that doesn't sit well. And the quiet in the cobblestone streets doesn't help. I can't ignore what's pressing me with its peculiarity: the idea of Merlin disappearing seems eerily natural, as though I could drink his Irish tea with a spoonful of salt and not even blink at its strangeness. I almost expected it.

Someone touches my arm. "Alms, my lady?"

I jump, my nerves more shot than I realized. A girl no older than me draws a fraying shawl over her shoulders while balancing a child on her hip. Plainly dressed, like the mechanical arts have not trickled past the walls of Camelot, she holds out a cupped hand. Her nails are dirty from lack of water, from ashes. Not like my fingers, charcoal-stained by choice.

"Please. Anything you can offer for bread." Her voice cracks. Behind her, several other pairs of desperate eyes watch from the infirmary.

"I don't—" They wait. I don't have any coins. Shame sets its weight on my shoulders for the hot meal I couldn't touch tonight.

"She'll return to Camelot," calls a honey-coated voice in an accent I can't place.

Through the dense shadows come the taps of a wooden cane, footsteps, the jingling of silver. A woman with tea-colored skin like Azur steps into the lanterns' light. She clutches a threadbare cloak around her shoulders with one hand, a twisted handle of wood with the other.

"Who?" Though I'm quite certain I know.

She inches closer, watching me with a curious eye as layers of jewelry chime with her steps. A small, rounded lens flashes from her palm, and she sets it over one eye to stare me up and down. "Begging your pardon, you wouldn't mind giving a lame woman your name in lieu of the coins that aren't in your pockets."

I wonder if answering her is the wisest thing to do, but the gypsy's crooked gait is eerily mesmerizing. I'm suddenly quite conscious of my empty pockets. *How could she know that?*

"It's Vivienne," I whisper.

Her eyes widen; she flicks the rounded glass back into her palm. "Vivienne? Hmmm. A good name. You wouldn't be the daughter of Carolyn and William, would you?" She gives the young mother a handful of coins that have appeared out of thin air. The girl is too relieved to question their origins and rushes off with her child.

I search for a purse, maybe a pocket hidden in the folds

of her cloak next to such an elaborate timepiece at her waist. "How did you know?"

She leans on her cane, and a knowing smile crosses her face, nearly reaching long earrings speckled with brass and steel starfish.

"Your mother used to play by the lake outside the city walls as a girl. You look as she did." She shuffles forward until she's mere feet away, her slightly curved back rendering her shorter than me, but not by much.

"Perhaps you have the same set of wits about you. In that case, pass on this warning: when the witch returns, magic won't be her only weapon. She has her fruit. Her creation. The dark magic machine that carries her blood in his veins."

The idea repulses and fascinates me at the same time. "Even so, there's a veil of protection over Camelot. Morgan knows that. Her magic won't be able to penetrate it."

The gypsy graces me with a slow smile. "Clever girl. You've been taught to think as Merlin's kind does. But he will soon realize Camelot's incantation isn't enough. Morgan knows what lies within Camelot, and she won't rest until it's hers."

Her eyes appear in the light: bright blue, shocking against her skin. I wonder if she might be blind, yet a jet black pupil stares at me with such intrusion that I step away.

"I'll pass on what you told me," I promise as I make my leave.

"To Merlin only!" she calls. "Though a former addict won't like hearing what it could mean."

I turn. "Who are you?"

She lowers her head like a servant would. "I'm a simple woman who once knew of another kingdom, one that hides as the world seeks it. Best to guard your mind, dear girl. You never know who might try to steal your thoughts."

Her necklaces and earrings ring in a harmony of notes as she leaves.

"Good night, my lady. To see Carolyn's child tonight was a gift." She pulls at the hood around her neck. "If you need me, I'll be at the lake outside the city walls, where I make my home. Give my regards to Merlin." She hobbles away.

"He used to be a friend."

———

I burst through Merlin's door without knocking.

"What weapon, Merlin?" I declare, shocking the tattooed man by his window. He chokes on his tea, and his boots dig into his woven rug to keep balance. Of course I was mistaken in thinking his feet had disappeared, but I can't be bothered with that just now.

"God almighty, what's the meaning of this?" he shouts. He strides toward me through his limp, his red cape floating behind him matching his angry eyes. "Has all of Camelot lost the sheer decency of knocking?"

I stand my ground, unwilling to let any more secrets be kept from me. "I can't watch life pass me by. I can't drink bad tea as a lady-in-waiting day after day until my time in the clock tower finally runs out, I marry God knows whom, and my life is a prison. If it would stop Morgan, I need to be a part of this."

"A part of what?" he growls as he paces.

"A part of whatever requires Arthur's Norwegian steel!" I confess to his shocked face. "You know I overheard you ask Lancelot for it. What could you possibly need his approval on? You're the one who made Camelot—"

"Enough!"

His voice reverberates against the walls, causing the leaves of gold on his desk to hum with vibrations. I swear his eyes go as red as a dragon's. He takes a calming breath. "Vivienne, you demand something you don't understand. The danger of being present in a forthcoming war, especially you…"

What about me? I want to scream. But I must remain calm, as Merlin prizes rationality over passion. Most times.

"And the Norwegian steel, the risk—" With a patient sigh, he takes my shoulders and smiles like an uncouth, black sheep of an uncle would. "You are so much like your mother sometimes."

I consider my mother's popularity at court, her easy smile and contagious charm rendering her my polar opposite. I'm about to strongly disagree with Merlin when he motions toward his table and a wealth of broken copper machines just waiting to be tinkered with. Blueprints I've never seen before lie amongst them, and he studies the papers closely.

"Truthfully, I will need my apprentice's help," he mutters. A long sigh erases the worry from his face. "Do you know the history of magic, Vivienne? The demigods created it to assert rule over mortals. But when mortals realized they, too, could employ its powers, the betrayed demigods were furious. They considered any use of magic theft. While mankind has free will, to dive into that thievery would bring about a terrible addiction and eventually require your soul as incurred payment. The simplest of spells were akin to tugging a mountain's weight behind you. And we couldn't help it. We'd die to feel that impossible pull of the land.

"But they allowed for requests, similar to how we ask for cooperation from the elements through alchemy. Though, granted, the demigods remain irritated about Arthur's Norwegian steel. We discovered long ago that its magical properties allowed it to be molded, and the only way to tear it is by way of diamond. Perfect for a weapon. But Lancelot fears I'll fall back into old patterns by being around such enchantment. Rightfully so."

"Then what will you do?" I shudder at the mention of Merlin's old vice.

He straightens, firming his jaw and setting down the blueprints on his table. "I will have that steel. This weapon I've had in the works for twenty years. Conceived when Camelot was threatened by the Celts and set aside as the peril dissolved and the kingdom prospered. Now that Azur's alchemic advancements are sophisticated enough, my creation will be the next great revelation in warfare and will fight whoever—or whatever—waits in Glastonbury for my incantation to lift."

When I blink, I see black-armored soldiers. My blood goes cold, and yet my eyes crawl with relish over the sheets of gold on Merlin's desk. Hungry fingers inch forward, but he swipes his hand at mine, and I jerk back.

"Ah, ah. Those have nothing to do with it. With Caldor

complete, I find myself restless." Merlin clears his throat like he's unwilling to say more and returns to his waiting tea at the window. He beckons me. "Please."

I pull away and pour myself a cup, only to have the sorcerer seize it immediately.

"Allow me to make a fresh pot." He smiles in a way that makes my eyes narrow. It's unlike Merlin to waste his Irish blend. But when the sorcerer empties the pot onto the fire, the flames don't fizzle; the fire blazes green before crackling back to orange. The scent of it wafts over, and I breathe in.

His tea has opium? "Merlin, what is that?"

He's a terrible liar and even worse at hiding things. Like a boy, he shrugs, gesturing the cup stupidly. "Tea. Cold now, but when an old man's been interrupted, you can't expect the warmth to linger forever."

It might be nothing more than a creative way to enjoy an old drug. But with Merlin's history of kissing absinthe glasses, not to mention the snuff box that might as well be welded to his hand, I wonder if it's not for a different purpose. Opium he doesn't readily smoke in private, only in the presence of inebriated company. He told me once it was a crutch when magic was destroying his mind and soul, but no longer.

My eyes must give away my thoughts.

"Nothing to be concerned with, my dear. Just rejuvenating the spirit with a gift from a traveling merchant I knew from the east. He passed through this part of the land tonight." He smiles, but it doesn't fool me. The pot of Irish tea ready, he pours us each a cup, shaking fingers careful not to spill.

"There was someone in the village, Merlin."

He flicks an eyebrow in curiosity.

"From the lake. She said Morgan would return with a weapon born of dark magic. A combination of blood and machine."

The sorcerer pales. He straightens in his chair, a crushing fist resting on the table.

"I didn't quite understand her riddles. But she knew you." I leave out her advice of steeling my mind.

He nods. "Well, then."

"What did she mean, Merlin? Who was she?"

He's slow to answer. "She's an enigma herself. We're not exactly on good terms these days, and it's not my place to tell you why. Huh. Azur will want to know of this."

We're quiet, drinking tea that might as well be the common blend from the banquet halls.

"Oh," Merlin says with slight surprise. He leans on the table, angling his head to get a better view of the gates. "Is that the boy you fancy?" He lifts his monocle to his eye.

I feel my heart in my throat at the thought of Marcus returning and scold myself for thinking something so foolish. Merlin keeps a telescope aimed at the stars on the window's ledge, and despite my pride, I tip it downward, peering through the eyepiece at the gates. Owen's words of caution aren't necessary, really. Marcus is only a fascination. Someone not from the castle who's seen the world. Nothing more.

He sits in a slouch, riding for the gates with an older woman crumpled in his arms. Her black hair is woven with gray, and her face sports a shape similar to Marcus's. Leather armor weighs on his shoulders, and he runs a hand over his eyes to clear away the exhaustion. The guards refuse to drop the drawbridge, but the clock tower is too high up for me to hear why. I watch Marcus's shoulders fall, but his resolve grow strong. He calls back, even foraging through his pockets for gold to bribe his way inside.

When the bridge finally drops, the woman's hand touches Marcus's cheek. His gaze seeks the towers, darting quickly from one window to the next, even glancing at Merlin's. Then he gallops toward the infirmary.

"Seems Arthur isn't the only one in the kingdom who'd put family above Camelot," Merlin mutters.

I feel the sorcerer watching me and curse myself for letting him get away with his description of Marcus in the first place. "You were about to tell me about the weapon, Merlin."

Merlin's eyes gleam, and what I told him about the gypsy is presently forgotten. "Indeed I was. To the cellar, then."

I frown. "The cellar?" The entrance to Merlin's tower has nothing in it other than dirt and the excrement of rats that find their way down there.

"Aye. Now it becomes necessary for you to know one of the many secrets of Camelot."

THIRTEEN

"Hurry, Vivienne!"

Merlin leaps down the stairs, and I'm ten steps behind the entire descent, moving as quickly as Guinevere's silver-heeled boots will allow without slipping.

When we reach the cellar, I rest my hands on my knees, swallowing mouthfuls of air: musky, absinthe-stained, and with another stench that gives me a colorful idea of what lies under my boots.

Amid some shuffling, the sorcerer speaks. "Here it is."

There's a ticking sound I recognize: the switching on of a gas lantern. It illuminates the small bunker for us.

I look up. "Oh goodness..."

I've never thought to glance up at the ceiling before. All these years, I've missed the chance to admire its beautiful, gentle markings like the Egyptian hieroglyphs sketched in Merlin's old, worn scrolls.

The etchings tell a story in drawings reminiscent of the

east, of bold sunlight and bright moonlight, of wide-necked snakes and shamans who look as though they've dipped into a knight's supply of cravats. Silver-bolted ears, tattooed necks. An alphabet unlike the Latin one, snaking up in dots and dashes. And in the center, a castle with happy subjects. A king and queen in a protective circle. Above, a separate kingdom, one of gold, looking down from the sky.

Merlin's voice is contemplative, even in such few words. "This way."

Behind the ladder to the blacksmith's shop is a stone wall, but when Merlin presses against the surface, it turns on an axis, revealing a set of descending stairs.

He grasps the wall before taking the first step, breathing in sharply.

"Merlin?"

He glances over his shoulder. "It's nothing."

Merlin descends, and I follow. A clack follows each step. I remember my silver-heeled boots, but no, it's coming from ahead. "What's that noise?"

Again, he looks over his shoulder. "It's nothing."

We continue on.

———

Hundreds of steps later, we hit a stone floor. I rub my cold arms and look around. The space is astronomical; the ceiling seems to go on forever, like a canyon in reverse seeking the surface. The landing leads us to a long hall where in the middle is a pyre built into the floor. At the end of the stone stretch, Merlin curls over his cane. When he sees me, he straightens, wiping away the strain. He stands next to a pair of doors, nearly as tall as his tower.

"While the catacombs have their own ways of keeping out unwelcome visitors, it's imperative you don't tell a soul what you see down here, Vivienne. I said there were secrets in Camelot. Some in plain sight, like the incantations engraved on the ceiling up there or the tattoos on my skin. Others are hidden here."

Merlin sets the lantern by his feet. The flame flickers and extinguishes. The world around us turns black.

But a bit of moonlight soon finds its way inside. Merlin comes into the light with an arm outstretched, as though he beckoned the moon to paint the door with luminescence, revealing sharp markings trailing down the frames. He touches the etchings and mumbles softly. The long sleeve of his left arm pulls back, letting him inspect a line on his forearm inked in another strange alphabet. Cane in hand, he points its emerald stone at the door and speaks in a whisper, letting strange words roll off his tongue.

"Ahkhaneehia ouvadrio."

There's not enough time for me to fully wonder if that was magic. The moonlight passes through the stone, sending emerald rays splashing everywhere. The door creaks open. Behind it, complete blackness.

Merlin picks up the dead lantern as though it could still guide him. The darkness swallows him whole.

"Merlin!" I shout.

Iridescent fingers of orange spring from either side of

him, traveling into the room. The fire leaps around the walls, and I rush to the threshold to watch as Merlin descends into a lair illuminated by hundreds of gas lanterns.

"Heavens," I whisper.

"Indeed," Merlin replies.

The walls are lined with stone sarcophagi: each face is different, from a masked monk with a wicked smile, to a lion with a braided mane. An enormous black furnace, charred and covered in ash, sits on the other side where the journeying fire halts behind an iron gate. Pipes climb the ceiling to a labyrinth of copper and brass cylinders interlocking, the pistons inside churning up and down.

The clicks of Merlin's feet draw me to the circular floor where the sorcerer regards a machine that must have been welded together ages ago, covered in the telltale ivy green and bitter red of tarnish and rust. It's a dragon's skeleton, black as night with a cogwork heart empty of blood and a lung system of patchwork leather. From inside, an iron lining peeks out. The neck curves up in a long swoop to a face with black eyes.

I step on a mosaic floor of embedded gemstones. Under my boots, the jewels shimmer and hum.

"What is this place?" I breathe.

Merlin smirks, feet clicking on the other side of the skeleton as tall as three horses and as long as eight. Around the walls, contraptions only found in the blacksmith's shop come alive, forming assembly lines, taking blocks of steel and pounding them into bolts and cogs that fall into buckets by the furnace. Weights strike against additional steel on those lines, flattening it into sheets. Cranks have songlike rhythm. There's a collection of copper discs for viewers, like the one in my pocket, stamped by a red-hot iron with the Pendragon emblem. A steam-powered roller curls flattened copper into cylinders for those viewers. Next to it, a larger one forming barrels for fusionahs. The new weaponry Azur brought to Camelot might become more prominent than swords one day. *Remarkable.*

"This is the birthplace of Camelot. A geographical crossroads between the old age of magic and the new era of mechanical arts. The founders lie in the caskets around these walls. Here is also the origin of the greatest weapon Camelot will ever know." He regards the iron dragon's skeleton.

I move away from the stone faces watching my every move. By the door, a crimson drape covers the frame of a looking glass. My head inclines toward such a rare object that found itself here.

Merlin is enchanted. "Everything in this place, from one request to open the door, to another that will forever silence the protective inferno: here's where the demigods made them. The words I uttered from the script in my skin were to request safe passage into these catacombs. Not a stolen spell as Morgan freely takes. As I once did, too."

He sees my face, how I must look petrified, and glances at the mirror.

"No need to get into specifics, mind you. Be careful not to touch the walls, as there are still traps about for curious fingers. And that looking glass is not for you. That'll serve you on another day."

I tear my eyes from Merlin for the piped ceiling. Behind

the brass and copper is the same reflective mosaic, the floor boasting rubies embedded in marble. The pattern is jagged and unclear, but when I look again, it morphs into a fire-breathing dragon with sharp talons and dark eyes.

"When the name Pendragon spread throughout the land after Uther's death in the war against the Spanish rogues, we declared the reign of a new king. I knew this old, forgotten place would be the foundation. A world of protection against evil, but as we know, it doesn't mean Morgan wasn't able to set foot in Camelot."

I frown. "Is she not wicked then?" The question is all wrong, but valid.

"When I knew Morgan, she wasn't a sorceress. Like I said, I told her about alchemy—I was excited to share that revelation with someone whose mind was also riveted by this sort of study—but from there she began to steal magic. I didn't need Azur to confirm that. I could feel it from afar." Merlin's eyes gloss over.

"It was foolish of me. I knew she, a healer, would be fascinated, but I didn't think it'd tempt her into the vice I'd just broken free from." He shifts his weight. From where I stand, I can't see what's caught his attention.

"Then Arthur and Morgan had a falling out," Merlin continues, "and the world became more dangerous as Lyonesse realized their curse: an entire civilization would drown with their castle, just when they'd turned their backs on magic for the mechanical arts. The kingdoms in these parts responded by Christianizing the land, expelling magic, and embracing the practical sciences. I knew in my heart Arthur would be king. Morgan was miles away, hiding from the mark on her head, trying to maintain correspondence with me, pleading for resources. When we decided to build Camelot and choose a king, many lost more than their pride."

I hadn't been born yet, but my father has told me about the examinations of consciousness only the bravest took to discover if they were worthy of Camelot's crown. Despite the sorcerer's warnings that the true heir of Excalibur would reign—and that would be Arthur—many were slaves to their pride, regarded the mystical sword in the anvil, and went to grasp it.

Excalibur is still kept far from the hands of the public, and with good reason. With a steel gauntlet soldered to the hilt, whoever grasps Excalibur must be the one of true worth.

Anyone else will have his arm sliced off from the seven whirring blades inside.

I imagine the terror Arthur must have felt when Merlin told him to trust his birthright, wield the sword, take what was destined to be his. Seize the opportunity to rule a perfect kingdom at such a desperate time in history without knowing for certain if he'd walk away a whole man.

"Considering what could have happened had Morgan tried to claim Excalibur, she really should thank me." Merlin leans on his cane as his feet click against the embedded gems. With difficulty, he makes his way back around the skeleton, pausing every few feet to study the handiwork.

A long wooden table behind me boasts journals with intriguing titles such as *The History of Eastern Alchemy* and *Warding off Curses and the Properties of Opium*. And another lying open as though someone was presently reading it: *The Mystery of Machines and Their Ghosts*. Curious.

"But Morgan always wanted more." Merlin draws his cloak around his body. "Now she's risked her soul to set a curse on the castle. All for a legend, one Camelot holds dear." He lifts his sleeves, exposing the tattooed charms on his skin, and regards them with a disdainful look. "A curse to counter my own protective incantation in the most creative way possible. Rather impressive."

Merlin picks up the volume on ghostlike machines, nodding and murmuring as he looks through the pages. "An excellent read. There's a fascinating part that outlines the moment of no return after a man about to fade into oblivion is freed from his body. His spirit becomes unconquerable if he can guide it into a machine."

I cannot think about ghosts right now. "What curse, Merlin?"

His bright blue eyes cannot hide the wealth of knowledge in his mind. "Nothing to worry about in the grand scheme of things, really. It's more on me than it is on Camelot."

"On you?" I tense at the memory of Morgan's white eyes and soprano words.

"Meant for a demigod, but I suppose it could apply to sorcerers, too. It weakens, then destroys, incantations associated with the one cursed. Now the veil of protection I stole for Camelot all those years ago has slowly begun to lift. A fault of my own, I suppose. I didn't know a curse like this existed. When I researched it, I was mesmerized by the intricate details, the active use of magic…" He inspects his palms as though blood lies on them. "Alas, this is why the farmlands could be destroyed. It happened rather quickly, so I knew my response needed to be just as swift."

"Alchemy broke the spell, then."

He glances elsewhere. "I haven't told you everything. I notified Azur when I felt the spell itching my skin. But to stop it now—" He shuts his eyes. "Hopefully there will be a cure, later. After."

My eyes sneak back to the journal on the table.

"Until then, there's a way to slow the process."

My throat is dry as I wonder what a former addict to magic has stumbled upon. "What process, Merlin?"

He narrows his eyes as though deciding whether I'll be able to handle what he'll confide in me. Then, with a breath, he lifts his cloak to reveal his feet.

And I step back in horror.

The remnants of the sorcerer's black boots lie torn beneath skeletal, bloody toes. The tops of his feet are nothing more than fresh meat: pink and sinewy, flexing as he cringes. Slowly, the skin atop peels upward and vanishes.

He's ... disappearing.

"I didn't know what to expect until I felt the change. Dreadfully painful as inch by inch I fade. It's sinisterly slow, and I won't vanish completely until the spell's reached all of me. Azur discovered, though, that opium is not simply a delightful drug: when drunk as tea, it's rather sophisticated in its ability to temper curses, but it's no permanent solution. No, not opium."

He sets a hand on my shoulder. "Vivienne, we must

complete this weapon before Morgan returns, and we must work fast. It's our best chance in a hopeless battle, especially with Azur's wing design, since Morgan won't expect Camelot to have the technology to reach flight. Even still, chances are the weapon won't be ready until I'm too far gone. You might have to finish it alone. It doesn't just need *jaseemat* to defeat Morgan, dear girl. It essentially needs a soul." He stares right through me as though hoping I'll understand the reason for his fright. "And you must prepare it for one."

"I don't understand—"

"You'll need to trust in what I tell you to do. And just as importantly, know what I keep from you will be for your own good. These days, certain knowledge might be dangerous. This is not compiling cogs and gears into a mechanical falcon, my dear. There's much danger here, and Morgan cannot find you." His gaze is unrelenting.

I squeeze my fists around the fusionah barrel I didn't realize I'd picked up. I won't be afraid of Morgan. Though I don't fully understand Merlin, I nod.

"Remember what I told you it'd mean for Camelot if we ever needed Azur's *jaseemat*?"

I nod again. It would mean Camelot was in grave danger.

"Simply wait. Once we've completed this, Caldor's timid flight will cease to be impressive. Azur's alchemy will be tested on the ultimate machine."

His eyes widen to take in the beast's cracking wingspan. With that, he's different from the man who showed me Azur's alchemic dust. I wonder if this weapon is more of an opportunity than a necessity. A truth Merlin would hate admitting to.

Skeletal feet clack like talons against the ground, and Merlin shifts painfully as he walks. He opens a set of scrolls atop the table. Fingers tremble from quivers of anguish. The pulse in his temple pounds against the inking of a Celtic knot. He traces the contents of the scroll until he spots a diagram of a key, long and twisted with a warped *fleur-de-lis* surrounding the key's face.

"This," Merlin says, tapping twice on the drawing. I look closer. It's not two-dimensional: it was drawn with a third angle to show the crossing lengths, rendering it four-sided. "Made of silver, and heavy as the devil's sin. For years I've yearned for its place to be upon my own incomplete ring. We need it to get Arthur's steel."

"Lancelot has it," I say, remembering their exchange while the farmlands burned.

"Aye. But he won't give it to me. I'm certain it's kept with the Round Table, as Lancelot keeps only flasks in his pockets. But I can't go there like this. You must retrieve it, Vivienne."

There's no reason for a handmaid to go to the Round Table; there's no way for me to get near it when complex mechanisms guard it, puzzles rumored to be unsolvable for most. Nevertheless, I nod. "My duties, Merlin. I'll let Guinevere know I cannot be her lady-in-waiting any longer. I'm sure—"

"No," Merlin interrupts with steeled eyes. "Keep to your duties, and help me when the queen retires for the evening. It's inconvenient, yes, but I'll manage what I can until your help arrives."

"But Merlin—"

"Vivienne, Camelot sees all, and Morgan cannot know of this. She's already weakened me with her damned curse, and she's made a point to memorize your face. I couldn't protect you if she were to know of your apprenticeship as well."

I can't tell Merlin she's already guessed it. But how could I possibly concentrate on my mundane duties while he suffers alone down here?

"Continue with your tasks in the castle. Retrieve the key." He frowns. "Damn it all, Lancelot. If only the Grail hadn't eluded you this time."

I freeze at the mention of the legendary chalice. Merlin notices.

"Yes, you heard me. I suppose it's about time you're let in on that secret, too."

"The subjects in the village . . . when a knight goes on the quest, they tell children he'll seek the Holy Grail, the chalice to balance the scales of magic and mechanical arts, but it's never taken seriously. It's almost a fairy tale." And a song whose lyrics I misremembered not days ago.

Merlin laughs. "Far from it. It's been Lancelot's obsession for the past five years. Not just a relic, but God's own fountain of youth. An alchemist's dream. Rumored not just to heal and prolong life, but end death." He considers his words. To have Morgan drink from that chalice and gain immortality . . .

"Naturally, it lies in Avalon, whose location is unknown to mankind. But its coordinates were supposedly hidden within Camelot's walls by a demigod who wanted Arthur to find the Grail. For such a bias to be discovered, she'd be damned to live a mortal's life in our mechanical world."

"She?" My eyebrows lift, and I run the song's words through my mind again.

Merlin's mouth shuts at the unintended slip. "No time for that. Not when there's a curse weakening the castle. Come, let me show you how this weapon will work."

He runs his fingers along the blueprints and scowls at the scrawled measurements.

My head swims from it all. In the monster, I see the chance to save Camelot in the inferno that would burst from its mouth. Set against pointed shoulder blades lies the possibility for firelances, keenly connected to a churning sprocket inside, which could blast out pre-made servings of bearings, deadly like a storm of iron hail.

This is something I can do. I clear my mind to focus on the task at hand.

One thought refuses to budge: *find something more practical to wear down here than a poppy-colored gown with a bloody corset.*

FOURTEEN

Hours later, I sneak into my bedroom, not sure what time it is and too tired to check if anyone is awake. My hands, blackened from the tongs I dipped into the volcanic furnace's belly, inch the door open, and then closed. I lift the hem of Guinevere's scarlet dress, pull back the impractical sleeves covered in soot, and tiptoe across the floor for my bed, giving up on the delusion of washing up first.

How could I fret over a bit of dirt at a time like this? When I first learned about alchemy from Merlin, I thought only Excalibur could rival its magnificence, but the catacombs have opened my eyes to possibilities even greater. I felt alive when Merlin sent me home, even with the daunting task of retrieving an impossible key, but now soft, clean sheets tempt me with the promise of sleep.

My bed creaks as I climb onto it. My eyes are heavy, and when I lie atop my sheets, they instantly turn gray from the dust in my hair.

"Vivienne!" comes a sharp whisper from the parlor.

My mother walks in, fully dressed for the day. I breathe in sharply and rise immediately. She eases the door shut, ensuring no one else has seen me return, the sight I am.

"Goodness, look at yourself!" she scolds. "Where in God's name have you been?"

"I'm sorry," I breathe. "Really, I am. But the queen requested I stay late." Instantly, I know how pitiful the lie is. And then the clock on Merlin's tower strikes eight, and my stomach twists. It cannot be this late. "Oh God. Guinevere." I run to the wash basin.

"Stop right there," my mother calls after me. I've already splashed cold water on my face and turned the basin black, but freeze at her tone of voice. She walks toward me, her footsteps with that unnerving echo. "The queen sent an orderly an hour ago to tell you she wishes to rest until half past four. She spent all hours of the night arguing with Sir Lancelot and at no point required your company."

I've been caught, but thank God nonetheless for the hot-tempered knight's ability to exhaust the queen, at least granting me the morning off to face my punishment. I dry my face and wait for any miracle that would first allow me a few hours of sleep.

But my mother's disposition is not gentle. "I nearly called the guards to search the entire castle for you last night," she says in a whisper she only uses when Owen and I have been particularly horrible. "I requested your compliance not days ago, and you have yet to cooperate."

I'm not sure what excuse would be better than the truth.

"I'm sorry," I say. I sound like a broken music box with a looped melody, but my head is too weary to offer anything else. "It won't happen again."

She eyes me carefully. "The castle is not safe, Vivienne. And I've been generous with your freedom—"

"I'll lock myself in these quarters, then. Should I also tell Guinevere that I cannot be her lady-in-waiting?" Now I'm not only exhausted, I'm frustrated, too. But perhaps some rebellion is just what I need to distract my mother from seeking the truth.

She sighs. "No, of course not." I watch her eyes shift from frustration to sadness, to an unusual look of hope. Just when I'm expecting worst of it, she steps toward the door, as though she's given up. "I'll call for you later."

No punishment. No warning. Just an aura of curiosity settling in my room as my frustration finally gives way to exhaustion.

I dream about mechanical dragons with bright violet eyes fighting a relentless witch.

═══════

Right before four o'clock, I leave for the main castle to pick up Guinevere's tea.

It'll steep while I balance croissants atop china. I will myself to focus, but the catacombs beneath my feet distract me. Besides, knowing Marcus is back, my eyes dart to anyone tall and lean, with dark, tousled hair. It doesn't help when every gentleman in Camelot sports the same style of blazer the knights and squires wore at the wedding. Lords tip their hats, saying "Good day, my lady." Their wives curtsy, eyeing with envy the sapphire gown my mother made for me, the copper-hued corset, the short and practical sleeves that barely graze my elbows.

Guinevere answers her door in a simple gray dress, corseted with leather. Willowy sleeves soften her tired smile. She sits by the fire and curls up her legs. I set the tray on a nearby table.

"Lancelot and I fought until dawn." She sips the tea I poured. "I never knew a person to be so *stubborn*."

"Just these days, perhaps."

"'Prepare for Morgan,' as though I don't know this myself. As though him leaving again would fix things."

I clear my throat, pretending I didn't hear the despair lingering in her words. "I think they gave us apricot jam." I pull open a croissant and spread the preserves inside, and then take a cup of tea myself. An English blend. Just horrible. "You must feel well-rested, at the very least."

She ignores the food I've handed her, and a bit of erratic lightness flits about in her eyes. It must be the late afternoon sun.

Then I realize she was close to a topic of conversation I could benefit from. "But perhaps the king was wise in making sure Sir Lancelot was left in charge. Not to leave again, certainly. I don't think he will."

Guinevere blinks, listening.

"The king knows Sir Lancelot would keep you safe at all costs." It's only meant to lead to the whereabouts of

Lancelot's key, but as I say it, a bout of uneasiness comes over me at the very true statement.

Guinevere shifts in her chair. "Keeping me safe would include endlessly poring over battle plans as he prepares to fight a woman of magic? Locking himself up with Excalibur and a plethora of metal toys?"

Excalibur. My lips part. "Why would he lock himself up with Excalibur?" It isn't as though Lancelot could wield the sword himself.

"All of Arthur's valuables are kept with the Round Table whenever he's away from Camelot. Treaties, seals . . . "

"Keys?" I try.

"Everything."

I sip my tea despite its tragic inferiority. Someone recently told me he'd seen Excalibur.

"Are you all right, then?" she asks, an unusual warmth penetrating her voice.

I meet her worried eyes. "Yes, of course."

But I'm not sure Guinevere believes me. Her eyes narrow as though searching, like Merlin did, for that which would entice a witch's curiosity.

A knock at the door startles us both from the uneasy memory. Setting my tea aside, I rise to answer it.

At the door, Percy acknowledges me with a familiar nod. "The queen is in?"

Guinevere comes to my side before I can call her.

Percy bows. He looks different without his usual kohl-lined eyes. "Lord Henry and I would like to call the council early, if that suits your majesty. I'm on my way to the knights' quarters to notify Lancelot."

Guinevere nods. "Of course."

At that I must speak. If finding Merlin's key means facing Marcus, so be it. "I can notify Lancelot."

Guinevere barely blinks, but a frown tugs at her lips when I say Lancelot's name. "Yes, Sir Percy," she says after a moment's thought. "My lady-in-waiting can send for Lancelot. I have some correspondence for him anyway." Her voice is unwavering. "Go straight to the main castle to prepare."

Percy bows and makes his leave.

At her desk, Guinevere finds her stationery. I've never seen her write, even when Arthur had parchment made by paper makers in the kingdom, set with a seal of her own. She scrawls in an inexperienced hand, folds the paper in half, and applies a wax seal. Long, sun-kissed fingers hesitate before the letter rests in my hand.

"Locking yourself in a room doesn't keep you safe from all dangers." She gives my hand a friendly squeeze, a timid smile following seconds too late. "I'll have the orderlies send up my dinner." At her dressing table, her coiled brass comb is hot enough to steam her hair into flat locks. "Until tomorrow."

"Yes, my lady."

I close the door behind me, but not before catching sight of a lace scarf next to her comb.

━━━━━

Knights stand about their entrance to the main castle, leaning on fences surrounding shorn green fields. Several of them glance at the farmlands, shaking their heads at the tragedy that befell just a short while ago. The rest watch Sir Darcy take another knight in sword fight. Squires who know I'm Owen's sister spot me.

"Viv!" a boy with short black hair calls, jutting out his chin to get my attention. "How 'bout a dance, love?"

The lot of them laugh as I storm past. My eyes shoot daggers, and it's just enough to hide my nervousness.

The squire did promise you Excalibur. It is odd, though, that in all this time, Owen's never claimed to see Arthur's sword, while Marcus managed to do so within hours of arriving here.

One knight tells the outspoken squire to hold his tongue. Several more see me approach.

"Where's Lancelot?" I demand.

They gesture to the main castle and return to watching Darcy's shield slice at the other knight's, razor-sharp itself with fanglike blades on the edging that protrude as he engages a mechanism. The knight aims at the bolt in Darcy's ear, but knights learn quickly how to shield themselves from losing their ears whenever their helmets are off. Darcy jerks to the side.

The hall inside the castle is lined with bronze suits of armor, the decorative seal of Camelot stamped onto the breastplates. I follow the long, red carpet to a room lit by a golden chandelier. Twelve copper-piped arms reach out from the epicenter sprouting tapered candlesticks. A traditional touch in a newly mechanical castle.

And just down the way is a door with an iron ring in the—

A scream. A man's blood-curling scream halts me. It's like I've run into a brick wall. I choke on my breath, and Guinevere's letter falls from my hand to the floor. I feel my eyes widen, searching for the source of the voice.

Another sound: the crack of a whip. The man screams again, echoes just as gruesome as the cries.

I'm looking at the floor, at my blue hem against the carpet and the letter that fluttered to my feet. I pick it up but can't understand what's drawing me there. Then my breaths sputter out.

The screams came from below.

Instantly I think of Merlin's catacombs, but they don't extend this far. The walls have eyes, though, and there are secrets in this kingdom—

"Hey!"

I jump, now facing a guard in the hallway, his hand on his fusionah.

"You don't have permission to be here."

I hold out Guinevere's letter. "I'm the queen's lady-in-waiting. I'm to see Sir Lancelot."

He jerks his head in the opposite direction. "Sir Lancelot is on the verandah."

"I don't know where that is."

He points to another hallway.

I pass him, pausing with hesitation. Everything is silent now. "I heard someone in pain."

"Sir Darcy got quite the nick in the arm from Sir Vincent's blade."

But I know Darcy's voice. He spoke with Percy and Owen at the feast. It wasn't him, or any other knight I'd know. Was it?

I head for the door at the end of the second hallway, the silence assuring me it must have been nothing more than my imagination running at full speed. After seeing what lies beneath Camelot's surface, I expect that's natural.

From behind the door, I hear Lancelot spurt orders between clanks of striking metal. A knot tenses my insides, and my fingers twist the ends of my hair.

I knock three times.

Lancelot's voice is gruff. "Come in."

I push my entire weight against the door until it gives. Inside, Lancelot glances over from a wooden platform extending across a grassy courtyard. But instead of greeting me, he braces himself as Marcus runs at him and slams down a sword on the knight's blade.

My eyes go soft when I see Marcus, and tumultuous butterflies conjure a gale inside me. With a grunt, Lancelot crushes the blow and elbows Marcus in the ribs, causing the boy to keel over as the air in his lungs bursts out wholly. The knight wields his shining blade; Marcus looks up in time to shield himself, stepping backward as Lancelot follows. I let myself inside, my heart in my throat as I watch the ballet of clashing metal and black jackets.

Marcus circles Lancelot, but he catches my eye and loses focus. It lets Lancelot knee him in the stomach and push him over. Lancelot grabs the hilt of his squire's sword and crosses both blades against Marcus's neck, forcing him to his knees.

Marcus sighs. "I yield."

Lancelot shakes his head. "Don't let a pretty face cost you your neck."

He helps Marcus to his feet. Marcus sheepishly straightens his tunic and brushes the dust from his blazer and dark trousers. Lancelot gives him a supportive pat on the back and hands him the blades. "Well done, though."

Disappointed, Marcus takes the blades to an array of weaponry and shields on the other side of the platform. The slanted roof ends when the stage meets the grass. Crashes of waves hit the cliffs below the balcony.

"Guinevere's lady-in-waiting," Lancelot says with a crooked smile and devilish eyes. The wind has blown his dark, curly hair around his face, the unkempt look and several days' worth of stubble creating a handsome, if fiendish, cameo. "To what do I owe the pleasure?"

The way he uses my lady's name without her rightful title grates me. Nevertheless, I present the letter. "They've moved up the assembly with the council."

The mischief in his eyes disappears. He breaks the seal and reads Guinevere's shaken penmanship. Then he refolds the letter and sticks it inside the inner breast pocket of his jacket.

"Thank you for your prompt delivery."

He regards Marcus, who's swinging Lancelot's sword aimlessly while the other sits on the wall.

"I must take care of this." They look at each other, speaking silently with their eyes in a fashion I don't understand. "I trust you can keep this discreet."

Marcus's face is unreadable. "Of course."

Lancelot nods. "Good." He bows to me. My legs automatically dip in a reluctant curtsy. "Thank you, love." He cocks a sly smile.

Lancelot leaves the room without another word. As the door shuts, my eyes roll.

Then it dawns on me that I'm completely alone with Marcus.

FIFTEEN

I turn, confirming my suspicion that the squire was watching me. Suddenly my rash departure from the wedding lingers between us without a lick of subtlety. He casually turns away, swinging Lancelot's sword in slow figure eights. I open my mouth to confide in a complete stranger that I need his help, but the words won't come.

"Discreet?" I say instead. "Like it's a scandal for Arthur's champion to meet with the queen?"

Marcus smirks. "Lancelot has a tendency to be dramatic. He was worse when dealing with the gypsies at the Black Sea."

My eyebrows lift. Marcus, like the rest of Camelot's squires, would have traveled to exotic places. Merlin goes to the Black Sea often, despite his strong hatred for the gypsies who think he's one of them. I'm dying to know where else Marcus has been.

"You're all right, then? After … everything?" he asks, his eyes carrying undeniable proof he'd spent nights worrying.

My hand reaches for the scratch on my cheek, now no more than a pink mark.

"I heard the knights gave you bit of a hard time last night." He likely wasn't told about the snide comment made behind his back.

I force a smile. "They tried to, but even their finest attempts were pitiful."

He flicks his wrist so the sword's hilt shuffles around once, back into his grasp. "You should see them during scrimmages." He smiles back.

Then our silence is louder than crashing waves as I search for a reason to ask about Excalibur.

But Marcus is in the mood for a bit of showing off. He balances the sword's point on his palm. As it wobbles, he watches me through the hair in his eyes. He reaches for the hilt but misses, and the sword falls, the edge clattering against stone before landing at his feet.

"You might dull the blade if you aren't careful."

He shakes his head, ducking to retrieve it. "Lancelot had this made in the northern mountains. You don't know what weaponry the alchemists there can forge."

I frown at the insinuation there might be something alchemy-related I don't know. Blast it all, though. He's right. And Merlin doesn't have any literature on the northern tribes. Now I'm dying to know more.

"See for yourself." He stands close enough that I can feel the warmth from his skin. My throat clears, and I'm slow to approach the blade, having not entirely appreciated the last time a weapon was so close.

My fingers find the viewer in my pocket. It clicks open, and the rounded glass piece becomes a magnifier, running along the sword's edge. There's something peculiar here.

"Hold on." I still his wobbly hand with mine, ignoring his fingers long and scarred with rough nails he clearly couldn't bother to properly trim when teeth would suffice. I click my viewer again so another glass piece falls in front of the first.

The apparent smooth edge isn't smooth at all: it's lined with miniature hooks capped with razor-sharp tips flicking up at the point.

I look up in amazement. "How could you balance this on your hand without it slipping straight through?"

"With great care." He shows me the reddening spot on his palm where the tip had begun to pierce. "You can only hold it upright for a second. Never any longer." He holsters the sword.

I only mean to take a breath, but speak without thinking: "I saw you leave. While they were taming the fires. I saw you leave the castle."

His shoulders fall like a weight's been dropped. "I didn't realize you were watching." He hops down into the grassy courtyard.

Because curiosity has gotten the better of me, or because his secret gives me something I could use in exchange for Excalibur, I follow him to a balcony looking over the sea. Far off, the sails of docked aeroships flap against the breeze, Spanish insignias carved into their wooden hulls. More ships dive into the horizon, too far from Camelot to reach in a day's time.

He leans on the ledge, squinting in the sunlight. Sad eyes drift from sea to farmlands. What Owen said about why Marcus is Lancelot's squire must be true.

"Who's over there?" I whisper, leaning on the ledge with him.

A heavy breath clears his face of worry. "Actually, it's 'what.' And it's my parents' farm. It provides grain for Camelot. Your bread comes from our land." He smiles to lighten the mood. Merlin was right: Arthur wasn't the only one in the castle who prizes family over kingdom.

"Are they all right?" I'm not sure if I should confess to Marcus that I saw him return as well.

He nods. "Their home was spared, but many other farms were destroyed. Our neighbors are in the infirmary now. Never thought getting to live here would entail nearly losing their lives." He watches the crashing waves. "I've never met a more relentless villain than fire."

The breeze picks up, and the solemn mood passes. Marcus hops on the ledge, balancing as he tiptoes over stepped merlons. "Still, I'm sure some are at least mildly impressed by the castle, which is nice."

He glances back after every jump, like I might disappear as soon as his head is turned. It's hard to look at him without entertaining the fantasies that drift through my mind. Especially when he purses his lips, concentrating on not falling to the jagged rocks peeking through the whitecaps below.

He steps atop a rather rugged merlon whose surface is rockier than the rest. I eye his feet, wondering if there's any traction on his boots. "Are you sure you should be doing that?"

"Don't worry. Owen and I sometimes sword fight out here. I know the parapets like the back of my hand. Especially useful whenever he tries a sneak attack. Not exactly one for losing, is he?" On cue, he trips and swerves to the edge.

I scream and cover my mouth. He resets himself with a smile.

"I said not to worry."

I scowl in a way that tells him I'm not entirely angry.

He heads for the other end of the balcony, away from aeroships propelling over the sea and toward a view of grassy fields.

"How did you come to be Lancelot's squire?" Indeed, it's a strange choice. Not that Marcus's physique isn't, well, ideal for the task, but sons of nobility usually receive that honor.

"That's a long, dull story, actually…" His trick progresses to a harder one: he unholsters Lancelot's sword and balances the hilt on his palm and then jumps over the next merlon while keeping the blade upright. When a heavy wave hits the cliff beneath us, he nearly tumbles again, and my eyes dart to the horrible death he's inviting himself to.

"My goodness, if you were to fall—"

"Wait. Let me concentrate. I haven't been able to clear this ledge more than once without needing to step down." He focuses on the sway of the blade. "Fine. I was twelve when I stole a basket of limes from a healer in a northern village. Lancelot was there, and the scene distracted him long enough to get involved and take me on as his page. I was fifteen when Galahad became a knight, and Lancelot made me his squire two years ago, on my seventeenth birthday."

He makes it to the last merlon and jumps down, tossing the blade with a slight tilt so it flips in midair and he can catch the hilt.

"What I don't tell too many is that becoming his page had everything to do with making sure I avoided a few days in the stocks."

"A thief now squire to the most powerful knight of the Round Table." I coyly look away to consider how one boy's life completely changed because of a stranger's intolerance of petty thievery. "I've never met anyone who wasn't born and raised inside a castle."

"I'm honored to be your first." He winks.

I have to ask. We cannot dance around like this, and there might be no better time. "Excalibur," I breathe. He freezes, and I have to force the words out. "Show it to me."

"Why?"

I knew the question was coming, and I have no proper answer. In all likelihood he might think I'm just a foolish girl reassuring herself Arthur's kingdom has a weapon strong enough to destroy Morgan. Marcus wouldn't realize how right he'd be, in a way.

I smile. "You did promise to, as long as we'd run away afterward."

His eyes fall shut in that horrid embarrassment we both felt at the wedding. The point of Lancelot's blade pricks at the crevices in the cobblestone. "So I did. Said a lot that night, apparently. Proof Lancelot was right in Mongolia. To trust a man with a secret is downright foolish if he's more loyal to the pint than to you."

I know he's apologizing for the spectacle with Stephen and Ector in only a way a boy would, but the mere mentioning of his travels is far more interesting, enough to fight my sense of priority. "Mongolia?"

Marcus nods. "Perhaps the longest Lancelot has ever gone without a drink to sustain him on lonely winter nights." He shakes his head at the memory. "I nearly rode off for the vast tundra myself just to escape his foul temper."

My fingers wrap themselves around the ends of my hair. I imagine snow in my palms, furs around me, the sorcerer turning an old icy castle into a working factory more sensational than the likes of the catacombs.

But I force myself to remember why I'm here. Marcus cannot distract me like this. "Please, if you know where Excalibur is, I need to see it."

He breathes out in one slow go of it, and I know I'm asking for more than he can give. "For many reasons, it's a bad idea. I wasn't exactly supposed to see it myself, actually."

I ignore his confession. "You don't know me and have no reason to trust me, but I give you my word." I step closer. "I wouldn't be here unless it was important."

His eyes narrow. "It'd be a shame if this was the only reason you stayed."

His tenderness strikes at my heart. I suppose my words were a bit insensitive. "I didn't mean—"

"I'd understand if it was." He looks away. "Even if you weren't being watched as much as you are now, it'd be nearly impossible—"

"Then why say you would?" I laugh in frustration.

He shrugs and holds it, hands clenching the sword's hilt as a smile lifts his face. "Why agree to a scandalous escape?"

Beneath us, the ocean expands with its crashing waves to a place I cannot follow. "Because I might never see the world as you have." I consider confessing my plans to leave Camelot, but an exaggerated lie might better convince Marcus. When I face him again, I realize how close we are. "Camelot is all I'll ever see, and even then, I'm caged in. Unless you help me."

We're staring at each other, and I cannot break away. Too many seconds pass between us without a word spoken. We ignore the song of the ocean and silently plea with each other for the truths neither of us will share. But proximity removed can cause a drought in the heart, and this is becoming too hard.

He finally nods. Glances around. We're alone, and not even passengers aboard those sailing aeroships will see what he's about to do. "All right."

Lancelot's sword returned to his holster, Marcus grabs my hand and laces my fingers with his before we're on our way.

———

We race down a corridor. I dart a look over my shoulder in case someone were to see me run hand-in-hand with Marcus and promptly inform my father. But the hallways are empty, leaving me to thoughts of how rough Marcus's fingers feel pressed against mine. We run past the red and gold of endless tapestries. Him, with more steam than a whistling kettle practically tumbling out of his ears and from under the unkempt hair grazing his neck. Most likely, a comb is the last thing on his mind each morning.

The corridor narrows into a parapet taking us across an extended bridge whose keeper never retracted the steel steps, giving us easy access to the knights' quarters.

"Can't you run any faster?" Marcus calls over his shoulder. His hand pulls more than guides me, forcing my black boots to flit after him as quickly as I can manage. Thank God I was able to rescue them from Guinevere's orderlies.

The bridge leads us to a staircase I've never seen before, one that seems to hover in midair.

"How—"

"Iron arms hold it above the ground and carry it on a track to the landing of your choice."

We take the first step. He uses a lever to guide the staircase toward another parapet on the other side of the castle. We step off, and he peeks around the corner. "On my word, run for it," he whispers.

"Run for what? Who are we hiding from?" I hiss back, but all he does is press a finger to his shushing lips.

He pulls at my hand.

"Go."

I squeeze my eyes shut and let the sound of his footsteps guide me. At the last second, he dashes to the right, and my eyes flash open. A patrolling guard is distracted by something in the courtyard below.

We reach a hallway where the tapestries are longer, hanging from each window like curtains. Marcus eases the door shut with nothing more than a click. The ceilings inside are high. Lanterns, lit. Our footsteps are quiet, but what little noise we make echoes loudly. The grandeur of the hallway is remarkable.

"We're in the knights' quarters," he says as our hands release. "Thankfully, the guard knew about the servants' bathing house. Right on time, I'd wager."

"On time for what?"

He flashes an embarrassed smile. "Some of the ladies don't realize that from this level, the knights are up high enough to see over the curtain drawn across the window. From a certain angle, well…"

I lift an eyebrow. Something to tell the orderlies.

We turn a corner that takes us across a parapet to a thick, black door at the end. There's a brass contraption where a usual knob or ring would be.

"What is that?" It looks like a brace Merlin once built to keep his own study locked before he invested in his beloved vault.

Marcus cups both hands to his mouth, blowing once and rubbing them together. "*L'enigma insolubile*. An invention Arthur purchased from a master mechanic in Venice when the Round Table was founded. To unlock it, there's a sequence…" He takes the cane of the contraption and pulls it foward until there's an audible click. Then he assembles gears from the underside of the machine in a precise order and wedges the lever between two copper grooves. He releases it. A roller chain churns a sprocket clockwise, and the door thuds open, letting the echo wail up a dark staircase.

Marcus shrugs. "Though I'm not one for trinkets, this

one is particularly useful and didn't require Merlin's expertise. Keeps out unwanted visitors."

I settle myself closer to Marcus, blinking in the blackness. It would be awful to get him reprimanded if we were caught. It'd be even worse to get myself in hot water. And there are many ways a lady could entice trouble here. "You're going to take me in there?"

One corner of Marcus's mouth pulls up in a smirk. He shrugs. "My lady might consider rephrasing her question—"

I look away pretending I didn't hear.

"—but it should be fine. Knights never come up here unless there's an emergency."

I think of how close I am to Arthur's legendary sword. I know I must focus on finding Lancelot's key, but I want to ask Marcus everything: whether it's true the chopped-off fingers of the proud still rot away in Excalibur's gauntlet. Whether the blade really sings as Arthur strikes it.

A lit lantern greets us at the top. Marcus's hand grazes mine by accident, but he clears his throat and says nothing as stolen moments linger between us. I imagine his fingers around mine. How it felt as we ran through the corridors.

The vow, Vivienne. He belongs to the Round Table, your time is limited, and *for God's sake, what are you doing conjuring up such ridiculous fantasies when you have to find, and steal, an impossible key?*

The timid color of Marcus's eyes calms me from my fluttering thoughts. We start for a heavy door outlined by the tangerine sunset.

"You cannot tell anyone about this."

I nod. This locked door is different from the first. There's a set of gauges, a wooden wheel with brass axles, a plate over the center bearing Camelot's seal. He takes the wheel, twisting it clockwise until there's a click, and then counter-clockwise until it completes a full rotation.

Mark me, the sequence is built into the door.

He peeks back at me. "I'll need you to look away."

My gaped mouth shuts, and I turn. The last click is the loudest. I look back. Marcus pulls the door open, letting me inside first.

"Welcome to the Round Table."

SIXTEEN

The first thing I notice when I step inside is that there are no windows letting in the sunset. Instead, the walls curve as though taking the form of a massive crescent moon embracing a balcony above the kingdom. White Athenian columns bow toward an enormous table, heavy and old like the room was built around it.

I can't tear my eyes from the blue ceiling of shy stars. "I never imagined it was like this."

"We always forget about the view." Marcus checks the corridor before shutting the door and watches me take it all in.

The Round Table is one magnificent sheet of granite naturally speckled with bright salmon, stone gray, and pearl, all mixing around a delicately etched coat of arms. A vicious dragon is carved into the center, composed of featherlike streaks and two crossed blades. Beneath, meticulously carved talons plant themselves into the floor. High-back marble chairs surround the table, giving each knight an equal viewing of the men who would sit on his left and his right.

"The knights are all fools then," I say. "An army of fools."

"A *small* army of fools until the rest return." His eyes dart toward the door again.

My heart twists in a strange way, and I don't understand why until he looks back at me. I've become rather good at stealing glances of anyone tall and lean and messy-haired enough to be mistaken for Marcus. I wonder if he'd—

No. I'll think about that later.

The sun falls below the horizon, and the semicircled columns turn blue and purple and rose from the forgotten light.

"Excalibur?" I say.

Marcus's eyes continue to hold mine as he steps back, turning on his heel for the door and listening briefly, making sure for the third time now that no one's followed us. On the other side is a tapestry curling down the wall. He pushes it aside for another wheel, a smaller one. The cranks are blunt as he spins the lock. Inside the compartment is a small mahogany box, like my mother's music box. I half-expect a harp strumming a slow, sad melody as Marcus lifts the lid and withdraws a skeleton key.

My spirits lift, but it's not Lancelot's. "All that for a key?" I hope my shrug doesn't come off as disappointed.

He winks. Turning back to the hidden compartment, he counts the stones in the wall, three to the left, two above. He brushes that stone, more discolored than the rest. A bit of gold in the shape of a keyhole glistens.

Marcus's eyes are serious. "Your knowledge of this cannot leave the room."

I nod.

His eyebrows rise. "I can trust you?"

"I promise."

He submits the key to the lock, turning once. We wait. His eyes shift to a spot in the room. When a gentle whirring sounds, he relaxes.

A few feet away, the stone cracks back into thin, flat panels, one after the other. I hold my breath at the first loud strike of rock on rock and wonder how Marcus, after being inside Camelot for mere hours, was able to discover this.

The other side is wood, turning the wall into an elegant display of pine. Only when the panels set themselves into their proper places does Marcus walk toward the center, gauging the middle panel, reaching for the highest point. With his height, he can easily grab a small, silver ring embedded there and pull it down. The panels surrounding that piece follow, like an accordion, until the space reveals a glass display facing the Round Table.

There are documents and treaties and wax seals and medallions. But all I can see is a stone plaque in the center with elegantly-curved edges. Hooks hang on it, and from them dangle keys of all shapes and sizes.

Marcus walks toward the display. I scan the keys, but can't find the one Merlin showed me in the catacombs.

"Watch," Marcus says. He opens the glass display, reaches for a gold lever underneath the plaque, flicks the lever in the opposite direction, and looks at the Round Table.

Another rumble, and it jolts me. I hold my breath without knowing why, listening to the sound travel under the stone floor. "What's happening?"

"You'll see." He moves to my side.

Camelot's coat of arms turns clockwise; the outer border of the seal moves, lifting from the granite surface. Stone scrapes, and I'm nearly positive sparks will fly out. Then shines a glint of gold, and I gasp. The hilt! The hilt of Excalibur!

A glass canister rises, magnifying the four-foot-long, silver-hued blade. When the entire sword is visible, the churning halts, and Excalibur rests mightily atop the Round Table that looks, by comparison, almost pitiful.

An overwhelming pull draws me closer to the blade. "Merlin's envious of the craftsmanship. That's why he chooses to ignore its existence," I say with a wobbly voice.

Marcus smirks. "What?"

"Nothing," I reply quickly. Then I look closer. The hilt is a dazzling gold even in the darkening light. The grip is shining and slippery-looking, like an ornament. A peculiar detail, actually. "What about the sleeve? The gauntlet? Was it all just an exaggerated legend?"

Marcus's expression tells me I'll be far from disappointed. He gauges the sky's light and draws from his pocket a long copper cylinder. When he presses a small lever, it hisses.

"It's like having a pocket-sized gas lantern everywhere you go. I hate how useful it's proven to be." He holds down the lever and strikes the end against cobblestone. A small flame ignites and holds. He steps toward a dark lantern by the door and lifts the fire to the lamp. "A birthday present from Lancelot last year."

A quicklight. Merlin has thousands in his tower. They don't take more than an hour to make from scratch. I've made a few myself.

The flame carries over to the lanterns just as it does in the catacombs. Copper shades are structured so rays of light beam toward the center of the Round Table, hitting it perfectly, shining against Arthur's sword.

When each column's lantern is fully illuminated, the light reveals an ash-gray hand gripping the hilt. The symbol of power and might forces me back several steps. There are layers and layers of sheeted metal connected with shining bolts that would reach Arthur's shoulder and let the steel bend with his arm. Frightening, yet regal.

"Oh my God." I rest against the table. My eyes dart from one hinge to the next, chasing the shine of the sword.

"It forms to Arthur's body," Marcus says. "When he seizes Excalibur, the gauntlet nearly comes to life. Arthur is as much a part of Excalibur as it is of him." He leans against the wall with his arms crossed and watches me admire the sword.

I know we can only risk a few more minutes. But I have to see Excalibur from every angle. "What about the rumor—"

"The farmer's hand?" He shakes his head. "Could have happened, I suppose, but his hand isn't there." Suddenly, he drops his arms to his side.

"What's wrong?"

He freezes in anticipation of something coming. Or someone. "Get behind one of the columns."

Footsteps. Without questioning it, I run for the balcony and set my cheek against a column so one eye can peek out and watch. Marcus switches the lever, muttering curses. Excalibur whirs as it lowers back into the Round Table. Too slowly it moves, but Marcus ignores that and races to the shelves, seizing a pile of faded, dog-eared blueprints and sifting through them. One catches his eye: one as thin as papyrus with measurements and diagrams in the shape of a sword. He thumbs it free, and I remember my purpose here.

The key. I still haven't found it.

"Wait!" I whisper, running back. I have to get Lancelot's key. Even if it means telling Marcus my secret.

Marcus shoves the blueprint into the plethora of dusty papers. His eyes go wide, and the voices draw nearer. "I can't do this. And you cannot ask any more of me. Please."

There's no time to reverse the stone panels. Marcus mutters another curse under his breath, surely not intending for me to hear, and pulls me by the waist behind one of the columns, lifting me several inches until my feet rest atop his scuffed boots and we're out of sight. I open my mouth to protest, but his hand silences me.

"Don't move," he whispers. He drops his hand from my mouth and rests a finger against his lips. Now that the sun has set, night camouflages us.

The door clicks open—it automatically locks again when shut, brilliant!—and, from the sound of it, two people walk in. I hold my breath and wait.

"The lanterns are lit. Who's here?" a voice calls. Lancelot.

Marcus lets his head fall back, and his eyes flicker toward the sky in disbelief.

"No one," says another. Marcus and I lock eyes with the same thought: *Guinevere?* "Percy sent orderlies not an hour ago to retrieve Arthur's plans. They left things as they were to save time, surely."

That seems to suffice. They walk further into the room. I pull myself from the edge of the column, right against Marcus while we wait to see if they'll try the balcony. Instead, chairs scrape across the floor, and Lancelot sits with a loud sigh. In front of a lady. In front of the queen. The scoundrel.

"The wizard wants Arthur's steel," he says plainly.

Guinevere's shoes clack with her steps. "Why?"

"Who knows? Like me, he doubts Arthur will find Morgan before she returns for Camelot—"

"I didn't ask you here so you could belittle my husband's decision." Guinevere's voice is sharp. "What did you tell him?"

"Told him no."

"The key?"

"Safe, and with me."

I frown at Lancelot's words. My hands, once lazy fists against Marcus's chest, clench in disappointment. Marcus clutches the small of my back in response as though trying to get my attention, but I pretend not to notice, willing away the prick of blush on my cheeks.

Guinevere's clacking shoes go silent. "If you went after Morgan, the wizard might try to go after the steel and—"

"Impossible, but even so, that alone is not reason enough

for me to stay. If I disobey Arthur, Morgan would be dead tomorrow. We both know this. No matter what magic she has, she wouldn't expect a lone assassin. The knights could seek the Grail, with or without the coordinates."

"Nevertheless," Guinevere says, "I don't know what Merlin might do if you were to leave."

Lancelot hesitates. "We cannot fight a war against magic, Guinevere. This isn't why you asked for a private assembly, I hope. To convince me otherwise. William and Henry are waiting—"

"You can't leave, Lancelot. Don't you realize you're needed here?"

A long minute passes without any exchange of words. Marcus and I freeze. His arm holding me is unwilling to let go. His jacket is soft under my fingers, and I can feel his heartbeat quicken under my hand. Lancelot's arguments and Guinevere's rebuttals are echoes that pass over us. I ignore their strange tension and instead consider the intimate thought of being privy to Marcus's inner workings. My fingers stretch across his chest, and I watch them twitch like a drum being struck. His eyes fall to my hand.

But then, "Lancelot," Guinevere says with an unusual informality in her voice. "I never did thank you, all those months ago after Lyonesse fell."

There's some shuffling like the roguish knight is uncomfortable before he clears his throat. "Not necessary. I knew the truth and spoke against any accusations. You'd have done the same."

Her voice is eccentric now. "Yes, I would have."

Marcus and I share a frown, and a pang of guilt hits me. We didn't mean to eavesdrop on a private moment, certainly, but while their exchange feels wrong, it's even worse to listen in. But Marcus shakes his head, like my ability to feel his heart has given him passageway to my mind.

I wonder what would happen to the woman he brought inside Camelot if they found us here. If those at the infirmary only took her in because of Marcus's connection to Lancelot. If losing that connection would cast her out.

The unease between the queen and knight is thick enough to reach us. Lancelot walks aimlessly, and I can't tell where he's headed. Marcus and I hold our breath. Our bodies tighten as footsteps come closer.

"All right. I'll stay." Lancelot stops before the balcony, and his gas-lit shadow falls upon Marcus's tense shoulder. The crashing waves below, so heavenly earlier, are violent and threatening now. "But the knights won't like hearing it."

"Thank you," Guinevere breathes.

Lancelot stands still for too long. "You're welcome." But they aren't talking about Arthur anymore.

"They're waiting for us," Guinevere whispers.

"Yes, and Marcus has misplaced my sword." Lancelot's steps take him away from the balcony.

When the door shuts, Marcus exhales with relief and pulls back to see me better. "That was close."

"Too close," I whisper.

He blinks, and his lips contort into a hesitant frown to go with his eyebrows drawn together.

Be careful, Vivienne.

His gaze trails from my lips to my sapphire dress to my eyes that match it. I feel his other arm tighten around me and think of how at the wedding, it felt just as intimate to touch only his sleeve. But what foolishness is this if the boy is about to give his whole being to the Round Table? Why give in to the heartbeat thundering against mine?

"Not close enough." He leans closer, but before anything can happen, I pull away.

"You forget the vow you will take." And as soon as those few words slip from my lips, I regret them.

He smiles, and it turns into a groan, letting me know of his physical torment. A long second later, he releases me, and I step off his boots. In the open space of the balcony, I smooth my gown, wishing away the rosiness on my cheeks. I have no key on me, but at least I know where it is. That must count for something.

"My lady?" Marcus sneaks a thumb to his lip and then flocks his hands to his pockets as my eyes catch his. Embarrassed, he looks away. "I'll walk you back now."

Guilt hangs over me from what I asked of him and what it could have cost. "I think under the circumstances, you might start calling me Vivienne."

His smile is a quiet one. "No, not yet."

SEVENTEEN

For several days, it feels like everyone in Camelot is keeping secrets.

On my way to Guinevere's towers, or to the market or
the court, or even to my own tower, there's someone who
regards me with a strange look, like they know something
that's managed to evade me. To top it off, children parade
through cobblestone streets singing the song of Avalon
with words so different from what I know.

> *"By the trees in Avalon,*
> *Machines guard that which Camelot's son*
> *Will one day find should all go well,*
> *And rogues of España don't dwell*
> *On seas beyond three countries past.*
> *Follow roads 'til you find at last,*
> *Kingdoms meeting with but a kiss,*
> *The Grail, our hope, cannot be missed."*

No skies or clouds or enlightened thinkers. But I can't have remembered it wrong all these years.

This is maddening.

Thank God for the clock tower to keep me sane.

Merlin divides his time between clock tower and catacombs, hidden from the whole castle but me. Endlessly he works as though nighttime doesn't exist—nor does his need for food, drink, or sleep. He refuses any Irish tea, though he does agree to the occasional miniature goblet of absinthe to chase his necessary opium drink, foregoing any chance to retell the story of how Azur introduced him to wormwood and how his own ties to French royalty spun it into a fine, if ethically questionable, spirit prone to causing harmless but entertaining visions. Just as quickly, though, Merlin is back to work. He finds solace in hiding behind his soldering mask, the fire, and its sparks.

Whenever I arrive, he gives me the same worried look, the same grunt saying he'll tend to any concerns later, like his vanishing feet and hands. It's the same look Lancelot and Guinevere have in court.

No news from the king. No news from her husband.

———————

"I let Caldor fly today," Merlin tells me from his armchair.

I'm poring over blueprints and welding together metal beams for the weapon's feet. Oil stains my hands, but I ignore it and glance over at the sorcerer's eerily stonelike form.

When I told Merlin where the key was, he grew quiet

and sat deeper in his chair, contemplating our next move. Our construction is at a standstill without Arthur's steel.

I haven't asked the sorcerer about the misremembered song lyrics. Nor have I told him about the strange images I saw when Morgan's magic seized my mind, because I don't understand them myself.

And something about them feels all too secretive, even for my mentor.

"As the silly bird flew over the gardens, I saw how weak my protective incantation has become. Flowers dying, leaves yellowing." Skeletal fingers clutch a hot cup of opium tea.

"The steel, Merlin." My gloved hand flattens sketches of retractable talons and cogs that would wheel a sharpened point of iron into a hollow cylinder. My other hand lifts my mask. "We can't do anything else until we get it."

He sips his tea. "It'll be ours."

"Lancelot has the key himself. How am I supposed to get it? Should I rob him in the middle of the night?"

"Huh. So he's carrying it in case I would try to steal it from the Round Table." Merlin holds up a palm. "Patience."

I breathe a sigh. Restless, I fiddle with a pair of bolts I'll use to wedge the talon against a spring connected to the weapon's foot. "Azur's *jaseemat*?" I try instead. According to our plans, one small box locked away in Merlin's safe is not enough.

"He's been notified. To create more will not be easy. Have you come up with a name for the weapon yet, dear? I'm surprised one hasn't struck your fancy this far along. With Caldor and Terra, you'd insisted upon naming them instantaneously."

"Merlin..." His small gesture shrouds me in guilt for

planning to leave his side for Jerusalem. The old fool might be intolerable sometimes, but his stubborn heart is a kind one.

"Now, now. It'll distract me. I suggest 'Uther' as the plans require a rather enormous ass in the making."

I sigh. A name for the mechanical dragon looming in the catacombs. A name that could bring hope to the poor sorcerer and handmaid working together. "He shall be called Victor."

From his chair, I practically hear Merlin's eyebrows shoot up at my declaration. "Victor?" he says in a quieter voice. "As in *victorious*. Not only bold and strong, but optimistic, too. I rather like it, Vivienne."

I hide a smile from the old man and look back at the specifications, the paper thin in my hands, but strong with mechanical revelation. My fingers trace the sketched firelances in the weapon's shoulders, pulleys and sprockets connected underneath that alchemy will set into motion. Countless test runs will be needed, even this early in the weapon's construction. No mistakes can be made.

Then I blink toward the rest of the weapon's—Victor's—design, feeling the wheels turning in my head, drawing me to a glitch in the plan.

A glitch.

I look again. Then a third time.

"Merlin," I whisper. He doesn't look up. "Merlin!"

He sweeps his gaze to me.

"It won't fly once it comes to life. The plans don't account for it."

Ignoring the strain on his feet, and now shins, he takes to my side quickly, brow furrowed. "Impossible."

I point to the sketch of the machine's spine. "The propellers will move Azur's *jaseemat* from the heart's chamber through the copper veins. But the wings have a separate mechanism for flight—the steam valve in the lungs, and that has no connection to the heart. The *jaseemat* won't touch them. Normally, it'd make no difference because we control movement and flight separately using wires. But this isn't Caldor—when Azur's *jaseemat* brings Victor to life, its mechanical wings will be useless. It'll only be able to walk, and what good is that if it's surrounded? We need to fix it."

He shakes his head. "There's no time for perfection."

"Merlin, be reasonable! We need to rewire—"

"No." Old, wrinkled fingers trace the blueprints. "Any sort of additional rewiring would take too long to assemble against the heart, and it'd take even longer to de-vein. Look—we'll connect the steam valve to the heart, but it'll have to be activated by hand once the *jaseemat* takes control. A lever, perhaps, one set between these shoulder blade firelances. Wouldn't take more than an hour to incorporate into the design."

My eyes widen. "You can't be serious. What you've designed is not something one could simply jump over like a set of merlons on a balcony!" I catch my breath as the allusion comes out of me. "We need to find another way. Use Azur's *jaseemat*—"

"Azur's alchemy cannot help with this! A lever cannot be brought to life because it has no possible life to begin with!"

"Then someone must help us with this task! The blacksmith, perhaps—"

"Puh!" he growls. "It's bad enough thinking your father

might come after me with my own pistolník if he were to discover your apprenticeship. To have help would draw attention and alert Morgan to what I'm trying to do."

"You would send someone in a war against Morgan's magic onto the back of a mechanical monster? Merlin! Victor's purpose is destruction! Kill anything that comes near it!"

He leans closer, shining eyes combating the clouds that want to take over. "Do not think we have the luxury of months or years to be ready. On the contrary, Vivienne. Morgan will strike when the incantation's gone, and at the rate I'm fading—at the rate the damn flowers are dying—we might have little more than a week."

I'm silent, staring at the blueprints in hopes another solution would reveal itself. I draw the mask over my face and reignite the torch. I solder hinges to a copper plate drilled into an iron talon. A heavy hammer pounds six nails into place, marrying the parts to a skeletal foot. My fingers run the teeth of two like-sized gears together.

Too many veins to pull apart from Victor's skeleton: Merlin is right.

I bolt the gears to one hinge, spinning them lightly. The predictability of these mechanical arts is a soothing reminder that some things will always act as they should, no matter what chaos the rest of the world might face.

I think about what other options there could be for the wingspan—anything that would prevent someone from risking his life.

But the answer is simple: *I need more time.*

Merlin returns to his chair. "We'll need someone strong.

Someone who can climb, keep balance, and run—fast enough to escape the onslaught after activating Victor."

I know someone who fits that description, but I won't acknowledge it. Not yet.

═══════

My mother weaves the cream-colored ties of my gown's silk bodice into a knot at my lower back. Sitting on my bed, I pull on my boots and lace them up.

"Why not wear your hair up?" my mother says, a tendril between her fingers. "All other young ladies of the court have taken to that style."

I shrug as my loose hair hangs like a curtain in front of my face and atop the V-neck of my periwinkle gown. The new fashion of sporting metallic nettings over long hair would mean my skin is exposed. All I need is to think of Marcus's rough hand clasped with mine and a gentle blush hums over my face.

"Not today," I say. "I mustn't be late."

"Actually, you're early," she says with a laugh that feels forced, pointing at Merlin's clock tower where there is still half an hour before eight o'clock.

We smile at one another, and I feel like I should try to be the daughter she wants. One who'll have her hair done properly, who'll happily take to a seamstress's life once she marries the lord her father chooses. Will it break my mother's heart when I leave Camelot?

"Errands." My trusty lie. I subtly check for my viewer in my dress pocket before I go.

The catacombs, the peculiarity about Avalon, and any question of getting Lancelot's key drift in my mind like an invasive thunderstorm all too welcome in a dry heat.

Before I report anywhere for duty, I need to clear my head.

And what better way than to work on my crossbow?

———

The gardens, though dying as Merlin said, refresh me instantly. Passersby of the morning don't take note of who I am. Instead they keep to their own conversations under parasols and tall hats, gentlemen in fashionable black tails despite the warm weather. They don't notice the fading gray, not with primitive mechanical falcons for entertainment. They watch the wire-controlled machines soar into the air for sport, hunting the spoils of the land. Life is easy when you blind yourself with fantasy.

My boots trample the grass as I head for my elm. Tucked under one of the large roots is a rolled-up strip of leather fastened shut with a clasp. I unpack it, feeling the excitement of seeing my curved applewood bow—no longer than the length of my forearm—peek out. It mounts on a leather cuff that doubles as a compartment for arrows. Three buckles lock around my forearm. A ring that fits around my index finger is connected to a pulley that releases the latch by my elbow.

Arrows stolen from the knights' fields are a tight fit for a cross-bow this small, but workable if I snap them in half.

I draw the string around the latch. The polar ends of the bow are close enough to embrace as I set an arrow in place. I shut an eye, looking through the sight at the tree. I'm standing further away than usual, but I have to know the strength of this weapon. My index finger yanks the ring, and the arrow flies free, slamming straight into the bark, but then it falls to the ground, not making a dent.

I slouch with disappointment, but after some adjustments, this could still be of practical use to the knights. Granted, I'd have to pass it onto one of Camelot's mechanics to take the credit, or the blacksmith, or even confess to Merlin this side project of mine. A lady-in-waiting would never construct such vulgar weapons out of wood and leather.

I rotate the underside of the cuff until another arrow clicks into place. Two more are still concealed. Pull the string taut, fire again. The arrow bounces off the tree and strikes the ground. Soon a third whistles through the air, the only other sound accompanying it the song of a bluebird.

The arrow gets caught between two pieces of jagged bark, and the bird sings again. But it's not a bluebird. Someone's whistling.

Footsteps crunch on the ground behind me. I free the buckles from the cuff and turn to Marcus strolling from the knights' quarters, smiling as he cups his mouth, sending me high-pitched whistles. His dark, tangled hair falls to his neck; the front frames his eyes as though he couldn't be bothered with the luxury of sight. He's changed his usual tailored pants for brown trousers that don't burden him with a holster or weapon, and his tunic is light. It matches his casual black blazer that's somehow still too restrictive for his energy. With his smile, though, you'd never notice the discomfort.

I'm smiling, too. For some reason I'm relieved it's him. As though he wouldn't think too much of such a strange hobby. I fold the crossbow back into the strip of leather. "With the falcon above, I feared for the life of the bird whose call I heard," I say in a stupid, bubbling voice.

"That was the plan." He stops a few feet away, running his fingers through his knotted hair. He eyes the rolled-up leather, lifts an eyebrow, and points.

"Oh," I say in a soft voice. "It's just—"

"The latch needs to be further back. The string isn't as taut as it should be." He unravels the tiny bow and tugs at the string, revealing too much elasticity. "See?"

My lips curl in disappointment. "It worked fine last time. That explains the wobbling arrows, though."

He blinks. "Bolts."

"Bolts," I agree. I know the proper term for a crossbow's arrows, but bolts are found in Caldor's wings, not on the battlefield. It's never sounded quite right.

He's smiling in a strange way. But I don't say another word. Instead I take back the crossbow and stow it under the tree. Now two know of its whereabouts. At least I'll know who to go after if I find it missing.

The silence is heavy as we ignore the secret I won't share. Those strolling the gardens soon abandon them to watch a game of cricket in the courtyard. We're alone.

"Thank you for the other day," I say, my fingers twitching as I wonder if I dare speak of Excalibur. Before continuing, I glance around in case someone were to hear. "For—"

"Directing you through the knights' quarters so you could carry out your errand?" Marcus finishes, like the memory makes him nervous. "Funny how easy it is to get lost in a castle you've never left."

I've been getting lost too rarely in my life. "And now that I know my way through its mazes and hallways, I'm forever in your debt."

Marcus digs the toe of one boot into the ground. "I'll remember that. Store it next to Owen's difficulty with ale."

I wonder why Marcus is out here. "Did you follow me?" I ask with a smile. Marcus's own seems to radiate light. He must have been born smiling.

"Actually, my lady, I'm investigating a criminal archer with a personal vendetta against Camelot's oldest elm."

"These trees can be unsuspecting foes, *my lord.*"

He scrunches his nose. "You can call me Marcus."

"You can call me Vivienne," I tease. He nods in a way that tells me it won't happen, and we retreat to our own thoughts for a moment too long.

"How is Owen?" I ask, grateful my voice doesn't tremble. Marcus ushers me to a secluded path.

"Haven't had the chance to speak to him. He's been in archery training nonstop. Why?"

"Ever since he became Galahad's squire, he hasn't made much time for family." Unless he's handing out unnecessary advice, that is.

Marcus nods. "I don't think Owen wants to sit back and wait for Morgan when dreams of being an assailant in Glastonbury are much more appealing." He smirks in an apprehensive way. "He might have done well with Lancelot and me on the quest. Maybe we wouldn't have ended up continents off course."

Marcus pushes a low branch out of the way, letting me pass through poppies and violets as he follows.

I wonder what other memories of foreign lands he has from the quest. "What place was the most unforgettable?" I twist the stem of a purple bloom between my fingers until it snaps off and into my palm.

Marcus wraps himself up in my eyes as though trying to will me to see the memories for myself. "Since you're forever in *my* debt, I feel I'm owed a detail about you before I answer."

I smile. "There's really nothing of interest."

He studies me as though I might be lying, and of course I am. And he should wonder what kind of lady-in-waiting boldly asks a squire to show her Excalibur or is caught in the gardens with a makeshift crossbow. But he indulges me nonetheless and responds to my query.

"Perhaps the north, where wild horses run maniacally through fields before a storm."

I imagine the wild beasts stampeding through grass and snow. Nostrils pulled wide, mist spraying from their mouths— a little too close to unruly steam valves with dark eyes that don't show where they're looking as fluids spatter wildly. Ugh.

"What is it?" he asks with a smile.

I shake my head.

His eyes flicker wide. "Thunderstorms?"

I shake my head again. "Horses."

He looks at me as though I'm joking. "What, you don't like them? You can't be serious. Everyone in Camelot rides."

"Not everyone. Vile beasts." Aerohawks are much more civilized.

He lets his head roll back in slow laughter. "They're not so bad. Perhaps you should give them another chance."

I think not. "No other place you'd deem unforgettable?"

All seriousness comes over his eyes in a devastating way. "Lyonesse, before she fell."

That surprises me. "Lyonesse!" He gives me a strange look. "Just that, Guinevere's from there." And it's odd he wouldn't have told me this sooner. Not many saw Lyonesse.

He nods. "Yes, I know." But he doesn't say anything else, like the memories are ones he doesn't want to recall. "And today," he adds, "she is tragically locked up in the main castle with Lancelot." He flicks a mischievous eyebrow. "I'd rather you not tell anyone you saw me out here on my way to the farmlands without permission, so to speak, when I should be back in the knights' quarters teaching Percy's squire how to sword fight."

I share in his smile. "The farmlands? Then why have I found you wandering the gardens?"

I cannot read his face for a long time, until he glances ahead where the walls of Camelot give way to the farmlands spared of Morgan's wrath. The green sprawls eastward, toward mountains that cut off Camelot from the rest of the countryside.

And in front of us, a large birch leans against the wall, its branches sneaking overtop, into the fields.

"This way is faster. When I'm not on horseback, I climb up and jump down. No need to sneak through the gates."

I nod. "Brilliant. Much more efficient. I happen to appreciate that."

"I had a feeling you would."

"Visiting family?" I wonder if he'd ever tell me about the woman he brought inside Camelot.

He finds interest in the foliage surrounding us. "Only for the afternoon. It's best if I'm not gone too long."

I suppose he could be visiting his father, but I temper my curiosity. He's unarmed and leaving the castle, so he'll have to be back before nightfall. But what would make him risk the trouble Lancelot might give him if he's discovered missing?

When I look at Marcus again, we're quiet. Behind him, Merlin's clock tower ticks away another minute, prying me from the temporary escape of these gardens. But then Marcus steps closer. His eyes lock on mine. Two violets, like the ones oh so beautiful and in bloom sprinkled alongside blood-red poppies.

"The queen will likely dismiss you as well, yes? Considering all the commotion in the main castle?" he says with a shaky voice.

"I have to report to her nevertheless. Perhaps she needs me to notify the kitchen of any changes for afternoon tea." I swallow in sadness at the very mundane idea.

"Of course." He looks away. "You know, I have a strong feeling my mother would take a liking to you."

It must have been her; I'm certain now. And I'm sure Marcus can hear every thunderous beat of my heart, not to mention how guilt clenches it when I think of how the woman he brought to Camelot touched his cheek as he found a way inside. But I cannot tell him I saw that. I nearly wish he'd said nothing at all. "Why would that be?"

He sneaks closer until space is too scarce between us and the increase in proximity binds our eyes. Only then does he think about my question.

"She'd be put off by your looks, of course," he begins in a slow, teasing voice. His eyes narrow with exaggerated judgment.

"My looks?" My fingers flock to their comfortable spots at the ends of my hair.

His mouth pulls up in a satisfied smile. "Of course. You're too beautiful for her to trust with me. She'd call you a siren whose sole mission in life is to tempt me away from knighthood." His words shine with a lightness unable to hide any honesty. He doesn't know how close he is to the truth I want.

"Then perhaps I'll go with you and assure her I mean no trouble," I whisper. "Surely the farmlands are safe now."

His eyes flicker widely in disagreement. "Not while Morgan's alive."

"Then perhaps you shouldn't go either, as you wear no weapon."

"Don't worry about me. It's only for the afternoon."

I look at him with embellished suspicion. As I smile, my teeth inhale my bottom lip and hold it. He clenches his jaw, and his eyes linger on my mouth. Then he looks away as his ears and neck warm.

"I speak lightly, but to be honest," he says more seriously, "my mother can spot an interesting mind when she meets one."

"Sounds like you've given this some thought."

"No," he says rather too quickly. "Not like that. Just since I know Owen. I see how you two are different."

Owen is arrogant. An ambitious soldier. Practically a reincarnation of Ivan the Great.

Marcus steps close again, the leathery scent of his clothes washing over me, and whisks my hand into his. The violet flutters to the ground. His eyes bore into mine as he presses his lips to my fingers. He doesn't blink, he doesn't look away.

"Have a good day, then."

He drops my fingers and walks past me, hands in his pockets as he strolls toward the birch. Then with a quick run and a jump, he's up the tree and drops to the other side.

I exhale the shuddering breath I was holding and run for the main castle before I can change my mind.

EIGHTEEN

The blush on my cheek has faded by the time breakfast with the queen has passed an hour later. She'll meet with Lancelot shortly, and to give myself a break from her suffocating quarters, I dismiss her orderly and take her empty tray back to the kitchen myself. I've walked this path so many times that I can allow myself to daydream of Marcus's eyes when he smiles and how he moves about like he cannot be still under any circumstances.

When I take the first step to the main castle, my landing echoes loudly enough that I stop, feeling my brow furrow. I blink at the leather of my boots. No, that wasn't an echo, but footsteps, many, marching—

Like an army.

I tear my eyes for the northern gates. From these steps, I can make out a sea of shining armor marching for Camelot from the hills. The tray falls from my hands, metal cutlery clattering loudly against stone.

A guard atop the city walls turns to the castle. "Send for Lancelot! Man your posts! Prepare for an attack!"

Around me, nobility fall into a state of restless panic.

"What's happening?"

"What broke the peace?"

They don't know about rumors of Morgan in the land.

"Where is Merlin?" calls Lord Henry as he storms through the doors behind me, crowds of dandies and noblewomen spilling past him. "If you're going to be Arthur's head advisor, act like it! Confound it all!"

The curtain covering Merlin's clock tower window is drawn, but I know the sorcerer is there. I dash through the courtyard, to the village, through the blacksmith's cellar. There are no sounds coming from the catacombs, so I run to the summit of Merlin's tower, where the sorcerer has already cast open his curtains and stares out at the intruders only minutes from our gates.

"Merlin! They're calling for you!"

He doesn't turn at the sound of my voice. He holds up a finger that pleads for seconds we cannot afford to spare. "Come. Come look at them. Tell me what you see."

Slowly I inch toward the window. I don't know why he's wasting time. But Merlin gestures for me to move faster, and so I reach him at the window and peer through the telescope at the soldiers' conformed march.

"Wait." I look again. These aren't the black-armored soldiers I saw when Morgan arrived. There's something different. They're less organized, more human. "These aren't the same men. It's not Morgan, it's—"

"Corbenic," he says, a heavy fist smacking on the stone of the sill before stepping away. "Pelles's army, attacking Camelot."

My eyes widen. "They heard of Morgan's arrival," I breathe. The war King Pelles vowed is finally here.

"I don't know how. Word of Morgan in Camelot shouldn't have left these gates. While a bunch of nitwits, the knights at least understand the meaning of confidentiality."

I feel my stomach twist in dread, and when I turn, Merlin's already set a silver breastplate across his chest. Foregoing his fine pistolník and sword, he finds a more utilitarian battle fusionah that served as a prototype when Azur introduced Merlin to his revolutionary warfare design.

"You're going to fight? As you are?"

"And how."

Despite Arthur's failures, Merlin will not surrender to Pelles. And I've worked too hard to lose the chance to bring Victor to life. One of Merlin's fire irons finds its way into my grasp. Its fine copper handle reflects my look of panic.

I follow the sorcerer down the stairs and through the streets filled with guards keeping peace and ordering everyone indoors until the danger has left. "Noblewomen to their chambers!" cries one of them.

They'll barricade us inside. What if this isn't resolved quickly and I'm kept in my chambers for days? Merlin said we might have less than a week until Morgan returns—I cannot afford to be kept from the catacombs.

We rummage past a shop selling lush textiles of bright colors and patterns for dresses and morning jackets. A stand of long, silk handkerchiefs falls when a trio of fleeing dandies runs past it. I seize a scarf from the ground and set it across my shoulders and hair, eyes cast down and away from guards who'd recognize me as the queen's handmaid.

It seems to work. No one spots me. Or no one is foolish enough to run *toward* the danger, rather than away.

Merlin beelines for the courtyard, and I stay close behind, an abundance of frenzy coming over me as I internalize the impending attack. I must get to the other side of the courtyard; from there, I can keep a strong eye on the village in case an intruder were to find his way to the blacksmith's cellar. They can't find Victor.

In front of the gates, Lancelot bellows orders to knights and squires. A loud clap of thunder makes me drop the fire iron and handkerchief. I slam my hands over my ears. But the sky is bright and free of clouds. It wasn't a storm.

At the gates, the guards have divided. Some form a semicircle around the entrance, firelances ready and aimed at the gates. More stand atop the wall firing nonstop at our attackers. A locking sound, tasting like metal on my lips, slams into the air. Three sharp points puncture the gates from the other side and twist.

"Steady!" is the call from the city walls.

Pelles's men are drilling their way inside.

The guards firing from the gates give up before their ammunition does. "These men will not be killed with bullets!" screams one.

And now my brother is having at it with Lancelot amongst the unit armed and ready before the walls. I reclaim my dropped fire iron and run further into the chaos of stoic knights and nervous squires.

Owen's tone is ruthless. "All of this could have been avoided if we'd invaded Glastonbury when the opportunity presented itself!" Eyes fall upon Lancelot as I reach Owen's side. No one notices me for my outspoken brother.

Merlin's eyes narrow on Owen. "Silence, squire. Learn your place."

I'm waiting for Lancelot to defend himself, to strike Owen's jaw for his insubordination, but he's oddly quiet. Like he might agree. The knight gathers himself. "Positions! Press them back once they break through. Keep Morgan's bastards cornered at all costs."

"Not Morgan," Merlin growls with annoyance. "From my tower I saw the blue of Corbenic advancing for Camelot. Who told Pelles that Morgan was brought inside our kingdom?"

Lancelot pales. He tries to speak, but stumbles on the words. "Can't be." Once the shock fades, he sneers. "You lie, wizard! Corbenic is our ally. Pelles is Arthur's friend, and mine. His family is my family—"

"Why would I lie, you stupid man?" Merlin snarls as he seizes Lancelot's vestments. "Corbenic marches to attack Camelot, and by the day our kingdom becomes more vulnerable as we await a more brutal war. We fight today to keep our kingdom standing, but know this, Lancelot: any future stupidity on the knights' part will result in *my* wrath, forget Arthur's!" With a heavy shove, he throws Lancelot back a few feet.

Lancelot furrows his brow in attempt to stay strong with so many regarding him as their leader, but his devastation is undeniable. The interlocking teeth of the drilling ram bites harder into the gates. Lancelot straightens. "Marcus! My sword!"

Marcus.

I gasp. And it's only now that Owen notices me.

Lancelot looks back amongst the squires. "Where's Marcus?" They look for him, but he isn't here. He's in the farmlands, and I could be the only one who knows this. Now, who knows what might happen to the woman he brought inside the kingdom?

"I saw him at the infirmary!" I burst out. All eyes turn, looking me up and down. I bite my lip and pray for a stronger lie. "The guards were tending to the people, and he was helping. He had no sword on him, certainly not yours, my lord."

The drilling ram slices at the gates, and warped metal flies across the courtyard. The sharp edges glide along the skin of those standing guard: the men struck fly into the air with the impact, letting their own blood paint the grass.

Suddenly, Owen's eyes are the strongest I've ever seen them. He glares like the warning he gave me was made in vain. And perhaps it was. "How serendipitous that you managed to cross paths with him, *my lady.*" Owen steps closer and speaks so only I can hear. "Get away from all this. What if others were to see you lingering here, a girl striving for a man's place in battle?"

I should slap him for such a comment and feel my fingers clench into a hard fist. "Not now, Owen," I say through gritted teeth.

Pelles's men press the drill into the remains of the gates, and now Lancelot has more pressing matters than an absent squire. Merlin unsheathes his sword and walks with it straight through the barricade of remaining guards, Arthur's champion following. The sorcerer finds a place at the front and waits.

The gate is near destruction. They're coming through.

"Ready!" Merlin bellows in a loud voice that rings through my skeleton.

It's happening. How can I stand tall in the face of what lies beyond those trembling doors? My feet step backward, inching toward whatever safety I might find. But the churning of the locking mechanisms in the nobility's quarters is loud. I cannot leave. I need to make sure no one finds Merlin's catacombs. So I firm my jaw and stand strong.

The drilling ram bursts inside on a massive wagon, an iron barrel that might fit the circumference of the Round Table. It slams into our soldiers with leftover force, running them over. Three steel teeth twist outward and rotate faster and faster like a knife obliterating an apple core.

Merlin lifts his weapon high and runs into the army spilling inside. He leads guards, knights, and squires into the throes of this attack, his long cape camouflaging his limp. Pelles's men wear the crisp blue of their kingdom's flag over plated armor, visors pulled down. If their king is amongst them, there'd be no way of knowing. They forego pistolníks and firelances for long, steel swords. But their armor is tough, and even with Merlin's heavy blows to the natural weak spots in the elbows and knees, he's unable to do damage.

Eyes wide, Merlin pulls back, and perhaps this is Morgan's curse showing itself, reminding him why he sent me after Lancelot's key instead of going himself.

Pelles's soldiers are ferocious. When one soldier drives his sword into Stephen's shoulder, I jump. The squire gurgles awfully and clutches his arm. Other knights likewise feel the cool blades of Pelles's men pressing into their necks and chests.

"Steady!" comes from above. I look to the brigade of guards atop the citadel where a cannon tilts toward the gates' twisted remains. Three guards ready the cannon at a precise angle. "Fire!" One guard's hand slices the air with his order. The weapon booms.

I jerk my eyes back to the gates and watch the cannon's blast envelope scores of Pelles's men. Nevertheless, they push through, breaching the knights' perimeter. I dash up the citadel's stone steps for a better look and to stay out of harm's way. But when I reach the top and glance over at those manning the cannon, the guards are less than happy to see me.

"Get to the towers, my lady, lest you be mad!" Their faces are covered in soot, and they grunt as they reload the cannon. But Pelles's men advance just as ferociously, like iron is able to bounce off their armor.

I can't understand how their weaponry could be so futile. "How are they still standing strong?" I shout.

"To the towers!" the same guard screams back, sweat beading on his neck as he rummages through his arsenal of pointless copper tools. He curses under his breath and regards the other two. "Are these men or gods?"

They're afraid. And now heavy footsteps approach.

"My lady!" another guard shouts.

As the shine of silver armor peels around the corner, my free hand finds an unexpected crossbow. It's heavy and bulky, and it's awkward to lift high. There are no bolts handy, but there is a copper knife amongst the guards' supplies. It fits improperly in the crossbow and serves as a pitiful last act of desperation.

Regardless, I fire the blasted thing straight into the unprotected neck of a Corbenic soldier who does not see a girl standing in front of him.

NINETEEN

The soldier falls dead, and I shudder still. It was only a copper knife and should not have damaged him in the slightest. An eager attempt to buy mere minutes.

Copper. Merlin couldn't touch it when he was a thief of magic, so he told me many times. But these are men of Corbenic, not the same black-armored soldiers I saw.

Still, I can't ignore this. "Use what you have," I tell the guards in a shaky voice, handing over the fire iron with its copper handle. I cannot think about the life I took. Right now, I have to follow my instinct that there's magic afoot here.

It might make all the difference.

The shocked guards haven't moved to take the fire iron from me, so I slam the weak spot between copper and iron over my knee until it snaps in two, razor-sharp at the edges. I throw the handle into the cannon's mouth. "Use what you have! Anything made of copper—spoons, pocket watches, viewers. Throw them into the cannon!"

They obey, and I stare out into the sea of battling men. When the guard calls "Fire!" this time, Corbenic soldiers fall to the ground and stay there.

Merlin regards the strange death because of my revelation. He looks unsure, as though all of this is a dream.

No, something else makes Merlin regard his raised sword like it's a stick of wood, useless in a fight. He pays no mind to the surrounding action. I wonder if he's realized as I have that magic sustains the soldiers' strength. He pulls back his sleeves to a patch of inked script on his skin, eyes full of wonder and fear—

BOOM!

Blast after blast after blast from the citadel, and more of Corbenic's men fall with each eruption of warped metal. Copper seems to be doing the trick, better than iron ever could. The guards cry out to those manning other cannons and the massive trebuchet with its steel crank, ordering them to change tactics.

From the ground, Lancelot hears this. "Drive them together!" he shouts. Copper soars across the sky, sending Corbenic's men to die quick deaths.

My ears are raw, but we're overcoming our foes. We've gotten hold of this attack and now we turn the violence onto those who brought it.

"Fire!" is the last cry from the citadel before silence falls over us.

My eyes are squeezed shut, and it takes an eternity to open them. When I do, I look out on an unsettling peace at the northern gates, at knights and squires and guards who glance at the human faces of their fallen enemies. I find Merlin's eyes from this distance and recognize the sense of uncomfortable relief he wears like a silk cravat. Somehow, I manage to breathe again.

The injuries are gruesome and plentiful; the deaths are few. And while Camelot has nevertheless won against Pelles's soldiers, it was done all too quickly.

———

I leave the citadel and find Merlin in the courtyard, staring at the jagged remains of the gates, the repairs of which have already commenced. Camelot will not appear weak, Morgan le Fay in the vicinity or not. The infirmary has rushed to collect the wounded, and the bishop has been sent for to orchestrate prayers for the dead.

Merlin isn't hurt, but nor is he at peace. He clutches his robe over his hammered armor, the old man Morgan's made of him returning as his adrenaline flees. "Well done, Vivienne. That was an inventor's way of thinking."

All I can see is the slow gait of the soldier I killed. My hands shake. "It was copper that did it, Merlin."

The sorcerer grunts. He understands what I mean, that copper will be instrumental in slaying Morgan's drones while Victor fights whatever dark magic machine the witch pits against us.

"Good for bullets or arrowheads, perhaps, but it's too thin for more sophisticated arsenal. And it's too impractical to load our cannons with spoons and viewers until the kingdom is red and raw from it. Against a woman of dark magic, at that. Huh. But useful information, nonetheless." His words are monotonous, like he might not realize he's speaking. "Especially considering—" A strange pause.

"What is it, Merlin?" But I already know. It was too easy.

"Morgan wanted something else," he says. "Something I've wanted myself for a long time, and nearly took just now." The sorcerer looks at the armored bodies to be buried outside of the city. No celebrations will commence when we've killed men we considered allies.

He'll convene with Lancelot and Guinevere in the assembly hall shortly. But for now, the sorcerer walks back to his clock tower alone to consider what happened. I watch him go.

Merlin never said what he and Morgan both wanted.

———

"My contact from Jerusalem is trustworthy. Pelles did not hear about Morgan escaping alive, that much is true. For now, he's all right, along with the rest of Corbenic's citizens, but all are under Morgan's control. The witch knows Arthur left Camelot to follow her, as I expected, though I can't shake this new suspicion that she might have a spy on the inside who confirmed the king abandoned his post, resulting in this ambush. Perhaps someone whose original purpose was to seek Avalon's coordinates. I could be wrong. Regardless, Arthur's attempt at peace will certainly fail. And Morgan will return sooner than we thought, Lancelot, I assure you."

Merlin paces in front of Lancelot and Guinevere. Though

their faces are wrought with panic, I have to imagine they'd be more upset if they knew they now stand in front of a fading sorcerer—never mind that he was fighting alongside the knights one hour past. Merlin hasn't told them everything, and clearly things are worse than he originally thought if it was enough to risk leaving the tower for the second time today. His scarlet cloak binds tightly around his shoulders, falling to the floor. The gentle clicks of his cane and skeleton feet—"Those boots were damn uncomfortable anyway"—are audible, but the tension in the room is louder. He inhales a pinch of snuff with no attempt at discretion.

Guinevere takes my hand. "The gates," she says.

"They've cleared away everything," I whisper. "And the gates should be reinforced in a day's time."

She relaxes wearing a look of bitter relief, and it's impossible to feel anything more than that. Stephen rests in the infirmary and should be all right, but others weren't so lucky. To prevent further panic, all of Camelot has been told it was a band of rogue soldiers whose poorly executed plan to seize Excalibur went horribly wrong. According to my father, Camelot doesn't need to know about the threat of le Fay just yet. It's dumb luck no one else recognized the blue of Pelles's flag.

"Does this Azur also think there's a spy in our midst?" Lancelot asks, his scruffy chin caught between his thumb and forefinger. He's forgotten his rift with Merlin, or is too overwhelmed by recent events.

"Well, if you need further evidence, Morgan left Camelot too easily, come to think of it. As though there wasn't much for her to lose in abandoning her plan that day," Merlin remarks.

"She left because all of us pointed our fusionahs at her without hesitation, only awaiting Arthur's command," Lancelot reponds.

Merlin strides toward the outspoken knight with tried patience. "A command he wouldn't give, and she knew it as we did, Lancelot. Even if I'm wrong, you cannot afford to let a suspicion like that go ignored."

Lancelot firms his lips into a tight line. "So what will I have to fight when the witch returns?"

Merlin thinks about the question. "You got a taste of it today: a legion of soldiers similar to those who first arrived with the witch, possessed by *Telum Paret* as Azur confirmed."

That spell. Merlin had called it "The Obeying Weapon" in front of Morgan, and his very disposition had been shaken by his memory of it: a spell that would allow a thief of magic to control the mind of another. But no. I shake my head. I have to speak up at this. "Forgive me, my lord—" It feels wrong addressing my mentor with such formality. "—but these men were nothing likes those I saw the night of the wedding." I stare blankly at the sorcerer. We both watched them approach from his tower. They were Corbenic's men, yes, but they did not assert the same unnatural magic as the black-armored demons at the gates.

Merlin might have cringed at my words in any other circumstance; now, he indulges me. "Your handmaid is sharp, your majesty. There was indeed a difference today, Lady Vivienne. Corbenic's soldiers were newer targets of Morgan's magic. Children, essentially. Cursed, but only in mind, not body. According to Azur, some unlucky fools in the Holy

Land were able to free themselves of Morgan's magic through nothing more than sheer strength of will, and when they returned home, they were wrought with insanity." His eyes fill with horror as though watching it happen. "The worst of it, though, how she went about enhancing and claiming them as hers, is too horrid to repeat. And so I know this was not a true attack for Camelot. No, this was won too easily. She meant to do something else."

Guinevere and Lancelot share a look of worry. "What, wizard?" he asks.

Merlin studies Lancelot, but ignores the question. He looks with strong eyes at Guinevere. "She's forged a legion, your majesty. Seems your maid's vision is better than your husband's after all. Lady Vivienne was a valid witness."

I beg to have been wrong. Those black-armored soldiers so much more ferocious than Corbenic's mindless men ... it was my imagination, it was because of the dark, or the moon-light. It can't have been *real*.

"My God," I whisper.

Merlin's eyes are on mine, but his words are not aimed at me. "We should be thankful Camelot was protected. Otherwise, *Telum Paret* would have made us her newest drones while the witch was in our presence."

Lancelot straightens. "We were able to beat Pelles's men this time. Surely, it cannot be as horrendous as you say."

Merlin firms his jaw. "Don't underestimate her. To use such magic on Pelles's men to create the soldiers Lady Vivienne saw would have required physical reinforcement. It would have taken much work and even more time. You have no idea what sort of weight a spell of that magnitude will force a thief of magic to carry."

Lancelot thinks about Merlin's words, and his eyes darken. I've never seen him so afraid. "Magic like that cannot still be amongst us."

Merlin tenses as he thinks. He doesn't like what he sees in his mind's eye. A hand sneaks into his pocket and withdraws another pinch of snuff, turning his eyes red and watery. He squeezes them shut.

"Yes. Torturous to the body, but nothing compared to the trapping of the mind, being unable to control your own actions, hearing the witch's voice overrule you. The legion that comes for Camelot will be different from Pelles's poor bastards. They'll be alive and dead, armor and flesh."

The queen's voice is laced with vengeance. "What must we do?"

Merlin studies her as he studied Lancelot. A frown comes across his face, a curled lip of distrust. "Prepare for war. And allow me the honor of building a weapon strong enough to fight her, your majesty." There's a touch of sarcasm, but he struggles for sincerity through a flash of pain he tries to conceal.

Guinevere glances at Lancelot in defeat. The knight steps forward. "It's not up to us, wizard. It's not my steel to give, and even if it was … there has to be another way."

I open my mouth to argue there simply isn't and, my goodness, after what we've just gone through. But Merlin clears his throat. He looks at the floor as he paces. A tiny shake of the head. Frustrated, I concede to the silent order the knight and queen missed. Lancelot's hand slips into his pocket and grasps something, and I wonder if it's not a key.

"There is," Merlin says. "Other kingdoms to the north have been ... unaffected, from what I hear."

"You said all—" Lancelot starts.

"No, not all," Merlin grunts. "Outside of the country, yes, there are other kingdoms Morgan has destroyed, but within Britannia, Corbenic is the only one unlucky enough to have felt her wrath. So now we rally Camelot's allies under the lie that Morgan is on her way. Castle Blanc and Beaurepaire, perhaps. The Caledonians, certainly. My Druid allies, most definitely. We'll need power in numbers. I'll go for help, and when I return, the blacksmith can aid me in enhancing any arsenal into sophisticated weaponry."

The queen and knight consider Merlin's plan while I frown at his obvious lie. Why the quick surrender? I need that steel. And I know Morgan's insanity. I saw her eyes, heard her voice, felt her seize my mind and everything in it. I can't imagine a world where Morgan finds Avalon.

Where sea and sky meet with a kiss, the Grail, our hope, cannot be missed.

We're a kingdom without magic facing a forthcoming hurricane of it, a taste of which we've just barely swallowed. Why would Merlin give up?

But now, Lancelot agrees. "We'll send a dozen guards to escort—"

"There's nothing your guards could do if Morgan were to find me. Save the manpower."

Lancelot huffs in frustration. "Then *I* will go—"

"No, Lancelot," Merlin says firmly. He steps close to the knight and sets a reassuring hand on his shoulder, casting his cloak over Lancelot's arm. My brows knit. "You were left to rule in Arthur's stead. One old man versus hundreds in Camelot. Your job is to rebuild the gate and finalize plans with Henry and William. I'll return before nightfall." Then, to himself, "I have to."

"We'll send for Arthur's advisors immediately." Guinevere steps down from her throne. Merlin keeps to the rules of etiquette and bows as she approaches. Lancelot can't tear his eyes from her. "We must be ready, Lancelot." She sets a frightened hand on his arm and without thinking, he grasps her fingers and nods.

Merlin narrows his eyes, stepping away as he looks out from under drawn eyebrows. He clears his throat, and their hands come apart.

"Your majesty, if you're to oversee the knights' plans, at least dismiss your handmaid. She's too young to be burdened with problems such as these." Merlin's eyes fall to mine, and I imagine the scoff he'd emit at the irony later. "Besides, she remains a face known to Morgan."

Guinevere nods. "Take your leave, Vivienne. Stay in your chambers whenever your duties are dismissed. I'll see you tomorrow."

I curtsy. "Yes, your majesty." I'll have the old fool's pistolník for that comment, even if we both know it's the furthest from the truth.

Merlin leads me toward the doorway, limping and clacking against cobblestone more noticeably as his step quickens.

"The mind should be strong enough to withstand that sort of traitorous thought, no matter what inhibitions were freed," he mutters.

"What?" I ask.

He shakes his head with a grunt.

———

In the courtyard, Merlin orders a guard not tending to the gates' reconstruction to fetch a horse, then reaches for his snuff box, inhaling several pinches. "Be in the tower by night-fall, in time for my return. I'll need your help to get the steel inside."

I blink. "But Lancelot refused it."

"Lancelot should know never to trust the promises of a thief." Merlin returns the snuff box to his pocket. When he withdraws his hand, a silver, four-pronged key dangles on a chain from his finger.

"Instead, he's a nitwit who thought this was safer in his pocket than locked up with Excalibur. Serves him right, deny-ing me this privilege mere hours after what befell. There's no one who can help us now. Britannia and the rest of Arthur's allies are under Morgan's control and won't be freed until the witch is dead. Thank God for that, I suppose."

He's walking through the courtyard too quickly, and I must ignore the wet blood finding the toes of my boots.

"All this time we feared the wrong war, Vivienne. How much simpler life would have been had Arthur's violation of Pelles's orders resulted in a war of machines instead of Morgan's scrimmage of magic. I must resort to desperate measures now. The Norwegian steel lies in a cave beyond the eastern woods, guarded by *l'enigma insolubile*, a mechanism also guarding Excalibur. Since the steel wasn't given to me when I asked politely—twice—I'm going to take it."

He catches the key in midair and returns it to his pocket.

The guard brings a horse, and I see a rare opportunity in front of me as the devastated gates pull free from the walls, exposing the open land. "I'm going with you!"

Merlin huffs. "Ha! I think not. Return to the catacombs. See what can be done with the blueprints." Merlin mounts the horse, but before he can ride off, I grab the saddle—to hell with the awful beast.

"No, Merlin, I'm part of this, too! There's nothing to do until Arthur's steel is in our grasp."

Merlin leans closer. His voice is low. "Then return to your chambers, as the queen instructed. Collect copper spoons, for all I care. Just be at the tower as I told you."

He yanks my hand from the saddle and guides his horse into a trot, but I follow.

"You go alone, a cursed man yourself! Do they know that? What if you were to fade further out there?"

He halts the beast. "And what would you do if that happened? Don't you realize that all of this goes beyond your selfish desire to leave Camelot? We all have roles to play in life, Vivienne! Whether we want to or not!" He shakes as he spits the words. "Morgan doesn't just need Camelot or Excalibur, or even me. It goes deeper than that! She needs *you!*"

"What have I to do with it, *pagan?*" I shout.

The slur hits Merlin like a club of iron. "I don't know. It

might be nothing, or it might be everything. And if it's the latter, it's something I cannot say aloud for fear of putting you in danger. The only one who'd know for sure—" He stops there, shaking his head. A staunch refusal to say more.

I stand firm. I don't know why I'm so desperate to stay by Merlin's side when only weeks ago the thought of leaving for another land was much more appealing. "Take me with you. I'll wear your sword."

Merlin takes a breath. "Look through the blueprints for a miracle."

A miracle. I imagine Marcus running toward the unstable Victor because of the glitch in Merlin's blueprints. The time I've spent contemplating a secondary plan while staring day after day at that manual lever can't be in vain.

The sorcerer doesn't flee. He waits for my final argument.

I lift my chin. "Give me a chance to see the world beyond Camelot just once, if you can give me nothing else."

Merlin straightens his back and tugs on his horse's reins, riding off. My shoulders settle in disappointment. The walls of Camelot close in on me.

Then he stops and turns. "Well? What are you waiting for? Get Caldor, and get the carrier from my desk. And don't forget my sword, but don't you dare believe someone as untrained as you would wear it. I'll have them send for another horse. Meet me at the lake." He gallops toward the gates, pulling a hood over his shorn head.

Hiding a grin, I run for the clock tower. It's nearing one o'clock.

We must be back before nightfall.

TWENTY

"Open the gates!"

"Let her pass!"

"No, that's not the queen's handmaid—she's the messenger the wizard vouched for! Bringing word of the attack
to the northern kingdoms!"

Goosebumps prickle my skin as I gallop across the drawbridge and breathe in the sharp metal smell still lingering
from Corbenic's drilling ram. The horse's mane strikes at my
hands. Wind whips around me, rustling the burlap cloak I
grabbed from Merlin's tower to hide my handmaid's dress.
The last time I was this far from home, I was terrified. Now?
Knowing it could be me Morgan wants?

Oh please, Merlin, be waiting at the lake...

A steam-whistled caw draws my eyes to the sky. Caldor,
beckoned to life by my rough alchemic request, soars through
the clouds toward an edge of the world I've never seen. The
horse moves just as quickly, and soon I lose my dislike of it.

Marcus was right about these magnificent beasts. I want mine to move faster, lift off the ground, into the sky. Returning by nightfall is not nearly enough time.

I want Caldor to bolt the sun in place so I can explore this world forever.

Forever would begin with the horrors of the farmlands.

I meet Merlin at the lake, and we ride through land spared of Morgan's wrath. But to the west are remnants of what used to be homes. Now ash, charred branches, copper harvesters that haven't lost their rust. Some survivors have returned to see what can be salvaged, walking atop graveyards of their former lives.

Merlin reaches the woods first. He drops from his horse and calls Caldor; the falcon lands at his feet, still alive with *jaseemat*, chirping wildly as copper feathers churn free the twigs stuck between them. The sorcerer takes a pinch of snuff, nose reddening, eyes even worse.

I catch up quickly, dropping my hood from my hair.

Merlin explores the leather carrier I brought. He pulls on a set of thick leather gloves and tosses another pair to me. I clutch them against my chest.

"When we reach the cave, you aren't to touch anything without these on." He lifts his goggles to examine Caldor's eye with a steel tool and clicks into place an extended lens. While we're inside the woods, Caldor will fly above the forest as our guide. "There we are."

Merlin whispers something, and the falcon flits into the air, arching over the woods' tallest tree. The sorcerer watches, lifting his goggles to his forehead. He holds a small dome of glass curved across a wild metal arrow.

"What is that?"

The arrow stops, and Merlin examines the direction. "Eastern science is at an all-time high in terms of discovery. Caldor is connected to this piece. He knows where the cave lies; I've told him as much. As long as we follow the arrow, we shouldn't get lost."

I smile, and Merlin sends me a proud wink. "Shall we?" He mounts his horse and gives a loud cry, igniting a gallop.

I don't hesitate in following.

━━━━━━━

The woods are dark.

Still branches morph into breathing shadows. The narrow path weaves in coils as though leading us back to where we started from. At times, Merlin studies the ceiling of leaves. He checks the arrow in his palm. Caldor whistles above us.

If I wanted to escape from this path, it would be impossible. The trees' trunks are thick; branches, twisted and hand-like, as though they were once men who now protect these woods.

"Stay close, Vivienne."

I pull my hood over my head and strain my eyes through the dimness. The viewer in my pocket would be of no use here. Even if I had a quicklight, it wouldn't be enough.

Instead, I keep my hand close to my waist, where I've fastened a miniature fusionah from the leather carrier. "Here's hoping you'll never need it," Merlin had said at the lake just as a satchel of ammunition flew from his grasp to mine. So different from my little crossbow. This weapon boasts a steel blade, long and elegant against the silver firelance rendering it swift and deadly. A capped barrel to indicate it was already loaded, ready when I'd be.

Just in case.

As though to distract, Merlin speaks. "We'll need Azur. He's graciously agreed to come to Camelot." He glances over his shoulder at me. "He flies by aerohawk, but he's quickened our model to be as fast as an aeroship." Merlin chuckles, but I don't miss the envy. "He should arrive tomorrow. Can you imagine?"

No, I cannot, but I'm relieved knowing Azur's on his way. With him working alongside us, construction of the weapon will certainly go as planned. For a moment, the entire madness of the woods seems to change into the peace of Camelot's gardens.

"He made more *jaseemat*, Merlin?"

"Aye, he did."

Merlin's horse fights through the trees. Soon, the sorcerer has to wield his blade to slice armlike branches from the path. As the limbs fall, a moan passes through the woods. There are a few seconds of silence before Merlin clears his throat, and we continue on.

"Pray we make good time, Vivienne. And remember what I told you about touching the steel. Leather gloves aren't an ideal solution, but better than nothing. Slower. And do not underestimate this kind of magic. I must admit, I'm—" He stops his horse. The inked patterns dark on Merlin's skin look out of place next to such vulnerable eyes.

"I'm terrified," he admits. "This steel is our best chance against Morgan, but she could still employ *Telum Paret* once Camelot's veil of protection has been lifted. How could I fight back? How could I ensure Morgan never gets the Grail?" He removes his goggles and studies them, forcing a quiet laugh.

"The only way to defeat Morgan would be to steal magic. She knows this. It's why she sent Corbenic's men to attack us: to lure me back to my addiction, knowing it'd make me a weak opponent—so out of practice compared to her. If you hadn't discovered her magic, and I'd given in, the demigods would put a stop to any future incantation I'd try to steal for Camelot's sake, certainly, unless the Lady of the Lake—" He swallows, a quick glance at the otherworldly trees that might have encouraged him to mention such an obscure fairy tale. "I cannot pretend being in the catacombs hasn't brought back an element of desire. Alchemy's been a godsend, but it's still a manipulation of nature. A cheat, if you will. And here—"

Here, we seek magical steel that could make things worse for Merlin. Even if it doesn't, how could it possibly guard against the demonic weapon the gypsy in the village told me of?

Morgan's magic let her combine blood and machine.

Merlin sharply breathes in the forest's air and closes his eyes. As though drunk on France's finest absinthe, he hums an Irish ballad. Something dark trails from his nose to lips. His eyes snap open. My horse backs away.

"Merlin?"

He tears off his gloves. The fingertips on his outstretched hands have disappeared for good. He runs them over his face, pulling his hand back as dark blood drips from his nose. I freeze at the sight of it, wondering if I'm about to be left out here alone.

Merlin pulls the gloves back on. "Hurry. We won't have the luxury of the sun to check the time." He yanks on his horse's reins. Slices away each branch blocking the path. Wood moans as it falls. But the trees don't fight back. The trees let us pass.

And finally, we reach the limits of the woods and ride into a blue sky with Caldor flying above us. The mechanical falcon whistles as it soars over Camelot's farmlands toward the mountains.

I glance back at the woods canopying over the path. The sun indicates it's well past three. Five hours until night, maybe six if the sun can hang on to the sky long enough.

———

The farmlands are abundant with fresh air and fields of wheat. We cross a stream toward the mountains. Caldor flies onward, disappearing inside a cave.

Merlin stops at its entrance and lowers himself from his horse. The cave stands nearly three times the size of the grand hall, and Merlin disappears into a blackness soon banished by the quicklight he snaps against stone. The orange glow illuminates a wooden door about a hundred yards off. On it, *l'enigma insolubile* gleams brilliantly through years of rust. Merlin sets Caldor—head cocked and still—into his carrier.

"Come, dear. Leave the horses. Let's see what the enlightened thinkers of Greece were capable of during their time in Venice."

I tie my horse's reins to a low branch by the entrance and follow Merlin. *Enlightened thinkers?* Like the song of Avalon.

He gauges the brass contraption, sprockets, roller chains with gears on their undersides. His hand sneaks into his pocket and pulls out a pinch; he turns away as a quiet snuffle escapes his nose. Then he withdraws Lancelot's key.

There's something different about this locking mechanism. "Hold on. Why would *l'enigma insolubile* have a key? It's just a sequence."

Merlin glances at me as though he might wonder if I finally saw Excalibur. "This one is different from the Round Table. Extra protection in case Arthur decided to hide absinthe from his knights, hence the very French *fleur-de-lis* design to honor the green fairy's homeland. Here, there's an extra piece..." As he speaks, he reaches under the gears and clicks them into place. He bends his knees, but it comes about painfully, and he breathes heavily as the pressure mounts. "I can't."

I step forward, holding out my hand. "Seems it was wise to insist upon my company."

He hands me the key. "The lock is on the other side. You won't see it unless the gears have clicked together properly."

I crawl under the massive contraption, my gown muddying at the knees. Merlin gives me his quicklight, and I lift it to the roller chain, seeing where the gears connect. A keyhole in the shape of a cross appears in the center, fitting perfectly. I turn the key clockwise. The roller chain winds; the sprocket rotates.

"Good girl. Up you go."

I hand back the key, and Merlin helps me to my feet. He takes the long brass lever and wedges it between two copper grooves. It releases, and the door opens.

As it slams against the wall on the other side, the horses whinny. Shocked by the loud noise, of course.

Then the sound of a foot snapping a branch sends Merlin in front of me in one fast motion. His fusionah clicks in warning at the intruder. "You have no business here, boy," Merlin says in a dangerous voice.

The reply comes in a brash whisper. "Oh fuck."

I look to the entrance from behind the sorcerer, my hood covering my hair.

By the horses stands Marcus, hands raised and eyes locked on my unpredictable mentor.

TWENTY-ONE

The sorcerer hid me for my own good. I know this.

Still, I step out from Merlin's protection before I can consider the dangers of the squire knowing my secret. Marcus's eyes fill with slow recognition upon seeing me.

"What are you doing here?" I breathe. Merlin's aim remains a readied threat, and Marcus must feel that, too. He makes no sudden moves.

"I was on my way to my family's farm and saw two riders reach this mountain." His eyes trail to Merlin's. "I know about the safe."

I turn to the sorcerer. Oh God, to reveal myself as the wizard's apprentice so rashly. "Merlin, lower your weapon."

Merlin ignores me. "You're Lancelot's squire, sent to follow me."

Marcus shakes his head as I step in front of him. "Lancelot doesn't know he left Camelot. I swear. He isn't even armed, for goodness sake." I set a hand on the sorcerer's firelance until it falls to his side.

Merlin's eyes finally break to mine. "It's not good to have people know we're here."

Marcus eases forward. "Why are you here? What's *l'enigma insolubile* guarding?"

Merlin's eyes snap forward. "That's not your concern." He takes a step as though his crooked gait would scare Marcus off. "Be gone with you!"

"No. I'm no fool, Merlin," Marcus says. "I see how weak the incantation over Camelot has become. And you're both out here alone? I'm not leaving. You're mad to think the world outside Camelot's walls is safe enough for anyone these days."

"Then you shouldn't be here either." Merlin straightens. "Yes, in fact. You shouldn't be. You're the one who was missing. You should have been back in Camelot while we were under attack!"

Marcus pales. "What?" He looks at me for an answer.

I think of the white lie I told Lancelot. Why did I feel the need to protect Marcus? "Morgan sent possessed soldiers from Corbenic to attack the castle only hours ago. After you … " I cannot finish the thought. Not when it could put Marcus in trouble with Merlin.

A panic sweeps over Marcus's face. "The infirmary. The people in the infirmary. Did anyone get hurt? Did—"

"Fine. All fine," I say.

Marcus's shoulders fall in relief. "Thank God." His eyes take him to a place where I cannot follow.

"But knights died today, and your absence was noticed.

If I were you, boy, I'd head back immediately." Merlin juts his chin toward Marcus. "Wandering the farmlands instead in a crisis such as this, and now speaking against me, daring to understand my work—"

Marcus doesn't flinch. "Tell me your work, then. If the lady's involved, I can't imagine it'd be something immoral."

"Magic's involved."

Marcus glances at me for any clues to diminish his incredulity. I will my eyes to silently tell him it's all right, but perhaps whatever good opinion he had of me has disappeared now.

If he knew more, perhaps he'd feel differently.

I speak softly to Merlin. "He's fast. A natural athlete." My heart sinks as I imagine Marcus struggling with the stubborn lever of a weapon I'm to build with the steel behind us. "He can help."

Merlin considers my whispered words. His cloudy eyes confirm what I fear Marcus's involvement in all this will be. "Fine. The wagon. Bring it forth." He points to a dark corner.

Marcus's eyes take an eternity to shut. "Merlin, neither of you should have left the castle. God. An attack when I was only miles away?" His eyes open and fall harshly upon the sorcerer. "The witch is out here."

"Huh, you don't say. In that case, you'd better hurry."

Marcus's eyes narrow, but he disappears nonetheless into the darkness, returning with a closed riding wagon complete with brass doors and locks. The vehicle is meticulously crafted and painted in faded shades of Camelot's red and gold, chipped in some places.

"How did you know that was there?" I stare through the window at the locking gadgets and components. It's a metal and wooden structure capable of extending into a million different forms.

Merlin limps forward and receives from the squire's hand a brass tug that would fit to a horse. "I built it, of course." He uses his sleeve to dust the surface of branches and dried leaves. "Long ago. It kept me busy so I wouldn't return to magic. Naturally, I'd started it with the secret intention of taking Arthur's steel. Now for an altogether different reason."

Merlin's quicklight casts an orange glow into the dingy air inside the safe. I search for a ceiling in a vault of infinite rock and stacks of sheet metal, long and rectangular, warping as Merlin roughly seizes an armful. It's a treasure trove of glistening surfaces reflecting matted firelight. A woman's hypnotic voice sings as he carries the steel to the wagon.

Merlin uses a key from the ring in his pocket to unlock it. Four seats of red upholstery easily transform into hidden compartments for smuggling purposes, expanding and retracting into a space outside of this world's. The sorcerer points at me. "Give the squire your gloves."

One finger at a time, I obey. Marcus looks at me with a million questions. But he settles for one. "What is all this?"

I hand him the gloves, unable to look him in the eye.

"This is how we save Camelot from Morgan."

———

It takes no longer than an hour to load the wagon with as much steel as it can hold. Arthur's supply seems endless, but "twenty stone, and nothing less," Merlin grunts. Thankfully, that's plenty, while barely making a dent in this reserve. The cave sings an entrancing sonata, but the song is nowhere nearly as distracting as the unnatural delight dancing on my skin.

The sensation intoxicates me, lifts me onto a cloud somewhere as Merlin fights the enchantment to keep his scowl. He's careful not to touch anything, but the steel's mysticism has nonetheless had an effect on his pain. The twists of agony are less violent; the relief is quick and cool. Still, he grunts at the squire to move faster so we can get out of this "bloody, bewitched place."

Marcus sets the last of what we'll take into the wagon, looking about in confusion as he shoulders our burden. Hints of red at his ears express unwarranted pleasure. He glances at me more than he should when otherwise keeping a look out on the cave's entrance, as though expecting Morgan herself to waltz right in.

The wagon locks. *L'enigma insolubile* whirs as the door slams and the song dies. Our ears are finally spared, but the silence after hangs low. Jaded exhaustion weighs on our faces as we hitch the wagon to Merlin's horse. The sorcerer mounts the steed, snuff box at his fingertips.

"Vivienne, we ride out." He glances at Marcus. "You've done enough, and the girl is in good hands. Your gracious services are no longer welcome."

"Wait," Marcus says before letting an eternity of silence pass, like a battle stronger than the magnitude of Morgan's forthcoming war possesses his mind. He steps forward in defiance. "You're not in Camelot yet. Le Fay might be near." And when he speaks, it's like he's betrayed another.

At my horse's side, I'm searching for words that would build a fortress strong enough to keep Marcus from the truth. "My lord," I say. Marcus glances at me. "Just go. Please."

Do whatever it is you're out here for, and stay out of the sorcerer's affairs.

Do this so that I can stop thinking about how I'll have to ask you to be a part of something that might kill you.

"I'll explain everything later." I'm not sure it's a promise I'm ready to keep.

Marcus takes a step. "Not two weeks ago, the witch threatened your life. How could I claim to be honorable if I let you return guarded only by a wizard?"

"I told you I'd be fine!" I hiss, feeling my eyes widening.

Merlin rolls his eyes. "Enough, boy. You've already seen too much. Guinevere's maid is perfectly safe in my keep." He won't mention how his apprentice of seven years is more than capable of dealing with his quirks. "Be gone now."

But Marcus ignores him. "He's an addict in possession of magical metal without saying what it's for—"

"It's not—"

"And you, boy," Merlin growls, "don't understand how deep this all goes! Vivienne knows what she's gotten herself into. She doesn't need you to save her."

"I know that, wizard." Marcus glares at Merlin, and then turns to me. "I'm not trying to save you. I'm saying I'm not leaving your side." With one look, he tells me he cannot be swayed in this.

Please, Marcus. Please just go...

Merlin's eyes flash. "And that is where you're weak. Why are you out here anyway? We both know it's not for family—isn't that so? I don't have time to waste on Lancelot's temper if he were to find this out. Be gone!"

Marcus gauges Merlin with suspicion. "I don't trust you, Merlin."

And I don't miss how Marcus ignores Merlin's question.

The sorcerer flicks an eyebrow, the few words the squire does speak able to bring humility over him. His horse stills.

"Strange how I wish you would." Merlin glances at the sky. Dusk will arrive in a few short hours. He gauges Marcus as though searching for clues. "Huh. You, on the other hand, I do trust. Perhaps your place in this plan is more detailed than I thought." He huffs a sigh. "Oh, very well. Ride with Vivienne."

He flees for the woods.

Marcus and I face one another. I look for judgment in his eyes, but find none. "There's no going back if you choose this road."

He steps closer.

"Things cannot be unseen or taken back. And I've seen much already without you by my side, you do realize?"

After a moment, he nods. "I know."

How would he know? But we cannot discuss this now. I return the nod.

Foregoing the stirrups, he helps me atop the horse. I lay

my legs to the side, and he climbs up behind me. "And here I thought you didn't ride," he whispers in my ear, his voice shaped in a smile. He seizes the reins and kicks the horse into a fast gallop. An arm goes around my waist. Though I'm certain we're going to lose our balance, I won't pretend it doesn't bring a bit of blush to my cheeks.

The sorcerer waits at the limits of the woods, looking upon our path with unease.

"What is it?" I ask. Then I see the difference myself.

The woods we left were forest green, speckled with brown and other natural colors. But now, a bright shade of emerald smears each tree. Their shapes are uniform. Branches bow over the pathway, but they're not armlike anymore, they're arms. Arms of leaves and fingers. Body parts with eyes that shut when you look for them. The woods are alive. The woods look nearly human.

"God save us," Marcus whispers.

Merlin clears his throat. "Nothing to worry about. Come now." He rides on.

We follow, dipping our heads as we pass under branches boasting skin on the bark, hair on the leaves. Moans have turned to rhythmic breaths. Merlin hacks at a tree in the way, and the branch swings down like a reaching arm, three prongs on the end like Morgan's red-apple nails.

Merlin withdraws his quicklight; Marcus does as well, handing me the reins. Two glowing spots of orange are the only conventional comforts in this place of natural and horrific beauty. Earlier, if only briefly, the woods reminded me of the gardens, where I usually feel at my most secure.

Now I find myself craving the familiar mechanical world of Camelot.

═══════

Our horses' footsteps are loud.

We've been riding for hours with no end in sight. With no extra *jaseemat* for Caldor, we rely on Merlin's memory to return to Camelot. But now we should find another route, use Marcus's knowledge of these parts to take us around the woods.

Before I can suggest it, Merlin points across the way to a tree—the very same one from no more than several hours ago, hanging dead with three prongs reaching for the ground. I turn in Marcus's arms to look at it, nauseating horror coming over me as taunting apple blossoms sprout into bright, tempting fruit.

Merlin glances about. "The path is looped. It's Morgan's magic." His horse patters to a stop. "We never should have taken this path."

Marcus breathes out in frustration. "There must be a way out. There cannot be—"

"There is a way out," Merlin says. He glances up at the ceiling of the woods, now black instead of green. "It's a simple spell. She doesn't mean to harm us, or trap us indefinitely. She means to do something much worse."

I fear I already know what he'll say. "What, Merlin?"

"This is how she'll force me to steal magic." He tilts his head. "So soon, Morgan?"

My fingernails dig into my palms. "Merlin, you wouldn't." Though I'm not so sure now. I remember how he looked in the midst of Corbenic's attack—he was tempted.

The sorcerer clicks his tongue at the stilled horse, which reluctantly starts again. "Perhaps I'm wrong. Let's go a little further as I stretch my mind for ideas." He studies the encased arrow on his gloved hand before remembering the immobile Caldor. "Keep an eye out for poppies. I could use a smoke." He laughs once.

I tug at our horse's reins to start again, but its steady pace can't temper my worries. Even Marcus's arm tightening around my waist does nothing for my nerves.

Merlin halts his steed.

"Merlin?" I straighten as though it would help me see better. It doesn't. "Merlin, we must turn around—"

"Shhh." Merlin dismounts, landing soundlessly on a bed of leaves. He limps toward something sitting against a tree.

"That wasn't there before," I whisper hastily.

Merlin kneels. Leaning against the skinlike bark is an armored man, still as death, sitting next to a fusionah covered in leaves. I shudder as the orange glow from Merlin's quicklight illuminates skyward eyes, a look of horror, the indication of hunger. Something hangs on the mouth of the soldier. Merlin removes the black helmet, revealing a gray face with a wound square in one temple. The man's jaw is covered in iron plates, nailed in place with steel bolts. Marcus and I look away.

"Morgan's legion." I shudder, my eyes turning back

with reluctance. Now more than ever, I'm eternally grateful I only saw a glimpse of them by the gates.

Merlin frowns. "So it appears. This is the real danger—not Pelles's mindless men. Azur was right. This is unspeakable." He takes the man's face in his hands, moving the head from side to side as he studies the bolts. "Poor bastard was still alive when she did this, but *Telum Paret* hadn't taken effect yet. God rest him."

From the dry wound, Merlin pulls out a small bit of copper cogs that were sharpened to incredible points. "It's from a pocket watch." Realization comes over him as he glances at the foliage-covered fusionah. "He must have been denied bearings, so he used what he had to end it." Merlin checks the man's neck and wrists: sure enough, long, dried cuts from a blade could not end the man's life. "The same ingenuity you showed during the attack, my dear."

I shut my eyes. I don't want to think about that.

"Escaped while his mind was still his own." The thumps of Merlin's off-balanced steps toward his horse are slow.

"What does all this mean?" Marcus asks.

Merlin rests against his saddle. "Copper, boy. I couldn't touch the damned stuff for years. Leave Morgan and whatever machine she sets upon the castle to me. The knights will have to use copper somehow to keep her drones at bay. Camelot could use the supply in my clock tower for bearings, I suppose, but I don't like the plan, Vivienne, as it's a horribly weak metal for—"

"No, not if you can make it sharp enough," Marcus says. The sorcerer's eyes dart to the squire's. "Lancelot's sword has hooks on the blade. Granted, not copper, but it's damn near impossible to have anything touch the edge without slicing through, even without force."

Merlin's eyes widen. "They forge weapons like that in the north. That's right." His hands search his pockets for his snuff box. "Crossbow bolts reinforced with copper edges. Bearings. I'll need to get started once we return. The blacksmith must know."

"The knights will need thousands, Merlin," I say. "That'll take time. We must turn around—"

Merlin drops his quicklight. The orange glow disappears before striking the forest floor. His body shakes. Marcus's light shines against the sorcerer's skin. I swear I see the blood rushing through Merlin's veins.

"Oh God," he mutters.

Something is wrong. The horses go restless. Marcus grips me tighter.

"Merlin!" I shout.

When Merlin doesn't respond, Marcus drops from the horse. He gauges the land with caution. "She's…damn it, wizard…"

Merlin's gaze drops to his quicklight, absent of its glow. "Even my inventions are at her mercy. How can that be?"

Marcus's quicklight is next to die, leaving us in near darkness. I drop from the saddle as Marcus pockets the useless tool. My fingers seize the miniature fusionah from my waist. Shakily, I uncap it and straighten my arm with the barrel scoping the land.

And seeing Marcus shake his head does nothing for my nerves. "There's no use for weapons."

Merlin quivers with whatever madness has taken him. "I wonder if Mordred screamed when she bolted his bones, too."

"Merlin, stop!" I shout, feeling the cool metal dig into my palm. "We have to turn around!"

Merlin breathes heavily, the only sound for several moments. "No," he says. "Vivienne, please. When we return to Camelot, I cannot leave my tower. Not for any reason."

He gasps. Icy fog bursts from his mouth.

"She's here."

TWENTY-TWO

Everything happens so fast.

Marcus yanks me out of danger's way, but Merlin is faster and casts his arm toward us with eyes glowing red. His lips struggle to form words, which slip along his voice like warm honey.

"Cachey havachah."

A wave of twisted light shrouds us with a translucent sphere, like we're underwater. Camouflage from the slow, approaching footsteps. I find a tragic sense of regret in the sorcerer's eyes. The realization of what he did sets in. Marcus's arms go tightly around my shoulders like a shield.

"No, Merlin!" I whisper in vain.

But he doesn't answer. He turns toward the path, where a hooded Morgan le Fay stands.

A low voice whispers in my mind. *Sensu ahchla tetay meo loqui havahchi…* The spell Morgan uttered to access my mind. It should feel invasive and mind-splitting, but it's soft, encouraging.

"You find yourself in a bind, Merlin," Morgan purrs.

Marcus pulls me close, remnants of angry curses on his lips. "We have to get out of here. What did he do?" he whispers.

To say it out loud would make it true, but now I'm more frightened of the familiar whisper in my head. "He stole magic to veil us from her."

"What?" Marcus hisses.

Merlin's eyes shut. A chill comes over his body. His eyes snap open.

Sensu ahchla tetay meo loqui havahchi…

I'm cold, and tornadolike winds whip around me. When I blink, I see a world of golden walls and streets. A dull chalice with iron studs and a leather grip. Under my feet, clouds and blue ocean.

The sorcerer looks at Morgan with contempt, but a small smile plays against his lips. *Merlin, no.*

"The only mistake I made was leaving Camelot," he admits in a smooth voice I have never heard him use, and I'm certain Morgan notices it, too. That slight smile vanishes quickly. "How dare you, Morgan? How dare you stand here wearing a cold smirk like a chain of fine gold mere hours after you made Pelles's men attack us?"

Her eyes shine. She practically beams with joy. "It was just to bring a healthy bit of fright to you, wizard. Nothing you couldn't handle."

"We were forced to kill brothers-in-arms because of your magic. Knights of Camelot died today!"

She lifts a finger. "Ahhh, Merlin. That was not my doing. You could have saved them. With one quick spell, you could have brought them back. The one inked on your skin in a script I cannot read."

Merlin's coolness fades, and he clenches his left hand.

The witch circles him, gesturing the trees. "And now another obstacle. But the spell to release yourself from these woods isn't difficult."

Merlin paces in front of where horses and his wagon once stood. All evidence shielded.

"No, it isn't. You knew it before I gave you that lesson on alchemy. What on earth was I thinking, Morgan? Did magic help you sense the vulnerability of the farmlands? Is that why you let the handmaid go? She was no longer the leverage you needed, was she?"

I grow hot with anger at the memory. I hate that Morgan held fear over me.

She doesn't blink. "There's more to her than that. You might have suspected it for years while those fools were out there searching. Don't think I didn't see her importance as soon as the idiot opened her mouth."

My eyes fall shut. I never should have said a word. Marcus shuffles, and I wonder if he's figured out my connection to Merlin.

"It's time to leave the forest now, sorcerer. Despite what magic I've mastered, controlling time is another question, and an informant waits outside these woods with the specifications of Excalibur for Mordred. Now, return to what awaits in Camelot."

Merlin's face is full of awareness, like he might know whom the witch means.

Azur was right: she has an informant. Someone Lancelot might scour the kingdom to reveal. And now Marcus tenses against me. I look at him with questions in my eyes and the memory of papyrus between his fingers. As his breathing strains, he looks back, and I see in those violet eyes how he managed to find Excalibur, how I was a convenient reason to see it again. Why he went to the farmlands today in the first place.

Merlin sighs as though calling a bluff. "And what will I find in Camelot, my dear? A newly built set of northern gates? Perhaps more burnt farmlands? More lives lost?"

A corner of Morgan's lips tugs up in a dark smile. "Arthur returns."

"His attempt at justice failed, I presume?"

"He never found Glastonbury. Britannia is under my control. All except for Camelot, but I can wait for your incantation to fade. Arthur entered these woods, too, Merlin. Incredible how they manage to stretch over quite a range of countryside. Conveniently so. My brother and his knights walked in, but never found their way out."

Merlin steels his eyes. "What did you do?"

She notes the shining red fruit hanging from skin-patched trees. "I kept him out of Camelot. Plenty of food and water in these woods. Of course, not understanding the trap was enough to plant seeds of insanity, but only temporarily. Now, he'll return to the betrayal I've arranged."

Betrayal. My eyes and Marcus's lock again, but now his beg for understanding. He runs the back of his fingertips across my burlap cloak.

Merlin is silent long enough that I can hear the gentle pattering of rainfall. A storm the trees shield us from. Oddly enough, it's comforting.

Sensu ahchla tetay meo loqui havahchi... A man's voice. I search my mind for foreign languages that would match it in hopes it might not be magic, but there's nothing. All I can think of are clouds three kingdoms past. Sea and sky meeting with a kiss. The sorcerer standing tall with both hands resting atop the emerald stone in his cane. Watching, studying the picture my mind paints. I shake my head of these scenes. Of everything bursting into a world of gold.

"Have you nothing to say?" Morgan taunts.

The sorcerer shrugs. His eyes flash at mine; he smiles. It'd be insane to think he saw the floating kingdom that appeared in my mind's eye. But it's Merlin, and he's a thief of magic again.

I know he did.

Merlin takes a satisfied breath. "I'm trying to decide which of these fields would most likely have poppies this time of year."

She grits her teeth, her voice poisonous against his dripping sarcasm. "You belittle my power."

"Huh! Born out of revenge for Uther stripping you of your name and of desperation for the king's bastard son, conceived through too much absinthe and not enough foresight. I've been wondering, Morgan: how do you keep your boy loyal? Do you use *Telum Paret,* or is that solely for those you forge into iron soldiers?"

I think of the skyward look of anguish on the dead man's

iron-plated face. The horror that must be the life of the witch's boy is nearly enough to make me feel sorry for Morgan.

But not for long. She casts her arm toward Merlin as he unsheathes the sword at his waist. The magic strikes ferociously, sending him to the ground and his blade lost amongst the trees.

"You'll never find Avalon, nor the Grail, and you won't have Camelot," he breathes. "It was built for justice and peace. It will never be yours."

"If you had asked me twenty years ago, I might have agreed," Morgan says, her voice shaking. "But now, I'm stronger than you ever were. All I need is the girl's mind and Mordred will have a fighting chance."

What does she mean? My heart races.

Merlin rises, hanging at the waist as tremors run over his skin. "Your boy is a machine, not a man, and he cannot live without the mechanical arts you've darkened for your own evil purposes. His mother is a common witch and wasn't a very good healer before that. You'll destroy your soul, leaving him to suffer alone."

At once she's inches from him, and the sorcerer's neck is in her grasp. She lifts him high with one hand while the other stretches across his face. When her palm touches his forehead, Merlin shakes in agony. I cover my mouth, holding back any screams of terror.

Then there's a flash, and she drops him. Merlin lands again on the forest floor. Blood pours from his nose. He spits more onto the leaves.

Morgan searches with piercing eyes. "There's another

here. You've hidden someone from me, Merlin. It's not the girl, is it?"

My blood goes cold.

She steps away, carefully studying each tree as though sensing the veil. Marcus pulls me close until I'm hidden in the warmth of his skin and the roughness of his clothes.

"No..." he whispers, but the words carrying an unbearable weight aren't for me.

"There's no one else here," Merlin drawls in pain.

"You're lying." She steps toward us. "Two. I feel their presence. Young ones. Perhaps they helped you leave Camelot while my attention was elsewhere. Perhaps one is foolish enough to risk one life for the love of another."

Another footstep in our direction. Marcus and I dare not move in case she could hear the crunching of leaves under our feet. She leans close to examine a tree. Studies its fleshlike bark and hairy branches with indifference. Marcus holds me tightly. The witch is mere inches from my ear, close enough to hear me breathe if I were to. Merlin's eyes find mine despite the concealment spell.

Don't move or make a sound.

It's his voice uttering the familiar words in my mind. The witch moves on to the next tree.

Merlin, I think, hoping to mercy he'll hear me back. *You stole magic to shield us.*

A wave of light comes over Merlin's skin. His eyes roll in ecstasy. *There was no other way.* The stronger the whispered spell beckons my mind, the clearer his unspoken voice. His eyes are a horrifying mix of sadness, desperation, and thrill, holding contact until he can bear it no longer.

Morgan continues searching. "Where are they, Merlin?"

"There's no one here, bitch."

Morgan flicks her fingers. Merlin tenses, and the veil around Marcus and me rustles. "Desperate enough, yet? Only a few simple words."

His lips peel back over his teeth. "You will never beat me."

She smiles, one of triumphant insanity. "I feel I already have. Keep the twits hidden. You'll have to steal magic to free them!"

Merlin twitches. He tears off his gloves. Invisible fingers seek his snuff box. Morgan watches, amused. And now the spell is more frantic. Panicked to stay inside my head.

I'm sorry. God forgive me I am, he whispers between the honey-tasting words I can't understand.

Merlin, please. I hold Marcus tighter.

Stay out of Camelot until nightfall. Only return under cover of darkness. Let no one see you. For God's sake, as soon as you're freed from this wretched place, make for Camelot's land, where I'll ensure Morgan is blind to your presence and the squire's. Trust the boy: have him bring you back to the castle! Don't be caught by the witch—she mustn't use magic on you!

Merlin's head rolls as though his neck has snapped clean in half. Marcus clutches me tighter. We watch Merlin pry open his snuff box, toss the lid aside, breathe in as much as he can, shaking his head like a wet dog of the blood pouring from his nose.

"Oh God, yes!"

Morgan casts her hand toward him. Skin peels back from muscle. Jagged shards of bone pierce flesh where shins and forearms should be. His body struggles to exist.

I can't bear it any longer. He must put an end to this. I know he can. "Merlin!"

Morgan's head snaps up in my direction. Marcus clutches me with a death grip, curse word after curse word streaming from his lips.

But as she storms forward, Merlin reaches us first, his hand seizing mine.

"Taharouverechkoh nobiserahmah!"

Merlin breaks through the veil, and we scream as the sorcerer's theft of magic churns a tumultuous wind and turns everything black.

TWENTY-THREE

Marcus clutches me tighter and tighter as the wind torpedoes around us until I feel as though we'll be torn from the earth and launched into the sky—

Then it stops.

My cheek against his pounding chest, I open my eyes and look around. We're in a wet green field with no sign of the woods breaking through such a ruthless gray fog. I gasp for air, forcing myself to take in as much as possible, but I'm trembling like mad, and Marcus is no better off.

"What the hell?" he manages with wild eyes.

White knuckles clutching my fusionah, I pull away, searching for any sign of Morgan, but she's not here. I pace the raw land as though it could somehow reveal Merlin instead.

"Merlin," I breathe in a wavering voice, wishing I had all but forced him to bring me here. "I'm so sorry..."

Marcus reaches for my arm. "He isn't here."

"Where did he go?" I scream, too hysterical to care

about Merlin's last words: run from the sorceress who knows my face. Return to Camelot's land before she finds us. "He can't still be in there with that—that *witch!*"

"You didn't hear him, did you?" Marcus shouts loudly enough that my attention is all his. He grabs my shoulders and brushes the tangled hair from my cheeks. "In your head—the wizard's voice? He said he'd return to the clock tower."

It stills me just the slightest, our proximity only helping. "The clock tower?" I whisper. Merlin used *Sensu Ahchla* on Marcus, too.

Marcus nods. "He spoke to me like I'm speaking to you now. Said to return you to the castle after nightfall because you don't know the path, and Camelot depends on your safe arrival." He blinks. "A strange thing to say about a lady-in-waiting."

Merlin never told him what we needed the steel for.

I look to the horizon, ignoring Marcus's words. My eyes search for markers that could direct us back to Camelot.

But the land is strange. The ground was just rained upon. A hopeful sign, meaning these parts were struck by the same storm as the woods. But I can't see Merlin's tower in any direction. "Where are we?"

Marcus shields his eyes from the ugly white sky and looks across the terrain as the fog lifts. "Beyond the farmlands. I don't know these parts."

I've never seen a sky so cold.

"Merlin told me she wouldn't be able to find us once we reached Camelot's land. It must have been too much to steal to get us—" I bite my lip at the thought. "He wanted to protect me. When I return, I must meet him..."

I've said a lot. Marcus takes my hand. He squeezes once and nods, and my eyes lock on the serene, sleepy color of his. Now he must know there's more to me than my duty as the queen's handmaid.

But he doesn't press further. "All right." He gauges the sky and drops my hand, pointing across the land. "There. That forest's formation I recognize. Three hours away, at most."

I look for the marker he's identified, but everything looks the same. And with such loud gallops—

I freeze. Hold my breath. Face the horizon behind us. Through the fog, I make out trees too far off to reach by foot. Galloping from them is a white horse. Riding it, a woman with frightfully long, white hair. A black cloak follows her like a flock of ravens flapping their wings. I feel the blood drain from my face.

"She's—" I cannot breathe.

Marcus whips around. "Go! Now!" His hand yanks me after him.

Morgan's screams blend into the wind. *"Wretched, ungrateful boy! Your betrayal will cost your mother her life!"*

We race through the wet field, able to hide from Morgan as we run under a shield of willow branches. Fusionah tight in hand, I twist to shoot at Morgan. I only have one shot. There'll be no time to reload. The barrel explodes with enough force to rattle my skeleton. I miss.

A bolt of lightning strikes my hand. I scream. My skin

singes, and the weapon boils from inside out into a puddle of liquid metal. Marcus shakes me free of it.

"Drop it!"

It falls from my hand, and now we're running unarmed. The witch's cries surround us with no source of their deafening tone. Light infects each tree's trunk, each branch, each falling teardrop of green foliage. Fire blasts them alive like the woods we escaped.

"Enough of this," Marcus grunts. His free hand finds a miniature fusionah in a hidden leather holster under his jacket. My eyes widen.

He fires once, twice, a third time, a fourth. All deflect off Morgan's upraised palm. Out of ammunition, Marcus strikes the ground with the now-useless weapon.

"Futile attempt, thief! Your mother's life for the handmaid!"

Marcus and I sprint toward a blessed meadow. I pray it's one he recognizes.

"Not yet!" he screams, like he's heard my prayer. Refuge from Morgan is out of reach. But there's hope. Marcus juts his chin toward land shrouded by clouds as black as charcoal. Rain devastates the grass. "There!"

The land is still far off, but I want to cry with happiness all the same. There's no air to breathe, and my lungs feel like they might collapse upon themselves. Slices of light singe the ground. I hazard a look back, but there's no sight of Morgan. I look forward: she's right there.

We come to a stop in the thick mud. My eyes go wide. My heart leaps with fear.

Marcus darts left. "This way!" We weave through trees surrounding the meadow.

I look back at the laughing face of the witch. She vanishes, but lightning slams into the ground. *Oh God, oh God, oh God.*

"Keep down!" Marcus shouts. We run and run and run, breathless now, headed for a cornfield. Marcus tenses with worry, but his voice lies well. "We're going to make it." And because Merlin trusts him, so must I.

My boots dig into the wet grass. My lungs rasp for air. Marcus clings to my hand, and we make it to rows of corn as a burst of heat hits us.

"Get down!" Marcus shouts.

We drop to our knees, hidden by stalks quickly decapitated of their fruit by bolts of fire. Push through until we're hidden. My palms flatten against wet earth. Marcus reaches for my elbow, keeping me close. We still ourselves as clouds billow over us. Celestial or evil light searches the land.

"Oh God," I whisper, catching my breath. Marcus's grip on me loosens enough that he can run his thumb over my skin. *We'll be all right. We will.*

Light vanishes, and bursts of thunder go silent. The land eases into its natural form.

"How does she know you?" I demand in a shaking voice. "Is that why you left before the attack? You told Morgan the king left Camelot!"

"What? No! God, no!" His face twists at the very thought of it.

"Why did you have a firelance when you said they'd be

useless against her?" I hiss. "How would you even know that unless you're one of those black-armored bastards?"

He's shaking his head. "You have to trust me. I'll never betray Arthur or Camelot or you."

"How can I trust you?" I demand, pressing closer, my fingers tight around his wrist. She mentioned betrayal. She mentioned an informant.

"Please." Wind torpedoes around us, and he yanks his wrist free to grasp my cheek. "As you won't tell me your secrets, don't ask me for mine. Not now."

We stare at one another, waiting out the heavy silence. I must let it go. At least until we return to Camelot. I comfort myself knowing Merlin trusted Marcus. "Is she gone?" I ask, my voice too afraid to go above a whisper. "Can she see us?"

Marcus won't risk standing. He peeks through the stalks. "Don't know. But we're on the edge of the eastern farmlands. Merlin said we'd be safe once we reached them?"

I nod.

The shine of brass catches my eye. I glance at a chain-link fence on the outskirts of the field, no more than fifty feet away. Wooden beams separate the wild, wet land from cultivated earth. There's a harvester on the other side with a copper cylinder serving as a primitive exhaust pipe, terribly blackened from smoke. A small furnace filled with whitened charcoal sits beneath the padded seat where underneath I recognize the fuel reservoir this contraption requires. Birds nest on the overhead iron arm with a large scoop, able to yank weeds from the earth. Merlin would never let something so dangerous or poorly maintained anywhere near his clock tower.

Marcus settles beside me. "I can't tell where the borders are. We need to keep moving."

As he speaks, the sky darkens with the same charcoal clouds as before. I blink as drops of rain find my face.

"My lady, please," Marcus says with a gentle pull of my elbow. Our faces are so close as the rain drenches us. The harvester creaks from the gale's wind. The scent of fuel wafts over to me.

Then the sky lights up with a harsh, green light. In the east, strange lightning searches. For something. For someone. Blasts of thunder have the voice of a witch. She won't stop. She won't stop until all of this is hers.

"No," I whisper through gritted teeth. "I won't be afraid of her." I boldly reach into Marcus's right pocket—

"What the hell—"

—for his quicklight. With it, I stand tall enough to tear through cornstalks for the forgotten, rusted contraption.

"Wait!" Marcus reaches for my boot, but I've already pulled away. I've seen contraptions like this harvester before. I have to buy time to perfect Victor.

I have to try.

"My lady!" Marcus shuffles to his feet after me. "You don't know what she's capable of!"

Merlin's told me what traditionally happens when contraptions such as these are under intense pressure. He's shown me what kind of damage they can cause.

Twist the exhaust pipe. Start a fire.

Light blinds me. I feel my way through the barbed stalks until my outstretched hand finds a cold, rusty chain.

"What are you doing?" Marcus shouts, not far behind.

"Just a few seconds…" I whisper. For this to work, Morgan must be close.

I step over the chains. Glancing past the harvester, I see Morgan le Fay in the wet field. Her eyes find mine. Her steps toward me are determined.

I wind up the crank on the machine. It spurts alive, but before it moves, I kick a rock under the wheel to keep it immobile. I hold my breath and step atop the seat. My hands find the copper exhaust pipe, and it's just as thin as I'd expected, especially with years of tarnish finding a home here, cool enough to soothe my reddening hand.

"My lady!" Marcus calls.

"On my word, run," I say, my terrified eyes locked on Morgan. There are blessed tools next to the farmer's seat, and below, an iron wrench with an adjustable gauge. Morgan is approaching fast, and her hand is cast forward. Her lips are moving. Every passing second feels like an eternity.

"What?" Marcus shouts, leaping over the fence like his legs were meant for it.

The wrench twists the pipe, sealing it off. I flick the quicklight against my boot. The flame keeps burning despite the downpour. She's close now. My eyes find Marcus's. He knows what I'm going to do. Seconds until her hands will find my neck.

I drop the fire into the fuel reservoir and shut the gate. *"Run!"*

TWENTY-FOUR

Marcus yanks me down from the harvester and over the fence. We sweep our arms across the stalks, clearing a path as branches scratch our cheeks.

Morgan screams magic behind us.

But then there's a blast.

We run faster and faster as the fire follows us into the eastern farmlands. Heat penetrates the air.

"Damn it all," Marcus whispers. His hand grips mine. "There!"

Ahead, where the forest disappears into burnt remains stands a lone, weather-beaten barn on Camelot's land, two stories tall with a creaky door slamming from the wind.

We reach it. Marcus yanks the door open and then slams it closed behind us. Our backs push flat against wood. The cries of the witch die as Merlin's thievery of magic hides us. The battering rain is silenced. Our breaths are in sync. Fast-paced, terrified.

"I owe you a quicklight," I whisper.

Marcus smiles. "My birthday's in December," he says through jagged breaths.

I glance at our fingers, still interwoven. He inhales sharply as though he's noticed just as I have. With hesitation, he unravels his hand from mine, running his fingers through the back of his hair and returning them to his pockets.

My hand is cold.

I take a long breath. I knew the explosion wouldn't be enough to kill Morgan, but I might have bought much-needed time.

I ignore the heavy thumping of our hearts and focus on the barn. The walls have been reinforced with iron beams to stand strong against farmland storms that would "drain the world in a blue mess, crack against the sky, and run across the fields, only to pick up speed as they went along," Marcus tells me.

"Whose place is this?" I ask.

He steps toward a narrow staircase. It leads to a loft hanging over some empty stables. "My parents and their neighbors sometimes keep mares in here."

We stand staring at each other, unspoken words fighting their own battle between us. He cocks his head to the side. "Spare blankets. Come on." I hesitate as tremors pulsate through my veins, but Marcus's smile is enough to calm me. "We'll wait out the storm. I'll ... tell you what I can." The stairs wind around a fireplace empty of ashes or any other signs of use. Marcus shrugs. "Need to keep the horses warm somehow. You've never seen farmland storms."

The landing brings us to a work station set up with tools and wrought-iron welded into decorative clocks and the like. Marcus ushers me toward a tall window where underneath there's a low bench. The sky flashes with strange lightning, but we're safe, and the awning at least keeps the space dry.

I sit, shivering and crossing my arms for warmth and modesty. My dress and cloak are soaked, and my skirt is horribly muddy. I open my palms to a thick layer of dried weeds and dirt and wipe them on the cold, wet fabric covering my thighs. Marcus shrugs off his blazer and sets it over my shoulders. He tears his eyes from the dress hanging off my skin to search inside a nearby trunk, pulling out a woolen blanket.

"Here." The blanket goes around me, and it's not terribly soft, but keeps out the chill. Marcus's hand lingers on mine as he closes the edges into my grasp. He pulls back the fingers of my right hand to check the red welt splayed across my palm.

"I'll live," I say.

He sits next to me, head against the window frame. One muddy boot rests on top of the other, and he crosses his arms.

We keep to our own thoughts. Lost in the idea of what could have happened.

I glance up. "You're not cold?"

He shrugs and then shakes his head. "I'm all right."

But I blew up a harvester as any amateur inventor would know how to do. Not a lady-in-waiting, certainly. Marcus must have questions about that, but as the quiet passes, it doesn't feel uncomfortable. His presence is calmer now that we're on Camelot's land, but still cautious, as though he might not trust Merlin's magic to do what was promised.

"The limes I stole all those years ago, the ones that could have put me in the stocks if Lancelot hadn't come to my defense ... they belonged to a healer," he says, fingers fidgeting in his lap. "Earlier this year, Lancelot and I passed through the same village, and there was the healer—Morgan le Fay, exiled, hiding from the rest of the world. She found me while Lancelot was off with some noblewomen and claimed she was owed for the opportunity to become a knight's squire. She promised me something if I could get her blueprints of Excalibur."

I'm quiet, my heart twitching from the treason Marcus is dangerously close to.

He looks at me. "I saw Excalibur after the wedding as the knights discussed what to do in case Arthur's sister returned. I was terrified that if she came back, it'd be to finish the job before I could do it myself. Too much time had passed, and Lancelot and I were late returning to Camelot. I thought she'd recant on our deal. I was desperate, but I couldn't search for blueprints with so many present."

I know this is because of his mother, even though he doesn't say what Morgan offered in return. I think of my own family, however insufferable sometimes, and I understand Marcus completely.

"I hated myself for this. And then you asked me to show you Excalibur, and it was reason enough to try again. But I saw her threaten your life. I saw the farmlands burn. I had to save my own mother from flames that reeked of the witch herself, and when I finally found Arthur's blueprints with you not three feet away, I couldn't do it. It's why I went to the farmlands this morning, to tell Morgan so, but now she'll ... "

He bites his lip. "You're sure those in the infirmary were not affected?"

"Promise." A silence passes before I find the courage to speak again. "My lord?"

He looks at me.

"We can't let Morgan claim Camelot," I whisper.

He doesn't answer. He stares past the awning at the black sky. "As soon as the rain lets up, we should run. The gales out here don't reach the castle."

I nod. "How much further?"

He looks at me in surprise. "Take your viewer and look."

I frown. My fingers find the inventor's tool in my pocket and aim it at the castle. I peer into the eyepiece and click down two extra lenses.

My lips part, but I can't find the words.

In front of me, through the rain, is a perfect view of Camelot untouched by storm and rebuilding itself stronger after Corbenic's attack. Clouds tumble across the sky, slow unfurling bodies of gray looking like they'll ambush the kingdom, but never do. From where I sit, I can see deep into the clock tower. And inside, curled by his window's ledge, Merlin sits holding a cup of tea. Exhausted, pale-faced, but alive.

Alive.

"He made it," Marcus says. "Miraculously in one piece. Told you."

I breathe, letting the weight of it drop from my shoulders. Merlin disappears behind the curtain unscathed.

Marcus takes a breath, too. "From here, you see a lot. You learn the faces of Camelot, their passions, their secrets. For example, how many blonde girls are up in the castle's tallest point, building gadgets with a wizard?"

I face him, my lips parting in surprise as I register his words.

He looks at his crossed boots. "I saw you for the first time months before I left to be Lancelot's page. I was only twelve. You might as well know you've fascinated me for that long." He confesses it in a low voice with no trace of lightheartedness.

But there's pride. He knew. When he saw me with Merlin, he wasn't nearly as surprised as he should have been, and this is why. Same goes for my crossbow or how I demanded to see Excalibur.

All I want now is to forget Avalon and Morgan and the dangers we faced today. I want to cast aside all responsibilities Camelot has given me and the charge of treason Marcus could face if someone were to know what he told me. I want to tell him everything about the clock tower, and even more of my willpower disappears as I realize how intensely he's looking at me and I feel myself looking back in the same way. His smile fades, and he glances at my lips.

Then, a crash of thunder. Marcus looks outside and then back at me. We read each other's minds, but he reacts faster. He grabs my hand.

"It's getting worse. We have to go."

My blanket falls, but I hold tightly to his blazer. I follow him down the stairs, out the door, and into the storm where, other than this barn, there's no shelter in sight. Instantly, he's in a sprint, and I need to keep up. Rain floods the land.

"This is absurd!" I shout as thunder overtakes the skies. I drop his hand, unable to imagine myself running in this impossible weather for a castle that's still too far off. My body turns to ice as the rain drenches us. "Let's wait in the barn."

Marcus looks about, ignoring the rain falling from each lock of hair in slow drips. His skin shines, and the linen of his tunic sticks to his chest. He rubs my shaking arms. "Could be hours. Morgan won't find you. I promise. The sorcerer trusted me to return you."

"You want to run in a storm such as this? It's much more sensible to wait—"

"No, it's not—"

"It's not even dark yet! Merlin said to wait until nightfall so no one would spot us."

He looks as though he'll give in, but when he catches sight of the barn something else keeps him strong.

I can't stop from shaking. "Please. I'm freezing."

His hands run over my arms again, his muscles pulsating for warmth. The linen he wears is now no more than a wet rag. When he gives me a small shake of the head, I know what he's afraid of.

"My lord—"

"I can't."

His fingers reach to touch my hair, but he has the good sense to stop himself. "I realized it when you set foot in there. When I finally met you, I didn't expect I'd…" He blinks wildly. "To be in there with you alone, for perhaps hours…"

I frown, cursing the temptation—the fire around us

I'm dying to embrace. Fire is a relentless villain. "Why did you tell me all this?" I demand.

He clenches his hands. "I don't know." He pulls away, the distance an eternity. "Because I had to know what it was like to be near you. Because I'd seen you so many times—"

"Why hold me behind a column on a balcony to… Why knighthood if…" I can't finish the thought, not when the reason is his mother. He doesn't answer, and I knew he wouldn't.

I feel like that moment after several drops of green fairy, right before you've had too much. You wonder what harm a little more could do, and when you have it, you realize it was for the worst the next day. But perhaps this could be the one—

His hand grabs mine and pulls me after him. He must be able to read my thoughts. "We need to return to Camelot."

I stand my ground. Owen's warning, and Merlin's, they scream in my ears. "We're already going to catch our death of cold—"

"Yes, we are. But there are many ways to make it worse. Please."

Owen was wrong. It wasn't a boyish fawning Marcus felt for me. I drop his hand. "More time to get warm. A fire to ward off the chill."

Marcus's muscles shake from the cold. The ever-present smile on his face has vanished. Now he stares at me with freezing red lips on a white face. "Do you know what might happen if I were to go back in there with you after what I told you? After what we just went through? Don't you realize I might fall further and then have to leave? Do you really trust us to be alone in there, and not forget the vow I will one day take? Do you trust yourself?"

To not lie would mean inevitable heartbreak; I don't know why I speak the truth. "No, I don't." My voice is barely a whisper. I drop my arms and give in to the sin in me that wants him more than heaven.

He moves toward me slowly but without pause. I hold my breath, unable to read his face especially with the rain.

"Hell," he breathes.

Then he's too close, and I won't move away—not when his hands clasp either side of my face and draw me flush against his body; not when he breathes against my cold mouth—whether it's out of hesitation or an attempt to savor all of this, I'm not sure.

He kisses me, fingers all at once in my wet hair, pressing against my back from under his jacket. The rain from his locks drips onto my lips, letting me taste parts of him I'd only breathed before. The back of his throat emits a moan traveling from his mouth to mine. Flashes of light pulsate in the sky, but we're hidden from Morgan, and nothing will find us tonight.

He lifts me, pulls away far enough to breathe against my lips. My eyes open. The violet slits of his eyes watch me with lust and disbelief. He carries me for the short strides to the barn, hastily forcing the door open. It shuts behind us, the refuge saving us from the ruthless, bewitching gale.

He sets me against the wall, his mouth lingering a hair's width from my own, palms on the wooden planks behind me. I dart my tongue across my bottom lip as my hands coil up in small fists against his chest.

His body leans into mine. We breathe in together as our kiss turns from desperate and sudden, to slow and full. His fingers trail down my arms to my waist. My balled fists stretch around to the back of his neck, under the hair dripping rain onto my fingers.

He takes my lip between his teeth and bites gently, breathing out as rationality takes him.

"I can't go any further. For your sake and mine."

I try to respond, but it's a whimper. His lips return to my lips, and my shoulders slump so his jacket and my cloak fall to the ground. His fingers clutch my waist and slide down the wet fabric to my hips as his discipline weakens. I feel the sides of my dress shift, the hem lifting as he rolls the pleats into his fists. My sensibility returns.

I still his hands. His mouth freezes against mine, but I'm the first to pull away, tasting my lips while he catches his breath. He squeezes my palms and then drops them, using the wall as leverage to push himself off. Our clothes are wet, and wrinkled lines decorate our bodies from pressing against each other. The linens are transparent. We each look away.

"We should have left for Camelot," I whisper. "I'm sorry."

He adjusts his tunic and trousers and flicks the rain from his hair. He runs his hands over his face, waking himself from a fog. When he turns back, his eyes undress me. When they see mine, they fall still. "Never imagined I'd hear an apology afterward," he whispers, a laugh escaping his lips.

I embrace him, resting my cheek against his rapid heart.

He exhales a pained sigh and sets his arms around my shoulders. "I've never done that before," he admits.

My lips find his neck, wanting nothing more than to press fully against his wet skin.

"Please don't." He lifts my chin. "Either that would be a terrible idea or a fantastic one." Another sad smile.

His eyes tell me of another world where things could have been different. Our skin could have dried from a fire he'd have built, and he could have finger-combed my hair as my back lay against his chest. We could have ignored the clock on the tower, the castle in the clouds. We could have escaped.

Escaped. Left Camelot. Run off somewhere, away from his duties and mine.

"Now what?" he whispers, breathing a smile to make light of everything. But the devastation in his voice doesn't fool me. Neither do his eyes.

He should know as I do. It has to end here, before it even begins.

But then he cups my face, and ending this is the last thing I want. "I've wanted to know you for so long," he says.

To be the reason he gives up on knighthood would be a devastating scandal. My reputation would be a harlot's, and he might be cast out of the kingdom as nothing more than a serf whose mother's life could be lost. This cannot happen, especially when the castle is destined to face another attack. Camelot would be left without a finished weapon to fight Morgan. Arthur's resources would be hers. The Grail would be hers.

"I don't…" Words fail me.

The vulnerability on his face is overwhelming. "I'm not an idiot. I know our time is limited, that your reputation's at stake, that after all of this, your father will want a respectable man for you. Not a serf. Owen's made that quite clear."

"That isn't it—"

"But that's part of it. I'm not trying to upset the social order in a castle I still have yet to understand. Honest." His eyes are far away. "But you don't know how happy you look when you're listening to ramblings about Mongolia and the Black Sea or when you're working in the clock tower. You don't know what that does to me."

I smile, running my fingers under my eyes to catch any traitorous tears of frustration or bliss. Duty is slowly surpassing happiness.

Marcus's face breaks. "Please, say something." He pushes the hair from my eyes.

There's only one thing I can say. "You're the only one who knows of the clock tower. Of the joy it brings me. And that's all right with you."

He smiles.

"But with your knighthood—"

"We'd have to say goodbye at some point anyway. Could be as simple as me walking out that door and into a ruthless storm. Or I could be slain by Morgan's legion, by the witch herself for siding against her."

"Don't," my voice rasps as I capture his face in my hands. I push away the image of his cold body on a battlefield of iron-jawed men, machines foggy with steam while he lies amongst them. "I can't bear it."

He tries to smile, but it's bittersweet. "What else?"

I'm not sure anything else I say would be logical or sound. For now, my heart is stronger than my head. I have to grab on to any hope I can. "There's nothing else."

His face inches closer to mine before he pulls away. Best not to tempt fate. He rests his lips against my forehead, setting a kiss there that's much too chaste. It's all we can ask for.

The rain shows no signs of letting up just yet, but still we're here, and we're alive.

"Come," he says, leading me toward a warmer spot. "I'll make you that fire."

TWENTY-FIVE

I'm walking down a sunlit corridor.

The light moves around me like a untrustworthy wind, ushering me closer to an altar, a dull chalice sitting atop. My hand reaches for it, but a voice tells me it's not mine to—

A door slams. My eyes snap open.

That golden world fades.

My fingers grip a gentleman's jacket and a blanket wrapped around me. I'm pressed against Marcus, my head in the crook of his shoulder, his arm across my waist. The fire has long since sputtered out. Wind rattles the barn's poorly made door. The storm has passed. Merlin's spell held; Morgan never found us. And now it's morning.

"Oh goodness!" I'm to my feet instantly, and the jacket and blanket fall. Marcus takes a few seconds to awaken. I leap from the bundles of hay for the door.

"Wait … hold on … " Marcus calls after me, sleep still woven in his voice.

There's a gentle hum of crickets as the sky turns from purple to blue, the sun threatening to appear at any second. My heart pounds, and my head is still between dream and wake, but it's enough for me to take in my surroundings and run for the castle. People might look for me once they realize I never returned. Guards will wander the streets, magnified goggle viewers and three-legged nightscopes atop the parapets in full force, with gas lanterns whose flames could stretch beyond five feet, only to find me in the arms of a future knight.

Damn it all!

I shake my head and mutter some of Marcus's favorite curse words. Then I realize the additional cost of being alone with him just once—I failed to meet Merlin in the clock tower. But blowing up the harvester might have slowed down Morgan, enough to forgive my failure.

"You keep running that way and you'll walk straight over the drawbridge!" Marcus calls, catching up. He laughs as I fold over, exhausted. "With a set of legs like that, you shouldn't have needed a horse yesterday!"

A lazy arm strikes out to hit him, but he moves to avoid it. "A lady of Camelot can do better than that, surely."

"It's not funny! There's probably a search going on right now!"

He crouches next to me, watching each pathetic gasp for air with shining eyes. "They're not looking for you." He helps me up, his arm around my waist. "Come along, you stubborn girl."

"You can't know that," I gasp. "My parents must be frantic."

"No one's noticed. I'm certain."

"How?" I grasp his free hand. Oh God, I love the roughness of his skin.

"Look," he says, pointing with the finger in my hand to the clock tower. "If they were searching for you, Merlin's falcon would be out, and the wizard would be scanning the entire kingdom with his telescope, but his curtain's drawn."

The curtain of Merlin's window is indeed drawn, although I'm not sure he'd need his telescope. But perhaps Marcus is right. Then I realize the subtle detail in what he said.

"Caldor." I thought the mechanical falcon was my secret alone.

His eyes are riveted with curiosity. "I've told you my travels. Tell me yours."

My smile numbs my cheeks as I start as far back as I can remember, grasping the memories in midair to show him, one by one. By the time we've reached the lake, we're clutching hands as I go on about the revelations in alchemy Merlin learned from Azur. The ulterior motive in seeing Excalibur, which Marcus had already guessed once he found Merlin and me in the cave. My crossbow side project. I mention vague details of Victor, and my heart screams at what I've decided to withhold for now. My recollections of heavy coughs and smoky air distract Marcus, but then I describe Caldor, and his fascination returns, at some points asking me to repeat what I've said as though the ideas are too much. I know the feeling.

I've never felt so freely happy before.

———

Guards patrol the wall closely, and a handful more smoke by the convenient birch. The gates have been resurrected overnight: the blacksmith must have worked nonstop to ensure our kingdom was strong again.

To avoid creating a scandal by risking the front gate, the only option for Marcus and me is to sneak in through a little known break on the other side of the gardens, where several blocks are loose. Squires go there to buy *shisha* from eastern peddlers, he tells me.

We disappear into some shrubbery, finding the break easily. No chaos has erupted inside Camelot. On the contrary, the gardens are mostly empty, save for older ladies encased by parasols watching their husbands play cricket. Tradition must be kept, even as the aura of fear still looms. Perhaps word never reached the subjects that men died yesterday, despite all somber evidence to the contrary. A few dandies refuse to bid the night farewell and take to morning strolls with maidens of the court, the bodices of their gowns low enough to be quite the distraction. The girls' eyes widen in awe at the dandies' exaggerated retellings of what happened.

"Oh God," Marcus says, his eyes falling upon the reconstructed gates. There's no sign of carnage, but blood has dried into a most unpleasant shade of brown on the northern wall. In the grassy courtyard, it nearly looks beautiful against the green. "What Lancelot must think of me," he adds. A long pause before he finds the will to ask. "Who was it that died?"

"I only know Sir Vincent was amongst them."

His eyes darken with regret and sadness. I step toward the

break, but Marcus's hand draws me back. "Wait," he whispers. "One more minute."

His hands settle on my back, locking me to him. My hands graze the collar of his tunic, and the pulse in my wrists leaps against my skin. He rests his forehead against mine. We close our eyes and just breathe, letting our hearts beat against the other's. His fingertips trace the outline of my face and brush back some of my loosened hair. "We're to be different people inside the castle, I suppose."

I nod.

"Then until we return to the farmlands." Marcus kisses my cheek, and this time, I don't pull away.

He slips past me into the gardens, walking backward for a second and managing a bittersweet smile before jogging for the knights' quarters to face Lancelot's wrath.

I gather myself, running a careful hand over my hair to make sure I don't look like the wildcat I feel I am after a night in the rain, sleeping in a bundle of hay with a squire.

A wilting peony greets me in the gardens, where there's more decay now than before. The bloom breaks and flutters to the ground. All around, more yellow and brown have sprung up. The gardens look closer to the wild farmlands than the fairy tales I always thought they resembled.

Merlin's incantation is waning fast.

———

My hand tugs on the ring of my bedroom door. I beg God to be spared of any creaking that might awaken my mother, who mistakenly believes my ritual of sleeping until late morning on Sundays has yet to be broken.

Inside, it's dark, and my bed lies empty, sheets untouched. But as soon as I take a step toward those soft blankets, the gas lantern in my room brightens. I squeeze my eyes shut with a wince. My mother's footsteps sound from the door, one light clack after another until I feel her presence in front of me. I listen to her long sigh.

"You were out all night only one day after there was an attack."

Blast. But her voice is calm. That's good. I open one eye in hopes it'd ease the trouble I'm in. "The queen was frantic after yesterday's events, and she asked—"

"Stop lying, Vivienne!" my mother shouts, eyes wide, cheeks flushed with fear. God help me if she found out where I actually was. I stare at our feet, mine covered in mud from the fields. Hers, properly polished and ready to appear at court. "Sir Lancelot and the queen were unavailable for most of the evening. I know you weren't with them. They requested no advisors, orderlies, or companions. I was terrified when I couldn't find you. I didn't know if you were hurt or—" She bites down on her words, her eyes filling with angry tears she's quick to overcome.

Guilt floods me for indulging in stolen moments with Marcus while the knights mourned their fallen brothers. "I wasn't hurt. I'm fine."

She nods once and then marches me to the dressing table, running a boar-bristle brush through my hair that still sports bits of sharp hay. "The council is due to meet in an hour. The queen will need you."

Over and over, she brushes my hair until it's smooth enough to fit into a bit of steel netting that yanks most awfully at my scalp.

"Has torture evolved to the state of fancy hair?" I whisper through the sharp pain.

"Your father wanted you to stay in your chambers when you weren't needed by Guinevere. The queen herself told you the same. Your disobedience might cost you a place in court, all for—" She yanks me around so we're facing each other, and I watch her thin lip try not to quiver. "You cannot think that your presence in Camelot goes unnoticed."

I frown. "What do you—"

But then a gasp escapes my lips, and when I realize what she said about Guinevere, a pang of worry strikes me. *No advisors, orderlies, or companions?*

In the woods, Morgan mentioned betrayal, and I was terrified she meant Marcus...

But the way Lancelot called Guinevere by name. The way their hands found each other. The way their eyes glinted white. How she sent for him to meet with the council, but they spoke alone at the Round Table first. How Lancelot's words seemed to indicate they'd known each other in Lyonesse, and quite possibly, he was the very person to save her from execution and charges of witchcraft. How the lace she cherished and then rejected was a token girls in Lyonesse usually received from their champions.

My mother studies my eyes. "Vivienne, what—"

"Open the gates!" guards bellow from the walls as heavy gallops lure our eyes out the window. The new ports churn open. "The king returns!"

Arthur.

I rush to the window. Hunched over his steed, Arthur's hair is a shocking white, his eyes frenzied with lines spidering outward. He disregards the unnaturally clean gates and any rubbish still present from yesterday's attack. His beard is gray, disheveled atop ruddy, sunburnt skin. He's an old man.

But strangely, he's managed to keep his clothes in immaculate condition, as though he fell to a level of hell where the body and mind were tortured while devils indulged in their appreciation for fine silk.

Galahad and more knights follow, not with the same physical affliction, but on the brink of slicing open the throat of the next man who confronts them.

My father runs to meet Arthur in the courtyard. Guards gape as their shaky king dismounts. Galahad and the other knights stay unmoving atop their horses. Several of them maddeningly declare they still walk in their foliaged, apple-tree visions, and we're all figments of terrifying nightmares.

"Your majesty!" my father bellows.

But as my father approaches, Arthur's blade threatens him, the hammer in his hilt clicking ready to fire.

"Arthur—"

My mother screams. I grip her arm. "Oh God." What sort of evil did Morgan put on him?

The king's head tilts unnaturally. "The witch told me what she did. In Lyonesse, and here. Where's Lancelot?

Where's the man I left in charge?" The line of Arthur's blade presses against my father's neck. His fingers are delicate at the hilt's trigger, drumming unpredictably. "Where's my wife?"

My father has no answer.

But I do.

I run to the basin and splash water on my face, and then change into a fresh gown of muted pink with a corset that's a mesh of silver, tossing aside the rained-on, slept-in garment from last night.

"Vivienne, stop!" my mother shouts. To disobey her now would be unforgivable. But I have no choice.

"I cannot stay here. I'm sorry." The stillness of Merlin's window weighs on me, but I need to find Guinevere. I need to know Morgan's talk of betrayal had nothing to do with her.

Without thinking it through any more than that, I run out the door.

———

I reach the queen's towers and burst through the group of guards at the foot of her steps, leaping up two at a time. When I reach the landing, I come to a halt.

She walks out of her bedroom wearing nothing but disheveled linens and bliss. White light segments her pupils, stretching toward gold irises that should be brown. Her hair is wild.

Lancelot walks out with her.

The knight—dark curls just as wild as hers and tunic open revealing a damp chest—takes the queen by the waist and turns her so her back is against stone. She touches his brow with tender fingers. He cups her face, and they breathe each other in with clashing lips.

"Oh God," I breathe.

It's loud enough for them to have heard me. Lancelot wrenches away from Guinevere. Their eyes flock to mine. The strange whiteness in their pupils disappears, and I see what must be the witch's curse with my own eyes.

Footsteps storm the stairwell. Arthur pushes me aside with such strength that I slam into the wall. Guinevere and Lancelot gape with horror at their king.

Morgan's promise of betrayal didn't concern an informant after all.

TWENTY-SIX

A sick chill blanches Guinevere's skin. Lancelot runs a hand over his face. And Arthur is calm. No man in his position should be this calm.

The queen presses her back against stone, and she shudders to the floor. Her lip quivers, and her eyes take her to a forgotten place, but even that is unable to quell her despair. "What have I done?" she whispers.

I thought I knew her. I thought she was madly in love with Arthur, and even though I'm certain this is Morgan's doing, part of me wonders if there wasn't any willingness on both their parts.

My father reaches us quickly, Guinevere's guards not far behind. Lord William's steps are unsure, his eyes ashamed by association. When he acknowledges me, I understand him immediately.

They might think of me as an accomplice. I could be in as much trouble as the queen.

"Get out of here!" he hisses. "Never come back to this place!"

My feet stumble over the first few steps, but I cannot leave Guinevere as she is.

"Lancelot?" Arthur asks, waiting for an explanation. Whatever Morgan taunted him with in the woods strikes against the incredulity in his eyes.

Lancelot's arms hang at his side in defeat, eyes cast downward, line of vision interrupted by the king's steady walk.

Arthur seizes Lancelot's vestments, slamming him into the parapet. Guinevere screams as the knight's back cracks against it. Lancelot winces. Arthur's eyes are solid white. He mutters incoherently under his breath.

My father rushes forward. "Arthur, there must be a trial!"

Arthur's teeth clench, inches from Lancelot's face. "Why bother? I failed as Camelot's king. An unfaithful wife, no legitimate heir! And now Morgan will claim what I couldn't find! Why deny me the chance to spill this bastard's blood?"

Arthur's fingers tighten around Lancelot's neck. The quickest flash of a smile pulls at the king's lips, and if I'm not mistaken, Lancelot sees it, too.

I step forward. I don't care what risk it is. "No, your majesty, you didn't see—" My father's fast arm holds me back.

Guinevere seizes her husband's hand. "Arthur! She's set madness upon Camelot! Don't you see it?"

The king throws her off. "That's what she told me you'd say!"

Then, reason falls upon him. He releases his hold on Lancelot, and the knight folds over, gasping for full breaths.

"Arthur," Guinevere weeps.

It's not with madness that the king pulls his wife to her feet and into his arms. It's with love. He regards her disheveled hair, crooked dress. His imagination might be running away with the details of their embrace. But still he holds her. "Treason, Guinevere. Punishable by death."

I push past my father. "No, you cannot!"

Arthur barely looks at me. "Silence, or you'll be strung up by nightfall!" His face is red-hot with anger.

I step back, defeated. Every second of passing silence screams at me for obeying a mad king. *Traitor, traitor...*

Guinevere sets Arthur's hand upon her heart. "This has always been yours."

As though seized by compassion, he leans close. "I'm sorry," he whispers against her ear. Her eyes widen. "Send them away. Both of them. Now." Arthur looks at my father. "Camelot cannot hear of this." He points at me. "And not another word from you."

My father bows, humiliated by the reality of the king disciplining his daughter.

Lancelot doesn't struggle as guards affix brass cuffs to each wrist, drawing them behind his back. Guinevere grasps her husband's hand, seeking clemency, her body shaking with its film of nighttime sweat. She sobs, hair across her face drenched from tears. "Arthur, please..."

My father's eyes catch mine again. "Go!"

They arrest the queen and her husband's champion. They'll be banished. A scandal Camelot can never know about. And as I run from the queen's tower, the weight hits me of how dangerous this could be for Marcus and me, their squire and lady-in-waiting. They could set copper cords swinging on the gallows for our necks just as easily if Arthur changes his mind.

But I know that's not why my father told me to go.

He was kind enough to think of my reputation.

———

When you affix cogs and copper to build a mechanical bird, following the instructions properly and taking your time, the falcon will surely take flight.

I repeat this mantra to myself over and over and tear free the constricting steel netting from my hair. The rules of the mechanical arts can be startlingly simple. I cannot think about torrid affairs, copper nooses, Morgan's curse, the attack on Camelot, or Avalon's location and how I'm tied to it. I cannot return to Guinevere's quarters. I might never see her again. Camelot is shutting me in. The faster I run, the more I hate the bindings of reputation that kept me from defending her. The only place I can go is Merlin's tower, serendipitous as it'll be the last place people will think to look for me.

I bolt through the gardens, my thoughts all twisted up.

Then I slam into a hard body.

Marcus.

"Lancelot's nowhere to be found," he says, lips cocked to the side. "Ector thought I was working in the infirmary. I guess someone told them—" His smile disappears once the anguish on my face breaks through my tousled hair. "My

God, what's wrong?" He takes my face in his hands. I cannot tell him of his knight's affair. To even speak of it when Camelot might be listening...

I grip his fingers, closing my eyes and breathing in his fresh clothes. "Everything." I lean into him. "Everything is wrong. I have to escape."

The clock on Merlin's tower chimes the hour. The sky catches the clouds, sending them flying across its canvas as falcons braid through. The gardens are still lush with life, but death is to come. Arthur knows, just as I know, what Morgan's capable of.

What would Camelot look like, trampled by demonic horses, splattered with even more blood?

And how different would everything be if the Grail were ours?

I imagine the kingdom coming together for Camelot's glory, but it's impossible to picture without Sir Marcus of the Round Table being praised as a victor of the holy task.

"Where should we escape to?" Marcus whispers, pushing my tangled hair behind an ear. "Let me take you there."

He sets his forehead against mine. I close my eyes. It would be so easy to cast away these cares. "No, I need to go to Merlin's tower."

"For what?"

My lip quivers as I consider my words. "Merlin has Arthur's steel. If I managed to slow Morgan in the farmlands, I can fix the sorcerer's weapon now. So much depends on whether..." Whether I could save myself from asking the unthinkable of Marcus.

His lips drift over to my temple. "Must you leave now?"

I'm quiet so I can enjoy the sensation of his mouth on my skin. But there are more important things at stake than a secret romance.

He pulls back to look at me better, and it lets me memorize him. Hair, clean but in long, messy strands across his brow. A white linen shirt with leather ties. The moment behind the Athenian column comes to mind, and I remember my hand atop his chest, the steady rhythm of his heart. I think of his rain-soaked body. His rough mouth clashing with mine.

"The Grail," I whisper. So important to Camelot. So important to Morgan, too.

Marcus's eyebrows rise. "What of it?"

"It was Arthur's intention. Before Morgan attacked the farmlands. To have the knights find it."

He frowns. "Yes…"

Our time might be up sooner than I wanted to believe. How stupid was I to think anything could come from this?

He forces a smile as though it would dismiss any somber thoughts. "But that might not be for ages. Is my lady tormented at the thought of sending her squire racing against Spanish rogues?"

In front of me, Marcus stands perhaps days away from making a vow so honorable, it's practically a straight path to heaven. And I'm the vice that could lure him down. "You aren't mine to keep."

He nods. His feet shift in place.

With a loud caw, Caldor dives over us, copper wings nearly catching my hair. Like the sorcerer exchanged his eyes for the falcon's, the bird watches me with suspicion. It returns to the clock tower.

I'm being beckoned. "Merlin calls." And I need to stay out of sight. I start again on my path but Marcus grabs my hand.

"Wait. What is this about? Why questions about the Grail?"

I'm terrified to know the truth. He embraces me again to suppress the worry flitting about in his sleepy eyes. My hands play with the leather ties of his tunic.

"If we were victorious against Morgan and you were knighted, would you be sent after the Grail, or stationed here?"

"I've been on the quest before. There'd be no reason to keep me in Camelot. Even if I stay a squire, I'd go with Lancelot. But it won't be until—"

"My lord?"

He hesitates. "Yes?"

"How long?" I ready myself for the answer. "How long would you be gone for?"

He clutches my cheeks. Hope disappears from his face, leaving behind responsibility. "Could be years."

I feel my eyes well up, but smile to hide it. The smoky, leathery aroma of him is so strong, and I want to breathe it in forever. But with each breath, Merlin's clock ticks louder. I weigh my options of losing Marcus to a vow of celibacy, to a marriage not of my own choosing, to war with Morgan, to the Grail. To never seeing him again. Or we could do as Marcus playfully suggested under a sky of bursting lights—

run off, leaving Camelot to face Morgan without Victor, the greatest weapon Merlin could ever build. We could let a witch claim the Grail.

"Morgan knows you won't infiltrate the kingdom for her." My face is grave, my voice wobbling. "Your mother. Her life depends on your knighthood. Especially now. Is that right?"

His eyes narrow. "How did you know that?"

"Why didn't you tell me yourself?"

Slowly, his hands release my face. "The wizard's reckless inventions weaken her lungs, which only worsened when Morgan burned the farmlands. My mother is in the castle's infirmary, but she cannot stay much longer as there's no room for someone who wasn't burned by Morgan, especially after yesterday's attack. If I joined the Round Table, it'd be the only way she could find permanent rest here, through strings only a knight could pull." He emits an ironic laugh. "Since my mother won't be healed by Morgan now, living in this mechanical world you think is civilized is the only way to save her from its harms. My father and I both know this."

My heart breaks at the ignorant astonishment I'd felt when I first saw Merlin's inventions. This is it. Enough never to see Marcus again. "Then why torment us both?"

He doesn't answer, or perhaps he doesn't know.

It's too much.

He must be able read my thoughts because he desperately grasps for my hands. "No, please—"

But I pull away, letting him see the tears in my eyes. I lift the hem of my dress and run for Merlin's tower, leaving Marcus in the gardens alone.

TWENTY-SEVEN

The last time I ran from Marcus, I witnessed a dangerous woman arrive. Those few moments changed everything in Camelot.

Now I rush through cobblestone streets away from our only chance of escaping that new Camelot, trusting it's the right thing, no matter how painful—oh God, how painful. The only way for Marcus to help his mother without committing himself to the Round Table is to escape Camelot altogether. But he'd need Morgan dead to keep his mother safe in the English countryside. Without Marcus activating Victor, there's no chance of defeating Morgan. She'd get the Grail.

I reach the blacksmith's workspace; the giant pounds away at red-hot steel. Upon closer look, I see the reddish shine of copper he's forging into twisted hooks just as intricate as Lancelot's sword. The blacksmith wipes his hands on his apron, and the gesture makes me stop. With the same height, it's easy to compare his gait to Marcus's. But I can't think about Marcus anymore.

I run past a familiar flying contraption standing behind the cellar door. Seeing an aerohawk would normally set me alight with excitement. But I have no will to fawn over creations such as these. I climb down into the cellar. My hands find the tilting door to the world below.

Below, where there will be logic. Where the world will be black and white. The sorcerer won't be there. No, not after what he did in the woods. Below, I can be alone to grieve, pull myself together before seeing Merlin. *No more than a few minutes, Vivienne.*

My fingers shake against the stony surface. I fall to the landing between cellar and stairs, a frivolous mess of a girl who can't face the world.

BOOM!

My cries go silent. It's the same thunderous shuddering of earth as when the cannons fired at Corbenic's men. The faded drawings on the ceiling flutter upon my sleeves. I glance down the stairs. Near the bottom there's a flicker of yellow light. It cannot be another attack—

BOOM!

Shaking me and the cellar walls. I hold my breath.

BOOM!

The thrust sends me over the first step. My fingernails dig into the stone crevices to keep from falling. It's not an attack. It's coming from the catacombs.

A rush of quiet goes about me. Merlin's omnipresent voice whispers, *"Downstairs."*

He can't possibly be down there.

Light dances below. Maybe Merlin was able to save himself from the magic he tasted. Maybe he's realized how much stronger he is. The burning pyre screams with each step. I search the catacombs' entrance through flames nearly twenty feet tall.

"Merlin!" I yell. "Merlin, I'm here!"

The flames scream back. Hot fingers stretch for me, barely missing.

"Ahzikabah," Merlin's voice breathes.

The fire goes silent. I wait, catching my breath. The flames disappear, the pyre once again a dark circle, whispers of smoke snaking upward.

"Merlin?" I whisper.

"Inside!" his voice booms.

The catacombs are red-hot. Merlin's rusty, intricate assembly lines churn iron into arrows and bearings. Barreled fire powder from the farmlands sits in the corner. Iron talons, perfectly formed against the skeleton, rest upon the floor's gemstones. Metal smoothed onto Victor's bones absorbs the light—Arthur's Norwegian steel, now shining skin.

My fingers reach for a smeared handprint on the weapon's belly, but before they touch, a gentle hum of heat and song warns me to pull away.

"Merlin, what have you done?" I whisper. Then, footsteps.

The furnace's fire casts a familiar shadow on the wall. Tall and thin and wearing a silk turban. I know there's a bronze clasp in the middle and elegantly styled goggles atop. Certainly, I should have realized it was his aerohawk by the cellar door.

Finally.

I breathe a grateful smile. Azur Barad stands there in a dark linen suit with a long saber at his side. A belt of hammered silver plates crosses his chest, a symbol of high status in Jerusalem. The wrinkles around his eyes have deepened. His beard has turned white since I last saw him two months past when he provided me with glass lenses for my birthday that Merlin used to forge my viewer.

Azur inclines his head. "Salom, Vivienne."

"Salom, Azur."

Then he sees my tearstained cheeks. "You have been crying." Azur sets a gentle hand on my shoulder.

I glance up at his poignant eyes. Only months ago, I begged to go with him back to Jerusalem to escape life here and the future that would not be of my own choosing. But now? How could I possibly leave Camelot?

"So much emotion," he says. "You are a different girl. You finally broke free of Camelot's mechanical world with the intention of escaping, but can no longer do so, can you?"

Tears overcome my vision, blurring the world and washing my cheeks. I've certainly seen what lies past the simplicity of the mechanical arts, and how painful it is. Beyond that, the truth is I'm not sure if I'm grateful or devastated to have met Marcus. Or to know Morgan's evil was born out of love for her son—how can I hate a woman who fights for that?

All of this has completely shattered my ability to think a rational thought.

Azur opens his arms to embrace me, and I catch my breath. "You made it." Now there's truly hope.

He smells like spices and tea, and his eyes carry the light of the sunrise that followed him here. "Merlin worried when you did not return last night."

I pull away, the back of my hand running across my eyes. "Merlin. Where is he?" And where did the loud booms come from? There are no cannons down here.

"He is in the clock tower, where he told you he would be." Azur approaches Victor, more dragonlike now than ever. He removes from his pocket a pair of gold-rimmed spectacles he sets atop a hooked nose. "Like a lunatic he worked, assembling this steel in one night's time despite being in dangerous shape. He should rest alone now. We must complete his weapon."

Merlin, in dangerous shape. A thief of magic once again. Unable to be in the catacombs because of the steel with magical properties. Fading into oblivion, and who knows when? Camelot is in no less turmoil: Guinevere's affair will cast her from the kingdom before I can say goodbye. And someone I care for will have to risk his life because of a flaw I can't fix.

"It's impossible, Azur." My hand covers my mouth. "I can't build something that might kill—" I bite my lip.

Azur watches me from his periphery. "Marcus? The champion's squire? Merlin told me of your fondness for the boy who came to Camelot carrying Atlas's burden." He steps away from Victor, and his soft, old hands reach for my arm. "Merlin also told me you were the one to trust. You are important to the future of Camelot, Vivienne. What you are capable of could save lives one day."

I breathe out. *One day,* since an evacuation is likely in order now, leaving behind an empty castle. There's only one reason to finish Merlin's weapon. "If I fail, we'll live in a world where Morgan finds the Grail."

"But if you complete Merlin's task, Camelot might claim it instead."

I think of my parents. Of Owen. Of Marcus. Of his mother.

"Now," he says. "Have you the strength to continue with all this?"

Numbly, I nod.

Azur gives me a moment and then regards my dress. "Your clothes, child, are not suitable." He gestures to the work table covered in torn journals, shards of steel. A folded black garment lies there. "A gift. Not from me or Merlin. Someone else knows of your work and thought it best to keep your court clothes in good condition."

I pick up a corseted dress similar to the style I'm wearing, lined with tough leather to withstand heat and an apron complete with pockets. A pair of new goggles with cogs that fold over the lenses are much smaller than Merlin's foggy pair. "Who are these from?"

"An anonymous benefactor."

Likely a wealthy friend of Azur's. I clutch the garments to my chest, lift my chin. No time now for tears. Azur straightens at my returned composure and turns to the blueprints on the table. "Take a look. Merlin made some adjustments. Make sure you understand what to tell the squire."

My fingers smooth out the edges of the blueprints. Right away I see the change Merlin made, and my mind calculates how long it would take to construct. The lever is not a challenging appendage to build and would solder easily to spine. The logic I developed over the years returns to separate my worlds of Camelot and clock tower.

But only yesterday, Marcus destroyed that separation and sought the real me instead of the Camelot version. I've never felt that sort of happiness before, even if it came out of secrets and eventual confessions, out of an unpredictable gray way of living rather than the simplicity of black and white.

How could something so illogical feel so right?

―――――

Smoke and oil stain my skin.

My new uniform has already frayed. It fits well, but Azur's friend didn't consider how impractical long sleeves would be when working next to a furnace. After an hour of fighting the blasted things, I took a pair of shears and cut them off, finding myself with spare rags I could use to mop my face of the constant sweat.

I withdraw prongs from the furnace and set down hot bolts to cool. In the meantime, I hammer out a thicker sheet of Norwegian steel. The assembly line will mold it into alternating barrels for the shoulder firelances, and Azur's *jaseemat* will flow through the copper veins, crawling toward six barrels per shoulder. The center shaft spins on a metal cog, connected to a leather belt of ammunition, and I have to smile.

Azur glances at a golden timepiece. Next to him are buckets of arrowheads, ready for the blacksmith to reinforce. "Vivienne, it grows late. Your day tomorrow will be long."

I lift my welding mask and wipe my hand across my eyes to collect the dust. Azur's words signal the day's end. Not long ago, I'd ask seven words each night to someone whose answer tonight would be significantly different. *Was today a good day, my lady?*

An edge of fear slices at me. "Camelot knows of the affair, don't they, Azur?"

Azur frowns. "A whisper passes through the castle, yes."

My fingers find a stray arrowhead, its edge already lined with copper. The small object looks like nothing more than a decorated triangle of iron, but my viewer's lens would show an intricate row of unsuspecting hooks. It pricks at my thumb. A drop of blood bursts free.

"Days of peace are few before it will all come to pass." Azur studies the weapon as though the task has grown more monumental. "Camelot might need more help than this."

And what if he's right in those few innocent words?

I regard Victor's humming steel, where the lungs and now-ticking heart lie obstructed from view. This weapon is a world of difference compared to Terra. It's incredible. Incredible, but likely to kill Marcus if he isn't quick enough. The fire next to me is a relentless villain, but love is a fine motivator. And work, a suitable distraction from tears.

I imagine Marcus outside waiting for me, and my heart hammers against my ribs. "I could work—"

"No, child. You are of no use to Merlin exhausted." Azur shuts down the furnace.

Though Merlin said he'd keep secrets from me, I must ask Azur. "Can you stop Merlin's curse? Please, be honest."

He pauses. "There are ways to stop it, yes, but Merlin wants a cure. For later."

"Why wouldn't he want something to stop it now? We need Merlin!"

"For some, power is obtainable only when humanity is no longer a limitation." His words are wrong, but Azur searches for compassion. "I will cure him afterward. I will exhaust all resources, I swear."

My fingers grip my apron. "What if you can't?"

Azur sighs in a way that strives for patience. After a minute to think, he leads me to the door. I cannot read the expression on his face, but the longer I look at him, the deeper doubt crawls into me, and the easier it seems to give up and abandon the castle instead for a life in Jerusalem.

"Let us not worry, Vivienne. Merlin knows what he is doing."

TWENTY-EIGHT

No one waits for me outside.

In my family's quarters, I peek inside my parents' bed-chambers at my mother wrapped up in her sheets. She might have given up on me now, and my heart breaks at that possible truth.

I hate the very idea of drawing Marcus away from his duty in Camelot. Any connection of him to Morgan might result in his mother's expulsion and his treason. I hate to think how badly I want to relinquish my own duty, even if aeroships would be sent for so Camelot's subjects can escape. If Morgan tries to claim Camelot, it'll be for an empty castle.

But we must defend that empty castle in the hope the Grail is real. Or else face a world where a witch could drink from the chalice to gain immortality and provide the same to her son.

I look to the knights' quarters in case their lanterns would still be lit. But the rest of the kingdom has fallen asleep, unaware that the billowing clouds resting above Camelot are there for good.

———

I hide my catacombs uniform in the folds of my ocean-blue gown and scrawl a note to my mother promising to explain everything later. At dawn I sneak through the castle. Everyone I pass buzzes about the scandal.

"Was it really the king's champion and the queen caught in a compromised position?"

"Are you sure you heard it right?"

"What will Arthur do?"

When I reach the gardens' edge, I stop. Coming out of the blacksmith's shop is Marcus, eyes dark like he never slept. His clothes are wrinkled, the same ones as yesterday. He runs a tired hand over his face.

The blacksmith follows, iron mask drawn as he and Marcus have a few words. A serf's horse trots for them pulling a cart with the dark-haired woman sitting in it. I duck behind the tree, watching as she waves Marcus over. He lifts her weak body and holds her close. The woman clutches the squire's face, speaking as her boy nods in response. He helps her back into the cart and hands the serf towing it a leather pouch I know carries payment.

Marcus watches the horse and cart trail past the gardens. The blacksmith returns to his shop, and Marcus heads down the street, hands shoved in his pockets, shoulders slouched.

People pass me. No guards who might arrest me for being

the queen's accomplice, but nobility who lift their tall hats to greet me. Ladies who curtsy with soft hands to their bosoms. Yet eyes surround me, watch me. Mouths cup neighboring ears, whispering, and fingers point as I storm through the gardens. Once I hid in this very elm as a girl, but now, I can hide nowhere.

Especially as the cart passes and the woman's face turns toward me, sharp blue eyes like the sky piercing mine. With no reason to recognize me, she looks away, drawing the weave of her heavy shawl tighter around her frail body.

The gossip grows louder, finally bringing me to my breaking point. When the wagon disappears over the drawbridge and into the farmlands, I run for the blacksmith's shop, away from the world of scandal.

I rush for the cellar door and climb down.

"To the tower."

Merlin's door is already ajar, the red surface mocking me. Not just the color of Camelot, it rings of the bloodshed we'll face.

I open it to a disaster. Broken inventions, tools strewn about, and shredded paper everywhere, as though a hurricane passed through. Now not even a bit of wind to move the curtain about. A shadowy figure wrapped in a scarlet robe hunches over in the sorcerer's armchair.

"Merlin?"

His splintered cane pulls the drapery across the bedpost, hiding torn sheets and feathered pillows. "Caldor's flight is much more fluid now, Vivienne. It's like he's an actual falcon."

Outside, the falcon indeed soars like it's made of feathers

and bones. Spiraling through a flock of doves above the trees, it's hard to tell Caldor apart from the rest.

"I'd give anything to know how it feels to fly," Merlin croaks.

"You tested Azur's aerohawk."

His shoulders fall at my words. "That isn't what I meant." But he doesn't elaborate. "Two nights ago, you didn't return as I instructed."

I swallow. "I'm sorry. But you wanted me to keep to my duties. Guinevere—"

"Guinevere was not the one you spent the night in an old barn with, my dear. Remember whom you're talking to." His voice has changed. Slower, raspier. "Though, by my calculations, recklessly blowing up that harvester denied Morgan the immediate attack she so wanted."

The bones of his fingertips drum against his emerald stone cane. I step away from the shadows and listen to the old Celtic ballad he hums, one he'd sing at banquets from the bottom of his stomach and at the top of his lungs, if he'd had enough ale.

He flinches in pain. The song dies, and he tears his eyes from the copper falcon to his hands. "Oh, the beautiful steel that's like a siren's touch!" He inhales sharply. "Destroying me, and waiting for me to return!" Shaken, he climbs onto his chair, escaping the invisible threats of the floor.

The door opens, and Azur rushes in.

I seize Merlin's skeletal shoulders in the shadows, helping him into his chair. "His satchel, Azur," I hear myself say.

Atop Merlin's table lies the familiar purse of opium.

Azur spots it and cranks a handle for the pulley system over the hearth. The kettle clicks over, and Azur pours in water.

I'm terrified of Merlin's violent spasms, dangerous twitches, the invisible points of fingers tearing at the chair's upholstery. I'm even more afraid he'll disappear all too soon. "Merlin!"

He's shrouded in shadows and won't let me look at him. His breathing finally steadies, and his hand casts me away. "Give me space."

I step back as Azur drops several helpings of sticky amber pieces into the teapot. He whispers under his breath while fixing Merlin's tea, prayers or alchemical instruction to ease the pain. I stand by the window, looking down upon Azur's aerohawk and its wings of fine silk. Arabic detailing on the wheel has been dusted with decorative gold.

The kettle sings. Steam clouds our vision as Azur pours hot water into the teapot by Merlin's waiting cup.

"I'm glad you're all right, my dear. Truthfully." Merlin takes a sip and promptly spits it out. "Damn it all, Azur, opium has done *nothing* for my craving!" He sets the cup and saucer on the table and sits low in his chair until his robe has curled up under his ears. Shadows crawl over his face. I still can't see him clearly.

"What happened, Merlin?" I whisper. He knows I mean the woods and glances sideways at me.

After an eternity, he speaks. "I've cancelled out any attempt Morgan could make to cast *Telum Paret*. Now she'll have to fight as we will. Struck twice when she expected otherwise. Well done, Vivienne."

He's stolen more magic—so that we cannot be turned into Morgan's drones.

The scent of his tea, herbal and floral, wafts over to me. I breathe it in as though it could settle my own nerves as well.

In the gaze that flickers to me, I see the shining eyes of a blind man. "Still, she draws near. But not as swiftly. We both know your lover must be the one to activate Victor. His speed and agility are like no other's. But first, Camelot will call for a public trial of Lancelot and Guinevere."

I run my soiled nails across my leather garments, distracting myself from the waves of anxiety ambushing me. Waves I felt the day I met Guinevere when she chose me for her lady-in-waiting. I'd prayed she'd find a kindred soul in another girl, but her brown eyes blinked in my favor because I didn't care how poorly I could sew or write letters. I, too, felt like I didn't belong here. To keep from losing a friend like that, I'll forever be glad to be against the world.

My whispered words are cold on my lips. "They'll execute them." Exile wouldn't be enough for Camelot. Not when anyone else would face the gallows for the same crime.

Merlin doesn't speak for too long. "It's a shame, Vivienne. It really is."

There were moments when I just knew, but to say something might have given away my secret in Camelot or risked Marcus's sheer existence here, especially considering what Morgan held over his head. All the times Guinevere spent complaining about Lancelot while I dreamt of escaping to the catacombs…

This could have been stopped—I could have prevented

it. And now her life will pay. Now, more guilt weighs me down, and the only way to lighten this burden is to risk my place in Camelot. There's no way Arthur would listen to me. Not again. Not this time. Still, I back away for the door.

Merlin's sharp eyes find me. "Where are you going?"

Azur reaches for my arm. "Vivienne..."

I pull away. "The witch said there was betrayal waiting in Camelot. Lancelot and Guinevere, they'd been acting strangely ever since Morgan fled the castle. She's responsible, Merlin!"

Merlin cocks his head. "I know. And I should have done something as soon as it dawned on me, but it wasn't for certain until I heard Lancelot's name spoken in Morgan's mind."

"I must tell Arthur what Morgan said in the woods." I ignore the dangerous question I'll face: *What brought you outside to begin with?* and imagine my father's confusion, my mother's disappointed eyes, and Arthur's fury when he discovers the sorcerer took his steel.

Azur's mouth drops open. "For you to do so..."

To tell the court of my secret apprenticeship with a former addict of magic, I'd lose my freedom in Camelot. "What could happen to Guinevere and Lancelot is worse."

Merlin's clawed hand squeezes his temples. "Vivienne, I've spent the past two days fighting my desire to tear this shroud from my body and pore over my tattooed magic like it's water and I'm dying of thirst." Translucent fingers clench his temples. "We're already facing an impossible battle."

"That's precisely why we need Lancelot!"

"They made their choice, Vivienne."

I firm my jaw. "It wasn't theirs." Though it might be completely true that their feelings were real, I know Guinevere, and even if Lancelot is an appalling scoundrel, neither would betray Arthur. "If I can tell Arthur how far Morgan's curse goes, they wouldn't have to die!"

Merlin leans away from the shadows. Finally, I see what Morgan's magic has made of him. Cloudy eyes pierce mine, but that's not what causes the blood to drain from my face. The skin on his neck has disappeared for muscle that fades as he moves in and out of the light. The edge of his jawbone protrudes, the same bone-white as his ghostlike eyes. A copper mask, hammered with rage onto his skeleton and caked in dried blood, hides his vanished features, warping his voice, and promising me years of nightmares that would combat those of Morgan.

"If you do this—" Merlin looks elsewhere, unable to finish the thought. I know he's wondering how Avalon must weave into everything.

"Your apprenticeship would be as good as over," Azur finishes.

Merlin scowls. "Perhaps it is anyway." Unsurprised by my astonished eyes and parted lips, he turns to hide the monster he's become. "Now, now. Fret not about a foolish old wizard." He points to his work desk where a bouquet of wilted violets lies.

I touch each petal with care.

"Damn it all," he mutters. "Vivienne, I told you lives depend on Marcus's knighthood. Not just those in the farmlands, but in the castle as well."

The boy who kissed me in the barn and watched me in the clock tower for years must be the one to activate the weapon. Camelot needs Marcus as much as it needs me. Merlin is never one to be perfectly straightforward when allusion suits him better.

"The walls of this damned castle don't only have eyes, they also bear cruelty to the subjects within. Seems Camelot's veil of protection was more illusory than I thought."

Quiet sobs catch in my throat. I cradle my uniform, searching for the courage that leapt from my heart just moments ago. "Is there no hope?"

Despite the shadows, Merlin gives me a sad smile, and I rejoice at the human part of him still alive. "There's always hope when it's a question of whether we should love. You're a smart girl. You should have known that."

I hastily wipe away a betraying tear. "It seems impossible." Not just war against Morgan.

With the flick of an eyebrow, Merlin glances out the window and whistles sharply. Caldor lands squarely on the sorcerer's arm. It's become more lifelike each day.

"Not too long ago, we were able to contort the elements of nature and breathe life into an otherwise copper-and-brass bird simply for my own amusement." His stark eyes look into mine. "Nothing is impossible, Vivienne."

It shouldn't lift my spirits since I'm fairly certain the logic is unsound, but the hope he speaks of is stronger.

But then Merlin freezes, suddenly drawn back to the window. Caldor flits from his arm to a wooden stand. The bird twitches uncomfortably and collapses, steam whistling from its head.

The alchemist steps for the window. "What is it?"

A rumbling of thunder ripples over the kingdom. I clutch my violets until they fall apart in my hands, dead petals and crushed stems. Merlin pulls back the curtain to look over the land.

I inch forward. "Merlin?"

He glances over his shoulder. "My incantation has been completely washed away."

Caldor's inanimate eyes stare at mine, vibrating from thunder. My catacombs uniform flutters from my hands to the floor.

Somehow I move to where Merlin stands. I expect scores of black-armored men storming for Camelot. Men whose minds were condemned to purgatory after a witch hammered iron to their jaws. But not yet. Below, serfs and peasants storm the square.

Merlin looks at Azur. "Now, we watch Camelot fall."

A riot has erupted.

TWENTY-NINE

Merlin grasps the windowsill. "The calm is over." He seems almost relieved.

Azur sets a hand upon my shoulder. "Do not sacrifice yourself for this. Think of the greater good. Merlin's weapon will be instrumental in saving many in the years to come. Let the lives of the queen and her lover be the price. There is no dishonor in that."

I pull away from Azur's hold. The machine I build might kill Marcus. The freedom I'll lose in saving Guinevere and Lancelot will be my penance. I back away for the door, faster now. I need to do this. And I hate that I'm hesitating.

"The weapon," Merlin rasps. "You're gambling with its progress."

"We need the king's champion," I say. "Arthur needs Guinevere. And so do I. With all that's happened, you're right: my apprenticeship is as good as over." It's devastating to admit.

Merlin's cloudy eyes flock to mine. "Finish Victor. That is

your task. We won't need Lancelot if his squire can do what you ask of him."

My fingers tense into tight fists. How can I ask so much from the squire whose heart I'll have to break?

The sorcerer folds over. He huffs, clutching the arms of his chair for stability. Traces of shins and ankles peek through his cloak. Flash with light. Fade, taking with them muscle and bone. With one quick pull, invisible nails scratch the wood of the chair already cleaned of its upholstery. I jump at the sudden movement.

"Have I ever told you how much you remind me of your mother?" His voice drops to a whisper, an octave too low. "You're headstrong, inquisitive. You've inherited her brilliant mind, and if she hadn't given up her own apprenticeship to become Lord William's wife, she'd be arguing the same as you. But it cannot be so."

"She was also your—" I whisper. My mother.

My mother whose only connection to the mechanical arts I thought was her cedar music box that played a song: old, poignant, sad. Merlin's favorite Celtic ballad. Who fretted over my place in Camelot, brushed my hair. Who'd told me since I was a child not to forget how danger lurks in every corner. Who I thought was sent to torture me on some days, but understood the anguish that came with knowing so much about our mechanical world.

Impossible. It cannot be. But I regard my uniform and realize I should have known a master seamstress in Camelot would have ways of creating a garment fit for the catacombs.

Merlin's head wrenches back toward the wooden rafters

of his tower, leaky and old, where sunlight pries through. His teeth clench, his eyes squeeze shut. The skin on his forearms and neck pulls back, strip by strip.

Azur reaches for my hand. "Vivienne, you must stay!"

But I back away and flee down the stairs. I have to stop the execution.

Even if it means a copper noose around my neck.

———

I hurry past the crowds, fighting my way to the square. In the gardens, I hold my breath in case I were to run into Marcus—he's not there. The courtyard is filled with opium smoke and nobility preoccupied with a spontaneous cro-quet match. They whisper about the affair, watching the chaos with delight. A justice-hungry serf rallies the crowd, his fury growing like a renegade flame on spilled gas.

"...how long should treason go unpunished? If it were any of us, our corpses would already be rotting! But the king wanted to dismiss them quietly, perhaps hoping the foiled attempt to steal Excalibur would distract us..."

He is no older than I am. Scarred, blackened fingers only a serf would have point to the castle in accusation.

On the gallows' bare stage, two snakelike copper ropes hang as Arthur sits off to the side in a formal gentleman's jacket. His eyes lose themselves in a spot across the way, dark-circled and empty of conscious thought.

"...no choice! Treason must be punished, no matter serf or royal!"

The trial begins.

I push through, casting away any wonderment of what the sensation would be like, having my neck sliced open from a cold, twisted cord, thin as a bracelet of silver and braided with steel to make it deadly like an old-fashioned noose.

"Let me through!" I shout. "I need to see Arthur!"

But the judge has a voice louder than mine, and no one steps aside, certainly not when the queen and her lover could hang. The judge paces in front of Guinevere, shackled in a plain brown dress. My heart breaks when I see how defeated she looks, how humiliated that her nighttime sins are not secrets and could never be in Camelot. Next to her, in front of his own noose, stands Lancelot.

Somber and calm, only his eyes move about, gauging the aims of the guards from the parapets above. I've seen Owen's aim; I know the archers are just as precise. A handful of arrows would strike the heart if Lancelot were to fight back. They wouldn't need a second try.

The sound of a wet splatter draws my attention to the stage. Serfs hurl fruits past their prime at the prisoners. Guards press the people back, gesturing their weapons with empty threats. A wave of drunken nobility creates a mob in the open space. A woman with rouged lips laughs unceasingly, stepping in my way. She knocks me over, and my palms scrape against the ground.

I pull myself to my feet and race onward, weaving like a ribbon for the stage. "Arthur!" Each cry more frightened than the last. I'm not brave. Why on earth did I think I could do this?

On the stage, Owen is missing from the lineup of squires. He must be elsewhere, eyes trained on the scene without a stitch of emotion on his face. But Marcus is there. Of the squires, he's the only one not standing at attention. Instead, his arms are crossed, and he watches the judge sentence a brother to death for treason, a crime of which he was nearly guilty. The edge of his mouth purses with anger at his inability to stop this.

"The court finds Guinevere, Queen of Camelot, guilty of high treason . . . "

The crowd roars, and it's deafening. Many have stopped caring about the trial and point at the evidence of Arthur's new age: his gray hair and the deep lines in his face.

"Arthur!" I scream. Guards push a section of the crowd back, and we shift away from the stage.

The judge reads Lancelot's verdict. " . . . guilty of high treason . . . " More cries from the crowd.

No one gives a damn about letting me through. Their fiery eyes lock on the gallows as they scream for the sins of the privileged. They know nothing of Morgan's influence.

" . . . hanged by the neck until strangled, decapitated, or emptied of blood . . . "

The executioner sets the copper rope around Lancelot's neck. Drums patter the last song the knight will hear. He is lost in thought while Guinevere rocks in a fit of sobs. Perhaps she kneels on the very spot her dead body will lie. I cannot give up.

"Arthur!" I scream, managing to get by a handful of

smoking dandies making bets on the likely way Lancelot would die.

One of them, with tall hawked hair, grabs me. Marcus glances over as eager hands go about my waist. I throw my elbow into the dandy's stomach, but he holds tight.

There's no hesitation. Marcus pushes past those in his way for me.

No, no, no. He cannot be a part of this.

The dandy pulls me closer, fingers gripping my skin until it hurts. "Hello, pretty. Where are you off to in such a rush?" he growls in my ear. The rolled *hashish* between his lips twists with his words, catching on the piercing in his tongue.

Marcus fights the crowd for me as the dandy's lips move closer to my ear.

"What is it, girl?" he asks, condescension dripping from his words. "Can't be that there's someone else, can there?"

And Marcus is so close that I'm sure he's heard the question. He waits for my answer. I'm deliberate as I shake my head to convey a message I'm both desperate and terrified he'll understand.

"No one," I tell both, pulling the boy's arm from my dress. The roars of nobility and peasants alike fade into a hazy blur. Marcus is all that remains. Despite the people between us, my message has reached him. His mouth parts, and he returns to the stage. A hand runs over his face to clear his mind. My throat tightens.

"Any last words, Sir Lancelot?"

The knight shakes his head. I force myself to the stage.

" …God have mercy on your—"

"Arthur, stop!" I shout. Arthur's eyes find me, the lone voice in the crowd not calling for death or mercy, and lifts a hand to the judge.

Camelot looks upon the queen's rumored accomplice. My mother stands nearby, dressed in plain clothes. Clothes that wouldn't attract attention. She shakes her head to caution me.

Arthur seethes. "I should arrest you," he says as Lord Henry holds him back.

"Please, your majesty." I tremble from cold blood rushing through my veins like steel restraints circling my wrists. "The queen and champion are not guilty of these charges." Instantly, there are shouts of anger. One voice sounds like my father's.

Marcus is unmistakably visible in my periphery. I watch as he hesitates the same way he did in the farmlands and marches for me as though he's realized what I'm about to do.

I catch my breath. "Morgan cursed—"

"Morgan cursed not just the castle that day." Marcus pushes me back and steps forward himself. "She also cursed the queen and Lancelot. They didn't know what they were doing."

My voice is frantic. "Your majesty, the squire doesn't—"

Again, Marcus pushes me back. "I know this because I left Camelot without permission and heard Morgan confess it in the farmlands. She's responsible, your majesty."

I step next to Marcus, but he won't acknowledge me. He waits to hear if his place in Camelot will be the price for his confession. Arthur would declare a lesser punishment for a squire than a lady-in-waiting, surely, even if Marcus is a serf.

"No, your majesty, don't listen—" I shout, but my voice gets lost in the madness, and someone seizes my arm.

"Quiet, you foolish girl!" my father growls.

A bout of nervous chatter comes over the crowd at Marcus's audacious declaration, his mentioning of "the witch, Morgan." Arthur towers over him.

I pry myself from my father's grip, but he yanks my elbow back. "This isn't their fault," I say, not caring that eyes watch me, ears hear me. "Morgan's curse on Camelot—"

"You cannot barge onto a stage to argue something so ridiculous! Are you mad?" His angry whispers might as well be shouts.

Arthur crosses his arms, gauging Marcus. "Squires are forbidden to leave the castle without consent."

Gossipy whispers encase Marcus. He swallows. "I know, your majesty, but—"

"Not many *serfs* have been offered the privilege of Camelot, boy, and today's the wrong day to challenge me. I return to my wife and champion in each other's arms, and you dare tell me it was not their fault?"

Marcus rakes the back of his hair. All eyes are on him, all pointed fingers. I want to take it all away, and yet, if Arthur grants him mercy, I'll have to ask Marcus for more.

He shakes his head. "No, your majesty. Not like that. It's just what I heard Morgan say."

Fire erupts in Arthur's eyes. The chattering amongst the crowd is louder now. Too loud for their mad king.

"You had nothing to do with it, do you understand?" my father huffs. He pulls me further from the stage, one strong hand gripping my arm demanding my attention. "You will not make a fool of yourself. Hide in our tower! Go!"

"No," I say, pulling my arm free. "I cannot hide who I am." I put on a look Owen carries well. I'm not a child. I'm not my father's protégé. There's a place for me in the world, and there's nothing he can do to stop me from seeking it.

The crowd grows angry. Chants and heckles and all sorts of fury rise up from Marcus's words.

It becomes too much.

"Enough!" Arthur shouts. But he doesn't call for a third noose. His eyes bore into Guinevere's, Lancelot's. "Get them off this stage. I have to think. I cannot see this now..." Shaking hands cling to his temples. "Not now."

The shocked crowd is silent until the rallying serf loudly objects.

"They're guilty of treason! An embarrassment to your kingdom!" He slurs his words with hatred, and the crowd's reaction is violent.

Despite, Lancelot's eyes lift to the sky in thanks for the mercy he didn't think would come. Guinevere exhales a shuddering breath. The judge signals the king's orders to the guards, and Arthur's wife and champion are thrown from the stage. Marcus is lost in the crowd, but I'm close enough to reach Guinevere's hand as guards usher her past me. She smiles in thanks as our fingers touch. A lifetime of shared moments, gone. Impossible now.

Camelot is an opera of vicious threats and infectious violence.

But then from the gates, "Help!"

Someone has arrived. Wounded. They lead in a man I don't recognize, whose stringy hair is as black as kohl with a beard to match. He must have been riding nonstop for days. Armor branded with Camelot's seal, a faded dragon tattoo on his neck. A knight returned from the quest, clutching the guards in gripping pain as they take him to the courtyard. No one flocks to his side to gloriously welcome him. Shock stills us all.

"Get help from the infirmary!" one guard's blood-curdling scream demands. Blistering burns on the knight's face and neck shine against tattered clothing. One of his arms has been hacked off, and the poor man is delirious with pain.

"The king," he manages. "Where's Arthur?"

Arthur breaks through the crowd. The guards drop the knight to writhe in agony while they call for help to be swift. "Gawain," the king breathes, seizing the knight's vestments.

Red spittle streams from the knight's lips. "Your sister. She's days away with an army the likes of which I've never seen before." The pitiful man spews up bile and blood. "I only managed to escape after the Spanish rogues took my arm. She killed other knights, Arthur, ones who were about to close in on the Grail. We knew. Even without the coordinates, we could damn well tell. The euphoria, the temptation. You never came to help…"

Then he falls still, either dead or passed out from delirium.

THIRTY

Arthur stands.

No one missed the fateful warning. Some have realized that news like this after one attack is no coincidence and declare as much. The serfs are the first to move. They push through knowing Camelot's bitter truth: they're the least likely to get to safety first.

War, on its way. All of Camelot knows it now.

And I still need to talk to Marcus.

Father has forgotten me for Gawain, so I grab my mother's arm. "You must get to our quarters."

Her eyes see right through me. I wonder if her husband ever knew of her apprenticeship. "Vivienne, you're coming, too!"

I shake my head. She must know why I have to disobey her. "This is something I can fix."

I turn and shove through the crowd. People run in every direction, battering against me like a cruel hurricane of bodies. I fight through them. I find a break and make out Marcus's lean frame, black blazer, tangled hair. And anger on his face as he beelines for someone watching from afar. Someone I thought was at the trial, but I'd been mistaken.

Owen.

Marcus breaks into a run and slams my brother into the stables. I gasp. I have no idea where this rage came from.

"Damn it all!" I curse, running for them. A chopping sound briefly draws my eyes to the sky where, through the chaos, an aerohawk catches the wind and soars east.

I can't think about that now.

Owen won't back down easily. His fist strikes Marcus's jaw, and Marcus jerks back. Owen pushes him away. "Bugger off, serf!"

"Hit me again!" Marcus growls. He shoves Owen back into the stables. "Fight me, you coward!"

My brother's head smacks against the wood with a sick thump. He slumps and then clambers to his feet to run out of Marcus's way. Galahad and Percy sprint for them.

"Stop!"

"We don't have time for this!"

I nearly reach them, but Percy spots the harried look on my face and steps in my way. "Get out of here, Viv," he hisses. "They're sending for aeroships to take the subjects to safety. Keep to protocol—make sure you get aboard."

I ignore Percy. "Stop it!" I scream.

Galahad seizes Marcus's shoulder. "Break it up! Let him go, Marcus!"

But Marcus won't budge. "He told Camelot about Lancelot and the queen!" he declares, arm pressing into my brother's neck. "Only a handful knew, and you were already angry enough at him, Owen, weren't you? A knight wouldn't have made such a stupid move. It must have been a *squire!*"

My mouth drops, and I yield to Percy's stubborn barrier. He goes still, and Galahad's usual air of nonchalance turns into shock.

Owen...

My brother seethes. "Lancelot cared more about Guinevere than the threat Morgan was. We all saw it! He could have sent an assailant to Glastonbury, and all of this time wouldn't have been wasted. Instead he took advantage of Arthur's leave? Serves what he got." His voice wobbles, his hands shake. "And you..." Owen's eyes on his former friend are wrought with venom, as though he knows more than he lets on about Marcus. "You were nowhere to be found two days past. Perhaps you shouldn't talk about betrayal, Marcus."

Marcus's eyes don't waver. He seizes Owen's collar, tightening his knuckles into my brother's neck. Another tremor comes over Owen.

"Say what you like, Owen, but Lancelot is a brother to me! For years, he and Galahad were my only family," Marcus fumes. "You nearly cost him his life! And the queen's!"

Owen shakes his head. "You heard what Gawain said! Le Fay's nearly here! I–I didn't mean to send Lancelot to the gallows. I mentioned the scandal in jest!" He trembles. "I didn't mean for this to happen!" Owen swallows. "Percy, Galahad... I didn't mean for this."

Percy abandons me to set a gentle hand on Marcus's shoulder, pulling him from Owen. "You might as well have betrayed blood, Owen."

Owen's hand grazes his neck. "You look at me as though I were the one who humiliated Arthur, but I'm not the one in the dungeons."

The dungeons?

When I delivered the queen's letter to Lancelot, I heard screams rattling from below my boots. Whoever their prisoner was, I can only imagine it was someone whose sins were crimes against the knights' quest or an outsider who yearned to steal Excalibur.

But Camelot was supposed to be a paradise. My father once boasted that Camelot needed dungeons as much as she needed gallows—useless to a kingdom many considered perfect.

I breathe against the sobs in my throat. "Oh, Owen."

Owen's face reddens. His hands shake. "I didn't want him to die. I didn't want either of them to die."

A knight calls from the main castle, "Percy! Galahad! To the Round Table at once!"

Galahad steps close to Percy, as though whispered words could stay secret in Camelot. "We have no idea what kind of magic or weaponry—"

"Copper," Marcus says, unable to look at my brother again without hurling him against the stables. "Fire it into the temples of Morgan's army, just as you did to defeat Pelles's soldiers. I saw it in the woods." He looks at me, but not for too long in case it would be noticed. He might be wondering if

I'll speak, but we both know I can't. Not if I want to keep my place in the clock tower. "The sorcerer knows this. By now, he will have relayed instructions to the blacksmith. Our ammunition will be ready in time." He speaks as though he knows the blacksmith's capabilities.

Galahad nods. "We'll need you to tell us everything, Marcus."

Percy sprints for the knights' quarters, relaying the information. I cradle my arms at the coolness of my brother's betrayal and the squire's heart. Galahad holds back.

"This won't be brought to the court yet, Owen. We need you on the wall with the archers. Let's go."

Marcus leaves through the stables. Likely to cool off before he'll consider obeying Galahad. I can't imagine how he'll respond when the Round Table asks his reason for leaving the castle in the first place.

My brother shouts after Marcus, "Keep your head down as you ride."

Marcus looks back, steel-eyed.

"It's your Achilles' Heel," my brother says. "Just in case war comes before you'll speak to me again."

Then Owen looks at me with the face of the eight-year-old boy I once knew, one who had to fall from high branches every now and then in order to remember he was made for the ground and not the sky. He turns away like he can't bear the thought of his sister being present for such humiliation and follows the knights. I watch him go.

After a heavy moment, I run after Marcus. "My lord!"

In the royal stables, Marcus catches sight of me, clenching

his jaw and avoiding my eyes. I grab his arm terrified he'll walk away, unsure of how I would handle that. My fingers linger on his sleeve, wanting to feel his hand. He faces me with eyes that scratch like shards of glass.

I swallow. "Merlin needs your help, and it kills me to relay the message."

He blinks once, and his gaze drops. My hand has clasped his.

"Merlin is likely consumed by magic at this point, and it's no business of mine to be involved anymore. I have to report to the Round Table. I'm lucky I still can." His voice is distant. "My lady will be so kind as to let me go."

"Marcus, please," I breathe.

It's the first time I've used his name in front of him. He looks at me as though time has stopped.

"Merlin's weapon," I recite from the scores of moments when I practiced this speech. "It's nearly ready, but—" My fingers clasp his tighter, and for a moment I think it'll be impossible to let go. "What I'm to ask of you could send you straight into death's arms."

His violet eyes have faded to an angry gray, brokenhearted by the sacrifice he made to save my good name from the king-dom's gossipy wrath. Or perhaps Marcus is as logical as I am and did it so I could finish building Victor.

Whatever his reason, he yanks his hand free, but instead of storming away, his palms cup my cheeks, and he marches me to the stable walls until we're hidden from the anarchy of Camelot. His thumbs stroke my lips, and his face melts with sadness.

"Then leave with me. We did plan to." He forces a sad laugh. "Let's go to a place where you can be as happy as I saw you once."

I breathe in the thought. "The weapon, it'd go unfinished. Knights would be defenseless against Morgan. She'd find the coordinates to Avalon. What if she found out how to override Excalibur somehow so her son can wield it? And knighthood, how can I ask you to give up on such an honor? Even if your mother were never the reason, no one would sacrifice—"

"For love?" Marcus challenges. "I doubt that. Knights are selfish and fleeting, seeking a different bed every night in the kingdom that's not the paradise you think. If they knew what love was, they'd hold onto it like it could save their lives."

My hand inches up to graze the cheek now bruising from my brother's fist. He leans into my palm, closing his eyes but somehow managing to keep the anger on his face.

"Lancelot wouldn't even give it up," I whisper.

"Because he was cursed by Morgan. There's no hope in that."

The clock tower chimes the hour. Time doesn't wait. Shouts tell us the castle has sent for aeroships for those who would flee Camelot. Just as Percy said. Protocol. A chance to leave for another place, a better life. My fingers trace Marcus's rough, unshaven skin, tickling my hand. My cheeks sting with tears.

He pulls me close, grabbing under my hair with both hands. Lips barely touch mine. "Ask me to leave right now, and

I wouldn't give it a second thought. The knights are my brothers, but they don't need the son of a serf to defeat Morgan."

"You would just leave when Camelot's under attack?"

He shakes his head. "Camelot is its people, not towers or balconies. They call for an evacuation. Who cares about this damned place?"

"Morgan would claim the Grail."

"That's not for certain."

I shake my head. I know an evacuation of Camelot doesn't account for all. "Your family—"

"I'll find a way to get my mother out of here. This isn't the only kingdom." He pulls away in fear, as though I'll say no and he's desperate for the yes. "Here we'll live lives we'd never choose for ourselves." His eyes lift to mine. "You'll be married. To someone not a serf. Is that why?"

I'm furious it would cross his mind. "How can you even think that?"

"Then come with me."

He sets his mouth atop mine, ignoring the salty tears coating my lips, but I pull away before he can embrace the kiss. I wrap my arms around his neck and cry against his warm skin.

"I can't. If your family were to face Morgan unarmed, I'd never forgive myself."

He goes cold. Like a statue. If I couldn't feel the slowing of his heart, I would have wondered if he'd turned into one of Merlin's machines.

I breathe, hiding the sobs in my voice. "This is our duty now. We can't let her win."

"Duty. Right." He unravels my arms from his neck and pauses like he wants to make another remark, even parting his lips before changing his mind.

"Marcus—" I whisper.

"I'm needed by the knights."

He heads for their quarters, shutting the heavy door behind him, leaving me standing cold and alone.

THIRTY-ONE

Nighttime falls over the kingdom.

Angry voices from the day linger in the courtyard like an army of ghosts forever calling for blood. People pass me on my way to Merlin's clock tower like I'm just another phantom. Carts and wagons with children wrapped in threadbare blankets flood the streets. Serfs and orderlies take all they own to escape the castle haunted with madness and threat. Royalty can do no wrong, and they've had enough. They won't stay another night in this bewitched place, not when kings can age overnight and knights are treasonous. Not when some have already heard more accurate rumors about the attack the other day and speculate about what sort of war approaches.

They vow to head north. Together.

The sky is black with unnatural clouds. No star shines powerfully enough to break through. I imagine how Caldor's wings would have caught a few wisps to repaint the skies.

Inside Merlin's tower, the sorcerer stands alone by his

window, watching below. "It was the right thing to save them, Vivienne. Forgive an old man's cruel pragmatism."

My eyes burn with tears just hearing that. "Where's Azur?" I want his answer to be "in the catacombs, of course," but I know what aerohawk I saw fly off.

"Gone," Merlin says in a blank voice. "Left without even a goodbye. I'd thought he'd descended below, but he left the *jaseemat* in his stead. The aerohawk…" He gestures the window, and I look to the bare land where the ground is scuffed, the aerohawk, missing. Once again, Azur Barad has fled Camelot, and I've been left behind.

"He hasn't abandoned us…"

"I don't know." Merlin looks away, humming a song, mumbled lyrics passing his lips without coherence. Maybe he has none. Maybe he's too far gone.

Only I can finish the weapon. No escape for me. Or Marcus.

"The mirror, Vivienne, in the catacombs. *Jaseemat* turns looking glasses into windows between two souls. I haven't decided if it's perfect irony, being so damn similar to magic, or if Camelot's superstitious serfs got the mythology right." With heavy breaths, he wipes his sinewy neck of exhausted sweat. "It's how Azur and I kept in contact, and thank God indeed my soul was complete, despite what I did in the woods."

He nods at his work table where a small looking glass lies. Easy to carry and hold, the frame a tarnished copper. My breath stops at seeing such a valuable trinket. "And now?"

Several days have passed since the woods. Many minutes since Azur left Merlin to his own devices.

Snuff box in hand, Merlin inhales a pinch. "Go downstairs. Unveil the looking glass. I'll stay with you as you work."

———————

Below, flames dance on the pyre, fingers of fire reaching around me. The password is a whisper in my mind.

"*Ahzikabah.*"

The flames collapse, letting me pass.

Alone, I drop my gown to the floor and kick it aside. I put on the sleeveless uniform I know my mother made for me. The leather apron knots around my waist. I bunch my hair on top of my head and use a soft steel netting to keep it off my neck. Camelot's nobility would be delighted. I pull down my custom-made goggles and ignite the furnace. The flick of a switch starts the assembly lines, spitting out steel bearings and arrowheads. I'll bring them to the blacksmith for reinforcement at dawn.

I unveil the looking glass, which at first appears as any other. Seconds later it changes, a strange thing to watch: Merlin's blue eyes appear and vanish just as quickly. The surface absorbs the light as though water could seep into it.

With a shocking scream, the furnace blares. The valve and its rotating pistons send steam toward the mosaic ceiling.

"What if I can't finish in time?" I whisper. Fit one shoulder's firelance barrel against Victor's skeleton. A coil of six, perfect and untouched, ready to expel death at *jaseemat's* breath of life.

"You cannot think like that."

"Azur left..." I still can't understand why. Twist the bolt clockwise to lock the barrels in place. Align the interlocking sprockets. With one rotation of the handle, the firelance's magazine spurts out nonexistent bearings.

"It cannot matter anymore. You must have faith in yourself."

I nod bitterly, knowing Azur would ascribe to the same rationality. Solder the six spidering copper veins to the barrels so *jaseemat* controls the firings.

Victor is nearly done. Its nose is a pointed drill strong enough to slash through pipes and break through the ceiling. Firelances in the shoulders are fit with their proper gears and triggers. The monster's talons will dig and kill. *I can do this.*

I set my goggles aside and fit a protective mask to my face.

"You didn't tell the squire."

I pretend I didn't hear. Diamond cuts red-hot steel with precision, sending sparks around me.

"It has to be him, my dear. There's no one faster."

My eyes well behind the mask. I manage a quick nod, and Merlin goes silent, letting me work.

A hammer bangs out the edges. Piping fits under Victor's body, right by carefully crafted propellers that will move the monster to the surface, into the air. Heat sends thick rivers of sweat down my skin, but I stay focused, every burst of steam one step closer to something I pray will work when I'll ask Marcus to risk his life to activate it.

It must work.

I'm forced awake by the sputtering furnace cracking loudly against the air.

My eyes open to near darkness. On the table, my arms serve as a cushion for my head as I sit atop a stool. There's an unpleasant crick in my neck as I straighten. My limbs are sore; my muscles are stiff.

"Perhaps some tea will help."

My mother stands next to me in an ice blue gown. She offers me a porcelain cup out of which steam snakes into the air, smelling faintly of Merlin's Irish tea. In her other hand lies a wooden box boasting cryptic symbols scratched into the surface. "Merlin thought you might need the early kick."

"What is that?" I motion toward the box, but take the tea. "Azur—"

"He's not here." She sets the box on the desk out of reach. "Spare a few minutes to gather yourself properly." Her eyebrows lift in a motherly fashion.

My fingers trace the rim of the teacup. "How long have you known?"

My mother tilts her head as she thinks. "You destroyed Merlin's hookah at a feast when you were ten, and you were damn well lucky he was too drunk to care. When morning came, and he'd sobered up, he asked me permission to school you in this world. How you were able to see a toy aeroship in parts of his pipe was beyond him."

I smile. The following week, Merlin approached me with assignments I'd have to complete before I could learn more in the clock tower. Destroy Lord William's bifocals, turn the pieces into a working telescope. Rearrange the construction of Lady Carolyn's loom so that with the crank of a wheel, the threads would weave themselves. But I wasn't to tell a soul any of this, not even my mother. Propriety had to be kept.

I sip tea as she studies the completed weapon I spent all hours of the morning testing and retesting. Victor is shelled and shining like a glorious statue in an emporium, its inner workings as intricate and deadly as the rules of life. An armored neck lifts to a black-eyed face with a domed eye that controls navigation, using the same eastern science Merlin showed me in the woods. My own touch.

While a terrifying monster, Victor also serves as an elegant representation of mechanical power. The wall is proof of that—one side is completely obliterated into rubble. I didn't realize what sheer destruction the firelance shoulders were capable of when I set the gauge to a stronger firing speed.

The world certainly hasn't seen anything close to the likes of this before.

My mother sweeps a layer of metallic shavings off the table, wiping her fingers onto her dress. A tiny smile seduces her lips. "I haven't stepped down here in years." I realize why she never told me she knew—any mention of a place like the catacombs in Camelot wouldn't remain secret for long.

Her eyes drop to my uniform, ripped at the arms and now shortened. A scandalous length as it shows my boots and knees entirely, but it was the only way to avoid suffocating in the heat. The corset atop is belted with a strip of lace Merlin found in the catacombs years ago, as though someone from

Lyonesse ventured inside once. "I see my dressmaking skills are not up to par these days." She flicks an eyebrow. "For the catacombs, anyway."

I set down my tea, and we share a smile. She looks back at Victor, a scrutinizing eye on every detail of my work.

"Merlin told me of the flaw in my design. To be fair, alchemy was a mere theory instead of what Azur has made of it today. Purely the possibility of gold from charcoal, nothing more."

I open my mouth to reassure her the blueprints have been changed to account for the glitch, and then blink. "Your design?"

"Made during the Celtic threat." She searches the blueprints and points in the bottom right corner to where her signature lies. "Merlin's conception, my ingenuity."

I stare at the handwritten notes of my mother. "Why didn't you continue?" Did she never consider leaving Camelot like I have?

She looks around at the chaos of the lair. "This was not the place for me, especially as your father was Arthur's advisor. There's nothing wrong with following your heart, Vivienne. It let me contribute something special to this kingdom of ours."

"It is a fantastic invention."

She shakes her head. "I was able to give them you." She kisses my forehead. "Be cautious. Camelot is chock-full of secrets. Knowledge that could change the course of history might be hidden right in front of you. Our world is not what you think."

I know that now. The past few weeks have shown me a

different side of the home I thought I knew. Ever since the day Caldor truly came alive.

My mother frowns. "Something else troubles you."

I look away. Now is not the time to speak of broken romance.

"I always knew dandies of the court would be nothing but foolish boys to you. Whoever he is, nobility or not, you don't want death reaching him before you have the chance to tell him the truth."

I'm about to ask her how she could possibly know, but no secrets in Camelot seem safe anymore.

I have to change the topic, and perhaps my own mother could shed light on the mysteries in my mind. "What do you know about Avalon?"

Her lips part in surprise, but before she can speak, Merlin interrupts from the looking glass. "Vivienne. Morgan draws near. Use Azur's *jaseemat* to bring Victor to life. Then run like mad."

THIRTY-TWO

Merlin's words encase me in fear. An eternity of silence passes before I speak.

"How?" My voice quivers as the seconds tick away. "Merlin, how do I do it?"

"Calm down." I don't miss the flinch of pain on his ghostly face. "Crawl inside the vent and light the fuel in the heart's chambers. Once lit, pour in the *jaseemat*. Azur's incantation will be released when you open the box. Go!"

I grab my mother's arms. "You must escape. God knows how this will turn out!"

"No, Vivienne, I won't leave you here alone!"

And she's firm on that.

The wooden box in my hand feels like one of Merlin's flimsy teacups, delicate as crystal. On his desk is a quicklight I set into my apron pocket. Black leather gloves fit to my elbows. There's a hatch on the underside of Victor's belly. A lock spins as it would on *l'enigma insolubile,* and the door swings down.

"Let me help." My mother cups her hands together for a boost.

She lifts me into the belly, Azur's box in my hand. Each breath I take inside reverberates with warning.

Victor creaks under my weight, but Merlin's craftsmanship is durable. One hand guides me through twisting pipes and sprockets. The ticks of the cogwork heart grow louder with each step. My fingers drift across the gears. Every mechanism is there for a purpose—to run Azur's *jaseemat* through copper veins. To give Merlin's creation a strange bit of life.

My fingers brush leather. Patchwork lungs containing two separate iron reservoirs of fuel and steam: one to breathe fire, one to propel the body. I reach for the tube connecting the fuel reservoir to the ticking heart, finding the chamber. Above is the lever, extended for Marcus's grasp. I push that thought aside. My fingers seize the heart's lid. I grunt as I try to release it.

"Vivienne…"

"Another second," I plead, quiet words like thunder in my ears.

That second passes, and then another. I can't remove the lid. To keep the chamber from leaking prematurely, the thief Merlin used an enormous amount of strength to tighten it.

I set the box at my feet. With both hands, I put all my weight on the lid's turn.

It gives, and I breathe out in relief. "Good."

The smell of fuel sets me back a few feet. It's a slow-burning gas Merlin manipulated specifically for this endeavor. There won't be an explosion, but a gradual, fiery trickle that will transport the *jaseemat* and control the weapon's outburst of flames.

I pick up the box, my quicklight ready. "Please work." I press the lever, and it hisses. My boot rests upon my knee. I swipe the quicklight against the bottom until a flame catches. Around me, Arthur's Norwegian steel shimmers, translucent enough that I see my mother's shadow on the other side.

I carry the flame to the chamber. The fire turns blue, orange, and yellow, moving deeper throughout the gears. I open the box, and the *jaseemat* dances like lights in a northern sky.

Azur's voice speaks. *"Yaty ala alhyah."* Come to life.

I waste no time in pouring in the *jaseemat*. It falls out like water, moving in swirls onto the iridescent tongues, wrapping itself around them, pulsating as though a ticking heartbeat. I'm fascinated and set my hand against the steel to gather myself. My skin rings with song.

The *jaseemat* moves in a ballet. I feel myself falling—

BOOM!

Victor jolts, sending me onto my back. I sit up, my feet pushing me backward.

BOOM!

"Vivienne!" my mother screams from the hatch.

I climb to my feet and run.

Victor's violent kicks force me to dive for my mother's arms. She pulls me to safety, and we watch together as the horrifying fruit of Merlin's imagination shakes with breath. A long protrusion at the base flickers as its tail. The heavy appendage slams down on the mosaic, sending gemstones into the air.

BOOM! with each strike, like the ringing thunder that brought me down the steps.

The tip of the tail grows into a five-prong spike. Each prong duplicates and resets itself on a growing spherical bulge, equidistant from one another. And then again. Then again—until it's a full glorious morning star, a weapon of destruction and heft. The sharp tips twist into deadly hooks, threatening to rip apart any living thing that touches it.

"Run!" Merlin cries.

His voice is drowned out by the thumps of the creature's front talons, dagger-sharp, scooping up gems in fast, easy swoops. Firelance shoulders come to sharp points, the skin over the barrels peeling back to reveal long, black tunnels. Bronze-colored plates on its body turn to scales. A massive head lifts up from the folds of awkward, triangular arms. Smooth and long and pointed, Victor's eyes are infernos staring at mine above the nose, a mighty drill longer than Excalibur. Its mouth sends devastating blows of fire straight for the ceiling.

I push my mother toward the door. "Go!"

We reach the stairwell in time to hear a newborn dragon screech for blood. As we climb, the cobblestone rattles as though the monster could create an earthquake. Dirt falls into my hair. I scrape my knees and palms as I climb the trembling steps.

At the ladder, we stop, out of breath. The etchings in the ceiling chip away and fall onto our clothes.

"Go now," I tell my mother. "Leave Camelot on the aeroships."

She firms her lips. "Vivienne, there's something you must know about Avalon—"

The cellar door lifts, and we look into the masked face of the blacksmith who's found us behind his workshop.

I know it's because of the shaking ground that he's here. I know this even though I can't see his face. But there's no time to explain. "Take her!" I cry, pushing my mother toward the ladder. "Take her to the aeroships!"

She pulls away from me. For a second, I feel the blacksmith's eyes behind his mask stare as though questioning why a girl would stay in this damned place. But he obeys and seizes my mother's arm, lifting her easily.

My mother's eyes go wide with fear. She twists in the blacksmith's arms to no avail. "No! Vivienne! You cannot do this! You have to run!" Unafraid of the masked man, she grits her teeth. "It cannot be this way! You know this!"

But he ignores her and slams the cellar door over my head.

———

I throw my goggles onto Merlin's desk. His window captures Morgan's black-armored legion in its frame, haloed by the flapping wings of the same black birds that followed her from the woods. But I don't know whether to be more terrified of her or of what the sorcerer has become.

He is no longer monster or man. He rests in the limbo

between: skin, muscle, and bone faded away, only distinguishable from his chair by occasional flashes of light. His mask cocks to the side, and every few seconds, he twists in his suffering.

I step forward. "Merlin?"

He opens a cloudy eye. "Well done, Vivienne. You have one more task."

"Marcus."

A gloved finger points at the window. "He's down there."

In front of the city gates, knights line up. Galahad, Arthur's new first-in-command, barks orders with his usual nonchalance. The ground rumbles; the knights ignore it. But they can't ignore the screeches.

"Victor will be a fine weapon, Vivienne. A machine with a soul of its own."

"It'll wreak havoc on the entire kingdom," I say in exasperation. I'm unleashing a monster into the world. What am I thinking?

"Trust me."

I swallow my frustration.

In the thousands, the red and black flags of Morgan's legion wave, carried by soldiers that will seize Camelot for their witch.

Calls from the cliffs draw my attention to a crumbling break in Merlin's clock tower wall, letting me see the other side. The view's incredible, better than the balcony circumventing the Round Table. An aeroship docks at the cliffs, floating in the wind with pristine sails flapping wildly. Above crashing capped waves, the people of Camelot flee for safer land. My tear-struck mother boards the closest aeroship. I breathe a brokenhearted sigh.

"Vivienne, it has to be now." What's left of the color on Merlin's dying skin fades to gray. "Do not be caught by Morgan. Camelot needs..." He sputters violently, as though suffocating.

"Merlin?"

A twist of pain comes about him. Two cloudy eyes stare me down. His breaths are heavy. He wants to speak, but can't. I draw my lip inside my mouth and bite until I taste blood. *He mentioned a moment of no return, when the soul was free, indestructible...*

"Not like this," he rasps, and I'm searching the entire clock tower because he's vanished, and his voice is omnipresent—

Then he materializes in front of me as the complete Merlin I once knew. Without even his limp. Only full white eyes that look as Morgan's did when she tried to steal magic here.

"Merlin—"

His face changes into a reptile's, and he lunges at me with a hissing tongue. I scream, backing into the desk behind me, letting all atop come crashing to the floor. He hears my voice and his face returns, save for the white eyes, two burning suns.

"Go! I can't risk my last minutes of sanity keeping from attacking you! That rage must be for Morgan!"

I run for the door as smoke surrounds the ghost he is. Taloned feet thump across the floor, and pointed black nails slice the air between us. I run as fast as I can down the spiral steps, leaping over them, covering my ears as the terrifying roars of something otherworldly threatens to follow.

Then comes the explosion.

The tower succumbs to a greater inferno than the harvester I destroyed. The heat of a fire I've never known catches up with me, and I scream again, nearly plummeting to my death. Oh God, something has gone terribly wrong. It must have.

The flames disappear as soon as I reach the cold ground of the cellar. The harsh roars ring in my ears, and I shake uncontrollably.

Trust me, Merlin had said.

I nod and will myself to my feet, remembering my last task before we'll trust Azur's alchemy for Camelot's salvation.

I spring up the steps and bound through the cellar door to look for Marcus.

———

Blasts of artillery and cannons devastate the gardens.

I run for them.

Run, run, run, and don't think it through any more than that.

Arthur stands at the forefront, observing as Galahad next to him sends a dozen men at a time across the drawbridge while the rest maintain formation at the gates.

Leather-gloved hands straighten sheeted-metal armor and belts carrying the blacksmith's reinforced ammunition. I can't find Marcus, but I know he'll be fighting in Lancelot's place as long as Owen's enigmatic remark never amounted to anything.

But if Marcus has already been sent in...

Galahad growls orders as the men ready themselves for possible death.

I duck under branches, race through beds of flowers, stomp them to the ground. My elm has been uprooted, my crossbow exposed. There's still one bolt in the compartment—I think. No time to check, regardless I yank my crossbow from its roll of leather and snap the cuff to my wrist. Put all my strength on the latch until it bends backward: a temporary fix for long-range shooting. Twist the bow on the cuff's cog so it follows the line of my arm. To my feet, then. I pass knight after knight as I run, but each is a stranger.

Then, as I near the edge of the gardens, I see him. "Marcus!"

He's in the last unit, armored in sheet metal and thick leather, standing by his horse, his hand on Lancelot's sword at his waist. A face too distracted to have heard me above the screams of war.

My heart pounds as I gauge the skies where Morgan's cannons fly, crushing the merlons of the castle's parapets, heading straight for the quarters where people once lived. I pray my mother is far enough away that she doesn't hear the destruction of our home. I search for Merlin, for any signs he survived whatever blast happened in his tower—and for the monster he promised would rise.

I have to push myself to try again. "Marcus!"

Another blast. I cover my head and crouch, my eyes

squeezed shut as the ground shudders. Once it's passed, I look to him.

He's heard his name. His kohl-wrought eyes fall upon mine. He's still at first and then sprints toward me. I run from the gardens, meeting him in the middle.

"Get back!" He catches my arm. "Get to the aeroships!"

I pull myself free and throw my arms around his neck. He smells like smoke and leather, and his hair's delightfully tangled. "Thank God they haven't sent you in."

"What do you mean? I'm going in next!" He grabs my arm again to send me to safety. For a moment, he's distracted by my exposed skin and tries his damnedest to look away.

"Marcus, you have to listen to me." I search the beautiful violet eyes I would look into for all eternity if I could. "Merlin's weapon—"

He lifts me to my toes, his face no more than a breath away from mine. "Please, don't do this. Not now. Let Merlin come down himself."

I grasp his stubbled cheek. "It can get to the surface, but you have to activate its wings. You're the fastest runner in Camelot. Listen to the earth below us. I'm sorry, Marcus. I'm sorry you're here and not escaping with your mother. I'm sorry this is why Merlin needs you. But when the weapon surfaces, you have to pull the lever on its back and then you need to run, Marcus. You need to run!"

The land rumbles. Our eyes lock for too long. He tightens with worry and surely it's for his own life, but he nods nevertheless. I hold on as long as I can, but he drops my arm and runs back to his horse.

My mother's advice rings in my head. "Marcus."

He's reluctant to face me.

"If duty weren't ... " No time for explanations. I take a deep breath. "I'd go with you. I wouldn't look back." I've always dreamt of escape, but it's not my path anymore.

His posture doesn't change, nor does his face. And that's what makes my breath hitch. Tears prick at my eyes.

"When you pull the lever, you'll activate the wings. You'll know it when you see it." And I have to trust Victor will live up to its design: attack the drones, kill Morgan.

I wipe my cheeks on my dirty gloves and run the other way, back through the colorless gardens. I force myself to accept this passed moment as a likely goodbye.

Then, as the trees envelop me, as my feet tread upon dying violets, footsteps follow. His voice speaks in its sad way.

"Vivienne."

I turn, and he's right there. He pulls me under my elm where no one will see us. His hands clasp my face, and his mouth crushes against mine. My arms go around his neck, and I pull him close, promising myself I'll never forget this.

He pulls away, and the enormity of this task escapes neither of us. But even stronger is the wonderment of what Morgan would do to her spy, the traitor, in this war.

The lace around my waist is full of charcoal and smells of smoke. I rip the tail into a piece long enough to wrap around his wrist. My fingers mingle with his. "Godspeed."

Marcus captures my face again. Our cheeks tearstained and dirty, he leans in to kiss me once more and then runs out from under the tree. The waiting horse jerks when Marcus leaps onto its back, but he grabs the reins and steadies it. His eyes find mine one last time before he rides for the gates.

He's the last to follow Galahad and the knights, but catches up quickly and disappears beyond the threshold.

I look upon the dull gray of our new Camelot, where once it was lush and green. I'm not sure of my purpose now, of what happens next. All I know is I'm supposed to stay out of the witch's way, lest she were to capture me. The gardens are eerily silent as the ringing of war numbs my ears.

The weapon pulsates from below. It still hasn't surfaced.

But in the sky, a new threat.

THIRTY-THREE

It's not an aeroship, which was my first thought when I saw the celestial body flying against the sky.

But my attention is quickly seized by firelances from Camelot's walls sending staccato blasts across the land. A guard cranks a wooden wheel, speeding up the split-second firings. I duck to avoid the falling shells.

Boulders of iron fly over the gates. I race to the walls as they strike the gardens. Dried leaves burst into the air like wooden snowflakes. My body flushes against cold stone. On the other side is Marcus, and perhaps he's already fallen.

I can't think that way.

Why hasn't Victor risen?

I curse and look back at the serpentine smoke from the destroyed clock tower, at the stark glint of ... something flitting around like an angelic mosquito. Part of me wants to hope Merlin was right when he told me about ghosts and their machines: there was a point of no return.

The smoke soars through the clouds and then plummets, a distinct set of translucent reptilian wings and a long, fluid tail nearly twice the length of its body. It beelines for the gates. I gasp as a ghostlike dragon with cloudy white eyes hovers like a hummingbird, head cocked to the side and peering at me. Its scales are fluid with wind. Remnants of tribal tattoos and facial piercings shimmer like white light.

It forces a screeching breath of translucent fire. Angular wings strike the air, sending trees and branches flying into the castle. The face is familiar. The face is reminiscent of the monster Merlin and I forged out of metal.

The spirit flies into battle. I follow, running over the drawbridge. The ghost breathes white fire into the drones—so many, they're like locusts atop the land—turning them into magnificent flames.

Knights and revenge-hungry serfs send copper-lined blasts into red-hot enemy eyes. Arrows through helmets. The strong figure of the blacksmith slashes a drone's throat using an iron hook plastered with a copper point.

At the forest's edge, Morgan sits atop her stallion with an endless parade of demonic steeds behind her. A burn, fresh and crimson, falls down her neck, courtesy of the rusty harvester I blew up. The armor covering her wounds is black like the drones', but lined red. Two swords cross her back in a studded leather holster. An entire fence of wagons boasts erupting cannons, enormous like the gallows.

"Merlin! You thought you could defeat me without magic! You're powerless!" She wields one of her long blades, pointing it at the ghost and uttering a loud cry indecipherable in its tongue. The hilt has a golden firelance with a long double barrel. She fires. The dragon tumbles back nearly a hundred feet. Through sputters of flashing light, it materializes into a cloak-clad Merlin, on hands and knees, keeled over with pain.

"Merlin, get up!" I whisper through gritted teeth.

Merlin's head hangs low, but with a sharp cry, he stretches his long, reptilian neck toward the witch, shifting into the dragonesque ghost once again. His lips pull back revealing dagger-sharp teeth. Iridescent wings sprout from his back and strike the air, sending tornadolike winds across the fields. Merlin soars for the witch, breathing fire. She casts her palm forward. Flames ricochet back, forcing Merlin to vanish and reappear several feet away as a man.

An idea comes to me: if I got close enough to fire my crossbow, Merlin would have the chance to finish off Morgan.

It could mean my death.

I take a breath. My hand flies to my forearm to click my last arrow—bolt—into place. I gasp. Nothing. I'd thought there was one more. I could have sworn there was one more.

But a quiver does lie on the other side of the drawbridge...

The ruffling of wind accompanied by a long horn pulls me from Merlin's fight. I glance at the sky.

"Azur..."

An entire fleet of aeroships soars straight for Camelot, all bearing the telltale white-and-gold flag of Jerusalem, luxurious sails beating down the breeze. At the forefront is Azur. He grasps the mast at the ship's bow, goggles drawn over his eyes. Behind him, a band of sailors eases the ship lower. He cries out in his native tongue and unsheathes the saber at his waist, pointing at Morgan.

The warriors in the fleet likewise lift their sabers. With a loud battle cry, cannonballs sail to the ground, forcing the witch and her drones away from Merlin.

My spirit strengthened, I tear my eyes back. Morgan will be defeated in no time.

For now, she is amused. She retrieves the second blade from her back and points the crossed tips at the ghost. "I admire your tenacity, Merlin. You have the persistence of a mindless machine."

Merlin smirks. "No, Morgan. Machines lack heart."

The propelling wind counters the heat from battle. I pull from the gates as Azur's aeroship lands. To get ammunition from him is a better plan than the quiver across the drawbridge. Azur runs for me, gripping a saber plated with copper. He lifts his goggles.

"The weapon, child! Where is it?"

"It hasn't risen yet!"

"You cast the *jaseemat* into the heart? As Merlin told you?"

"Yes, yes, I did exactly as needed to be done! It came alive, but—"

His eyes tilt toward the rumbling ground. "The weapon still digs." He firms his jaw. "Very well. My warriors have come to help Arthur. Jerusalem does not want to see a world where Morgan finds the Grail. We will die for Camelot first!"

"I need bolts, Azur!" He must have some on board.

"No, Vivienne!" he shouts, worry lacing his words together. "You cannot be caught!"

He turns back to the aeroship. His warriors have jumped from its plank wielding copper-plated sabers. They unsheathe more weapons and storm past to fight alongside Arthur's knights.

I search through the smoke for the quiver, but knights kick it aside as they fight. Drones stomp atop the bolts until I hear the snapping of wood. *Blast.* My eyes scan the archery front for some that might have been forgotten.

Azur's orders reach the anchored aeroships in the sky, all with cannons creating a rainfall of iron, crushing the drones. "Destroy her infantries!" he shouts, switching to English. "Leave the witch to Merlin!"

They call back, "Yes, sahib!" The sky goes black from their attack. Morgan bares her teeth.

Merlin, shifting from man to reptile, casts fire upon her. Morgan deflects it. He vanishes, reappearing an entire field away, running and leaping into the air. Talons, long and sharp, are ready to slice at whatever flesh steps in his way.

The sorcerer and the witch are close enough that perhaps I could get a good shot in. The nearly demolished quiver has three unbroken bolts. "I have to try."

But Azur holds me back. "Do not die a foolish death."

Morgan crosses her blades with a loud clang. "I'll have the girl, Merlin. Mere seconds inside her mind will show me the coordinates to Avalon!"

I freeze at her insane declarations.

I don't know where Avalon is. The images of golden cobblestone streets, a castle floating on the clouds, a matte chalice with iron studs: all the result of Owen's fairy tales told through shadows and gaslight.

"I don't know what she means," I whisper. Azur tenses.

Morgan whispers magic. Merlin advances. Her voice inaudible, she drops one sword, grabs the second with both hands, and when Merlin has leapt for her, she pierces the dragon's breast. The ghost materializes back into a man of flesh and bone, her sword threatening to dissect him.

"No!" I scream.

Azur grips my shoulder. "There is nothing you can do."

"There could have been!" The copper-tipped bolts gleam their hardest through the smoke.

Morgan squeals with glee as she plunges the blade deeper into Merlin's heart. He falls to the ground, coughing up clots of blood. Shuddering with pain, he cocks his head toward the castle with fading eyes.

I can't believe what I'm seeing. I'm losing all sense of hope. And perhaps Merlin knows that. He lets warbling white flames extend from his nose and mouth like hot vapor. He rolls his head on his neck, shuts his eyes, and reopens them to complete fire.

"No, Merlin," Azur whispers. "Death would be more favorable, old friend. You know this."

But it's too late.

"The girl is the least of your concerns." Merlin's eyes redden until iron-hot. "You failed, Morgan. Now Camelot's victory is imminent."

Even Morgan steps back.

"Essah tah je evanescehah oblivnohamehcha! Convertaha mesha in manesqui intokiah apparatuseeh!"

The blade pushes out from Merlin's chest amid a tornado of wind and white fire.

"Oh God," I whisper.

Morgan grasps her fusionah and points the barrel at Merlin. Her irises swirl with red and gold. Her teeth grit. She clicks the hammer back and fires.

But too late: Merlin's body flashes into a wisp of white light that slams into the sky and strikes the earth. The world shakes, and then all is still. Morgan stands wide-eyed and furious, eyes searching. She screams in defeat and retreats to her soldiers, shouting at them, activating them. Enslaving them.

"Merlin stole more magic, Azur," I hear myself say. "Didn't he?"

I glance at the alchemist. He's lost in thought. Refusing the clear truth in front of us. His old eyes narrow on Morgan. "Right now, we have a witch to slay." He pulls down his goggles, lifts his saber high, and runs to help the king.

It's a scene of good fighting evil, and I'm not sure who will be victorious. Just beyond the gates, Arthur slices at Morgan's soldiers as cannonballs slam into the ground. Excalibur is not only an unthinkable conquest for Morgan, it's stronger than her magic, and Arthur's copperless blade slays drone after drone as he seeks his sister. Gauntlet seizing his entire right arm, the king plunges Excalibur into another drone's chest. Dark, steaming blood pours free. Flashes of white light overcome the iron jaws. Eyes turn red like a deadly sun and then fade.

The thunderous booms go silent. It's enough for some of the knights to stop, pant, and wait.

Then the ground caves in.

THIRTY-FOUR

Possessed soldiers, warriors of Jerusalem, Round Table knights—they scream as they fall into the abyss. My hands cover my mouth in horror as I watch them fight to climb the avalanche of dirt. Most fail.

As they fall, Victor rises. I'm flush against the wall as taloned claws pull up Merlin's weapon, grip the dirt, crawl to a slow stop. Wings lie at its side, cold and mechanical, untouched by Azur's *jaseemat*.

I sputter for air.

Because Victor's blue eyes are rimmed with gold.

Morgan falls back to avoid the collapse of land. Her soldiers shift in direction once they see the magnificent monster.

I backpedal to the castle, unable to tear my eyes from the Victor. Once inside, my hand slips against the wall.

"Oh!"

I've pushed open a door to a massive wooden wheel looking over the moat, where drones barrel through to avoid Victor's—

Merlin's—blasts of fire. My eyes dart to each detail of the mechanism. I know what cranking it would do. "Raise the steel platforms."

Next to me, blood splatters. A drone falls. Before I can scream, there's a blast, and Percy is there, a smoking fusionah in hand. His face is thick with dirt and blood. There are heavy footsteps on the drawbridge, and Percy turns toward them. Two of Morgan's soldiers appear, all too close to the gates for comfort. Percy's fusionah kills them fast.

I want to escape this madness. But if I did so, I'd be waiting for Morgan to corner me, extract bewildering coordinates from my mind, and torture me, even if she can't use *Telum Paret* on anyone here. I'd be waiting for her to enslave me through her thievery of magic, to claim the Grail, and then what?

Three bolts left. Drones are dreadfully close to Camelot's walls, and I have a plan for them, but the bolts are more urgent. I race across the drawbridge. Once I reach the other side, my shortened dress lets me slide in the dirt, grab the quiver, and set it across my back. I stand, snap the bolts to shorten them, and fit one to my crossbow.

I catch sight of Arthur by the outskirts of the forest. Excalibur raised above his head, he freezes when he sees Merlin's machine. But as he gawks, something black moves behind him.

"Arthur!" I scream.

The king turns in time to slam Excalibur against a drone, but he's caught off-guard when another appears, its saw-like blade a caveman's version of Lancelot's hooked edge.

Arthur isn't fast enough to strike twice.

The blade comes down, ripping Arthur's skin from

neck to waist. The bolt falls from my crossbow as it happens. More drones come after me, but I cannot aim, I cannot fire. I'm not a soldier—I'm a bloody handmaid playing war. How could I possibly make a difference?

In front of Arthur, a copper-tipped shaft strikes between the drone's red eyes. The plates of the point snap open on the other side, trapping the bolt to the skull. From the city walls stands Owen, an empty crossbow in one hand, a second copper-tipped bolt in the other. He fits it in place and aims again, should the drone's dying feat be in retaliation.

But Morgan's soldier falls dead.

And my eyes burn with shameful tears.

Arthur limps away, blood on his lips. Pushing emotion aside, I grasp another bolt, ignoring the sharp edges of the point slicing through my glove and into my palm. My breathing heavy, I affix the bolt to my crossbow and ready myself to fight through this.

"Send for the infirmary!" Owen calls over his shoulder. Below, my father overseeing the archery front reiterates the cry.

Owen leaps rashly from the wall, straight into a sea of armored bodies. A cannonball flies through the spot where he once stood. It slams into the gallows. Shards fly through the square, forcing me to cover my head and run until I reach the gates. Victor's screeches chill me. I race over the drawbridge back to the stone wall. I can't breathe, might never breathe again. Knights spared from the long drop to the catacombs curse brashly and jump out of its way.

The wheel connected to the iron platforms is right next to me—

"Destroy it!" Morgan screeches.

Victor extends its limbs in an attacking stance nearly two hundred feet from Morgan's legion. Fire blasts from its mouth. Drones continue through the flames. Knights, warriors, and serfs stand their ground for as long as they can, but their bravery is limited and most inevitably flee.

Only Marcus remains. And Morgan is no fool—she's spotted her traitor. "Serf! I'll have your mother's blood!" She summons more drones. When they hear her screeched magic, they straighten and march forth.

Three black-armored soldiers rise in the fog. One slices Marcus's face, cutting a fine line from his eyebrow to chin. Marcus slams Lancelot's sword against the drones' backs, sending them into the depths of the crater.

More storm toward Marcus, but they'll have to pass through the moat's murky waters first. I race back to the wheel and set my weight against a spoke the length of my body, gritting my teeth and crying out as the mechanism slowly gives. Black boots splash through the water. The wheel churns, and I lead it clockwise. The drones are too simpleminded to notice iron platforms extending from under the castle, covering the water. Too slowly they move and so are crushed against the bank of the moat. I lean against the wheel, catching my breath. Percy and Galahad kill Morgan's trapped minions.

Marcus sends his horse running into the forest. He sprints toward Victor as Morgan's cries summon more slaves awake from the inanimate machines they were. He crouches low in case Victor's tail were to swing and knock him clear into the long, black drop.

"Marcus ... " What have I asked of him?

A drone races across the steel platforms for me. But I don't scream this time. I push away fear and lift my right arm. Red eyes flash at mine. A blood-soaked blade lifts to strike. My finger yanks at the pulley. The bolt flies perfectly into its head, and suddenly, I can't remember if it's the second or third life I've taken. I'm horrified, but I cannot think of it anymore than that.

I cannot think anymore.

I have to make sure Marcus isn't killed.

Pulling tightly on his thick leather gloves, Marcus grabs hold of the scales and lifts, but then drops with a wince. His gloves have ripped. His hands are covered in blood. The scales are razor-sharp.

He ducks to avoid Victor's spewing flames. Lancelot's sword in his grasp, Marcus sets the blade between the scales. Hilt clenched in one hand, point in the other. It presses against the tearing leather on his left palm.

Using the sword to lift himself, he maneuvers the hilt higher on Victor's scales, then the blade. The steel's strength does the work for him. Shining spots of red peek through the leather, making his grasp slippery—the blade is clearing a path. With a pained face, he moves the sword higher.

The beast sways in frustration as Marcus climbs. To steady himself, he grips a large triangular scale running down the spine. Bright-blue eyes too human watch him. Only the sorcerer has eyes like these, and Marcus is stalled for too long not to realize that. He takes a breath and pulls down the long lever protruding from the shoulder blades, using every bit of strength. The dragon goes silent. Its eyes close. Marcus leans over, breathing heavily.

Then Victor bursts with movement. Wings come to life from Azur's *jaseemat*. Fluid, strong, the wingspan extends into two crescent moons of humming metal.

"Get off, Marcus! Run!" I scream. I don't know if the ghost in the machine can control the danger it is. There's only one bolt left in my grasp. I'll need more to cover him as he runs. Slicing through the smoke is another set of red eyes. My crossbow fires, and those eyes turn white from death.

As Victor leaps into the air, Marcus stumbles onto its back. But when the monster is too airborne for him to fall safely, his bloodied hands grab the scales. Rabid blasts pepper away at drones below. Angry blue eyes flare as Victor's creaking body twists toward the ground.

"Merlin!" Marcus screams. But he cannot scream again and keep his hold.

The dragon alights the soldiers with fire, swooping over the ground. Low enough now for Marcus to drop. He lands on his stomach, rolling away just in time to miss the length of the wing snapping down as Victor returns to the sky.

Marcus backs away on his hands and knees, close to the crater's edge, but turning in time to avoid the drop. Then the tail's mace slams against the ground, and the land breaks under Marcus's weight. He hangs from the edge. Only his elbows serve as leverage as his legs dangle wildly.

"Marcus!" I scream.

I race into the thick of battle. Cannon blasts make their way toward me. Drones in the thousands, knights slaying them. There are more bolts on the field, and I seize a handful, reserving one for a quick kill. *Don't think.*

I slide in the dirt when I reach him. "Marcus!"

His hands grip mine. "You can't hold my weight," he says through frightened, chattering teeth.

"Yes, I can!" I lie, unwilling to let myself see the future of finding his cold body below.

He shakes his head. "We'll both fall."

I'm losing my grip from the swirling blood on his palms. But then a strong hand grabs Marcus's arm and lifts.

It's Owen.

Dirt on his face, empty crossbow in hand, he pushes me aside and grunts as he helps Marcus to stable land just as the edge breaks away.

The three of us watch the split-second in front of us fade to what could have been. I lean my head against my brother's shoulder. *Owen, you've returned.*

We stand. Owen gauges Marcus. "You all right?"

Marcus's face is shockingly white, but he nods.

Owen turns to me. "Viv, send anyone you find to get Arthur to safety." He grabs my hand, and for a split second, I wonder if he'll tell me again this is not the place for a girl. "Be careful. Morgan calls for the handmaid of Camelot." He steps closer. "She's ordered her soldiers to take you alive."

No order from Owen to escape myself—the wise thing to do. But I cannot think about his terrifying words now. As drones turn their empty faces toward me, I regard Arthur, hunched over, depending fully on Excalibur for strength. Azur calls to him, fending off advancing drones as Arthur twists in pain. With one final look to Marcus and Owen, I run.

I run straight for Arthur. Everyone in the kingdom fights to keep Camelot from Morgan. I know this. If I can help it, I won't let all we've sacrificed be for nothing.

I circumvent the crater. My ears listen for the whistling of cannonballs. The heavy footsteps of the drones—

A pair of red demon eyes breaks through the smoke before me.

My hand flies to the quiver on my back, but a bit of shining silver whipping through the air is faster, copper edges turning it into a ball of fire. The throwing star strikes the drone's head and sends it into the castle wall with a loud clang.

From across the field, Galahad turns back to battle. And I rush for the king whose singing blade impales the stomach of a demon-eyed soldier. Azur next to him decapitates two more.

"Your Majesty!" I stumble at the sight of Arthur's skin curling away from his wound. A drone's shield slams into his jaw, throwing the king off balance.

Excalibur flies into the air and lands a foot in front of me.

"Give it to me!" Arthur bellows, hand outstretched, green eyes frantic.

The blade shines through the smoke, a spectacle of power, just as when I first saw it. I inch closer. The gauntlet is enormous, as Arthur is a man nearly twice my size. But as I think this, the gauntlet seems to shrink until it's small enough for me to wield Excalibur. My lips part with desire.

"Girl, now!" Arthur screams. More drones advance.

I seize it by the blade right where it meets the hilt. I grasp it tightly even when the edge presses into my palms. Excalibur is dreadfully heavy, but perhaps even more of a burden to Arthur. I'm careful to avoid the steel gauntlet gripping the sword that knows I am not the king. The whirring blades inside spin with a maddening, bone-slicing pitch. The euphoria of its gleam...

Excalibur wants me to claim it, I realize. *My sliced-off arm would become legend, like the skeptical farmer's.*

Shaking free of such insanity, I reach Arthur and slam the sword into his hands before the temptation is too great to refuse. The blade chimes as it leaves my grasp. The gauntlet locks itself around Arthur's shoulder. The king swings Excalibur at those two oncoming drones, stealing the lives of both.

Arthur's face is white like his hair; his mouth and teeth coated in crimson. He lays a heavy hand on my shoulder.

"He is hurt!" Azur calls through the noise.

"I still have some fight left!" Arthur shouts back with strained effort. He glances at me with eyes too pain-stricken ever to survive.

It has to be now. "Your Majesty, you need to get inside the castle!"

Arthur shakes his head. He regards the danger around us. "Forget me. Get Lancelot. In the dungeons. Send my wife to safety."

I fear for Arthur's well-being, but nod. I won't think what it could mean for his life.

"Go to where the knights practice sword fighting—"

"I know where the dungeons are."

He doesn't ask how. With a quick nod, he dismisses me, and I run to the castle, praying the cannons won't find me there.

———

Inside, one could nearly forget Camelot was under attack.

It's quiet enough that the thumping of my boots reverberates loudly against the carpeted floor. My stomach lurches at the memory of agonizing screams, how they splintered the air.

By the trees of Avalon machines guard that which Camelot's son will one day find.

Arthur cannot die.

At the end of the corridor, the door awaits. I take the iron ring in hand and pull, descending into a dismal, mildew-smelling cellar, colder than the blacksmith's could ever be. Through little light, I make out thick iron bars. Labyrinths to and from each cell of torture.

Stretchers with iron handcuffs, tables with delicate tools boasting too many sharp edges, wires connected to apparatuses I know are steam-powered, ones that would send nasty shocks to metallic strips on a prisoner's arms, legs, neck. Hooks used for anything a creative mind could conjure up.

My foot slips on some condensation. "Oh!" I gasp. It echoes.

There's some shuffling in the east end. Some whispers. A woman's voice. But it's a man who speaks. "Who's there?"

It's gruff. It's Lancelot. Chains clank. "God save you if you're one of Morgan's." The voice drips with vengeance.

I shut my eyes from the horrible devices. "It's Vivienne."

"Vivienne!" Guinevere calls.

I follow her voice through the maze and past copper poles as thick as a man's waist. A furnace at the bottom—ashes of God knows what pouring out. Owen told me once of a contraption like this, how chains would bind a man's reluctant embrace to the burning metal. The stench of charred flesh hits me, and I'm terrified to think it might be fresh.

"Here!" Guinevere calls. I find the cell they share, Guinevere with her back against the putrid wall, Lancelot standing in front, sweat on his brow but coherence in his eyes. Red blisters peek out from under his tunic and sleeves, like he was forced to hold fire.

"The hell are you doing here? You should have left with the aeroships!" Lancelot growls through a thicker beard. Guinevere's eyes are dark with fatigue. Her hair has been cut to her chin, the first form of torture to a lady of the court, but she's alive and she's safe. And I could say goodbye now.

"Arthur's hurt. They need your help, my lord." I grip the iron bars. "And you, my lady. We need to get you out of Camelot!"

Lancelot doesn't think twice about answering. "The keys are on the wall. Hurry!" He points down the dark corridor. I want to laugh or cry at the thought of searching for more keys, but an iron ring is right where he said it would be with several keys strung onto it. I yank it down. We fit the proper key to its lock and swing the door open.

Guinevere rushes out to embrace me. "Oh, Vivienne."

I hug her quickly. But I can't make this any harder. I must act as a lady-in-waiting, not a friend. "We have to hurry!"

She lifts her chin. "I left Arthur once. I won't do it again."

Lancelot grabs her arm. "Guinevere, don't be foolish. All that is Camelot is gone. You can still make it. There must be some aeroships left."

She looks as though she might cry. "Lancelot? Save him."

Lancelot stares at her too long for only friendship and pulls her close in a tormented embrace, kissing her forehead once and setting off.

I can't bear to be in this hellish place any longer. "Guinevere, please! At least to safety above!"

She nods, and we run for the stairs.

———————

Outside, smoke and flames twist together. Steam bursts from Victor's back as it dives upon its prey.

The smell of clashing metal fills my nose. The whirring of aeroships' propellers and the cannons thundering ring in my ears. The knights have saved the drilling ram from Corbenic's attack and drive it into the iron men who press back just as gruesomely. Morgan's soldiers advance, and they couldn't care less about their armor or mechanical parts spiraling out from the drills' sharp points, breaking through their skin and impaling them. They were forged to do but one thing—take Camelot for the witch.

The only way to convince Guinevere to take shelter is if

I go with her. Lock myself away, ponder how I could know the coordinates of Avalon. Keep far from Morgan at all costs. Lancelot runs for the stables, returning with a horse and riding to the gates, no time now to get armor. He grasps a fusionah and carries it into the field.

I'm watching everything happen from a place outside my body. I'm not really here, I'm in the clock tower with Merlin. And we're about to send Caldor into flight.

In clouds above three kingdoms past, following enlightened thinkers vast.

"Vivienne," Guinevere sobs from the castle's steps. Her hand reaches for mine. "Please. I can't lose you, too."

But I can't ignore so much death on the fields. The men the witch stole are limitless to pit against us.

Morgan screams against the noise of war, *"Mordred! Seize what is rightfully yours!"* She stretches her black-robed arms toward the mechanical dragon, but Azur's *jaseemat* stands strong against her magic. Victor, likewise, cannot kill her.

A shimmer of gold catches my eye from behind Morgan's battalion. I look again. The figure steps forward. I rub my eyes, making sure I'm seeing clearly.

Through the smoke, a man of solid gold steps toward Camelot, wielding a pulsating sword the length of his body.

THIRTY-FIVE

A desperate woman, whose son was born not expected to live…
Her magic made it possible to combine blood and machine…
The gypsy's words did no justice to Mordred. Though his armor is plain, his face is the color of sunshine with vibrant hair to match. Like his mother wanted Mordred's human side to rival that which keeps him alive.

That which keeps him alive is a machine.

With white eyes and a face reinforced with iron hinges, he marches for the king. Arthur sends Excalibur into a drone's heart with no idea his son stands behind him. War is too loud, even without the deafening whir of Mordred's blade. A lever on the hilt activates a burst of steam, propelling rows of deadly hooks to orbit the edge.

Guinevere shouts my name, but I race from the castle despite her cries, as though anything I could do might change Arthur's fate. Mordred lifts his hell-made sword with arms whose joints are metal rods impaling the skin. He swings the heft of his blade at the king's unguarded back. The blunt impact sends Arthur to his knees.

"Fire to the land! Force them inside Camelot!" Morgan cries. The drones keep coming.

Mordred prepares to kill. But Arthur misses the sawing blow and finds his feet again. He faces his attacker, staring in horror at the same shape of eyes, the same jaw as his. Excalibur chimes as it strikes Mordred's sword. The twisted hooks catch on the ethereal blade. King and machine fight to conquer the other.

Thick smoke swallows any sign of Marcus or Owen. Lancelot is missing. I search for Galahad, for Percy, for anyone I know, but cannot bear to face the fallen bodies. One might belong to the blacksmith who's kept my secret for years.

Mordred wields his saw-like sword with never-ending strength. I cover my mouth, tears striking at my eyes. The boy's mind might have been human once. Perhaps he begged his mother for death instead of mechanical life. I gasp for air and watch him hack away at the faltering king. How foolish I was to think something as weak as my damned crossbow could ever contend against the weaponry in this war.

I don't care. There are more bolts by the archery front, and I store them in my quiver. I run straight into war even if it means I could be killed. Or worse, taken alive. I can't ignore how afraid I am that torture or death may not be far off. But Morgan cannot have Camelot.

Arthur disarms Mordred, slamming his heel into his son's gold-plated chest, sending him to the ground.

"Mordred, get up!" Morgan calls. "Claim what is yours!"

My will is stronger now. Three drones storm after me with the same empty eyes as the rest. They're to take me alive. My crossbow kills each of the poor bastards before they get the chance.

Mordred shakes unnaturally as though the wires holding him together are coming loose. Perhaps Morgan's demands are too much. Certainly she cannot think he'll take Excalibur—only the king can wield that sword. And Marcus never gave her the blueprints that would allow her to create an identical blade.

Morgan charges toward her fallen son, white hair rippling. She regards her brother and extends her hand, screeching in a foreign tongue. It sends Arthur straight into the air, then straight to the ground. His bones crunch with the landing.

Morgan's eyes roll into whiteness. Her voice rustles the wind.

"*Telum Paret dederresha tete ahnimum. Non quia sum paret tibishi. Tu mihi Telum Paret. Esta abiit avesho liberos-hikah arbitrio.*"

Each word clenches my temples like an iron vise. But it's nowhere nearly as wretched for me as it is for Mordred. My heart sinks with pity for the boy whose eyes roll back in human pain. Whose limbs shudder as though staving off blades and arrows.

He goes still. I'm frozen in place, watching. Silently, his heels edge him upward, and he's a machine once more.

Morgan's eyes shine with insanity. Dread crawls over Arthur's face. A drone slams me to the ground with the hilt of its sword. A shooting pain electrifies my body. I wince. The red-eyed demon reaches for me. My arm stretches. My finger tugs the pulley back. Bolt through the neck. The drone shudders until death claims it. They will not take me.

Lancelot rides through the smoke, sword in hand. He decapitates an unsuspecting drone. "Arthur!" Lancelot kicks the huffing steed to go faster, though it's nearly hopeless.

Victor soars over us, lashing fire onto Morgan. But the witch guards herself with a shield of magic against the white inferno. Hopeless or exhausted, Arthur trembles, and Excalibur's gauntlet slams against the ground.

"Take it, Mordred! You have Arthur's blood, my son!" Morgan screams. Her boy faces the dropped sword and his dying father. Their victory is within reach. And when the mechanical dragon claws at the air, climbing back into the sky, I know I've failed. Morgan is stronger than anything I could ever build.

Victor hovers unsteadily above Morgan as though hurt or in anguish. But then it opens its mouth and speaks. "Arthur!"

Merlin's voice. Calling for the king as Mordred storms for Excalibur, the boy looking unsure of his destiny even with such stoic features. Arthur's eyes widen. His lips shape themselves around Merlin's name, the name of the man he saw as a father, the man who sacrificed his soul so Camelot could win.

Merlin hasn't given up, and my hope is stronger upon realizing that. Now it's time to end all this.

Arthur shudders to his feet as Victor—*Merlin*—circles the sky. But Mordred reaches Excalibur first, his own saw-like blade fallen and forgotten. Mordred's arm slips inside the gauntlet. Arthur recoils in horror as the boy's face flashes white in sick pain. The blades whir inside, slicing off Mordred's arm. I clamp both hands over my mouth. Blood spurts from Mordred's lips, but he chokes it back.

Morgan casts her arm high and screeches desperate magic louder than her boy's screams.

The boy-machine shudders still and looks at his shoulder where gauntlet meets armor. He bites down on his bloody lip. But Morgan never needed Marcus to bring her blueprints— Arthur's blood was always enough. And if not Arthur's blood, then an arm mostly metal. The gauntlet solders to Mordred's body. The blades inside cease their whirring as they concede to Mordred. Arthur's jaw slackens in disbelief. I can barely breathe. Mordred grips Excalibur like the sword is part of him. His eyes lock on the king.

Morgan gleams with joy. But Arthur is quick to rise and seizes Mordred's dropped saw-like blade. The madman he was in Morgan's wood has vanished now that Merlin fights alongside him. That all of Camelot fights. Our lives might be lost in this battle, mine as well. But that can't matter. Now, we must fight together.

At the forest's outskirts, Marcus's dismissed horse searches for refuge from the growing smoke. I jump into its saddle, take a breath, and kick its sides. We leap over fallen bodies. I pry my eyes away, heading after Arthur through the ascending fog. I listen for the weapon, for Morgan's screeches, for the king's fight. Balancing atop the horse, I let bolt after bolt fly through the air.

We break through the smoke, but the witch's magic has

spooked my horse, and it won't run anymore. I kick its sides, but it whinnies angrily, and so I leap off its back, running for my king on foot.

Mordred and the witch advance for Arthur. Lancelot is a fast target for black-plated soldiers. He fends off arrows using the blade of his fusionah to shield himself. Eardrum-shattering blasts invade each drone's skull between clicks. Armored hands likewise reach for me, and I must be faster with my crossbow.

"Kill him, Mordred! Kill him now!" Morgan foregoes her swords for magic, her hands moving in circles. An orb of light glows between her palms. Victor swoops low and blasts her with fire, forcing her magic gone. She lifts her scream to the sky. A desperate look of triumph comes over Arthur's face.

Arthur swings the caveman's blade at his son. Strikes Mordred's solid chest. Seizes Mordred's throat. He lifts the boy. Mordred grips Arthur's neck in return, refusing defeat. In one fast move, Excalibur saws at Arthur's chest. The king shudders, but steels his eyes on his heir. "I'm sorry, boy, for what your life became."

Arthur yanks Mordred's head forward, exposing his son's neck. Victor soars toward the king. Copper-ridged bearings in the hundreds pepper against Mordred and Arthur himself until the boy's spine is sliced open. Blood and wires spill free. Mordred's eyes go still as the connecting passageway to his mind bursts with steam and fire. Excalibur melts away from Mordred's shoulder, the steel warped and ugly. Arthur stumbles back a few feet and then collapses to the ground. Mordred's blade in Arthur's grip runs out of steam. Saw-like hooks dig at the bloodied dirt and stop. And then Mordred himself collapses, falling over dead.

Morgan cries into the smoke-filled air. She is at her boy's side instantly, shaking his body. "No, Mordred! Look at me!" she cries. "Look at me." Her fingernails bore into his skin, turning blood-red what was human, only scratching what was not. *"Yaty ala alhyah,* Mordred, *Yaty ala alhyah."*

Come to life. But it's too late for Mordred.

Morgan shakes with fury. She stands, emitting huffing breaths, low and demonic, and pushes her palms together as though forcing two crashing rivers into each other. An invisible power bubbles and twists, like air distorted above a flame. She eyes Lancelot, galloping for her.

He'll die. Perhaps I will soon after. Another drone rises in front of me. The bolt in my crossbow frees itself into its temple. Lancelot bellows a name.

Marcus.

My heart presses against my stomach. I can't tell if Lancelot calls Marcus for help or cries for his squire. Victor dives, spitting bearings and alchemic fire. Smoke clouds my vision, and I don't know where to run. I back away from the swarms of drones with their eyes on me. I barely have time to reload my crossbow's bolt compartment.

"Marcus!" Lancelot screams again.

I run onward. I send bolts into the skulls of as many drones as I can. Smoke parts in time for Lancelot to speed toward the witch. I can't see Marcus anywhere.

Morgan snaps her face toward the oncoming knight.

She'll kill him.

"No, Lancelot!"

But he doesn't hear me. He lifts his sword to attack, and a translucent sphere in Morgan's hands readies for it. Morgan throws the weight of her magic at Lancelot. He's knocked off his horse and slams against the ground.

Blades lost in the fog, Morgan unsheathes a dagger from her thigh. My boots dig into the wet ground as I run, crossbow loaded. She's ready to send the blade flying into Lancelot's heart. I check my bolt and pull the string taut as she lifts the shining blade high—the bolt might not damage her in the slightest, or perhaps would bounce off her and come sailing back at me.

Oh God.

But across the way, my king lies dying because of her.

"No, you will not win," I whisper. My only regret is not advising Merlin to add more fuel to those harvesters.

I fire, and the bolt flies true, straight for her brow. But her hand is quick and snatches it in midair. Her white eyes flash at mine with recognition. The burn falling down her neck, like a rejected dragon tattoo of Camelot, fades to snow-white skin. "Not quick enough, *apprentice*. Tell me, is his mother's life a price worthy of your love?"

I don't know what she means, but there's no time to question it. A loud blast is followed by a ribbon of smoke, silhouetting her against grayness. Behind her stands the blacksmith. A fusionah rests in his hand, aimed at the witch.

Morgan keels over, and her dagger falls to the ground. Her skin falls with age. Lines and spots splatter across her face. I hold my breath, not daring to move.

In a fit of anger, she tears the armor from her body, where a sprinkling of red spills from the skin atop her heart. The blacksmith advances, reloading his weapon, but too slowly. Drones fall in line behind him, and he has to turn quickly and seize the heavy hook at his waist to slice into their barreled chests.

Morgan touches the blood on her skin. Eyes narrow as though I was the one who fired. "This isn't how Arthur's sister dies." Angry tears spill down her old face, catching in the wrinkles, spidering outward. "Not when I'm so close. Not if my son can be brought back."

Horror overwhelms me. What would she do to her dead boy's body?

She sets her hand flush against the wound. The outline of her fingers bursts with diamond light. Her hand falls from her skin, perfectly healed.

Immune to copper. She lifts my bolt, and it turns to dust in her fist. I quickly affix another. With the wave of her hand, the crossbow rips from my forearm and flies across the field. It smashes into a tree.

She advances faster. Morgan le Fay, after a lady-in-waiting. *This is how I die.*

I back away on soft, bloodied ground. Her fingers reach for my mind, and her eyes go white from the words *Sensu Ahchla,* and I must guard the part inside me that's hiding the world of golden cobblestone and a leather-wrapped chalice. I trip over dead knights, fusionahs still tight in their hands, my heels digging into the dirt. With each stride, escape from Morgan becomes more impossible. A sharp piercing splits my skull, and I feel her invade my mind. I wrench away from her magical hold. There's no dagger or sword to stop her. Nothing in my apron's pockets. Not even my damned copper viewer.

Another blast strikes Morgan in the neck. She falls to her knees, one hand pressing against the bright red blood spilling down her collar bone, a wince crossing her face. I tear my eyes to the direction of the shot.

Marcus stands not far off holding a smoking fusionah. His eyes go wide when he sees me. "Vivienne!" He breaks into a run.

Then Morgan's blood-soaked grip is tight around my throat, forcing me to stare into her demonic, white eyes. Marcus fires again. He misses. I dig my nails into Morgan's icy wrists. The blacksmith turns from the dead drones at his feet and throws his fusionah into the air. It lands a good distance behind me.

I reach back, and my hand falls upon its familiar shape of twisted metal—

The fingernails of Morgan's other hand grasp my temples, and there's a flash of light—

But then another fusionah blasts. This time straight into her forehead. This she cannot avoid. Her fingers drop from my skin.

She stares at me in confusion. Her eyes narrow on the hot fusionah in my hand. "An apprentice?"

Morgan collapses like a rag doll at my feet. Through a break in the smoke, the blacksmith nods, folding over to rest his hands on tired knees. Marcus slides in the dirt to my side as the smell of burnt trees and grass envelops us. I throw my arms around his shoulders, and he pulls me into an embrace.

"It's all right," I say. When I look up again, the black-smith is gone.

But around us, drones disengage, one at a time. Shut off, fall dead. Freed from their magical bindings. Human again.

Finally.

———

Victor glides above the land, burning the bodies of Morgan's dead, leaving knights and warriors intact for proper burials. Then it lands in front of Azur. War has taken a toll on both man and machine.

"Well done, old friend," Azur says. "You can let go now, but not for the next world. Meet me in Jerusalem and I will restore you. The Grail awaits."

The monster falls still, its mace-like tail shortening to the mechanical one I built, eyes black and lifeless. A burst of steam escapes from the valve at the top and whistles to nearly nothing.

The ghost within finds the sky, the form no longer a man. I can hear Merlin now, "Let the Trojans have their horse while Camelot has her dragon." Like rhythmic tides under moonlight, he flies in waves as though he's done it for centuries. As though he always had a monster dwelling inside.

With a final look to the fallen castle, the great weapon of Camelot soars east, letting a strong current guide him to Jerusalem.

"Goodbye, Merlin," I whisper in amazement.

Azur walks amongst his dead, kneeling and uttering prayers. He closes their eyes. Those who survived sing funeral hymns.

The stillness is peppered with slow, agonizing cries of the dying. I walk amongst them, knights and squires and serfs I've known my entire life now in desperate need of the Grail's protection against death. Blood spills from their mouths. Eyes glaze over in pain at the loss of hands or entire arms. Stabs to the chest. Peeling skin. Most hopeless with fatal wounds. Warriors from Jerusalem, tranquil.

Up ahead, a bloodied Lancelot collapses in front of the king lying by Mordred's shriveled-up body, now an ugly tarnished bronze. The poor boy looks nearly too human with pitiful mechanical features.

Behind me, Guinevere races out onto the field with Galahad following.

"Arthur!" The queen falls to the blood-drenched ground and lays the king's head in her lap. I crouch next to her, and my hand finds her shoulder, squeezing gently, not feeling the thin fabric of her garment for the devastation surrounding us.

As Arthur wrenches Excalibur from Mordred's body, Lancelot kneels. "It can't be that bad," the knight says.

Arthur cringes as he lifts his armor, pulling his tunic with it. Blood stains the queen's dress. I want to look away, but I catch a glimpse of purple and black skin peeling away from his serrated wounds, and my heart sinks.

"Can't say I've had worse." Arthur's voice balances on a fine line between frightened tears and mortality. With this, he regards his champion. "Find Avalon, Lancelot. Send the knights to help Gawain's infantry. We've abandoned the legend that the coordinates are inside Camelot, but we can no longer afford to. Make sure all this wasn't done in vain."

I should speak, tell the king we're close, that with Merlin's help—oh, *Merlin*—we could understand how it's all connected to me. I squeeze my fists around Guinevere's sleeve, but say nothing.

Lancelot nods. "We could have used you on the quest." He forces a smile only a brother could offer, and I'm grateful my outpouring tears are quiet.

Arthur returns the smile. "If you'd been king, and I'd been your champion, Camelot would have found it long ago, my brother."

Galahad stands close by. With a rough incline of his head, the king sputters, "Make sure it is so." The knight nods.

Guinevere touches her husband's cheek. The king presses her hand to his lips. "Had this been your home, I'd have made sure you never suffered like you did in Lyonesse." Arthur shakes with agony, pleading for a few more breaths. But death hears nothing and shuts his eyes. The king's hand falls to his chest, limp and lifeless.

Lancelot rises, running a hand over his face. Guinevere holds Arthur close and cries. I stand, looking across the land that is Camelot. Arthur's land. I wonder if all of this was for naught—if those here fought and died so Arthur would die, too. So strange it is to think only moments ago he was still here.

Then, across the way and through the trees, I make out a

grayness that wasn't there before. "Oh God," I breathe, running to the forest's edge.

The eastern farmlands originally spared, the barn we slept in, his family's home. On fire. All is gone but the remains of those who tried to escape. Even more ruthless is the horror that he who double-crossed Morgan would face.

I look back. Marcus approaches Guinevere and Lancelot, jogging from a band of squires helping the wounded inside the castle. He catches my eye and reads the dread on my face. When he looks past me, his lips part, and he rushes toward the fire and smoke.

He's swift and nearly passes me, but I hold him back.

"Gone. They're gone, Marcus," I whisper.

He tries to free himself, teeth clenched with mania. Then he inhales a breath and holds it, the truth of it washing over him. He spurts out violent sobs as we fall to the ground. I wrap my arms around his neck and press my lips to his bloodied cheek as we watch.

THIRTY-SIX

The living retreat to the castle in silence.

I don't know how many survived. Perhaps thirty knights, forty serfs. Maybe more if I were feeling optimistic.

My brother catches up as Marcus and I pass over the drawbridge. Owen throws his arm around my shoulder and kisses my head. He doesn't say anything about Marcus's hand in mine. He wouldn't. Not now.

We're surrounded by memories of Morgan in a paradise now lost: shattered gallows, destroyed streets, and crumbled towers. Guards carry the bodies of fallen soldiers to lie in the gardens for now. Behind us, Lancelot and Galahad push a small wagon carrying the body of the once king, hand grasping Excalibur's hilt, sword's point at his feet. The gauntlet is warped from Mordred's hold. That which gave Arthur Camelot, a burden he never wanted, was the very thing to have seized his life. By way of his own blood, no less. The queen follows in tears, having quietly refused when I asked if she'd wish to have me by her side.

My father staggers at the king's corpse, clothes tattered even from the supposed safety of the archery front. When he sees Owen and me, his shoulders fall with relief. He assists Ector and Bors with carrying in the wounded.

Marcus and I meet Azur in the courtyard. The alchemist sets his goggles atop his turban and takes my hand. "Jerusalem will mourn Arthur's death. But those who died today died with honor. Never forget that."

He waits, possibly to see if I'll ask to escape this wreckage for Jerusalem, to work alongside him to bring Merlin back— and how could that even be possible? But I don't ask to leave Camelot. I hug Azur goodbye, and with that, he knows I'll stay here for now to mourn the home we once knew.

Azur boards his aeroship, and it lifts off, sails beating the air, propellers guiding it east, following the rest of the fleet. The flags of Jerusalem lower to half-mast. A salute.

Marcus drops my hand. His eyes are red. "I'll take to the knights' quarters now."

I nod, and he leaves.

━━━━━

We convene by the cliffs where the anvil that once held Excalibur stands covered in moss, skirted by long grass. Waves crash into the rock. I squint in the sunlight, searching for aeroships that might carry my mother and the rest of Camelot's subjects. But Owen says they'll likely take to the north for now. No one would want to see their home like this.

Few dress for the occasion, even if it is the funeral of Camelot's king.

As the earth falls over Arthur's shrouded body, Galahad reminds Lancelot of the king's last request: the Grail. The thought of *why bother?* drifts until the king's champion speaks.

"If we rebuild Camelot and find the Grail, our home can be the paradise Arthur wanted it to be. I owe him that."

Lancelot holds Excalibur's shining blade, avoiding the armored sleeve. He regards the sword with an unreadable face and slams it into the anvil. It sparks as it slides into place and goes still to wait for the future king.

Guinevere stands next to her husband's champion. She finds me amongst the people, letting me see in her eyes how grateful she is for my part in this war. Lips form the words *thank you* even though the idea of gratitude feels foreign. I nod once.

Marcus clutches my hand. It's the first time I've seen him in days. He went to the farmlands after the fires died and stayed there for a long time. Now he's distant and looks as though he's abandoned food and sleep. The slice on his face is a faint red line now. His eyes are dark.

There's another crash from the ocean. I look over the cliff and watch birds fly through the clouds. I think of Caldor. I think of Merlin.

━━━━━

Marcus leads me into the gardens.

In the privacy of barren trees and trampled flowers, he

searches for words. My elm has been shattered to a splintered stump.

Finally, he speaks. "I have nothing left to fight for."

I brush my fingers across his cheek. I have no words of comfort.

He takes a breath. "My mother was the only reason I had to become a knight or betray Camelot. I didn't even get to properly bury her. The last minutes with my father were ones of—" He stops, biting his quivering lip still. "Her apron was all that was left, tied to her waist." His eyes finally meet mine. Oh God, their sadness. "I will seek the Grail."

A tremor hits the back of my throat. My own lip quivers now. I wonder if this is the last time I'll look into his eyes and, if so, how will I remember them in the years to come?

He squeezes my hands. "They offered me a place in Galahad's infantry after my role in activating Merlin's machine. Gawain said there are rogues in Athens. Three months away at most before the Grail is within our grasp. Maybe I can make it up to Arthur. I did nearly hand Camelot over to Morgan."

I turn so he won't see me cry. His arms circle my waist, and his chin rests on my shoulder. "Please, Vivienne."

After a deep breath, I nod. "We knew this day would come."

═══════

Guinevere's gown is modest, the color of sand. A veil covers her shorn hair. In the grand hall, she stands where she took her wedding vows, ready to see through her final act as queen before leaving for a nunnery in the north, leaving Lancelot to oversee the kingdom.

The blade in her hand is identical to the knight's. With hooks of copper instead of steel, it's the appropriate sword to knight Marcus with.

He kneels in front of Guinevere in a leather-lined blazer atop silver breastplates. Eyes kohled, fingers clenched around the tail of some dark fabric peeking out from his sleeve. He'll leave tonight in Galahad's infantry as a knight of Camelot. It could have been a very different outcome for Marcus, had the farmlands not burned, had his loyalty not swayed to Arthur's side.

Perhaps that's why she chose to burn them again.

I wonder if Marcus thinks of that.

I'm next to my father and brother by the window where the night is finally clear of smoke, showcasing a starry sky I haven't seen in days. Something flies across the moon, and for a moment, I think it might be Merlin and not the last aeroship to the north my father will insist I board. I suppose I should be elated that I'm finally leaving Camelot for another kingdom. But why do I feel empty instead?

The blade in Guinevere's hands touches Marcus's shoulders. He watches the queen with full eyes. "I knight thee Sir Marcus of Camelot."

We applaud as Marcus rises. Lancelot embraces him, and Marcus smiles, but it's a different smile now. His eyes find mine just briefly, but I would swear we stared at each other for an eternity. Mine well from happiness and grief as I recall the joyous seconds we stole under the tree. In the barn. When he asked me to run away with him. His very words "For love?" the closest we got to saying it aloud.

A dark figure by the doors catches my eye. Outside, a tall man heads for the village.

It's the blacksmith, the masked man who gave me the fusionah that ended Morgan's life.

———

Inside my family's tower, it's quiet.

Smoke looms over my mother's dressing table, dusting her jewelry with ash. Guinevere's lace veil sits next to the music box, mended by my mother's meticulous hand. A spool of thread winds down the carpet. Outside, there are no aeroships bringing her back. No joyous voices above the crashes of waves. All that remains is the story of Avalon. A tale different from what everyone else knew.

My mother meant to tell me something before Morgan's War. What was it?

A knock at the door. Owen steps in. "You missed dinner."

"Blood-thirsty handmaids do not live by bread alone." I smile in hopes it could rid me of nightmares of Morgan's haunting death at my hand.

My brother reaches me at the window. There are unspoken words between us, but we leave it alone. I owe him everything for saving Marcus's life. "I didn't expect to see you at the knighting ceremony," he says. The silver bolt in his ear is missing.

I watch the clock on Merlin's tower tick. The numbers are still there, save for the ones between the ten and the two. So strange to be away from it.

"It meant something to Marcus, having you there. You should know that."

My fingers wrap around my hair and drop the tendril just as quickly. I know this. I don't want to be reminded of it. "You fought, too. You weren't knighted."

"Don't deserve it. Maybe the quest will be my penance." He smiles as if he isn't hurt by the snub.

I return his smile with as much happiness as I can manage. It isn't a lot.

Outside, the knights are preparing to leave. Setting off after dusk gives them a head start without facing daytime heat in armor right away. They talk amongst themselves, possibly sharing the news of Morgan's curse being lifted from the rest of the land. The alliance with Corbenic has been reinstated now that Lancelot sent word of Morgan le Fay's death. But news of Arthur hasn't left Camelot. Not yet.

Beyond the drawbridge, Marcus leads his horse to the lake. I look elsewhere, not about to cry at something as silly as the thought of never seeing him again.

Owen adjusts the furs about his shoulders in preparation for cool northern nights. His kohl-lined eyes are smudged. He takes my hand.

"Vivienne, there's something else you should know."

THIRTY-SEVEN

Owen's words trample my mind as ferociously as my boots striking the gardens' brittle grass. I run with the will I thought I'd lost, but so much could depend on whether I find Marcus, whether I can see him one last time, no matter—

No matter what his reason.

My heart twists in a painful knot as I think of how he didn't tell me himself. My own brother had to.

I sneak through the break in the wall. The lavender dress I wore to the wedding oh so long ago catches on the rough edges, but I pull free. He's by the lake. I need to get there.

I catch sight of shimmering waves as the wind blows across the water. Standing there is Sir Marcus of Camelot.

He turns when he hears me approach, eyes still smudged with kohl. The skin on his neck is pink where his new tattoo crawls toward his jaw. Silver bolt through one ear. Thick furs hanging on his shoulders. Scuffed black boots on his feet. Leather on his back.

I'm out of breath but too angry to care. "You weren't going to say anything? You were just going to leave? Without telling me you and Lancelot made an agreement?"

He refuses to look at me. "My lady—"

"No, Marcus!" Every step toward him is more painful than the last. "I had to hear it from Owen."

His eyes fall shut and then open to mine. Sad and beautiful. "I'm still leaving."

I draw even closer. "Because you think you owe it to Arthur's memory. But if the knights bring home the Grail, you'll cast away your title, just like that?"

"If *I* bring it back. If *I* do it." His eyes bore into mine until he's certain I understand the difference. "I never wanted to be a knight. But Lancelot is my brother. He promised this to Arthur. And if my parents had to die, it shouldn't be for nothing." He won't look at me as he says it. "Say what you'd like about serfs in the countryside, but we know pride just as well as anyone."

"What will you do after, Marcus?" I challenge. "Why not stay a knight?" My eyes sting with tears. "It'll be hard to scratch off that tattoo anyway. You'll be a hero in Camelot. Honor, glory, women."

"I don't want that." He sighs in exasperation, looking around as though he could pluck the right words from dead foliage. "My heart belongs to someone I can never have. So if I'm off to find some old chalice instead, I need something...an escape to keep me alive. Something to give me hope when there's none."

"Hope," I breathe. "How could there be hope when you wouldn't even tell me?"

His eyes hold mine. "It's for me, not the girl I'm leaving. Camelot will soon forget me, and you shouldn't wait to see how long that takes, especially if you're to leave for the north. I don't ask that of you. I can't."

My fists clutch the furs around his shoulders. My throat chokes at the idea of his memory having no bearing on my ticking heart. "Northern kingdoms be damned. You're stupid not to ask."

His breathing goes choppy. "Vivienne—"

"Ask me."

He takes my chin in his fingers. His hesitant eyes blink with uncertainty louder than anything he could say, but still he presses his lips to my temple. After an eternity of silence, he pulls away. "Wait for me," he whispers with a spark of happiness, to which I nod fervently.

"I will."

He tilts my head toward his and kisses me, breathing me in as though he could take me to wherever his road might lead. I lean my forehead against his. "You didn't say goodbye."

"I could never tell you goodbye."

"The vow?" I have to hear him say it.

One side of his mouth lifts in a smile. He shrugs. "Clearly, I'm no priest. Free if I claim the Grail for Camelot."

It's quite the condition, but nonetheless he smiles, and it's as close as he can get to the violet-eyed squire who tried to kiss me under a starlit sky with the Round Table not feet away. I sputter on happy tears and bliss. His lips find mine, and my fingers weave through the hair at the back of his neck.

Ours is a moment of perfection in this new world.

"Good news, then?" a voice says.

We pull apart. Standing before the land gives way to the lake is the gypsy, leaning on her warped cane with burlap about her shoulders. She inches toward us, jingling silver loud with each step.

"You're Merlin's friend," I breathe.

She nods. "An old friend. It's been ages since we last spoke. Once he became more interested in alchemy, he stopped stealing my magic. Doesn't even try anymore." Metallic starfish earrings chime as they fall past her shoulders. She darts her eyes to Marcus, who regards her with caution. "Don't fret, boy. I'm of good use to you. But perhaps a formal introduction is in order. In the old language my name was much more eloquent, but to Merlin, I was always the Lady of the Lake."

I shake my head, though logic warns me not to doubt her.

She catches my incredulity and casts her hand over the water. The smooth ripples churn into a vortex until we see the wet, sandy bottom covered in hairlike seaweed and more. Marcus and I hold each other as wind whips around us. With a lift of her hand, the vortex erupts and paints the sky midnight blue, speckled with starfish as constellations. Then it falls into a smooth, glasslike surface. The wind goes silent. The sky, back to its usual nighttime state. Marcus and I breathe heavily.

Goodness, I see how Merlin was an old friend.

"The alchemist from Jerusalem sent word that Merlin's

soul is still of this world, through much effort on both their parts."

My heart feels as though it's been brought back to life. There's hope. There's so much of it now.

She steps closer. "Merlin's incantation was broken. Now, nothing protects the kingdom. But that's where I come in." She stares at me with ocean blue eyes. "I will protect Camelot. You, Vivienne, will continue with Merlin's work now that you've completed your apprenticeship. Through that, you'll help Sir Marcus and the knights."

My mouth falls open. "Me? I'm not an alchemist. I only took an interest in Merlin's craft as an apprentice. I'm not—"

"Was it not you who built Camelot's greatest weapon? That feat was not for the unskilled. Trust yourself!" Then the hope in her voice turns to warning. "But mind the responsibility that follows. The discovery of Avalon depends upon you, and so, you must stay within Camelot's walls until the Grail is found. Civilizations will hear of Merlin's successor. They'll seek you, just as Morgan did, for coordinates hidden in the safest place possible."

A lady-in-waiting doesn't have enemies. I could escape right now to a safer life in the north, as I've always wanted. From there, I could go to Jerusalem, if I could manage to get word to Azur. There'd be nothing to hurt me, no danger to face.

But I look at Marcus, and any desire for an easy escape flies into the sky. A life without all I love would certainly be an empty one. *To return to the clock tower, no less!*

Marcus squeezes my hand. "That you're important to

Camelot doesn't surprise me one bit. It's one thing Merlin and I agree on."

My destiny is clear. I'd much rather face danger or isolation in Camelot than safety aboard northbound aeroships or amid the hot sands of the Holy Land. For now.

The woman's bright eyes lure mine back. In them, I watch a scene. A young mother, three months with child, takes her yellow-haired boy to the lake outside the castle. It's Owen, who climbs a high tree and falls to the water, taken by a zealous wave too far from land in a lake too deep for him ever to survive. His mother cannot save him, but they're not alone. A gypsy brings her boy to shore. As payment for saving his life, the gypsy makes an unorthodox decree to Lady Carolyn, the former apprentice of Merlin.

"Your daughter will be of strong intelligence and heart. She'll know the coordinates of Avalon. Scores of kingdoms seek the Holy Grail, but Camelot is the one that would use its powers for good, creating a joyful coexistence between magic and the mechanical arts.

"When the time is right, your daughter will know exactly where it hides. While knights battle pirates of the skies, she'll work in Camelot, hidden from the world.

"Then, she'll lead the Knights of the Round Table to Avalon."

I gasp at the wealth of information in my mind. Enlightened thinkers. Sea and sky. The song I misremembered. The safe guarding Arthur's mystical steel, built in Greece, according to Merlin. All of it fits together like a pair of rotating sprockets.

Coordinates hidden in the safest place possible.

"Athens... Greece?" I breathe. Yes, that's what Marcus said in the gardens. "That's why the Spanish rogues are there. Avalon's a castle miles above the Great Sea of the Mediterranean." But how would they know that?

Marcus blinks at me. "You're sure?" He looks at the gypsy for validation. She flicks an eyebrow that confirms it.

I nod. "It's in the sky. I've always known this." I move to leave with him. "You'll need my help, Marcus. It's not of our world!"

The gypsy sets a hand on my arm. "Wait. Gawain's infantry fights a bloody battle against the Spanish rogues. To defeat them will take months. Long enough for someone in Camelot to build a vessel that would fly high enough to reach Avalon. How else could Sir Marcus claim the Grail?"

I blink. "You want me to build an aerohawk? Like Azur's?"

The gypsy inches closer, forcing me to peer into her stark blue eyes. "Think bigger, dear."

Then I see it. Something of my own conception and ingenuity. I know exactly what to build. I knew it when I was ten, bored at a feast with crying children surrounding me. I knew how the pieces of Merlin's hookah could interlock in such a way that a toy aeroship would be born of them.

I could do it again. Only this time, Merlin wouldn't have to worry about his favorite smoking device. An aeroship to reach the high altitudes of Avalon. I could surpass

Azur in this feat, whose kingdom's aeroships soar just below the clouds but cannot safely rise above them.

I nod at the gypsy.

"The catacombs have all you'll need." She backs away into darkness or legend. The lake returns to gentle ripples.

Then the moon glows too brightly. Light bursts at an incredible speed, aimed for Camelot, hitting the castle, painting it with luminescence. The crater in the land fills with soil. Trees in the farmlands sprout buds, flowers, leaves. All that was organic in Camelot has been restored. In the distance, the knights' cries are ones of joy.

Joy.

Owen arrives on horseback. "We're leaving." I reach his saddle, and my brother leans over to kiss my cheek. "But it's clear you aren't. Take care of Father. And send word to Mother when it's safe."

I nod. "Return home."

Owen gallops off.

Marcus takes my hand, drawing me into his arms until there's no space between us. His nose brushes against mine, his bandaged hands run through my hair. I lean into him, and he breathes me in as though he can't bear the thought of letting go.

I want to stop time.

My fingers find the lace around his wrist. I close his hand around the tail, recalling how lace was celebrated in Lyonesse. "Find your way back."

He shakes his head. "Find your way to Greece."

Marcus kisses me once more and sets another to my forehead. Then he mounts his horse and gallops off.

———

A normal girl would cry.

She would weep and perhaps run after him. She'd mourn for days, pining at the window. She wouldn't sleep or eat. And, really, that's such an illogical response. Still, once Marcus is gone, a strong desire erupts in my heart to see him again.

Like mad, I run back to the castle. I rush through the gardens and the village's abandoned shops and empty streets. I throw open the cellar door to the clock tower's summit. My legs twist and twist as I ascend. At the top, Merlin's tower is now roofless. Wind is my only companion.

I pass the desk, blueprints scattered throughout the wrecked space, telescope knocked over. The antiqued sword that was once Merlin's pride finds its way into my hand. I smile.

Journal entries torn from their spines are filled with erratic notes about the possible dangers of alchemy. About the Spanish rogues and whether they heard of the peril Camelot was in.

About Guinevere, the secrets she brought to Camelot, how the magical legacy of Lyonesse caused its watery end. How she was never cursed by Morgan since she never set foot outside the city walls.

But I push those aside. I extend my viewer and watch my beloved ride off, breathing in relief when Galahad's infantry reappears on the other side of the woods Morgan enchanted. Wind propels the knights north.

When they've blended into the furthest mountain, I collapse my viewer and set it back in my pocket. I look about the castle where the shimmering of the Lady of the Lake's protection glows.

I don't miss the cage in Guinevere's empty tower window, the canary's door now wide open.

My apron is on Merlin's desk. I tie it around my waist and pick up the goggles made especially for me. With one glance at the burnt skeletons of Caldor and Terra, I smile at the possibilities, foregoing any mourning of what was. My heart pounds at the wonderment of what other secrets might exist in Camelot.

There's only one way to find out.

I pull my goggles over my eyes and descend into the abyss.

The End.

Acknowledgements

To Justin. Thank you for being my toughest critic, despite what they say about spouses as beta-readers. Thank you for helping me make Excalibur awesome, for teaching me about Medieval weaponry, and for Chipotle runs so I could work on revisions. But most importantly, thank you for walking through life with me. I love you, sweets.

To Mom, who never seemed to mind that I wasn't to be a doctor or a lawyer. Thanks for everything, Ma. To Dad, my Padre, whom I greatly miss. The reference to good Irish tea was for you. To my sisters, Sarah and Monica. You inspire me. I've never met two women so strong and so present in life. Thank you for changing the world. To Papa Devlin, for teaching me everything there is to know about books. Thank you for Christmas carols in Stratford, for wheelbarrow rides, and for some easy wins at euchre. To my entire family, my in-laws, and my friends in Toronto, Kitchener-Waterloo, and Los Angeles. Thank you for your love when you found out I was actually a writer. I'm truly humbled by your support.

To my mind-twin and best friend, Carla. There is so much good in my life that I owe to our friendship. Here's to the amazing adventures still to come! Onward!

To Brittany Howard, for believing in Vivienne's story. To Marisa Corvisiero, my agent, for your wisdom, support, and the fantastic partnership we've begun. To Brian Farrey-Latz, my editor and partner-in-crime, for your patience, your collaboration, and your incredible ideas. To Ed Day, Mallory Hayes, and the entire team at Flux, for going above and beyond for me.

To Elizabeth Briggs, Rachel Searles, Jessica Love, Dana Elmendorf, Amaris Glass, PK Hrezo, and Sara Raasch. Thank you for amazing critiques, for always being there when I needed you, for retreats and brainstorming sessions, and for patiently obliging when I asked you to read my book JUST ONE MORE TIME I PROMISE I'LL NEVER ASK FOR ANYTHING ELSE AGAIN. I love you all forever.

To my online friends, and a special shout-out to my rad OneFours. YOU GUYS. Thank you for the friendship that is possible because of this strange new internet world.

Thank you, thank you, thank you.

© Jenn Verma

About the Author

Kathryn Rose was born in Toronto, Canada, and grew up in the Kitchener-Waterloo region of Southern Ontario. After graduating from York University, where she studied literature and philosophy, she relocated to Los Angeles, California.

When she isn't breaking up fights between her cat and dog, Kathryn can be found writing and reading mostly speculative fiction, cooking with her husband, or listening to rock music.